AN EDUCATED DEATH

Kate Flora

A TOM DOHERTY ASSOCIATES BOOK
NEW YORK

This is a work of fiction. All the characters and events portrayed in this novel are either products of the author's imagination or are used fictitiously.

AN EDUCATED DEATH

A Forge Book
Published by Tom Doherty Associates, Inc.
175 Fifth Avenue
New York, NY 10010

Forge® is a registered trademark of Tom Doherty Associates, Inc.

ISBN: 0-812-57156-8
Library of Congress Card Catalog Number: 97-18696

First edition: October 1997
First mass market edition: May 1999

Printed in the United States of America

0 9 8 7 6 5 4 3 2 1

To my three guys, Ken, Jake, and Max,
who light up my life.

More to be desired are they than gold.
—Psalms 19:9

ACKNOWLEDGMENTS

THANKS TO ALL the people whose generosity helped me write this book. To my friend Carl Johnson, who designed a police station for me and who told me what a cop keeps in the trunk. To my readers, Nancy McJennett, Jack Nevison, Christy Bond, Christy Hawes, Diane Englund, Carl Johnson, and Robert Moll, who criticized, corrected, and supported me through the writing process. To Kendra O'Donnell, a superb headmistress, for reminding me that when students are upset, they need to be fed. To Gerry Zagarella, M.D. To Sgt. Tom Le Min, of the Newark, Delaware, police department, who patiently answered my questions. To my mother and hero, A. Carman Clark, who continues to believe in me, and who lets me cry on her shoulder when things go wrong. To a wonderful writer and friend, Barbara Shapiro, who helps me keep my perspective. And thanks, most of all and once again, to Meg Milne Moulton, Thea's mentor. The Bucksport School exists only in my imagination. You didn't go there.

PROLOGUE

LANEY TOOK ANOTHER step. The ice cracked ominously under her foot and a spurt of water came up through the crack. The dusting of snow on top of the ice made it hard to assess its thickness or choose her footing. Her little black suede shoes had been a foolish thing to wear out here. If she'd known she was going to be walking in the woods, she would have worn her boots. She wasn't a nature-lover at the best of times, which this was not. She was only doing this to get the money. She really didn't have any choice; she had to have it. She'd worn the shoes because she wanted to look pretty, young and girlish and pretty. At sixteen, she was all of those things, but she hadn't felt pretty lately. She'd felt trapped and frustrated and furious at herself for having unprotected sex. At the time it had seemed inviting and dangerous, and Laney loved breaking rules. Now it just seemed stupid.

She stood still and looked around. It was so quiet out here in the woods she might have been the only person in the world. Sometimes she wished she was. It wasn't as if she got along with many of the stupid girls in her stupid dorm. In the moonlight, the snow-covered pond was a serene white oval surrounded by the black trunks of the trees leaning out over it.

She looked back at the dark figure who hovered behind

her, who was angry at her, and not acting much like a friend. "You were right. It's beautiful," she said, trying to hide her annoyance. She wasn't particularly interested in scenery and couldn't see why they'd had to come all the way out here just to conduct a business transaction. Adults could be so ridiculous sometimes. Kids were always being accused of being unrealistic but it sure wasn't her idea to turn this into a moonlight walk. She wanted to get the money and find Merri before her friend got disgusted and left without her. Maybe she already had. If so, she'd catch up with her at the movie.

"You have to get farther out. Right into the middle. Then you can really appreciate it," her companion urged.

"The ice is too thin. It keeps cracking. You can risk your life if you want. I'm going back."

"Just a few more steps. Even if the ice breaks, it's very shallow there. There's no sense in bothering if you aren't going to do it right." Her companion put a hand under her arm and urged her forward. "I never thought you were such a scaredy-cat."

That was another thing. Grown-ups were always teasing and saying dumb stuff when they were nervous, yet they always accused kids of being silly. She didn't want to take another step but her natural caution warred with Laney's desire to please. She needed to be braver. She knew that. She was going to have to be brave to face what she had to face. No one else was going to be on her side. Sure, Merri would be there, she'd promised Laney that, but Merri wasn't being supportive, not really. She was just doing this because Laney had begged. She disapproved and she was very open about it. She'd been totally unsympathetic when Laney told her that she was scared of doctors and nurses and blood. It just wasn't fair anyway. Why should she have to go through with this? She answered her own question. Because the alternative was worse.

"I have to be getting back. I'm meeting someone," she said, irritated that her voice sounded so small and shaky.

"Can I please have that money now?" She turned back but her companion grabbed her arm and held on. "Hey! What do you think you're doing?" Laney tried to jerk her arm away but the other's grip was firm. "Let me go!" Suddenly she felt herself being shoved forward. She staggered a few steps, slipped, and fell.

The ice snapped and groaned and suddenly gave way beneath her. She expected to hit bottom immediately but she went down and down and her feet touched nothing. She flailed about with her arms, grabbing the edges of the ice to stop her plunge. The ice just crumbled under her fingers. She gasped as the water closed over her chest.

Frantically she turned toward shore for help, waving her arms and calling, "Wait! Come back. You can't just leave me here." The retreating figure neither wavered nor looked back before disappearing into the trees. "Hey," she called, her fingers scrabbling for a purchase on the ice. "This isn't just my fault, you know. I didn't mean to hurt you. . . . You can't do this to me!" There was no one there. Nothing on the silent shore but the trees. "Help!" she screamed. "Help! I've fallen through the ice." Her sodden flannel skirt kept tangling around her legs, making it hard to tread water. She flailed at the edges of the crumbling ice, trying to find something to grip, until her fingertips were numb. She panicked, thrashing wildly around and screaming for help, still expecting her companion to come back and rescue her.

"Okay, okay, you've made your point. I was stupid and I hurt you and I'm sorry!" No one came. She was getting tired. It was getting harder and harder to keep her head above water. She went under while she was trying to scream, swallowing a mouthful of water.

She tried to make herself be calm. Her chest hurt from the cold and coughing and her arms and legs were getting heavy and unresponsive. She sited on the shore and tried to swim toward it. It seemed very far away and she was tired. Terribly tired. Her arms and legs were stiff and awkward and didn't want to do what she told them. She'd swallowed so much water it felt as though she were going to be sick. She tried not to think about what that water looked like. Dark brown, muddy, and smelly. She couldn't keep her head up so she held her breath and bobbed. She'd breathe whenever she came up. It was confusing. She kept mistiming it. Gasped for air and took in water instead, kept struggling for air and kept getting water. The stupid jacket that she'd borrowed was so heavy it was pulling her down. She tried to struggle out of it and got hopelessly tangled.

She was suffocating. She fought frantically to get to the surface. Her burning lungs demanded air and every time she tried to breathe she got water. Despite the commands from her brain, her arms and legs had stopped responding. "I'm drowning," she thought. "My mother isn't going to be able to handle this. Not on top of everything else."

She saw her mother's face bending over her. "Don't worry, Delaney," her mother was saying, "everything is going to be fine." For once, Marta Taggert was smiling reassuringly, the way mothers are supposed to. For once, there was no stream of criticism coming out of her mouth. Laney began to feel better. She gave up fighting and relaxed. It was going to be okay. She could let her mother take care of her. It was what she'd been wishing for anyway, these past few weeks. She'd so badly wanted someone to take care of her, to help her out. Someone she could talk to who didn't make her feel bad and dirty and wrong. The operation scared her. Now she'd have her mother there to comfort her, tuck her into bed afterward, bring her soup and ginger ale and magazines. Laney didn't want to be a mother. She wanted to be mothered. Too bad it took such a dramatic event to get her mother to pay attention. She smiled up into her mother's face. "I'm glad you're here."

CHAPTER 1

ANDRE WAS SILHOUETTED against the night, his big body a dark bulk against the enormous window. Behind him the lights of the city fell away toward the ferry terminal. Beyond it, sparkling like a jeweled tiara, the Bay Bridge carried late-night traffic to Oakland. I couldn't see his face because we'd turned out all the lights but I knew just how it looked. One whole side was a patchwork of scabs and the vulnerable pink of new skin. It was the kind of thing people stared at but they didn't stare long at Andre. Underneath the scabs his face was hard and unwelcoming. His dark brown eyes, which, when he let his feelings show, truly were a mirror of his soul, were dull. He looked like a man who'd suffered one too many bad things. He looked like exactly who he was. A cop. The man I loved. A man who'd been beaten, dragged behind a car, and lost his best friend.

Cops always live with the possibility that something will go wrong. So do their wives and lovers, their mothers and fathers and children. Andre is a detective with the Maine State Police. I met him when he was investigating my sister's death and it was the farthest thing from love at first sight. I thought he was a typical cop asshole and he thought I was a prissy obstructionist. It took a screaming match, an uncomfortable dinner, and hours of talking for us to realize we were wrong about each other. That was two years ago. Since then we've had our ups and downs but we've been pretty steadily together. One of the things I valued about him was that he'd always been open and willing to talk to me. If we could talk, we could always work things out. But he wouldn't talk about this. Since his buddy had been shot he'd pulled himself into his shell like a turtle. The only way I even knew the details of what had happened was that some of his friends had talked to me hoping I might be able to do something for him.

The situation had been filled with the usual volatility of the cop's life. Andre and the dead man, Ray Dolan, had gotten too close to a walking time bomb named Jed Wheeler and the bomb had gone off. An informer had told them Wheeler might be the guy to talk to about a murder they were investigating. In Maine, state cops handle all the murder cases. Their informant had told them Wheeler, a heavy drug user, was crazy and dangerous and they'd approached him cautiously but there isn't enough caution in the world when you're dealing with someone as strung out on drugs as Wheeler was. They'd gone to ask some questions and met the angel of death. Ray Dolan, a good cop, a good father, and a good man, had bled to death despite Andre's efforts. The angel of death took five rounds and kept on coming, trying to run Andre down with his car. Andre had been dragged a couple hundred yards before Wheeler finally died. Ray Dolan had been Andre's mentor and close friend. Even though Andre knew he'd done everything he could, even though he knew none of it was his fault, he couldn't forgive himself for not dying, too.

The ironic part was that six months ago, the angel of death had brushed Andre with its wings and he'd bounced back from that in remarkably good spirits. Maybe part of his recovery was due to the fact that I'd finally agreed to live with him, but I think that gives me too much credit. Or too much responsibility. After Andre had been shot in a hostage situation and I'd had time, sitting there in the waiting room, to reflect on all the opportunities I might be missing, I'd yielded to his pressure for us to live together.

Cautiously, I admit. It went against my fear of commitment and my reluctance, having already lost the husband I had loved so dearly, to take a chance at getting hurt again. After all, if Andre's getting shot proved anything, it was that he was in a risky business. It had also focused my heart and mind in a way no amount of talking ever could.

So I had sublet my beloved oceanfront condo to a co-worker's friend; Andre had given up his bachelor pad complete with devoted landlady who worried about whether he was getting enough to eat, and we'd committed ourselves to an experiment in domestic bliss. The experiment had included two killer commutes, incompatible working hours, and a surprising amount of fun. Until recently.

Even before the Dolan thing, our domesticity had been fraying around the edges. I'm not the jealous type, but it had been hard to overlook the amount of time that Andre's work was throwing him into the company of a bouncy blonde named Amanda. And Andre, who *is* the jealous type—ask him, he'll admit it—didn't appreciate all the calls I got from Denzel Ellis-Jackson. Denzel is a client and Amanda is a co-worker. They were just symbols of a larger problem—the fact that we were too busy to nurture our relationship or to even talk about it.

For the past two weeks, we hadn't been together. Andre the turtle had wanted to be alone, and I had had a bunch of work to do in Boston, so he'd stayed in Maine and I'd stayed with my partner, Suzanne, and we'd talked more, by phone, than we had when we were together. Talked all the way around things, but not connected. I'd finally begged him to take this trip with me to see if we could break through the barriers and find the partner we loved.

We were also in San Francisco, which is about as far as

you can get from Maine, because Andre's boss had begged me to do something with him. I'm neither a Pollyanna type nor a Florence Nightingale—few people make the mistake of thinking me warm and fuzzy—but despite our ups and downs I loved the man and I was willing to try. So far it had been like going on vacation with a stone. He'd met me at the airport in Boston, greeted me with a kiss that would have disappointed a grandmother, and lapsed into brooding silence. The scrapes on his face were almost healed and he walked with only a slight limp but the internal injuries were all too apparent. His spirit was bruised and bleeding. He had a black-and-blue soul.

I'm not a type A personality, only a B+, but I have pretty frantic work habits. I'm a consultant to independent schools—a euphemism for private schools—and I'd just finished a big project culminating in an enormous report. When I'm meeting a deadline, I tend to forget minor things like eating and sleeping. As a result, I'd rushed to the airport directly from the printer, running a sleep and meal deficit big enough to rival the national debt. I wanted to put my head on his broad shoulder and sleep. Instead I trotted out tricks from my traveling road show until my jaw ached from smiling. I tried light conversation, snuggling up to the man who usually can't keep his hands off my body, and an outright challenge, and met with so little response I might as well have been talking to my foot. He had three drinks, showed an avid interest in the airline magazine and then fell asleep.

He had looked out the window when we landed and murmured some responses when I pointed out the things I could recognize and he'd roused himself to comment on the display of hats in the airport, but once we were in the cab he became the stone man again. He jumped when I accidentally brushed against his thigh and acted as if he couldn't hear when I pointed out the civic center, the shop selling sexual paraphernalia, and the various parts of the city. Finally I got sick of it. "Are you awake, Lemieux?" I said.

"Yes."

"Happy to be here?"

"Let's not fool ourselves, Thea," he said. "I'm only here because certain well-meaning people think this will be good for me."

"I hope it will be." I didn't push him. This wasn't the kind of thing that responds to a miracle cure. If the trip worked for Andre at all, I expected it to be a gradual thing. A slow loosening of his iron control. Besides, neither of us reacts favorably to being pushed. I was hoping he'd be pleased with the room. I'd stayed at the Clift while I was out there on a consulting job. It was the kind of place where all the staff must have Ph.D.s and everyone is always helpful and polite. While I was staying there, I'd discovered that up on the sixteenth floor there are some rooms with enormous windows and beautiful views. When I decided San Francisco was the place to take Andre for his rehab, I'd called the manager and wheedled one of those rooms. Andre had never been to San Francisco before and I'd been looking forward to sharing this view with him.

The bellboy had turned on all the lights when we checked in. It was just a room, not a suite, but it had almost as many lights as our whole apartment. Ceiling lights. Floor lights. Desk lights. Bedside lights. Plus a ceiling light and two fancy black-and-silver deco fixtures in the gray marble bathroom. The minute the bellboy left I turned them off. I wanted Andre to enjoy the view in all its glory.

"Nice," he said without turning. "Very nice. Only I wasn't expecting California to be this cold."

"It's because of the damp. Even in the summer, fashionable ladies wear their furs in this city."

"Did you bring your furs, Kozak?"

"You can call me Thea. And no, I didn't. I try to be sartorially correct."

"So I won't need my bathing suit and T-shirts?"

"I hope you brought some sweaters to wear over them. I told you that you'd be perfectly comfortable here if you dressed like you were going to Labrador."

"I was thinking sunny California."

"When you should have been thinking foggy California."

"Right now I'm not thinking sunny or foggy."

"Am I supposed to guess what you are thinking, Detective Lemieux?" It was the closest we'd come to intimate conversation since we got on the plane. Since the accident, in fact. Accident—that was a silly term for it. Since the incident? No sense in beating around the euphemistic bush. Since Ray died, I tried not to get my hopes up. Since then he'd been as chaste and distant as a missionary. He'd been recovering but it was more than that. He hadn't been incapacitated, he'd been disinterested. Sex was something people did when they were alive; Andre's mind was full of death. I joined him at the window. He put an arm around me and pulled me against him.

"If you can't, Ms. Kozak, you don't know me very well." He kissed me with a frightening intensity and began fumbling with the buttons on my blouse. They were too small for his hurried fingers. He grabbed the blouse and ripped it.

The doorbell buzzed. I'd ordered a late dinner from room service but why did they have to bring it now? At this hotel, the least they could do was read minds. "Saved by the bell," I said, trying for a light note as I headed for the door.

"Are you going to answer it like that?"

I glanced down at my gaping blouse. "I guess I'd better not." I looked around for something to put on.

"There are some robes in the bathroom." The buzzer sounded again. I grabbed a robe and admitted the patient bellboy.

"Room service," he said, wheeling in a cart and positioning it in front of the window. Andre had had the fore-sight to put on some lights. "The manager sent some chocolate-dipped strawberries with his compliments to welcome you back to the Clift." He lifted the covers to prove he'd brought what I ordered. "Will there be any-thing else?"

"The champagne?" I said, impatient with his careful attention, his slow and gracious way of moving. He was trying to give good service; I was wishing he'd get out before Andre lapsed back into indifference.

"Of course. Excuse me." He went to the door and came back with it. "Would you like me to open it?"

"Thanks. No. I can manage." I crossed his palm with silver and he graciously departed.

Andre was standing at the window again, his back to me. I hoped I hadn't lost him. I put an arm around his waist. "Champagne?" I suggested.

"I'm sorry, Thea," he said. His voice sounded heavy and forced. "I didn't mean to be rough with you."

I shrugged off the robe and tossed it toward the bed. "I didn't mind. . . ."

"I tore your blouse."

"You kissed me. I wish you'd do it again."

He picked up the bottle and stared at it thoughtfully. "Remember the first time we had champagne?"

The town I grew up in was built along the shore of a lake. The effect of the seasons on the lake left a lasting impression on me, especially spring when the ice was breaking up. When it finally happened, it happened fast. One day it would warm up and great cracks would grow in that solid, forbidding gray surface. One piece would shift and then another, and suddenly there would be open water. Maybe it was wishful thinking, but something about Andre reminded me of that lake. "How could I for-get a big macho cop backing me up against the counter and kissing me against my will?"

"The big macho cop," he said scornfully. "What the hell good does it do to be a big macho cop, to be a cop at all, to be anything, if you can't keep the good people from dying?"

"It wasn't your fault," I said, "there was no way you could have kept it from happening."

"'What difference does it make whose fault it was? Ray is just as dead."

"And you're not dead." I put my arms around him. He didn't respond but I didn't give up. I stood there and kept my arms around him, moving when he did but not letting go. It was like dancing without the music.

"I've been sitting there every night with my gun out," he said. "Staring at it. Thinking how much easier it would be to just shoot myself and it would be over. Then maybe I could get the image of Ray out of my mind. I tried to save him, Thea. I tried. But I couldn't get the bleeding to stop. It just came pouring out of him. I didn't stop trying until Cooper came and then I went after Wheeler. I did it all by the book. I warned him. I told him to stop. I fired a warning shot. Everything. And then I shot him. I kept on shooting him and he still wouldn't stop. Just went over to his car, got in, and drove it straight at me. When I was being dragged by the car all I was thinking about was that when he stopped I was going to get him."

"I know, Andre. I understand. . . ."

"How can you understand?"

He tried to twist away from me but I stuck right to him. "I don't mean I understand perfectly. I know better than to say that. But I've been afraid for my life and angry at the other person for making me afraid. And I've lost someone I loved deeply and felt guilty about surviving when the other person's dead. I'm not like you. I know that. We're very different. But I understand some of what you're going through."

"No, you don't!" He tried to push me away but I hung on. He twisted forcefully aside, broke my hold, and shoved me away from him, sending me crashing into the desk with hip-bruising force. "I should have done better."

"You couldn't have done better. You didn't do anything wrong. It just happened."

"If I'd only done things differently. If we hadn't gone—"

"But you had to go. It was your job—"

"There must have been something I could have done. . . ."

"There wasn't, Andre."

He put his hands over his face. "That's what I can't stand," he said. "That we could do it right and still have everything go wrong. I can't accept it. I can't accept that I can't fix it . . . that I couldn't fix it . . . that there was nothing I could do."

"You did the most important thing you could, from my point of view, Andre. You didn't let him kill you, too."

"Sometimes I wish he had."

"How would the world be helped by having two good men dead instead of one?"

"At least I wouldn't have been left here feeling guilty for being alive."

"Don't say that again!" I put my hands on his shoulders and pushed him until he sat down on the edge of the bed. I sat down beside him and grabbed one of his hands. I'd been kind and understanding long enough. It was time he heard my side of things. "I used to be married to a man named David," I said.

"I know that," he said impatiently.

"David meant everything to me. He was the touchstone of my life. Seeing him. Knowing him. Being with him was enough for me. I was very happy. It's probably a cliché but I felt satisfied and complete." He didn't say anything, but Andre's face was puzzled. He already knew all this, so why was I telling him again? "Then David was killed. I felt like the center had been ripped out of my life and I was sad for a long, long time. When I began to recover and to live my life again, I erected barriers and didn't let myself become involved with anyone because I never wanted to take a chance on being hurt like that again."

"What's that got to do with—" he began.

I put a finger on his lips. "Just listen to me and maybe you'll see." I thought I saw the beginning of understanding in his face. "Six months ago, I woke up one morning thinking about coffee and breakfast and the first thing I heard on the news was that there was a police standoff up in Maine where an injured detective was being held hostage. The announcement that I've been dreading almost as long as I've known you. I'm tough. Things don't shake me. You know that. And the thought of losing you reduced me to Jell-O. Luckily, I was with Dom and Rosie—"

"He's a good man—" Andre began.

"I'm still not finished. During the hours that we were driving to Maine, and the hours that passed before I finally saw you . . . during the endless hours at the hospital while we all waited to hear that you were out of surgery and that you weren't going to die, I experienced pain and fear that are beyond description." My voice was shaking and I wasn't sure I was going to be able to finish what I wanted to say. "Whether I wanted it or not, I knew then that I had let myself care about you, let myself have a stake in your life. I knew then that if you lived, it was worth making whatever sacrifices were necessary so we could be together. I'm saying that it matters to *me* whether you live or die and I can't stand it when you say it doesn't matter to you. You aren't all alone out there, Andre. That love and loss you feel for Ray Dolan—I know about that. I know how it hurts. I lived through it once and I stared it in the face again when you were shot. I'm not just talking when I say I know how you feel. If I lost you I don't know what I'd do, how I'd handle it. Maybe I would head for the sea like a lemming. Just walk in and keep on walking until the water closed over my head."

Sometimes you don't know how you feel until you hear

yourself speak. That was what had just happened to me. I hadn't meant to tell him this stuff. I'd meant to keep it to myself and not burden him with it. To just be there for him. I hadn't even realized that I was angry. "I'm sorry," I said. "I didn't mean to make this a contest . . . I wasn't trying to say that my pain was as great as yours. . . ." The tears that I'd been holding back were like a rising tide. I couldn't contain them any longer.

He turned and buried his head in my chest, his own tears warm and wet against my bare skin. I put my arms around him and this time he didn't push me away. He wasn't going to stop hurting just because we'd talked but it was a beginning. When he made love to me, it was with an intensity I'd never experienced before. I don't know if the earth moved—in California that's not such a unique experience anyway—but I'm sure that the people on the floors immediately above and below us were thrown out of their beds and rocked liked ships in a storm.

Afterward I was starving but too exhausted to move. Andre brought my club sandwich and some champagne. "I think I'm ready to join the living again," he said. I certainly hoped so. Always one to up the ante, I was beginning to wonder if we could rock the whole hotel and not just a few floors.

CHAPTER 2

THE ANDRE WHO woke up beside me the next morning was a different man from the one who had gotten on the plane in Boston. Not that there had been some sort of instant cure—even the very talented Dr. Kozak wouldn't claim that—but the healing process had begun. I didn't expect a miracle cure anyway. I know that recovering from the loss of someone you're close to takes time. When my husband, David, was killed I lost myself so compulsively in work that I barely came up for air and I withdrew from the world almost completely. I knew what it was to be locked up tight and I didn't push Andre at all. Not emotionally.

Physically I pushed him hard. San Francisco is a very active city. It demands that you get out and explore it. That's not so easy when the challenge is handed down by a city that's all hills, but it didn't stop us. Even though he was still stiff and sore, we trudged doggedly uphill and down, relishing the sudden surprising vistas, discovering hidden gardens and elegant bits of architecture. We rode the cable car to Ghirardelli, had lunch, and walked out to Ft. Mason, right under the Golden Gate Bridge. We stopped at the Marina and watched people flying kites, practicing tai chi, and exercising their dogs. Whippet-thin bikers and shiny spandex-clad joggers were everywhere, as were death-defying in-line skaters.

For the next few days, we forgot about work and practiced having fun. I took him to Post Trio and Fleur de Lis, through art galleries, to Gump's. We went Christmas shopping and airily asked to have everything wrapped and shipped. We bought dragons in Chinatown, laughed together over the coffee menus, which offered as much selection as the whole menu in many restaurants back East. We had drinks at the Top of the Mark, enjoyed mediocre food and a great band at Ghirardelli, and went boating in the park. We made no attempt to be anything other than what we were—tourists. When we weren't out walking or moving, slow and sated, from one food event to another, we were catching up on lost sleep, or at least spending a lot of time in bed.

I was beginning to feel like a regular person, not a crisis fighter with a phone glued to her ear. Andre had even smiled once or twice. We were both recovering workaholics. Unfortunately, time flies when you're having fun, and that's what we were doing.

At four o'clock Saturday morning the phone rang. I felt Andre go stiff beside me, expecting bad news, and not stiff the way I like him, either. They'd been happy enough to send him away to Mother Kozak's rehab but if the Department of Public Safety decided that it needed him, they wouldn't hesitate to interrupt his San Francisco vacation, haul him back to Maine, and throw him right back into the middle of the job that had hurt him so much. It wouldn't be the first time he'd been hauled out of my bed in the middle of the night. It used to make me nervous, having the Maine Department of Public Safety know who was in my bed. Living together, I got used to it. Now I don't worry about it at all. They don't care who he sleeps with as long as they know where to find him. Actually, he tells me that a lot of his friends think he's lucky to have found a woman as good-looking as I am who doesn't want to get married. He says they meant it as a compliment but I didn't take it that way. I'm still recovering from the trauma of being a teenage girl with a big chest. I need to be admired for my mind.

The insistent phone kept intruding on my mental meanderings so I gave up and answered it. I knew it wasn't for me. I work with a much more genteel clientele. During school hours, which start at the unacceptable hour of 7:00 A.M. or earlier at boarding schools, my phone is like an admissions crisis line. If I venture in at a civilized hour like nine, my desk will be buried under so many pink slips it looks as though we've had a rosy snow storm, and many days, if I want to get any serious work done, I have to wait until dark. But my clients don't call me in the middle of the night.

I'd forgotten that it was three hours later in the East. "Thea? Thank heavens. I was afraid you'd be out sightseeing or something and I'm desperate." Dorrie Chapin's well-modulated voice wouldn't convey desperation if she were hanging off a cliff by one slipping hand. Dorrie was the first female head of a stuffy old New England boarding school, and she had won the job by dazzling them with her competence, not her smile or her charm.

"Dorrie, it's four in the morning." Beside me, Andre sighed and put an arm around me, pulling me close. I hoped Dorrie wouldn't talk long.

There was an embarrassed pause. "I'm sorry. I'm afraid I got it backwards. I was thinking it was three hours later. We're having a bit of a crisis here. I'm not thinking very clearly."

I didn't point out that she was thinking clearly enough to have tracked me down in a San Francisco hotel in the middle of the night, which meant that she'd already talked with Suzanne and they'd decided this was my department. After years in the business, we collaborate on most things, but when the agenda calls for a classy, soft-spoken professional to charm and cajole a board of trustees, Suzanne goes. When it's a case of crisis management and perhaps bringing staff to heel, they call for me, or, as one trustee put it, send in the big woman with the loud voice and fierce eyes. That's not what I see when I look in the mirror, but it's what the client sees that counts.

"What's up?"

"One of our students fell through the ice in the pond last night and drowned."

Just as surely as if I'd been a knight closing my helmet, lowering my lance, and galloping off to joust, I shifted into consultant mode, my brain churning out a list of responses to Dorrie's crisis. Any serious injury to a student is a headmistress's nightmare. The death of a student, or of anyone in the campus community, calls for prompt and serious damage control. She'd called me because she knew I'd dealt with these things before. It had been a rocky autumn in the independent school world—only December and I'd already been consulted about a suicide; a student, with an obsessional crush on a teacher, who brought her father's handgun back from a weekend at home and tried to make him sleep with her; and a young athletic star on steroids who tried to force himself on his girlfriend.

Boarding schools were particularly paranoid—no, paranoid was a bad word since the fears were genuine— particularly worried about suicides because adolescents are so suggestible. Where there's one, there's a significant risk of copycat activity. "Was it an accident?"

Dorrie sighed. "I don't know yet, Thea. We're talking to her roommate and her friends, of course, and the dorm parents. She had been depressed but she wasn't a very happy girl in general and there doesn't seem to have been any significant increase in her depression." She paused and shifted into gear, unwilling to waste time speculating. Dorrie would wait until she'd gathered her facts. It wasn't that she lacked compassion, she just had a businesslike approach to life. Since I did, too, we worked very well together.

"Here's what I'm planning to do," she said. "The students will be gathering for breakfast soon. At breakfast we will announce an all-school meeting in the auditorium, at which I will inform them of their classmate's death. Morning classes will meet as usual but in the afternoon they will meet in small groups with their advisors and a counselor to talk about what has happened. The administrative staff, along with whatever trustees I've been able to assemble, will be calling the parents to explain briefly what has happened. We will follow that phone call with a letter. I wish you were here, Thea. It's her parents I'm really worried about."

"It sounds like you've got the situation under control," I said. "Keep the counselors available for a few days and be sure the students know where to find them. Even if it means you end up paying them to sit for hours with nothing to do. Evening hours are particularly important. It's after dinner, when they've been sitting in their rooms and had time to brood, that they may need someone to talk to. Keep the student center open later, maybe even all night. Tell the faculty to make themselves available, too. Often a troubled student will seek out a trusted faculty member. You'll need to run a workshop for the faculty and the dorm parents so they'll know how to handle this. They're your front line in this. Oh, and food. Call the food service and tell them you'll need lots of food. In the student center and probably in the lounges of the dorms. That's all I can think of right now."

I shifted myself up on the pillow, turned on the light, and grabbed the pad of paper hotels are so good about keeping by their phones. I always take them home with me to put next to my own phone, but at home there's no maid to be sure they *stay* by the phone. "Tell me what happened," I said. "I'll do some more thinking about it and call you later if I have any more ideas."

"I know embarrassingly little, Thea," she said.

"Don't tell the parents that," I said. "You've called your lawyer?"

"He's on the way."

Dorrie told me what she knew and it wasn't much. The dead girl's name was Laney Taggert. Margaret Delaney Taggert. A junior who had started as a sophomore. Pretty but standoffish. Manipulative. Secretive. She didn't have a lot of friends at school. She had a boyfriend but it was reportedly a stormy relationship. Dorrie was trying to confirm when she'd last been seen, but hadn't yet caught up with the faculty advisor who'd shared her table at dinner. She wasn't there at bed check but her roommate thought she'd gone away for the weekend.

As Dorrie gave me the few facts she knew, my mind raced ahead of her like a frisky dog. The pad in my hand was covered with notes on the questions I wanted to ask. About the system of checks they used to keep track of students. Whether juniors and seniors had greater privileges. What Laney's relationship with her roommate was. Was she in the habit of taking solitary walks? Was there a system in place to warn students about the pond? When she'd last been seen. Who had found her and why had they been out so early?

As soon as Dorrie finished, I started in on my list but she cut me off. "Those are all the right questions, but they can wait until you get here. I'm in the middle of fighting a forest fire now. As soon as you can I want you to come in and go over all this stuff. I've got to go. I've been standing out by the pond watching them fish her out with a grappling hook and trying to give her CPR. My feet are soaked, the rest of me is frozen, and if it weren't seven A.M. I'd say I need a stiff drink. And the police chief is in the doorway glaring at me. When are you coming back?"

"Tonight. We're taking the red-eye."

"Can you be here by ten?"

"Foggy-headed and bleary-eyed."

"I'd rather have you in that state than most people bright-eyed and bushy-tailed. See you tomorrow."

"Wait, Dorrie." I could feel her impatience across three thousand miles. "Stay in touch. And follow the three C's."

"The three C's?"

"Closemouthed, cautious, and caring. And don't let this turn into a media circus. Only one person talks to the press. Either you or Tom. Be sure that everyone knows that. Be sure the students know that they don't have to answer any questions. Tell them they shouldn't be answering questions. Tell the media to leave your students alone. Make sure campus security knows that and is prepared to back you up."

"I will. Anything else?"

"This will sound silly but it isn't. You might consider walkie-talkies."

"For what?" She sounded skeptical.

"For being able to move around the campus and still stay in touch with your office and campus security."

"I never would have thought of it," she said. "I hope it doesn't come to that, but I'll keep it in mind." She was gone but I could picture her crossing her pleasant office and dealing calmly and competently with the waiting police chief.

I knew what she was facing. I'd been on the scene almost immediately after the suicide, following the headmaster through a grueling eighteen-hour day. They're a special breed of people, heads of schools. I wouldn't want to be one . . . couldn't be one, I don't suffer fools gladly enough. I'm too impulsive and impatient. Too irreverent to keep a straight face when the bullshit is coming thick and fast. Too much of a loner to be around people that much. But I work well with them and my clients like me. Maybe because I'm allowed to call a spade a spade and then they can use my reports, in their refined but forceful ways, to effect the changes they want to make.

Andre stirred restlessly beside me. "Back to sleep," he murmured. "It's late."

I turned off the light and snuggled down beside him. My mind was running too fast to go back to sleep but if I got up, he'd get up, and he needed to rest. We lay in the sleepy darkness, our bodies entwined, while my mind was back in Massachusetts.

Dorrie Chapin was headmistress of the Bucksport School, a second-tier coed boarding school about thirty miles outside of Boston in the picturesque town of Sedgwick. Bucksport had an extremely photogenic campus with massive trees, rolling manicured lawns, and stately brick buildings, which had made it the setting for several movies. Its strong athletic program was reflected in the acres of well-maintained playing fields and the athletic physiques of the students. There were miles of walking and jogging trails through the woods and a pretty, tree-lined pond about a mile back in the woods that they sometimes used for skating. J. Crew, Eddie Bauer, Gap, and L. L. Bean did a big business there and all the young men owned blue blazers and gray slacks while all the young women had an adequate supply of dresses. The school had a slightly larger than normal population of students from broken homes.

Dorrie was the first headmistress—women are only beginning to make inroads into the inner sanctums of coed schools—and she was operating very carefully. She was only in her second year at the school, hired after an extensive national search that had gone through two rounds of candidates before the trustees found anyone they liked. Not that all of them had liked Dorrie. She was the majority choice of a split board, a difficult situation for anyone entering a new position. Her job had been further complicated because she'd had to clean up a serious fiscal mess caused by the inattention and inability of the departing headmaster and after that she'd faced a disturbing decline in applications.

She'd taken it all in stride. It was her nature to see things as challenges rather than problems, opportunities rather than obstacles. The fiscal situation was improving and my partner, Suzanne, and I had done an admissions survey and produced a report and recommendations that the trustees had accepted and were acting on. Still, she was just beginning to get on her feet. An incident like this was the last thing she needed.

I tried to picture the pond in winter. I'd seen it in April when parts of the wide path had been soggy wallows of well-churned mud and the overhanging trees just sprouting their first tiny leaves. Everything had seemed soft and gentle and the pond had been still as a mirror. I tried replacing that budding green with the gloomier browns, blacks, and grays of late fall, covering the ground with a light snow and the pond with ice. Maybe it was pretty but in my imagination it seemed grim and uninviting. I wondered why anyone would choose to walk there in December and why she would venture out onto the ice. Had it been an accident or had Laney been a troubled teenager looking for a final solution to her problems?

Eventually his warmth and the rhythm of Andre's breathing made me sleepy again. I left Bucksport and Dorrie and the sad end of Delaney Taggert behind and went back to being on vacation in my favorite city, San Francisco, and back to one of the things that I did best—sleeping. There were no more phone calls and when we woke up a bright winter sunshine was beating down on the fog and everything gleamed. I couldn't wait to get out and walk.

We wrapped up a splendid Saturday with drinks in the Redwood Room. Andre was staring pensively at his Armagnac as if there were a message for him hidden in the glass. "Are you glad you came?" I asked.

He took my hand and gripped it hard. "Let's not go back. Let's escape into the mountains and live off the land," he said, his dark eyes shining with mischief.

"I wouldn't know how to live without the sound of a ringing phone."

"You're a bright girl. You could learn."

"I'm not a girl, Lemieux, I'm a woman."

He gave me a thorough appraisal. "That's right. You are. Almost too much woman for me."

"What's that supposed to mean?"

"You use your womanly wiles to break down my defenses and make me feel things. You make me be alive whether I want to or not. . . ."

"Is this turning into a serious discussion?" He nodded. "But you aren't serious about wanting to run away?"

"Half-serious," he said. He put his hand on his forehead as if measuring depth. "Sometimes, when I feel like I've had it up to here with the awful things people do to each other, with the lying and deception and evil, the lack of any sort of fellow-feeling or compassion, I let myself daydream about how nice it would be to just get away from it all to someplace peaceful and quiet. Just the two of us. Maybe a dog. Maybe some kids. Crazy, wild, insolent, headstrong girls just like you, brown as bark with their hair flying in the wind. . . ."

I just stared at him, astonished. Andre loved his work, loved being a policeman. He'd never talked like this before. And while he'd mentioned children, he'd always been joking before. We didn't even talk about marriage. Close as we were, I'd been hurt so much by losing David that a part of me was still terrified of making another commitment.

I met my husband, David, in a bar where I'd gone with some girlfriends after a Bergman movie. The film, as Bergman will, had stirred us all, and we'd all felt we needed to have a drink and talk it over before we went home. Being alone with the bleak and disturbing thoughts his movies inspire can be downright dangerous. David had stopped at our table and said one of the stupidest things a man can say—"I knew three such gorgeous women didn't just come here to talk." We'd begun a three-pronged effort to put him in his place when he turned to me. "I admit it. It was a stupid remark and it was a lie. I was drawn across the room by your eyes and I've come to beg to be allowed to spend eternity in their orbit."

That was David. When there was something he wanted, he didn't let anything stand in his way, and he'd wanted me. I'd ended up going home with him that night and after that I'd never gone home except to pick up clothes. We got married and settled into an intense happily ever after. And it was happily ever after for two years, until the night a friend talked David into coming for a ride in his new Camaro. The friend, who had been drinking, wrapped the car and David around a tree. He walked away with a few bruises but he killed David. When he came to apologize to me, I broke his nose. It didn't make me feel any better. After that, I pulled myself into my shell and stayed there, unwilling to be hurt again. Loving Andre had broken down a lot of my defenses, but as the last year had shown, Andre's job was a very dangerous one. I couldn't bear losing someone again.

Sometimes I forget Andre has the cop's knack for reading people's minds. "Just let me talk, okay?" he said. "I'm not trying to put you in a cage. I know how you feel and I've accepted that. We're not so far apart on things, you know. After Melanie, I still have an intense fear of the prison door clanging shut behind me."

We sure are a romantic pair. I'm afraid of getting too close for fear that I'll be hurt. He's afraid of being trapped in another bad marriage. We'll probably still be like this when we're ninety, still circling warily around the central question. "I'm not sure I could live on a mountaintop with you. When you put on that inscrutable cop's face, lock yourself away, and put out the Nobody Home sign, I get so angry I—"

"Come beating down the door," he said.

"As I recall, sometimes you're not only not home, you've got all the other cops covering for you and nobody knows where you are. When you have a highly mobile job, it's really easy to be elusive. . . ." In the past, Andre had dealt with conflict by being unavailable. Now that we were living together, it was harder, but for the past two weeks, with me working in Boston, he'd become impossible again.

"I won't do that again, scout's honor. . . ."

"You were a scout?"

He puffed out his chest in mock pride. "Eagle Scout, ma'am."

I fanned myself with my hand. "Don't do that thing with your chest. It gives me palpitations."

"Sorry." He lowered his eyes and tried to look humble. Andre trying to look humble is like a Doberman trying to look friendly. He's too big, too physical, too intense.

"At ease, Trooper," I said.

"I am at ease. More at ease, anyway. You know that losing Ray is going to bother me for a long time. You can understand about that. But it's not locked away anymore. You may complain about the Nobody Home signs, Thea, but you don't let them stop you. Trying to keep you out is like waving a red flag in front of a bull. It just makes you try that much harder."

"When I was little, my mother was complaining to the doctor about how she couldn't manage me. Pigheaded and stubborn is what she said. The doctor suggested these might be easier traits to accept if she looked at me as determined and resolute. It's funny how often she still tells that story considering I was the good doobie, at least compared to Michael and Carrie."

"Your mother doesn't appreciate opposition." I gave him the let's-not-go-into-that look and he dropped the subject. Since our big fight in the spring, my mother and I have barely spoken. "I can picture a little girl like you. I'd like to have one someday."

It was the second time he'd mentioned children. "What's this with you and little girls all of a sudden?"

He leered and twisted the ends of an imaginary mustache. "I'm twisted."

"Seriously."

He finished his drink and stared sadly at the empty glass. Ten feet away, the waitress noticed and through an elaborate series of signals they agreed she'd bring him another. Women notice Andre. He has an aggressively physical presence. Big shoulders, deep voice, strong jaw.

The persistent five-o'clock shadow that screams too much testosterone. I used to resent it but I'm getting better. Except when I hear Amanda's honeyed tones on the phone.

"Coming so close to death makes me think more about life." It seemed odd that he was saying these things now and not six months ago, but people come to things in their own time, in their own ways. I waited for the rest but that was all he was going to say about it. "Speaking of life, how's Suzanne doing?"

Suzanne is my partner. Unless, since she started the business, I'm her partner. She's small and blond and even more of a workaholic than I am. I'm a better organizer and a better writer. She's an ace people person. Suzanne could get Godzilla to cooperate and think it was his idea. She had had a baby in January and was going crazy trying to balance motherhood and work. "Just as you'd expect. She's trying to nurture the perfect baby between projects and child-care crises. Trying to be the perfect stepmother. Coming in every day impeccably groomed and in despair because she has to wear size four clothes instead of size twos. She'll be lucky if the poor thing isn't neurotic. I imagine its first word will be 'survey,' unless it's 'enrollment' or 'statistics.' His first word, I should say. Little Paul Eric Merritt, Jr."

The waitress brought his drink and another bowl of smoked nuts and we stopped talking about children. With a gentle buzz on, we collected our luggage, let the doorman summon a taxi, and left San Francisco behind.

The plane was on time. We ignored the beverage service. Ignored the dinner service. Ignored the movie. I used his shoulder as a pillow, he used my head as a pillow, and we slept in a companionable heap all the way to Boston.

It was a sad parting. We should have been going home together to build on our hard-won closeness. We hated to say good-bye. Maybe it was a good thing we had such busy lives, such demanding schedules. Otherwise we would have gotten so caught up in saying good-bye we'd never have gotten around to parting and neither of us would ever work again, just a pair of happy, homeless street people, singing in the rain. Some days I think I wouldn't mind that at all and today was one of those days. "Take care of yourself, Andre," I told him. "No more cowboys and Indians." It was not a politically correct remark.

"Good guys and bad guys," he corrected.

"Just be careful."

"I will," he said. "You, too. No more Detective Kozak. You go out there to Bucksport and do your consultant thing and that's all, you understand?"

Since neither of us has a personality that takes kindly to being told what to do, we walk a fine line in the orders department, but this time he had a point. Since he'd known me, I'd required more stitches than a baby quilt and none of it had been any fun. All I have to do is think the words *emergency room* and I break into a cold sweat. "Believe me, that's all I intend to do. This is work, the stuff I do every day, not one of my mother's save-the-world projects."

"It better be. If you find anything even slightly questionable, let the police handle it. I've spent enough time hovering by your bedside waiting for you to wake up."

"I thought you liked me in bed. . . ."

"Not in hospital beds, Thea."

"I could say the same about you."

They announced that his flight was boarding. He gave me a hug that would have cracked the ribs of a lesser woman and a kiss that should have gone on forever. Then he picked up his bag and walked away without looking back. *Way to go, Lemieux,* I thought. *Leave 'em hungry for more.* I picked up my own bag and headed for central parking.

CHAPTER 3

IT WAS A bitter-cold morning. Clear and windy. Little bits of orphan snow blew around the parking garage looking for the rest of their drift, warring with the windblown sand for space in the corners. If this was a taste of the winter to come, we were in for a hard time. I was parked on the roof so I let the car warm up while I brushed off the snow and dirt that had settled on my windshield. As soon as the weather warmed up, I'd take her to the car wash. Under her coat of dust and road salt my nice red Saab looked pale and ancient though I'd only had her for six months. You can't own a bright red car and not keep it up. It wouldn't be right. Across the harbor, Boston looked surprisingly clean. Snow sparkled off some roofs and the wind was blowing great plumes of white smoke sideways and tearing them into pieces like a giant shredding cotton.

Even with a Saab, I hate driving on slippery roads, but luckily the roads were clear. Massachusetts highways are hard enough without ice and snow. They don't have driver's ed here, they have bumper cars. I negotiated the tunnel, merged onto the expressway and burst out onto I-93 ready to make some time. Unfortunately, the other cars on the road didn't share my agenda. I got stuck behind a trio of law-abiding citizens determined to make the rest of us go fifty-five. Very unlike Massachusetts drivers. They were lucky some truck hadn't flattened them like recyclable tin cans. I wasn't surprised that one was from Maine, another from Illinois and the third, I saw when I finally passed, was a tiny old lady who couldn't see over the steering wheel.

I'll never have that problem. Even if I do shrink when I get old, it'll only bring me down to five feet nine or ten or so, and maybe I'll finally be able to find clothes long enough to cover my knees. I don't wear short skirts from choice. I wear short skirts because when you're almost six feet tall, all skirts are short. My partner, Suzanne, who is short, says I'm wrong. She thinks all the clothes are made for tall women. Maybe clothes aren't made for women at all. One thing I know. If men had to wear skirts and dresses, they'd come in short, regular, and long, just like suits do. Sure they make something called petites, but Suzanne, who is petite, says they aren't proportioned for anyone she knows. Just as jackets are fitted to accommodate men's shoulders, women's should be fitted to accommodate our chests. I'm sick to death of blouses that bulge between the second and third buttons. Minimizer bras and double-sided tape are all that stand between me and ostentatious display. The challenge would be to find a form of sizing that wouldn't make the smaller-chested woman feel inadequate. Maybe we could size them like champagne? A magnum, a jeroboam, or a Methuselah?

Today I was not wearing a blouse. I was wearing a plain gray-green sweater dress, purchased by Suzanne back in the days when she'd had the energy to shop. It had the virtue of being able to be slept in and still look decent. When she first hired me, Suzanne had found my wardrobe deplorable. She'd tried nagging and nudging but I don't much care what I wear as long as I'm comfortable and covered. She finally solved the problem by buying my clothes herself, a solution that suited both of us. I didn't know what I was going to do now that she'd stopped doing it. Maybe I'd get a personal shopper.

I rolled off the highway, drove through the uncluttered streets of Sedgwick, and through the tall brick pillars that marked the entrance to the Bucksport School. As the narrow road meandered along through a stretch of swampy forest, I wondered how fire engines ever got in. Maybe there was a school rule against fires. More likely they just used another entrance. This one was to impress prospective students and their parents. The road widened slightly at the top of a rise and then rolled down between the manicured lawns and scattered brick buildings to the big, grassy circle that formed the center of the campus. It reminded me of a New England town common. I put the car in one of the visitor spaces in front of Metcalfe Hall between a police cruiser and a shiny black Lexus. The tall bell tower, faintly reminiscent of the factories of Lawrence and Manchester, cast a long black shadow across the snowy lawn.

In the large, open lobby, a gaggle of girls stood together, giggling about something. Their high-pitched laughter echoed in the big room. I went down the hall past them to Dorrie's office. Beside the door was a black-lettered sign that still unaccountably said Headmaster. Probably Dorrie had tried to change it and been stalled by the guy in charge of grounds and buildings. Curt Sawyer was openly resentful about working for a woman. Lori Leonard, Dorrie's secretary, was frowning at something on her computer screen. She looked up when I came in. From her smile, I could tell she was relieved that I wasn't someone else. "You can go right in, Ms. Kozak," she said. "Mrs. Chapin is expecting you."

Dorrie wasn't alone. Besides Dave Holdorf, the assistant headmaster, and Curt Sawyer, there were two other men I didn't know. "Good morning, Thea," she said, getting up and coming to meet me. "I'm glad you're here." She sounded relieved. Winter air travel is unpredictable. She probably had been afraid I wouldn't make it. Her hand, when I shook it, was cold, and she looked as though she hadn't slept. Still, she was faultlessly turned out in a rich wool pleated skirt, a white cashmere sweater, and a Hermés scarf. Her jewelry was simple, understated, and real.

She led me to a wing chair facing the group of men. "Coffee?"

"Please. That stuff they serve on the plane doesn't do a thing." Dorrie is the kind of person who learns how you take your coffee once and you never have to tell her again. It's just one example of the kind of memory for people and details that makes her so good at her job. She went to the door and told Lori what I wanted. The men already had their coffee.

"I'm not sure you've met our legal counsel, Peter Van Deusen, and the Sedgwick police chief, Rocky Miller?" I shook hands with Peter and Rocky, wondering why a grown man would continue to call himself Rocky. I should know better than to think things like that around cops. I know they can read minds.

"It's really Alan Rockport Miller, Jr.," he said, "but I've always been called Rocky and it's too late to change now." It was the kind of comment you might expect from a man in his fifties, but Rocky Miller wasn't that old. Maybe late thirties. Maybe forties, if he was older than he looked. "Forty-five," he said, reading my mind again.

"What's my next question, Chief?" I said.

"What am I doing here?"

Dorrie looked amused. "I see he does it to you, too," she said.

"They all do it," I said, annoyed at the way Rocky Miller was taking over Dorrie's meeting.

"They?" he said. There was an edge in his voice I decided to ignore. He probably thought I meant men, not knowing about my history with cops. Most cops have an us-them mentality. They assume a degree of separateness that really isn't justified.

The lawyer cleared his throat and ostentatiously checked his watch. "Can we get on with this? I have another meeting. . . ."

Maybe Rocky could read my mind, but I could read Peter's. He was thinking that he was an important and busy lawyer who wasn't going to let some two-bit local police chief steal the show. I glanced at Rocky and saw that he was thinking the same thing.

Dave Holdorf got up and brushed some imaginary specks off his pants. "Are you sure you need me, Dorrie, because I've got a lot of—"

"I need you." Dorrie and Dave respected each other's abilities, but they didn't like each other. Dave had wanted to be headmaster but the trustees didn't think he could handle the job. He knew it and resented it. I saw that Rocky hadn't missed that, either. Dave sat back down with an almost imperceptible flounce. A look of distaste flickered across Curt Sawyer's face. The administration at Bucksport, like bunches of disparate people everywhere, was a dysfunctional family, but it was coping well with its dysfunction.

Dorrie handed me a fat folder of papers and sat down. "All of you, Thea included, are pretty well up-to-date on the situation." They all looked at me curiously. They knew what their roles were, but except for Dave, none of them understood how I fit in. Dorrie caught the looks. "Ms. Kozak is an independent schools specialist. One of her areas of expertise is crisis management. I'm afraid this situation has just about ruined her San Francisco vacation and she was willing to come to us straight from the airport." She gave them a settle-down-and-get-along look and launched straight into the bad news. "Chief Miller has brought us another piece of bad news this morning. Do you want to tell them, Rocky, or shall I?"

His answer surprised me. "It's your show, Dorrie," he said.

She acknowledged the compliment with a nod. She opened the folder she was holding and took out some papers. "The autopsy report indicates that Delaney Taggert was about seven weeks pregnant." Curt Sawyer and Dave

Holdorf spoke together, their words crossing like rapiers in the air.

"Which suggests that she might have killed herself," Dave said.

"Why is that such a big deal, Dorrie?" Curt asked.

Close behind them came Van Deusen's question. "Do the parents know about this yet?"

"Not yet, but they'll have to be told. And it's a big deal, Curt, as you should well know, because the last thing we need right now is another indication that we aren't taking adequate care of our students. You might argue that it doesn't make any difference if Delaney was pregnant now that she's dead, but to her parents, and undoubtedly to all our parents, particularly the parents of daughters, it could make a big difference. We function here in an in-loco-parentis capacity. The parents trust us to keep their children safe—"

"Come on, Dorrie. You know as well as I do that if these kids want to do it they'll find a way," Curt said. A typical head of campus security, and, in Bucksport's case, head of grounds and buildings, he was a nuts-and-bolts guy. His grounds were impeccable; his grasp of the politics of school administration somewhat less so.

"Try telling the parents of a sixteen-year-old that, Curt," Dorrie said.

"We've got to be very careful how we approach the parents about this," Van Deusen said. He was sitting forward on the sofa, one foot tapping nervously. Everything about his posture was tense, his short, stocky body seemed barely contained by his suit. He reminded me of a terrier straining at the leash.

"I'm aware of that, Peter," Dorrie said. "I was hoping you could give me some guidance. But before we get to that, there's more. Something a lot more serious." Everyone stared at her in surprise, probably wondering what could be more serious than a dead student who had been pregnant. "You may recall the circumstances under which Delaney was found but I will review them for you anyway. An early-morning jogger using one of our woods trails spotted something pink out on the pond, paused to look at it, and noticed a large area where the ice seemed to have been broken. There were footprints leading out to the hole in the ice and none coming back. He went out as far as he could and poked around the hole with a stick. He came up with a pink glove and came straight to the campus to get Curt."

"We know all that, Dorrie," Peter Van Deusen said impatiently, checking his watch again. "And then a couple maintenance guys went out and fished around with shovels and found the body, which the fire department had to get out with grappling hooks. So what's the big news?"

I decided that I didn't like Peter Van Deusen. At that moment Dorrie looked as though she didn't, either. I knew that what was foremost in my mind was central in Dorrie's, too—the potentially devastating effect of a teenage suicide on the peer community. And suicide was the most likely thing, given a pregnant, depressed teenager. It was disappointing, almost criminally so, that neither the school's attorney nor the man in charge of campus security understood that.

Dorrie cleared her throat nervously, as though what she had to say was particularly difficult for her. "Chief Miller did a follow-up interview with the jogger yesterday and learned something we didn't hear the first time. He says there were two sets of tracks leading partway onto the pond, as though two people had gone out together, but only one set coming back." She waited for the import of her statement to sink in.

"So?" Curt Sawyer said. "So two kids go down to the pond. One decides to leave and the other goes farther out to explore the ice. What's the big deal?"

"I hope there is no big deal, Curt," Dorrie said quietly. "But it means that somewhere on this campus is the other person who was out there . . . someone who knows a lot more about what happened than we do and who isn't coming forward to talk to us. I'm wondering why."

The whole situation took on a darker tone as possibilities leapt into my mind. Had there been a friend out there unable to save her who was now huddled alone with a terrible secret? Had Laney needed support to get herself out there, then dismissed her companion on some pretext before taking that final plunge? Someone on this campus was burdened with a terrible secret.

I was about to ask a question when Van Deusen interrupted. "Can we take a few minutes to talk about handling the parents?" he said. "I've got another meeting to go to."

"Excuse me, Peter? On a Sunday?" Dorrie's voice had an edge it hadn't had earlier. "When I called to set up this meeting, didn't I make it clear that it might take all morning?" He nodded but I could see that he hadn't detected the change in Dorrie. "Then what's this business about another meeting?"

He shrugged. "Naturally, I'll give you all the help I can, but I have a very busy schedule this week."

Dorrie's palm slapped the arm of her chair. "This is ridiculous. If you don't have time to give Bucksport the attention it needs, Mr. Van Deusen, I'll ask Mr. Graves to assign us an attorney who does. Your cavalier attitude is both offensive and unwarranted. It implies that you do not value our business or appreciate the gravity of the situation."

It looked as though this was one midlevel associate who wasn't going to make partner, and he'd probably always wonder why. I watched Van Deusen deflate under Dorrie's steady gaze like a balloon with a big leak. John Graves was the managing partner at Graves and Doer. The very mention of his name made his subordinates tremble. At least Van Deusen had the good sense to admit his mistake. He apologized and used the phone to call his office and reschedule his meeting. The client, it appeared, was his disgruntled wife.

When he had rejoined the group, Dorrie tented her fingers on her knee and looked around at all of us. "Now, I am·not ready to take the radical step of assuming there was some sort of foul play involved in Delaney Taggert's death, and neither is Chief Miller. All I'm saying is that there is someone in this community . . . maybe more than one person . . . who knows more than they are saying about Delaney's trip to the pond, and we need to know what that something is. That's where Thea comes in."

All their eyes turned curiously to me. Somewhere a distant bell rang. Tomorrow the corridors would be filled with a hubbub of feet and voices. A headmaster's office usually isn't isolated from the student community. But today was Sunday. Through the window I saw the sunlight on a trio of bright heads crossing the circle. "Delaney Taggert fell thought the cracks," Dorrie said. "Maybe in more ways than one. Her parents are devastated and we can expect that devastation to turn to rage toward the Bucksport School. That we are not a caring environment. That we let their daughter drown because we weren't taking proper care of our students." She ran a nervous hand through her neatly coiffed graying hair.

"Our best protection, against a lawsuit, against an exodus of students, and because it's the right thing to do, is to conduct a thorough inventory of our system of parietals, checks, and faculty contacts, as well as our security system"—Curt Sawyer sniffed loudly and Dorrie ignored him—"to be sure that we are doing all we should, and to find out where, if anywhere, things went wrong in this case. To demonstrate that we are taking this seriously, we're bringing in an outside person, a crackerjack independent consultant, to assess the situation and confirm that our procedures are adequate to care for our students."

Curt Sawyer, who ought to have been particularly interested in this subject, looked bored. He was playing a game with his feet and the patterns on the Bokara rug. "Isn't that right, Curt?" Dorrie snapped him to attention like a drill sergeant. He stopped playing but continued to look bored and annoyed.

I waited for my marching orders, feeling slightly intimidated by her praise and slightly uncertain about the assignment. An audit of the school's procedures was well within the bounds of our usual work, but the fact that a death was involved did give me pause. On the other hand, I was just beginning to develop something of a national reputation as a competent troubleshooter in tricky situations like this. I was good at it and Dorrie needed my help. There was no need to get into the details of Delaney Taggert's death. My job would be the more removed one of assessing the procedures in place for monitoring students and their safety, and determining whether they had been followed. If it began to look as though there were anything suspicious about her death, that would be a job for Chief Rocky.

"Dave, I want you to work closely with Thea. Smooth the way for her. Tell people why she's here and try to ensure their cooperation. I have an ulterior motive in all this as well, which I've discussed with you, Rocky." Dave Holdorf's eyebrows went up when she called the chief by his first name. "I'm hoping, in the course of her interviews, Thea may be able to learn more about what happened to Delaney." This time it was my eyebrows that went up.

"I wouldn't advise you to do that," Van Deusen said. "I think any questions related to her death ought to come from the police. You don't want it to look like you're conducting an investigation. A superficial inventory for PR purposes is fine. A good idea, in fact. But not probing questions about Delaney Taggert. Suppose someone on the outside found out. Suppose Chip Barrett found out. He'd make it front-page news."

"Who is Chip Barrett?" I asked.

"Jimmy Olsen crossed with a pit bull," Curt Sawyer said sourly. "A nosy, interfering little weasel who doesn't understand the word no. Reporter for the *Sedgwick Sentinel*. A buck-toothed little rodent who fancies himself the Scud Stud." From this unusually voluble response, I deduced that Sawyer had had his share of run-ins with Chip Barrett.

I resisted the urge to point out that not understanding the word no was a problem a lot of males had, even though I'd just given a talk at the last Independent Schools Symposium on managing issues of violence and coercion by boys in the boarding school environment. I was as nervous about Dorrie's suggestion as her lawyer was but for different reasons. I'd sworn that I'd steer clear of anything that looked like an investigation. Even if Laney's death was an accident and not suicide, I'd already had my share of traumatic deaths. I wanted to stay at a nice clean arm's length from the details. I was here to inventory procedures and process. That I could do and that was as close to the death as I wanted to get. I didn't mind finding out the facts like what time she'd signed out and where she was supposed to have gone. What I didn't want to do was come to know Delaney Taggert. I didn't mind knowing her schedule; I didn't want to know about her life.

It sounded as if Dorrie had a different agenda in mind but that wasn't something that needed to be discussed before a roomful of people. We could have a quiet one-on-one later.

"Okay, that's it for now," Dorrie said. "Curt, you'll be working closely with Thea. I want you to be sure she has access to any of your people that she needs to talk to and I don't want any macho horsing around about not talking to her because she's a woman. And don't give me that look. I know how your people are. A few sessions of law-enforcement training and all they want to say is 'Just the facts, ma'am.'" Curt's face was belligerent but Dorrie stared him down and he went without saying whatever it was he wanted to say.

Dorrie sighed as he went out the door. "If that man

weren't so good at what he does . . ." She gathered up her papers and went back behind her desk. From the security of that position, she directed the rest of her troops. "Dave, would you show Thea where her office will be?" She checked her watch. "Thea, I need about twenty minutes with Peter and the chief and then I was hoping you and I could talk over lunch?"

I followed Dave out, noting the tense set of his shoulders. Lori wasn't at her desk. I took advantage of the fact that we were alone. "Has it been hell, Dave?"

He nodded. "It sure has. Dorrie's handling it well. She's doing a great job with the parents and the media. Her damage control measures are excellent and bringing you in is an inspired move. But she has no idea how shaken up the faculty is. Her focus has been on the students. I think the faculty could use some counseling as well. They take it very personally, as you can imagine. I guess I don't have to tell you what the boarding school environment is like. You know as much about it as any outsider can. It's kind of like a small town. We all live in each other's pockets here, and right now, everyone is looking in everyone else's pocket, trying to find a place to put the blame. They all feel responsible. You'll see what I mean when you talk to them."

He led me down the corridor and opened an anonymous door. "We've put you in here. A bit cramped, I'm afraid, but we've done what we could to make it comfortable."

A bit cramped was putting it nicely. The office they were giving me wasn't much bigger than a closet, but it had a window looking out over the circle, a rug on the floor, and chair that looked as if it wouldn't ruin my back. There were even a couple nice pieces of student art on the walls. "Whom have I displaced, Dave?"

"No one." I knew better. Private schools are always short on space. Offices don't sit around long before someone discovers them and asserts squatter's rights. "The assistant business manager. But she's on maternity

leave. Come next door for a sec and I'll introduce you to
Ellie Drucker, our 'Jill of all trades.' If you have a question and you can't find me or Lori, Ellie can help. She
does fund-raising and organizes faculty events and probably most important of all, she's responsible for our
perennial gardens."

"It's Sunday, Dave. Why is everybody here?"

He shrugged. "Like I said. It's a small town."

I followed him a few steps down the hall to the next
door. It was open, revealing a cubicle like mine. A
woman was sitting behind the desk staring intently at a
computer printout. "Ellie, can I bother you for a minute?
I'd like you to meet someone."

She put the papers down and smiled at Dave. "I'm always glad to be interrupted when I'm doing this," she
said. She stood up and leaned over the desk, her hand
outstretched. She was a tall woman with a wide, pleasant
face and well-cut gray-blond hair and had obviously once
been quite attractive. Now she was carrying at least sixty
extra pounds and the weight had puffed up her skin so
that her cheeks were squirrelly and her chin blended into
her neck. She was wearing the suburban matron's costume of flowery dirndl skirt and cotton sweater with
matching flowers. The cheerful colors suited her but the
skirt exaggerated her width.

"Eleanor Drucker, this is Thea Kozak."

She had a nice firm handshake. "Is this Dorrie's consultant?" Dave nodded. "Well, I hope you can get to the
heart of this thing quickly and reassure everyone that it
was an accident," she said. "My husband, Chas, was
Laney's advisor. It's been a terrible shock for him and I
know many of the students are upset as well."

"I told Thea that you were a fount of valuable information and advice," Dave said. "I hope you don't mind."

"I appreciate the compliment, Dave. I'd be glad to help
Ms. Kozak anytime." She smiled ruefully. "You can usually find me right here."

I realized then that we'd met before, or at least spoken, when Suzanne and I were doing our earlier consulting project, and I was embarrassed. The fact was, though, that Ellie Drucker was one of those people who toil quietly behind the scenes and don't get noticed. "We spoke before, I think, the last time EDGE was working here." EDGE was what we called our educational consulting business. She nodded.

As we were leaving she called after us, "By the way, you two don't know of anyone who needs an au pair, do you? My niece from Indiana just landed on my doorstep looking for a job. She drives me nuts, but she's great with kids."

"I'll ask around," I said. Dave just smiled and shook his head.

I followed him back to my office. "Let me know if you need anything, okay? And I think Dorrie's arranged for everyone to have lunch later. I'll check." Dave had turned to go but he turned back. "I'm glad you're here, Thea." Then he left. I was surprised. Dave and I get along all right but he'd never seemed particularly glad to see me before. Suzanne and I are kind of like doctors. People consult us because they need us, because we can help them, but they aren't happy about it since needing our help means that something went wrong.

I sat down at the desk, opened the file, and stared at the first thing inside. A picture of Delaney Taggert. It was a posed picture in black-and-white. But even in black-and-white, her huge dark eyes stared out at me with a frightening challenge. She had the kind of face that grows beautiful with time but is hard for a teenager to wear. High forehead, heavy eyebrows, jutting cheekbones and a thin, elegant nose. Her mouth was too wide, too well defined, and had a slightly insolent curl. Just from her name, Laney, I'd been expecting someone less challenging, sweeter, more innocent looking. She seemed to be asking me something. I leaned over the picture, studying the challenging, almost arrogant face, and it became clear what she was asking. "Come on, Thea Kozak, do I look like someone who would kill myself?"

I closed the file with a snap and leaned back in my chair, eyes closed. I was not going to let my imagination run away like this. I was here to do a job and I would do it, but that was all. Someone else, Chief Miller maybe, could figure out who Delaney Taggert was and what had happened to her.

Out in the hall I heard the rumble of heavy, hurrying feet. The door flew open and a disheveled teenage boy burst in and slammed it shut behind him. "Are you Thea Kozak?" he said, throwing himself into my visitor's chair. I nodded. "Good," he said, "I need to talk to you about Laney Taggert."

CHAPTER 4

AFTER HIS PRECIPITOUS entrance, the boy tossed his book bag onto the floor beside the chair, shifted an overgrown shock of hair out of his face, and stared at me with the total misery only an adolescent can manage. He had the fragile, ravaged look the young get when they go without food and sleep but even in his unkempt state he was beautiful, something that belonged in a glossy fashion ad for Gap or Benetton. We stared at each other for a minute before he remembered his manners. "I'm Josh," he said, thrusting a reddened hand toward me. "Josh Meyer. I was Laney Taggert's boyfriend."

His hand was unexpectedly callused and rough, his handshake brief and a little awkward. Adult conventions were a veneer that had been laid on him; they weren't really a part of him yet. He settled himself back in the chair and we studied each other again. He had an enviable mane of chestnut hair and gorgeous eyes, dark-ringed gray irises peering through impossibly thick lashes. I recalled as a teenager being convinced that guys always got the best hair and eyes. It was certainly true of Josh Meyer.

"You're the detective, right?" he said, and went on without waiting for my response. "Good. I had to tell somebody and there's been no one around to tell. I mean, no cops or anything, and I wasn't about to waste my time with one of their caring counselors." He made "caring" sound like an obscenity and seemed to assume that I understood what he meant. "Whatever they may tell you, Laney didn't kill herself." He watched my face closely as he delivered this bombshell. "Laney was a complicated person. That's a fancy way of saying real screwed up. She didn't have a lot of confidence in herself. But she was tough, too, and she had plans for her life. She knew being pregnant was no big deal. I mean, she was just going to get an abortion and be done with it. It wasn't something she'd kill herself about."

I had a million questions I wanted to ask him, chief among them where he'd gotten my name and the idea that I was a detective, but dealing with teenagers is a delicate business. It can be tough to get them talking. Once you do, you don't interrupt them. It's far too easy to say the wrong thing or ask the wrong question and have them clam up, end of conversation, good-bye. So I didn't ask Josh Meyer my million questions, I just leaned back in my chair and listened.

It was hard. Moderation wasn't a word in Josh's emotional vocabulary. In both physical appearance and manner he typified the word "edgy." A few sentences into his monologue, he jumped up, wrenched himself out of his coat, and flung it on the floor beside his book bag. Despite the weather, he was wearing only a T-shirt, dingy white with a repellent picture of skeletons and violence fading into gray obscurity, ripped at the shoulder. His long thin arms reminded me of a monkey, the muscles and bones sharply visible beneath the skin, and he was never still.

"People are going to tell you that Laney and I had a lot of fights and it's true. But how am I supposed to feel when my girlfriend tells me she's pregnant and I know the baby isn't mine?" He leaned forward, gripping his knees, and glared at me as if Laney's pregnancy, or at least her failure to comprehend his reaction to it, was somehow my fault. His knees were as bony as his arms and were coming through the holes in his worn-out Bucksport sweats. "Guys aren't supposed to admit stuff like this, but I'm not hung up on all that macho stuff. Laney was the first girl I ever slept with but I'm not so stupid that I wasn't careful. So, yeah, when she told me she was pregnant, I pushed her around a little."

He fingered the hole in his shirt. "Laney did that." I realized that wearing the shirt had nothing to do with the weather; it was a memorial act. He swallowed and raised his head, his bony jaw at once tough and vulnerable. "I didn't know how to feel, you know, I was, like, choking on my feelings. Laney understood that." He took a deep breath. I could feel the punch line coming. "What I wanted to tell you was . . . you find the father of her baby and you'll find the person who killed her."

He sat back in the chair, the starch going out of him, absently playing with one of the rings in his ear. He'd been carrying this message around for days searching for the right person to receive it. Obviously, that person had not been Chief Miller. Now that his task was done, he looked spent. Something vaguely motherly stirred in me. I wanted to give this kid a sandwich and milk and put him down for a nap. He might be old enough for sex but he couldn't take care of himself. This was someone's beautiful son. Unslept, unshaven, unfed, and underdressed. "May I ask some questions?"

His gray eyes regarded me suspiciously. "I guess." The set of his jaw was pugnacious and he perched on the edge of his chair, ready for flight. That was another adolescent thing—they said what they wanted to say and then they wanted to be gone. Suzanne, who is learning to cope with an adolescent stepson, calls it hit-and-run speech.

"What makes you think Laney Taggert's death wasn't an accident?"

"Laney wasn't stupid." I waited for more but that was all he said. Outside the window, the blue sky was clouding over.

"Has someone told you that they suspected her death was a suicide?"

He gave me one of those don't-be-an-idiot looks. "Everyone is so careful to tell us it's an accident. Why else would they do that, if they didn't suspect it wasn't?"

"Are you always this suspicious?"

"Grown-ups have a habit of thinking we're stupid," he said.

"Has anyone specifically told you they believe she killed herself?"

He shrugged. "Some people have."

"But you don't think so. And you also don't think it could have been an accident. Why not?"

"I already told you." Insolent and angry. "She wasn't stupid."

"Maybe she didn't know anything about frozen ponds."

"Oh, give me a break!" He sighed. "We're not talking about a young naturalist here. If she didn't know anything about frozen ponds what was she doing out there?"

"I was hoping maybe you could tell me."

"Meeting someone," he said.

"Any idea who?"

His face closed down with the predictable teenager's nobody-home look, the one where their eyes glaze over and their expression assumes an insolent blankness that makes you want to whack them. He made a show of checking his watch. "I've got to go. . . ." He picked up his coat and started to put it on.

"Just one more question, Josh." The gray eyes landed on my face and rolled down me like rain off a slicker. I was aware of my visceral response to his maleness, a strutting aura of newfound sexuality, and shamed by a faint desire to have him like me, an unconquered vestige of my high school days.

"Yeah?"

"What makes you think I'm a detective?"

Suddenly there was something in his thin frame that reminded me of a startled deer. A nervous tremor or something. "You are, aren't you?" The tones were those of a betrayed child. I made a slight assenting gesture. I wasn't a detective, but I didn't want to scare this boy into thinking he'd done something wrong. "You want to know how I heard about you?"

"If you want to tell me." I thought he was going to answer, but he'd been scared in that moment when he thought he'd delivered his message to the wrong person, and that had made him mad—at himself, and so, he thought, at me.

"If you're the detective," he said, "you can find out for yourself." He grabbed his bag and left.

Well, I thought, as I made some notes to myself, my resolution not to know anything about Laney Taggert's personal life had worked for about three minutes. I was going to have to do better than this if I was going to stay uninvolved. The last time I'd tried to find out why someone was killed I'd nearly gotten killed myself. Even if my spirit was willing, my flesh was weak. I couldn't take another round of physical abuse. I was going to have to be very clear that my task was a policies-and-procedures audit. I was not here as anyone's detective and it seemed to me that Dorrie had some explaining to do. I opened Laney's file again. This time I got through at least five minutes of reading before someone barged through the door.

I was expecting Dorrie, though she wasn't one to barge in anywhere, but to my surprise, it was Rocky Miller and he wasn't a happy camper. He dropped into my visitor's chair with such force the wood actually groaned, slapped his palms down on his knees, and glared at me. I guess I was supposed to quail before his wrath and beg to be enlightened but I'm not the quailing type. "I want you to know straight off that I don't like this scheme of Dorrie's at all." He waited again for my response, but since I didn't know what he was talking about I didn't have one. "I think this is a matter for the police, not some hot-shot woman consultant."

"I guess that pretty well damns everything about me,

doesn't it, Chief? Not that I'm entirely sure which attribute it is that makes me unfit for the job. The fact that I'm a hot shot? Or a consultant? Or a woman? I might be able to clear things up for you if I had some idea what you're talking about."

"Using you as a detective is like getting a pig to direct traffic."

There it was again—the word "detective." It appeared that in our bicoastal conversations about how to manage her campus crisis, there was something Dorrie had neglected to tell me. Another agenda beyond the one she'd shared with me, which was that she wanted me to do an inventory and assessment of their systems for keeping track of the students and keeping them safe. Something Dorrie and I needed to talk about before I tried to explain myself to Rocky Miller. But Rocky Miller was sitting right here insulting me and in a flash of weakness, I yielded to my baser impulses. People who begin conversations with personal attacks ought to expect a less-than-pleasant response. "There are a lot of people who would say that's exactly what you're doing when you send a cop out to direct traffic. Others might argue that you're insulting pigs. Pigs are very smart animals, you know."

As soon as he'd said the word "pig" Miller knew he'd made a mistake. "I didn't come here to trade insults," he said.

"Why *did* you come?"

"To try and talk you out of it."

"This may come as a surprise to you, Chief, but I don't know what you're talking about. What is this thing that I'm supposed to be doing that you think I can't do?" It didn't come out as clear and lucid as I'd hoped and Rocky Miller just stared at me with a puzzled look on his face. It wasn't an unattractive face, if you like blond men. He had good features, curly blond hair, a ruddy complexion, and a pugnacious jaw. He looked boyish and slightly preppy and stubborn as hell. I would have laid bets that he was heavily into court sports and had a little trouble keeping himself from being too competitive. Right now his chin was down and pulled back into his neck like a bird about to strike. I didn't wait for him. I struck first.

"You heard what Dorrie said in there. I'm here to do an inventory of the system of parietals, checks, and faculty contacts, as well as take a look at campus security, to be sure that Bucksport is doing all it can to ensure students' safety. What makes you think I can't do that?"

This time it looked like he understood. "That's not the part I'm talking about. I'm talking about this damn-fool idea of Dorrie's that we have you play detective and try to figure out what the story behind the story is. Who the father of her baby was. What happened after she signed out that day. Why she went down to the pond. Who else was down there. If there's anything to be investigated here, it's police business, not the job of some zaftig civilian who's good at writing reports. There is nothing you can do here that we can't do better. You can go ahead and do your little cosmetic audit"—he waggled his fingers dismissively—"but stay the hell out of the way of the professionals who know what they're doing."

He delivered the speech to my chest instead of my face. "I've met some arrogant SOBs in my life, Chief, but you just went to the head of the list. Do I infer from what you said that you believe there's an inverse relationship between chest size and brain capacity or is this just a cops-versus-civilians thing?"

Someone in the doorway cleared her throat. I'd been so intent on arguing with Rocky I hadn't even noticed the door open. "I was afraid this would happen," Dorrie said, coming in and closing the door behind her. "I'm sorry, Thea. This is terribly awkward. I'd meant to bring this up over lunch and explain things to you before I asked you to consider broadening the scope of your project. It's not as inappropriate as Rocky makes it sound." The looks they exchanged made it clear they'd discussed this before and hadn't reached agreement. "I think you can quite naturally fit some probing questions into your interviews, if you're willing to do so. Despite what he just said"—her tone got positively frosty—"Chief Miller has agreed to cooperate and help us any way he can. Now, they're setting up a nice private lunch for us in the trustees' room. Let's go and discuss this in a civilized manner."

Rocky Miller got up and followed her out, tight-lipped, resentment in every line of his body. He didn't let me go first. Whatever his opinions of women, and I thought I'd had a glimpse of those, they didn't seem to coexist with any old-fashioned notions of chivalry. I wondered how he could be a police chief when his emotions showed like that. Most of the cops I knew could show no more emotion than dead fish when they wanted it that way. Maybe it was a hereditary position in Bucksport. That wasn't unusual in small towns.

They had set three places for us at the end of a long mahogany table. Dorrie sat between us in the customary mother's place. She was going to have her hands full keeping peace between us. Because he'd gotten my back up, and because I was feeling mellow and kind, it being Christmas, the season of love and joy and all, I stuck out my size nine foot, expensively clad in Italian leather, and took my first step down the slippery slope. "Explain what you had in mind about this detecting business."

Rocky Miller looked like he wanted to kill me. "I wish you'd listen to me, Dorrie. I think the whole idea is stupid," he said.

Somehow, it sounded a whole lot like the conversation I'd just had with Josh Meyer. Maybe Rocky's problem was simply an extended adolescence. I knew therapists often considered it as extending well into the twenties, but into the forties? "I'm afraid I can't comment, since I haven't even heard the idea yet," I said.

"Eat your soup before it gets cold," she urged.

Dorrie had dealt with adolescent behavior long enough to recognize that's what she was seeing from us. Like a wise mother, she ignored it long enough to let us simmer down a little bit and get some food in our stomachs before she tried to deal with us. It worked fine with me. I'm a rational human being. It didn't work so well with the chief. He scarfed down his lunch like a deprived Great Dane and then tossed his fork onto his plate with a clatter. I suppose it was a symbolic form of throwing down the gauntlet. "I don't like it, Dorrie," he said. "She's just a kid. She hasn't any experience. At best, it's a waste of time; at worst, it will muddy the waters so badly we'll never get this straightened out."

Phooey, I thought. If I'd had a badge and a gun, he would have been even more unhappy. This wasn't about experience; it was about control and turf. I was almost flattered by being called a kid. I'd faced the big three-oh with a mixture of courage and depression, aided by Andre and a bottle of champagne, and I was not by any stretch of the imagination a kid. Not even in comparison to a baby-faced forty-five-year-old. What really stung, even though I knew it wasn't what he meant, was his remark that I had no experience to do this job. I was better qualified for it than he was, however Dorrie defined it. I knew I had a lot more experience in the private school world than he did. He probably couldn't even identify the school hierarchy or understand the rhythms of boarding school life, and I was sure, from his manner, that he'd be no good at interrogating teenagers unless half an hour of name-calling counted as interrogation. They'd label him "pig" or whatever kids these days called cops and clam up tight.

When someone gets my back up, I don't always act as smart as I should. I should have kept quiet. "Chief Miller," I said sweetly, "how many murders have you solved? I don't mean cases where the murderer confessed, or where there were witnesses, I mean cases that were genuine mysteries?"

He looked uncomfortable. It wasn't the sort of question he expected to be asked. He cleared his throat and studied the room and finally he said, "A couple."

"Me, too," I said. "And how much experience do you

have working with the faculty, staff, and students of private schools?"

He gave me a look that was a mixture of dislike and curiosity. "Have to deal with them all the time, being police chief here."

"I have about seven years, myself," I said.

Dorrie, who is one of the quickest readers of situations that I have ever met, figured out what I was trying to do and asked a question that sounded completely out of left field. I knew that it wasn't. There was always a purpose behind Dorrie's questions. "How did the trip to San Francisco go? Did things work out for Andre?"

"Pretty well, I think. It was pretty rocky at first but by the end he was doing better. Physically he's recovered. The emotional recovery will take some time. Andre is Detective Andre Lemieux, Maine Department of Public Safety," I explained to Rocky. "He's my . . ." I groped for an appropriate word. Boyfriend sounded too trivial, roommate too distant, lover too intimate. An article I read once suggested POSSLQ—person of the opposite sex sharing living quarters—but to me that sounded like something cute and small and fuzzy. Andre was fuzzy but he was neither small nor cute.

"Significant other," Dorrie suggested.

"My significant other," I said. "His close friend was killed a few weeks ago . . . you might have read about it in the papers . . . they were interviewing a murder suspect who was strung out on drugs and the suspect tried to kill both of them." I didn't elaborate. It wasn't Rocky's business. The purpose of the conversation had been to establish one of my unique credentials—cop's girlfriend. I wouldn't have thought of it, or rather, I wouldn't have broken the protective seal I keep on my private life to share it with a lout like Rocky Miller, but Dorrie had known, with her instinctive knack for knowing what's important, that it was information that would impress Rocky.

"State cop?" Rocky said. "How'd you meet him?"

"He was the investigating detective when my sister was murdered."

"So he solved the crime and the two of you rode off into the sunset?" Rocky said.

"So *I* solved the crime," I said, "and no one rode off into any sunsets. It was raining."

"You solved the crime?" Rocky's tones were dripping disbelief.

"I wish the two of you would stop spitting at each other like a couple of angry cats so we could talk this over sensibly," Dorrie said. "Rocky, we've already discussed this at length and you agreed to cooperate yet you've been at Thea's throat ever since you met her. What on earth has come over you?" It was another of Dorrie's virtues that while she could be exquisitely subtle dealing with the trustees, she could also be very direct. She hadn't been subtle dealing with her lawyer and she wasn't being subtle now.

"I didn't expect this," he said, waving a hand that was supposed to indicate me.

"I probably remind him of his ex-wife," I said, meaning to be sarcastic. I accidentally scored a direct hit.

Rocky Miller's slightly protuberant blue eyes glared at me across the table. "How the hell did you know that?"

"Maybe I'm a better detective than you give me credit for?"

"All right, you two, that's enough!" Dorrie said, her voice so low it was almost inaudible. As the ad says, when you want to be heard, whisper. "Rein in your egos and listen to me. First, Thea, I apologize for the way this was sprung on you. I didn't mean it to happen this way but it seems that very little is happening around here the way I want it to. What I want from you is an assessment of whether it was an accident or if there is any reason why Laney Taggert might have wanted to kill herself. I don't even know why we're talking about murder investigations here. As far as I know, there is nothing to suggest foul play. Rocky thinks the way to handle this is to bring in a few of his men and send them around the campus to interview people. Frankly, I don't think that approach would work. Your best information will come from the students and most of them are so antiauthority they aren't going to cooperate—"

"We talk to kids all the time, Dorrie," the chief interrupted.

"It's the power relationship that's the problem," Dorrie said. "I know how good Thea is at talking to these kids. I want them in a situation where they feel safe. She's going to be talking to them anyway, about the security procedures, the sign-out process, faculty checks, all the things she needs to ask for her audit. It'll be easy for her to slip in some extra questions about Laney. Once the students start talking, they're going to want to continue. If they have concerns or suspicions, they'll want to share those . . . with the right person."

"Which is a trained police officer," Rocky said.

Dorrie sighed, a sigh of gentle exasperation. I admired her patience. I wanted to throw something at him. "I'll go over this one more time, Rocky, but I'm beginning to feel like a broken record. Bucksport is a well-known and well-respected private secondary boarding school. Our endowment is growing, but it's still small and it takes a lot of money to maintain a campus like this. We are dependent on tuition and annual giving to make ends meet. Both tuition and annual giving are dependent on how the school is perceived by parents, alumni, and potential applicants. Even the hint of a scandal can have a significant impact on our applicant pool, our donations, and even our current population. Therefore, any inquiry that takes place must be done with the utmost discretion." She paused and looked at Rocky, who was playing with his fork. For a second, I thought she was going to tell him to stop fiddling and pay attention. Instead, she reached out and took the fork away, leaving her hand over his.

"My choice of Thea to conduct this inquiry does not reflect a lack of faith in your department and you shouldn't take it that way. I intend for us to continue to work with you very closely. Everything we learn will be shared with you immediately and if anything suggests Lancy Taggert's death was neither accidental nor suicide, Thea will immediately bow out and let you handle it. I assure you that Thea's experience with murder investigations has left her extremely cautious." Dorrie's reconciliation technique reminded me of the way I was taught to darn socks. First you circle the hole with thread and gently pull the thread tight until you've closed the gap as much as possible. Then you begin to weave threads back and forth across the gap until the hole is mended.

"I know that Thea reminds you of Sharon and you've translated that into young, inexperienced, and untrustworthy. But she isn't Sharon. She's a mature, extremely able, and accomplished professional woman. In my opinion, she's the best person we could get for this job and we're lucky to have her. By the way"—she paused and gave me a curious look—"I didn't tell her about Sharon. That was just a good guess on her part." Rocky took his hand out from under Dorrie's and put it on top, giving her hand a squeeze.

It didn't take a detective to see that there was more between them than just a professional relationship and it surprised me. There must be more to Rocky than the juvenile, belligerent, sexist man I'd seen. I'd only known Dorrie in a professional context, but we'd spent enough time together to know each other's stories. Although she was older—about Rocky's age, I realized—we had a lot in common. We were both somewhat reserved, workaholic young widows who took our professional selves very seriously. Dorrie and Rocky seemed like an odd pairing to me.

"You didn't tell her about Sharon?" he said.

"Of course not."

"Sharon, as you probably guessed, was my wife," Rocky said. I thought I was going to get a story but that's all he said. I let it go. With Dorrie's help we were slowly working our way toward a truce, and a truce was what we needed if we were going to be able to work together. Besides, there was no way I was going to undertake any sort of investigation into an unexplained death without a policeman in my pocket. I'd taken a lifetime's worth of chances already, first with my sister, Carrie, and then with Helene Streeter and my mother's protégée, Julie Bass. I knew that life could be very dangerous. But with the caveat that if things got dangerous, I would bow out and hand the job over to Rocky, I could see that I was needed here. In her career as headmistress, Dorrie would probably never face a more challenging and delicate situation. I had just spent seven years developing the expertise and reputation to be selected as the consultant of choice in such situations. In a small, crass corner of my professional self I realized this was an important opportunity.

Over dessert, which was a succulent apricot tart, we discussed some of the specifics and Rocky reluctantly agreed to Dorrie's plan. After lunch, he strode off to attend to some business elsewhere on campus and Dorrie and I went back to her office to talk. I was to start the next morning, as soon as I'd checked in at my office, talking to a list of people that Lori Leonard had already scheduled. We reviewed the hierarchy and I took copious notes on how the parietal system worked, how the day's schedule flowed, and at what points a faculty person had regular contact with students, how sign-out worked, and bed check, and what sort of special privileges upper-class students had. I also had an overview of how the campus security system functioned.

I'd gotten as much sleep as I could on the plane but the red-eye is aptly nicknamed. By the time I left her office I was bleary-eyed, my throat felt scratchy, and I was sick of the clothes I'd been wearing for almost twenty-four hours. I rushed down the brick walkway to my car, oblivious to the dangers of smooth leather shoes on ice. Just as

I reached the door, my foot slipped. A strong hand under my elbow stopped the fall and pulled me gently to my feet. "Returning to our conversation about pigs," Rocky said, "a woman in high heels is as unstable as a hog on ice." He got into his car and drove away.

CHAPTER 5

I AM NOT, by nature, a morning person, so it's a peculiar twist of fate that I've chosen a profession where everyone gets up with the birds. Nevertheless, I was up with the birds on Monday and in my office by eight with a cup of steaming mochaccino and a chocolate croissant. I occasionally give in to my chocolate impulses. It's either that or join Chocoholics Anonymous and I don't have time for that. I figure, why spend time in some dingy church basement listening to other people's tales of woe and addiction when you can just eat the stuff?

By eight-thirty, everyone else was in, too, and things at the office were unusually chaotic. Magda, Suzanne's secretary, was shouting something into a phone in a language I assumed was Hungarian and taking notes in something that looked like hieroglyphics; calm, cheerful Bobby had been pulling at his hair so that it looked like a fright wig; and my secretary, Sarah, was yelling at a pair of legs that emerged from behind the copying machine. I debated grabbing my stuff and hurrying to Bucksport, but I hadn't been at work for several days, so instead I waded in and started sorting things out.

My desk looked as if someone had stood over it and shredded a roll of pink insulation. Even from the doorway I could see that many of the messages had Urgent! written on them in red. Sarah stopped screaming at the man and machine and charged into my office. "I thought we got a new copier so that we wouldn't have to have the repairman here all the time," she said.

"So did I. I'm afraid I haven't been paying attention. Has it broken down a lot?"

"A lot? It's worse than the last one."

"Have you kept a record of all the repairs?"

"In the file," she said. "Every last one of 'em."

"Bring me the file, then, and I'll look into it. Anything else I should know about?"

Sarah indicated my desk with a wave of her arm. "Other than this? Someone sent you flowers. Yanita Emery called while you were in the bathroom and says she has a crisis. And Mrs. Merritt is in her office crying because her day-care lady quit and Junior is crying right along with her. Maybe you can help. Call me if you need me. I'm going to go back and yell at the repairman."

"Does it do any good?"

"No, but it makes me feel better."

I decided to deal with the last item first. Mrs. Merritt was my partner, Suzanne, who started the business. Not a woman given to tears and weakness. I found her behind her desk scowling at something she was reading. There was no sign of breakdown other than a slightly red nose. "So, partner," she said, "how did it go? Romantic days and nights of unbridled lust?"

"Of course."

She smiled at her son, who was sitting in the corner playing with an elaborate contraption of beads and colored wires. "Better be careful. Here's graphic evidence of where all that can lead."

"Well, Andre has been getting a strange gleam in his eye lately and talking about children. Speaking of children, Sarah says your day care has fallen through again?"

"It's like a nightmare, Thea. I spent a week interviewing people to find just the right one . . . and then she lasted, what? Five weeks? Whatever happened to work ethics? The way things are going, the kid's gonna end up crazy from having no stability in his life. What am I supposed to do, quit?"

"Could you stand having someone live in?"

She shrugged. "Depends on the person. And you'd have to give up your room. Why? Got someone up your sleeve?" She sounded hopeful.

"Maybe." I told her about Ellie Drucker's niece and gave her the number. Then I went back to my office to call Yanita Emery. The flowers on my desk were pink, accompanied by a card from Andre's boss, thanking me for my rehab job.

I got waylaid by pink message slips. I was sorting them into urgent, needing attention, and discard categories when the phone rang. It was Suzanne. "I am constantly reminded of how smart I was to make you my partner," she said. "Her name is Marion. She loves babies. And she's on her way over right now."

"Good luck," I said. "I hope things work out." I had gotten as far as lifting the receiver to call Yanita Emery when Bobby appeared in the door, looking miserable. Yanita would have to wait. "What's up?" I asked.

He shook his head hopelessly. "I don't know where to begin." He lowered his big body into a chair, sinking down until he managed to look small and pathetic. I waited; he didn't say anything.

I looked at my watch. "Well, you'd better spit it out, because I'm due at Bucksport in an hour. I don't have time for twenty questions."

"This is no joking matter," he said.

Seeing how upset he was, and knowing that Bobby was gay, it crossed my mind that he might be about to make an announcement about his health. I braced myself for bad news, hoping that wasn't what was coming. We all loved Bobby. In a lot of ways, he was the emotional soul of the office, the only one of us who usually managed to be good-humored and nice to everyone. The tension level in the room rose tangibly. "What?" I said.

"It's about your condo," he said. "That you sublet to my friend Ryan?"

I was so relieved I almost laughed out loud. "What about it?"

There were tears in Bobby's eyes. "Oh, Thea, I'm so sorry. I'm so awfully sorry. I feel like it's all my fault, but honestly, I never knew . . . I never expected . . . I didn't realize what kind of a person he was underneath, or I never would have suggested . . ." He trailed off, his hands clasped tightly in his lap, unable to meet my eyes.

I couldn't stand it. "Get to the point, Bobby," I said. "What's happened to my condo?" I loved my condo. It was the first place I'd ever had that was really, truly mine, that I didn't have to share with anyone else, and that was arranged just the way I liked it. When I moved to Maine to live with Andre, I'd sublet it to Bobby's friend Ryan. I'd been too busy to notice, but now that I thought about it, I hadn't had a rent check this month.

"He trashed it. Things are dirty, things are broken, things are missing. There are holes in the walls, spots on the rugs . . . the shower door is broken, the toilet tank is cracked . . . I was there for a party this weekend, and I couldn't believe it. Such a beautiful place and he'd treated it like a dump. I lost my temper and I . . . uh . . . well, I'm afraid I didn't make things any better." His voice fell until it was almost inaudible. "I pushed him right through the slider."

It was only then that I noticed that, in addition to the two Band-Aids on his face, one of his hands was wrapped in gauze. Oh, boy. And the neighbors had thought I was bad. I flipped to Ryan's number and picked up the phone.

"Are you calling him?" Bobby asked. I nodded. "It won't do you any good. He moved out yesterday. I spent the whole day trying to find him. No one has seen him, or will admit that they have. The rotten pig. I can't believe—"

"Stop." I said. I only meant I didn't want to hear any more because it was too painful but Bobby took it as a personal dismissal. His face ashen, he bolted from the room. I flipped through the cards again, found the one I wanted, and dialed a number. In the course my of adventurous life, I've had occasion to need the services of people who clean up apartments after a disaster. I had just the man for the job. I got him on the phone, reported what had happened, and told him to see the manager for a key. Then I called my insurance agent and did the same. I'd been in the office for an hour, hadn't even gotten to the pressing things, and already it felt like eternity.

I picked up my messages again. Sarah stuck her head around the door. "It's Yanita Emery again. You want to take it? She sounds desperate."

"I'll take it."

The King School was an alternative private school for black males and I'd sent Yanita there to be the assistant head. Since I felt responsible, I couldn't ignore her pleas for help. I knew she wouldn't claim something was urgent unless she believed it. She sounded flustered, a state distinctly at odds with her usual poise and calm. "Well, Thea," she said, "it's hit the fan this time."

"Denzel?" I said. "And a woman?"

"What else?" She sighed. "No. That's not fair. I honestly think that he's been set up. That the woman is lying. But he's stonewalling me, won't talk about it except to say that she's lying and he's not going to lower himself to her level. Along with everything else, we've got a serious case of wounded pride here. Help!"

I wasn't surprised by the nature of her problem. Denzel Ellis-Jackson was an absolutely gorgeous man. Magnetic. An educational visionary. A brilliant speaker. And unfortunately, a man who liked women too much. Yanita and I and Arleigh Davis, the head of the board of trustees, had worked hard to make him mend his ways, and for the most part, we'd been successful. He seemed to understand that these days even a hint of sexual harassment could bring the roof down and that one man's friendliness was another woman's harassment.

I thought about my schedule and looked at my watch. "Yanita, I'm up to my ears with that drowned student out at Bucksport but I can squeeze out some time tomorrow. I'll need Denzel and Arleigh, too, okay? I'll call you again at the end of the day to go over things, and then we'll do the face-to-face?"

"Are you sure you can't do it today?"

I sighed. In her position, I would have asked the same thing. "I'll see what I can do, but I'll have to call you later."

"Whenever you can make it," she said.

Time to go. I'd told Lori to start scheduling my appointments at ten. I had to leave before anyone else came along and dumped another problem on me. I already felt like a camel with a challenged back. I took another look at Laney Taggert before I stuffed the file into my briefcase. A Slavic face, I thought. She and Josh must have made a striking couple. I glanced through it. Bucksport was not one of those places that pretended it didn't believe in tracking and Laney had had all honors courses. She was also seriously involved in drama and played field hockey. It seemed odd that a strong athlete could have drowned but I didn't know much about death by drowning. Maybe Rocky could help me. And let me read the autopsy report. Probably he'd think I was too young for that sort of thing. I realized that I'd never asked Dorrie what might have led Josh to think I was a detective. That was one mystery I could solve today.

The first person on my list was Dave Holdorf, impeccable as always. I noticed that he'd been biting his nails. He handed me a schedule. "We've got your day all planned, as you can see. I hope you don't mind."

"No problem, Dave. Want to give me a rundown on who they are?"

"That's what I'm here for. You heard my instructions.

I'm to smooth the way. Right now I'm afraid it's like spreading chunky peanut butter, but I'll do my best." He shrugged helplessly. "You can probably guess where I'm having my biggest problem."

"Sawyer?"

"Of course. When he just did buildings and grounds he was fine but now that he's also in charge of security, he's developed this absurd paramilitary attitude. I'm afraid one of these days we're going to have an incident we'll regret. . . ." His smile was thin and unmerry. "Other than this, I mean. He understands trees and grass but teenagers are beyond his grasp. He doesn't realize that they're our raison d'être. He regards them as a threat to his carefully groomed environment. Every time he finds a condom in the underbrush he practically dies of apoplexy."

"Is that a big problem around here?"

"Condoms or apoplexy?" I just raised my eyebrows. "No. Not a big problem. But these are kids in the full flower of youthful lust and things do happen. The best we can do is limit their opportunities and challenge their inventiveness. It's part of our creative-thinking-skills curriculum."

"I see you haven't lost your sense of humor."

He managed a wry smile. "Bruised but not broken. Like I told you yesterday, everyone here is deeply affected by this. For me, joking is one way to keep depression away." He got up and dusted off his pants. Either he was obsessive or the air was full of things that I just wasn't seeing. "You'll have to reach your own conclusions on this but I don't believe we were careless about Laney. She just used her ingenuity to slip through the cracks. You will discover, I think, that she was quite ingenious." There was a knock on the door. "That'll be Joanne," he said. "Good luck."

He was replaced in the chair by a petite, aggressive-looking woman with black hair and black eyes. Joanne Perlin was the dean of students. By reputation, a very good one. We'd worked together before. We went over the basics of Bucksport's system for keeping track of students. In addition to the evening curfew and routine bed checks by the senior proctor on each floor, there were several occasions during the day when a student's absence would be noted. The faculty took attendance in each class. There were faculty members at each table in the dining halls who regularly ate with the same students and faculty members were also the athletic coaches so that a student's absence from sports would be noted. In addition, all students not on detention were allowed to sign out in the afternoon and evening to take a bus into Sedgwick—the bus stop was at a local ice cream store—and juniors and seniors could sign out on weekends to go home with friends who were day students. Someone diligently checked to be sure that all the students who had signed out for town returned.

"I've got the general picture. Now let's focus on Laney Taggert. At what point on Friday was she last seen? Was she there for bed check?"

Joanne sighed. "We think she signed out at the end of the afternoon to spend the weekend with her friend Merri Naigler. Merri is a day student."

"What do you mean, you think?"

"I mean we think but we don't know," Joanne said defensively. "No one can find her sign-out card. The students are also supposed to verbally check out with their dorm parents but I'm afraid someone was a little lax about that."

"When did you notice that it was gone?"

"The card?" Joanne hung her head. She looked deeply ashamed. "Sunday."

"So no one expected her at dinner or was surprised to find her gone at bed check?"

With every question I asked, Joanne looked more like a guilty child. "I'm afraid it's a little more complicated than that."

"Complicated how?"

Joanne spread her hands in a gesture of submission. "Okay, I know I'm being silly, trying to keep this from you. You're going to be talking to all these people anyway. I won't do anyone any good pretending this isn't an incredible mess. I wish you luck. It would take a detective to sort this one out."

"That reminds me of something," I interrupted. "Yesterday I had no sooner gotten into my office than a kid called Josh Meyer came in, threw himself into that chair, and asked me if I was the detective. Where could he have gotten the idea that I'm a detective?"

Joanne was wringing her hands together so vigorously her knuckles were white. It hurt to watch. "I'm afraid that's my fault, too." I waited for her explanation. This nervousness and hesitation were unlike the Joanne I knew. "Well, Kathy Donahue, one of the house parents in Laney's dorm, was extremely upset because she did the bed check Friday night and when Laney wasn't there, she accepted the roommate's explanation without checking. She's sure that Laney's death is her fault. She said that she and Laney had been talking about how pretty the woods are at night when a full moon shines on the snow. She thought as a result of that conversation Laney had sneaked out to see the woods and fallen through the ice and if she'd only paid more attention, Laney might have been saved.

"I told her I was sure that wasn't it, that the situation was a lot more complicated than she realized and that Dorrie was bringing in a private school consultant to act as a sort of procedures detective. I'm afraid I wasn't particularly careful about what I said. Josh had been waiting outside the door to see Kathy. He must have overheard."

"I see. Okay. Tell me the rest of the story."

"I hope I don't miss anything, there are so many twists and turns. Let's see. Laney finished basketball sometime between three-thirty and four. You know that all our students do sports the first two years. . . ." She jammed an unruly strand of hair behind her ear. "Laney was a junior, but she'd missed a term her sophomore year, so she had to make it up." She hesitated. "Not sick or anything, she just managed to miss it. That, as you will learn, was Laney's talent, avoiding what she didn't want to do." The hair slipped back down, tickling the end of her nose. "Damn!" She pulled a bobby pin out of her pocket and pinned it into place.

"I'm going to get a crew cut one of these days. On her way to the locker room one of her coaches, Mimsy Spence, asked if she was going to the movies that night. A whole busload of them were going. Laney told her that she wasn't sure she was going to see the movie because she was planning to go home with Merri for the weekend and she didn't know what Merri's plans were." Joanne stopped and counted out some numbers on her fingers.

"Have you talked with Merri? What does she say?"

"She says she was expecting Laney to meet her in front of the administration building so her mother could pick them both up, but Laney didn't show and when she went over to Laney's dorm, no one had seen her. But she says Laney had been moody and hard to get along with lately and they had argued in the locker room after basketball, so she figured maybe Laney was sulking and if she got over it, she'd know enough to call. Merri doesn't live far from the campus. Then Merri left."

"Did anyone see Laney Taggert after sports?"

"Yes. Josh says he saw her on her way back to her dorm and tried to talk to her but she was distracted and in a hurry and she told him she had to meet someone and she'd see him later at the movie."

"What time was that?"

"Sometime between four and four-thirty."

"And then?" Joanne didn't say anything. "Is that it?" I said. "Was Josh the last person to see her?"

"No. Chas Drucker, the faculty member she sits with at dinner, who is also her advisor and her English teacher, says Laney came up to him when he was on his way to the dining hall and said she wasn't feeling well and was going to skip dinner." Joanne lapsed into silence again. She seemed far away.

"That's all?"

She roused herself. "Not quite all. There was one more thing . . . I mean there may be one more thing. One of the maintenance men saw a girl heading off toward the jogging path around five o'clock. He didn't know Laney and it was too dark for him to notice much about her clothes, but the girl was wearing a long skirt like Laney was when they . . . when she . . . when she was found."

"Are all these people on my list?"

"All except the maintenance man but Curt Sawyer's on your list. If you need to talk to the man directly, Curt can arrange it. Look, I'm sorry, Thea, this has probably been the most disorganized interview you've ever had. I can't seem to make myself think clearly about this stuff. I start to think about that poor dear girl and all the order just goes right out of my thoughts. Ask me anything else and I'm sharp as a tack. I don't know what's come over me."

It sounded like shock. Shock and guilt. As dean of students, Joanne was probably the one most directly responsible for the welfare of the students. Being placed in a situation where someone might accuse her of not caring was the ultimate reproach. Even if no one else had said it, she was saying it to herself. It looked as though Dave Holdorf was right. It wasn't just the students who needed help handling this. Joanne and I went over some of the details of the sign-out system. Even though I hadn't been hard on her, she left looking like someone who'd been called on the carpet. When you hold yourself to a high standard, no one can hurt you more than yourself.

"As far as you know, five was the last time she was seen?"

"If it was Laney that he saw, yes."

Joanne's place in the chair was taken by Warren Winslow, director of residence. He was a quiet, self-contained man who volunteered nothing and showed no signs of emotion. It was rather a relief after Joanne's angst. He confirmed that house parents are supposed to be informed if a boarding student is spending the weekend off campus, whether it is with a friend or with their parents. There's a card the students fill out with their host's name, address, and phone number. For absences other than to the home of a day-student classmate, a note from the boarder's parents was required. In addition, the house parents try to keep a close eye on the emotional well-being of their students and there is a policy that they will have at least minimal contacts with each student daily.

"What do you mean by 'minimal contacts'?" I asked. He seemed annoyed that I was asking and grudgingly described them as contacts where words were exchanged.

"Are good-mornings sufficient?"

"We're looking for something a little more substantive than that."

I guess I needed to shake him out of his nonchalant attitude because I still didn't quit. "Such as 'How are you?'"

"There isn't any magic formula," he snapped. "It's not something you can define in a manual. It means enough contact to form an impression of the student's state of mind."

Satisfied that I'd finally gotten a reaction, I didn't press further even though I'd known teenagers you could try to talk to all day and still have no clue about their state of mind, unless surly counted. "Tell me about her dorm parents," I said.

He told me that Laney's resident faculty couple had impeccable credentials. Bill Donahue had gone to Middlesex and Dartmouth and his wife Kathy had gone to Rosemary Hall and Wellesley. In his eyes, I could see, this meant they were above reproach. Not that their pedigrees told me anything about them as people, such as whether they were caring and conscientious, observant, diligent or lazy, but Joanne would have seen to that when she approved his choice. Assuming that credentials were synonymous with character was common in the private school world.

I'm not a prep-school product myself, although Suzanne is. I've learned to bite my tongue when confronted with the likes of Warren Winslow. He was the kind of guy who, when I used to meet them at college mixers, always wanted to know where people had prepped. He had the costume—wide-wale cords, oxford cloth shirt and rugged outdoorsy sweater, the gold-rimmed glasses, and the slightly laconic manner. All in all, it was an unexciting interview but I wasn't there to be excited.

Winslow didn't take long and then I took a break to, as people euphemistically put it, freshen up. About an hour and a half after my morning coffee, I always need to freshen up. I took a minute at the mirror to return my hair to the confines of a barrette. I have a lot of hair. Not as much as Sonia Braga, but a lot of dark, curly hair, and it has a mind of its own. I am always trying to restrain it and make it look professional, while the hair itself favors a windblown look. We often compromise on the majority in confinement with a few tendrils allowed to escape and curl at will.

I went back to my desk to wait for my next appointment and found a small vase of daffodils. A hastily scribbled note underneath them said, "Something to chase away the winter gloom. Thanks for remembering Marion. Ellie." I began to understand why Dave had said she was in charge of morale. The flowers did wonders for me. My list said I was meeting Genny Oakes, Laney Taggert's roommate. She was late. There were voices out in the hall and then Joanne came in, followed by a girl whose face gave new meaning to the word sulky. She dumped herself into the chair, jammed her hands into her coat pockets, and sat there glaring at me. "Thea, this is Genny," Joanne said, and beat a hasty retreat. Being good with adolescents doesn't mean you can always get along with them. It looked like a saint might find it challenging to get along with this girl.

"You're Laney Taggert's roommate?"

"I was."

There was something in her tone, just a hint, really, that made me think she didn't entirely regret having lost her roommate. "It was nice of you to be willing to talk to me, Genny. I know this must be very difficult for you. Did anyone tell you what I wanted to talk to you about?"

She gave me a puzzled look. She had lots of good, honey brown hair, much of which hung across her face, forcing her to peer through it, and a big, aggressive body. Born to play field hockey. "No. I assumed it was about Laney. I might as well tell you this, since Mrs. Donahue will tell you anyway. Laney and I were not friends. I had asked them to give me a new roommate."

"Why?"

"Why weren't we friends or why a new roommate?" Her voice was steady and flat but I knew she was waiting to see what I'd do.

"Both."

She shrugged and tossed back her hair. "We weren't friends because we had nothing in common. I wanted a new roommate because of that and because I was sick of living with someone so secretive and sneaky and manipulative. She had no morals."

"In what ways was she sneaky and secretive?"

"Her life was a constant game of trying to beat the system. She had a whole repertoire of illnesses and excuses to get out of tests and papers, to get her teachers to cut her slack. She was always cutting classes. Going off campus without signing out. Borrowing clothes, jewelry, and money, with or without permission. Trying to get me to cover for her when she was going to be absent at bed check. And she wasn't friendly. She was cold. I just got sick of it! I was always afraid I was going to get into trouble because of her. It felt like I was getting an ulcer." She wrapped her arms protectively around her stomach.

"Was she often absent at bed check?"

"Sometimes," Genny said sulkily.

"How often? Once a week, once a month? What?"

"Maybe four or five times since the beginning of the year."

"How did she manage that?"

"I lied for her," Genny said. "I'd say she was in the bathroom, or down the hall, stuff like that."

"If you didn't like her, why did you lie for her?"

She twisted her body around restively. Like anybody, she didn't like being pressed for details. "I just did," she said unhelpfully.

"You 'just did' isn't a very helpful answer. Could you elaborate on that a little?" I used my best authoritative voice, the one Genny was used to after a lifetime of schoolteachers.

"She just had this way of making you want to please her. It wasn't only me. Even though she treated us all like crap, we kept trying to please her." She parted with this information grudgingly, obviously reluctant to admit that Laney had had this power over her. We digressed then to a discussion of bed checks and contacts with the dorm parents. Despite the ease with which Laney had sneaked out, Genny seemed to think they were sufficient.

"Any idea where she went?"

"To meet Josh, I suppose. To crawl under a bush and screw." She eyeballed me quickly to see what I thought of that. "Until the weather got too cold. She hadn't been doing it lately. Skipping out after curfew, I mean. Not that she shared the details of her sex life with me. But I knew."

"Is that what you meant when you said she was secretive? That she had a clandestine sex life?"

"Oh, come on! I wasn't that interested. She was secretive about everything. Like I'd notice she seemed depressed, mopey, you know, and I'd say, 'Hey, you seem depressed.' She'd give me this icy look and just say, 'Oh, really?' I mean, everything was like that. If she got a package from home and I asked what was in it, she'd just say 'Stuff.' " She spread her arms wide. "She was the most closed person I've ever seen. It was impossible to know her."

"Did she know you wanted a new roommate?"

Genny nodded. "I told her. And I told her why, too. I guess that maybe I was hoping she'd change, you know. That maybe if she knew I wasn't happy, she'd come around and be the kind of roommate I wanted. But all she did was shrug. She said, 'Do what you want, I don't care.' That was Laney in a nutshell. She didn't care about anyone but herself."

Getting to know someone through interviews is a lot like painting by numbers. As you add each color, a little more of the picture appears. When you're done, the result is a rather crude approximation of a real picture, the pieces don't quite work together, but you get an idea of how things are supposed to look. All I'd had before was the stuff in the file, reports from her teachers, generally favorable and showing a bright and interesting girl, and Josh's quick psychological assessment—that she was complicated, which meant that she was all screwed up.

"Was there anything you liked about her?"

"She had a wicked sense of humor. She could do an impersonation of any teacher and have them down perfectly. We used to call them her twenty-second master-pieces. She liked to perform. Give her an audience and she came alive. It didn't matter whether it was an audience of two or two hundred." Genny scowled. "She had a twenty-second version of me that she did. I mean, I could see myself instantly. You ever meet her?" I shook my head. "Well, she was slender and dark and graceful but when she did me she became big and horsy and terribly cheerful. The first time I saw it, I was stunned. I felt like I'd been stabbed. I wanted to kill her." As soon as she'd said it, she gasped and put her hands over her mouth. "I didn't mean it like that," she said.

"She knew you'd seen her?"

"Yes."

"Did she say anything about it?"

Genny nodded. "Yeah. She said she knew I didn't like it and she was sorry I'd seen it. She hadn't meant to hurt my feelings."

"That sounds like an apology."

She nodded again. "But it wasn't, don't you see, because she wasn't sorry for doing it—that was the hurtful thing, the way it showed what she thought of me. She was only sorry for getting caught."

"Had Laney been depressed lately?"

"No more than usual. She hadn't been feeling well. She'd been missing a lot of classes. But I didn't bother to ask her about it. I'd given up bothering. She never answered me anyway."

She looked so miserable I hated to press her further, but her information was important. "When did you ask for a roommate change?"

Her head came up angrily and her eyes narrowed. "A week before Thanksgiving. I kept asking Mrs. Donahue about it but she just kept saying these things take time. I finally had to get my mom to call Dean Perlin." She hugged her arms around her body and stared at the floor.

I wondered about the school's inaction. Making Genny stay with a roommate she detested for a month after the desire to change was announced seemed extremely cruel and unfair. I'd have to ask Joanne what had happened. "Let's talk about last Friday. Did you know she was planning to spend the weekend with Merri Naigler?" She nodded. "When was the last time you saw her?"

"I don't know. I mean, people keep asking me that question and I don't have an answer. I saw her back in the room around one. She was putting some stuff in a bag and when I asked where she was going, she said to Merri's. Then I thought I saw her going off across the circle later, carrying the bag, so I assumed she was going to meet Merri, but when I got back to the room, Merri came up looking for her. I said I thought I'd seen her out on the circle with her bag, but Merri said she'd never shown up. So I don't know. When I saw her at the circle it looked like she was waving to someone. I couldn't see who it was. Maybe it wasn't even Laney. I can't say. Whoever it was was wearing my new pink jacket, though. And I haven't seen it since." She looked very pointedly at her watch. "Can I go? I've got a class."

"Of course. Thank you for talking to me, Genny." She got up and rushed to the door. As she opened it, we could hear angry voices coming down the hall.

A man's high-pitched voice was protesting loudly. "Take your hands off me, you militaristic thug," followed by a scuffle of feet and another protest. "I said cut that out! It is completely unnecessary. I said I was going to cooperate."

Genny turned back toward me, her eyes bright. "Looks like Rambo Sawyer and his sidekick, Lennie, have nabbed ace reporter Chip Barrett again. This ought to be good." She threw the door open so I could see what was happening. Curt Sawyer, his face tight and angry, was coming down the hall, his hand firmly on the arm of a smaller man who looked like a grownup Beaver Cleaver. The Beave's other arm was in the clutches of a slightly Neanderthal-looking fellow in a maintenance uniform who dwarfed both the reporter and Sawyer. I joined Genny at the door and watched the strange procession go by. Ellie Drucker was in her doorway, too.

Barrett was obviously not one to be deterred by circumstances. As the trio drew abreast of us, he stopped, nodded to Genny, fixed his greedy little eyes on me and said, "You must be the detective. I need to talk to you. I've got some very interesting questions for you about this whole Laney Taggert business."

"Come on. Move it," Sawyer growled, dragging ungently at his arm. His hulking companion, the one Genny had called Lennie but who had Chris stitched above his pocket, dragged on the other arm, and the resisting Barrett was hauled away.

He turned and called back over his shoulder, "Hey, detective, anyone find Laney's overnight bag yet?" as they disappeared into Dorrie's office.

"Maybe you and Chip should get together," Genny suggested. "I hear he's got some interesting theories." She hesitated. "You did get the Lennie reference, didn't you?"

"I'm sorry, Genny, I'm afraid I didn't."

"Of Mice and Men," she said scornfully, slinging her bag onto her shoulder. "And they say *my* generation isn't educated."

There's nothing like confrontation and confusion to stimulate the appetite. After my cheerful morning's work, I was starving. I was supposed to be having lunch with Dorrie and hoped she wasn't going to be tied up too long with Sawyer and his prisoner. While I waited, I attached a sheet to each person's interview notes recording their version of Laney Taggert's last day. According to my schedule, after lunch I was seeing Laney's friend Merri Naigler, her advisor, Chas Drucker, and last but certainly not least, Curt Sawyer.

I wasn't looking forward to that. Even when Curt and I want to work together, we have these naturally antagonistic personalities that set us at each other's throats. It takes all my maturity and self-control to stay civil, and Curt has less of each of those attributes than I so he can't stay civil. Dorrie or Dave, whoever made up the list, should have known better than to throw us together at the end of the day.

As it turned out, I didn't have to meet with Curt at the end of the day. The commotion caused by the capture of Chip Barrett, who, at the moment of his seizure, was trying to steal records from the school files, was eclipsed by a shriek worthy of a diva, followed by the broadcast, in the loudest possible voice, of a piece of information Dorrie had very much wanted to keep secret. "Pregnant! Jesus, God, William, Henry! What do you mean she was pregnant? How could you have let that happen?"

Laney Taggert's mother had just had some more bad news.

CHAPTER 6

UNABASHED, I STUCK my head back out into the hall. I noticed that Ellie Drucker was doing the same thing. We got to see Dorrie Chapin bring Mrs. Taggert under control in her best headmistress style. "Are you quite sure," she said, her voice full of scorn, "that you want that information broadcast to the entire Bucksport community? If not, I suggest you come back into my office and try to get yourself under control." Although headmasters and mistresses bend over backward to treat parents well and keep them in good humor, it is also true that parents—some parents, at least—will take advantage of that balance of power and treat the administration as one group they can abuse with impunity because they're paying customers. It was that instinct that Dorrie was nipping in the bud.

Marta Taggert, silent, but her face a mask of fury, followed Dorrie back into her office, trailed by a man I assumed was Mr. Taggert. He didn't say anything but there was something in his manner that told me he was the one who was truly suffering. I returned to my desk, reviewed the notes I'd taken, and made a list of questions I wanted to ask the next set of interviewees. It looked as though Dorrie was going to be tied up for a while. I was considering driving into Sedgwick and looking for a place to have lunch when someone knocked on my door.

Lori Leonard stuck her head in. "Can you come down to Dorrie's office?" No more information. If I didn't already know what I was getting into, they didn't want to scare me off. I grabbed my notes, stuffed them into my briefcase, and followed her.

The atmosphere in Dorrie's office was so highly charged the air practically crackled. Dorrie and Peter Van Deusen and the Taggerts were grouped around the coffee table, just as we'd been the day before, but there wasn't a shred of warmth or congeniality. Dorrie drew me into the group like a survivor grabbing for a lifeline. "Thea Kozak, this is Marta and Jack Taggert. You've already met Peter."

I shook hands with the Taggerts. Her hand was cold and seemed to be all sharp nails and bones. She had the same build Genny Oakes had described as Laney's. Slight, delicate, and graceful. Instead of dark hair, though, hers was a brittle blond. He had a grip that could crush cans without effort. It matched his stocky workman's body and big wide face. They looked about as well matched as Barbie and Hulk Hogan.

"Thea, I've explained to the Taggerts what you're trying to do for us—"

"What I want her to do," Marta Taggert said, cutting her off, "is to find out who was responsible for getting my daughter pregnant. It is unthinkable that such a thing could have been allowed to happen here! That's one of the main reasons we sent her here . . . to get her out of our small town and away from its negative influences. A lot of good that did! Not only dead, but pregnant, too. I don't know how I'm going to explain that to people. To all the people who thought I was putting myself above them, sending Margaret away to a fancy private school."

For a minute I was confused about who Margaret was, until I remembered that Laney's full name was Margaret

Delaney Taggert. It also seemed to me that Mrs. Taggert had her priorities all screwed up, if she was more concerned about the fact that Laney had been pregnant than that she was dead. Still, I grew up in a small town, and I knew how people could talk. "No one needs to know that your daughter was pregnant, Mrs. Taggert," I said.

She raised a thin, trembling hand to her forehead. "They'll find out," she said. "People always do. What you must do is find the boy who did this and then we'll let Jack deal with him. It's probably that awful Jewish boy she liked. Joe or Jay or Jake or something. He probably seduced Laney and then denied responsibility. That's what young men do these days. Not a shred of morals or a sense of duty. When I think of poor Margaret in such terrible trouble so far away from me . . ." She paused and dabbed at her eyes with a tissue. I hadn't seen any sign of tears so I assumed it was part of her grieving-mother act. "It's not right that he should leave my daughter in such despair she took her own life, and walk away without taking any responsibility himself. He must be brought to justice."

"We don't know that Laney's death wasn't an accident," Dorrie said. Her eyes met mine and I could tell she was thinking the same thing I was. Marta Taggert's grief was mostly posturing but according to her dramatic interpretation of the role, she ought to be seeking revenge for her wronged child. Undoubtedly, her idea of a proper resolution would be something along the lines of a public castration of Josh Meyer by her husband in front of the entire school community. Without doing much more than raising an eyebrow, Dorrie was appealing to me to do something.

Dutifully, I waded in, not expecting it to do much good. "Has Mrs. Chapin explained to both of you what I've been brought in to do?" The Taggerts looked blank, probably because they'd so dominated the conversation, or at least she had, that no one had had an opportunity to explain anything to them.

"I'm here to conduct a review of Bucksport's procedures for monitoring students to determine whether they are adequate." I could feel Peter Van Deusen's glare so I avoided meeting his eyes. He didn't want me to reveal the audit to these people because they might misconstrue it, but I thought I knew what I was doing. "As part of that process, I'm trying to develop a picture of Laney's life here. Who she saw, where she went, what she did. We don't believe the school did anything wrong with respect to your daughter but we need to be sure, to get a very clear picture of what happened, for the sake of all the other students as well."

"Well, it's obvious you did something wrong or she wouldn't have . . . or that terrible thing wouldn't have happened to Margaret," Marta Taggert said.

Experience has taught me that sometimes even the most vindictive-seeming people are only angry because no one has ever bothered to say they're sorry. "Mr. and Mrs. Taggert," I said, "I know this in no way makes up for your loss, but I want you to know how sorry we all are about Laney's accident." Jack Taggert made a sound like a strangled sob, murmured something, and lowered his eyes. I shifted my attention to his wife to give him what little privacy I could. "Were you and your daughter very close, Mrs. Taggert?"

A good lawyer will tell you not to ask questions if you don't already know the answers. I'd made a calculated guess about what Marta Taggert's answer would be and she didn't disappoint me. "Very close," she said. "We were more like sisters than mother and daughter, really. Maybe because I was so young when Margaret . . . Laney was born."

I took her unappealing hand between mine and held it there. "Then this must be doubly difficult for you, losing a daughter and losing a friend. Maybe it's too soon to ask you to do this, but would you be willing to come along to my office and talk to me about Laney?"

She took the bait the way a trout takes a fly, unable to

resist another act in the grieving-mother show. It wasn't like me to be so unsympathetic but I was willing to bet that Laney Taggert's mother knew her daughter less well than she knew the label on a whiskey bottle and that Laney had been sent here not for her own benefit but for her mother's and over the objections of Laney's father. "Would you like to join us, Mr. Taggert?" I asked.

He shook his head without looking at me. His wife might be into the whole scene but Jack Taggert was just a man who'd lost a beloved daughter. He needed to be alone with his grief and no one was giving him a chance. As we left the room, I heard Dorrie suggest he might like to take a walk across the campus and look at the chapel. He just raised his big shoulders and sighed. He didn't seem like a man who was passive about decisions but grief can often transform people. I'd seen it happen to my father. My sister Carrie's death temporarily changed him from a real take-charge guy into a helpless, shambling old man.

At my office door, she excused herself to visit the ladies' room and when she came back her breath was a fragrant combination of alcohol and breath mints. The only person she was fooling was herself. She settled herself into my visitor's chair and assessed me with the practiced eye of a woman who doesn't welcome competition. "You're awfully young for this, aren't you?"

It was the second reference to my youth in as many days and I didn't take this one any more kindly than I had the last. I'd seen my face in the mirror this morning and I didn't look like a kid. It was the same face I'd been seeing for years except for the beginnings of smile lines around my eyes and mouth. The only thing even vaguely youthful about it was an irritating pimple that was starting beside my nose. I hardly thought she was referring to that. "I'm not as young as I look," I said. "This is my seventh year in the business."

I got a fresh sheet of paper and prepared to take notes.

"Laney was a junior, right?" She nodded. "You and Laney were in touch on a regular basis?"

"Of course," she said. "I told you. We were very close."

"Tell me about her. What was she like?"

Her eyes widened in surprise at the abruptness of my question. Then she shrugged. "Like any teenager, I suppose. Difficult."

Okay, so this was going to be like pulling teeth. I wasn't going to get a description spilling out, I was going to have to work for it. "Was she more the bookish type or a social butterfly?"

Marta Taggert crossed her thin legs and pondered that one for a while. She was wearing a very short navy knit skirt with a long navy sweater over it. She was slim enough to wear it but it was, to put it discreetly, rather too youthful for a woman of her years. The look was finished with navy stockings and extremely high sling-back pumps. Had I been her daughter, Marta Taggert's attempt to hang on to her youth would have embarrassed the hell out of me. "Neither," she said. "Laney—I might as well call her Laney, I suppose, as that's how she was known here. I always preferred Margaret. She was the arty type. Moody and flamboyant. She craved attention but she didn't like to let people get close to her." She hesitated. "Except me, of course. My friend who has a daughter Laney's age is always saying, 'I don't know how you do it, Marta. Cheryl won't tell me a thing.' Laney always confided in me."

"You say she was moody. Unusually so? Was it normal teenage moodiness or was she depressed?"

"Normal," she said quickly.

"Was she often depressed?"

"Yes," she said, then changed her mind. "No."

"How long had she been at Bucksport?"

"This was her second year."

"So she didn't start as a freshman. Where was she before?"

"At home. At the Ellanville High School."

"Did she have any trouble adjusting to high school?"

"Laney didn't adjust," her mother said bitterly. "She liked the world to adjust to her."

"In what way?"

"She had an aversion to rules. Any rules. Curfews. Chores. Deadlines. Social conventions. Any attempt to impose authority on her met with resistance. And Jack encouraged her. He thought it was great, said it would make her a stronger adult, but I couldn't stand it. She was unmanageable."

"You had trouble disciplining Laney?"

"I didn't say that."

"I'm sorry. I thought you just said she was unmanageable."

Marta Taggert pressed her lips together and didn't respond.

"Was her resistance to discipline one of the reasons you chose a private school?" Resistance to discipline sounded like one of those carefully chosen phrases from a teacher's evaluation selected to try to convey the message without sounding too judgmental. No one had the guts to write the bold truth anymore. It might damage someone's self-esteem. As a result, we were building a world where everyone would have high self-esteem and absolutely no ability to judge themselves critically or take responsibility for their actions or work toward self-improvement. No one is bad. No one is lazy. We are all just different and it is important for us each to recognize and appreciate those differences. Oops. I was letting my mind wander. If I let it go too far down this path, I'd lose my concentration and steam would start coming out of my ears. I snapped my mental whip and brought myself back into line.

Marta Taggert was glaring at me, a pale cousin of the look I'd seen her give Dorrie. She'd said all she was going to about her daughter's discipline problems. She didn't like people who pressed her or argued with her.

Yessir, I could imagine exactly what kind of close, intimate, confiding relationship she'd had with her daughter. Like two fishwives, more likely. "Why did you decide to send Laney to a private school?"

"So she wouldn't be alone so much."

"Is she an only child?" Her mother nodded. It was the only answer I was going to get so I dropped that line temporarily. I'd see what they'd said on her application and what her public school teachers had said about her. "Who were her friends here at Bucksport?"

She pondered that one. "Merri Naigler, of course. And her roommate, Genny. They were very close. Genny was like the sister she'd always wanted. That boy, what's his name . . . Josh. She always had boys as friends from the time she was a tiny child. So there was Josh and there was another guy, Charles or something, and her house mother, Kathy Donahue. She really liked Kathy a lot. She said Kathy took very good care of her, kind of like a substitute for me. I think she was trying to make me feel better. She knew how much I hated having her away."

"Did the two of you usually communicate by phone or by letter or what?"

"Phone. And letter. Both. I mean, what else is there?"

"Some parents also visit fairly often."

She shook her head. "No. No, we didn't visit much, I regret to say. Mr. Taggert and I are awfully busy. That's why we thought it was better for her to be at a boarding school. So she wouldn't be alone so much."

"I take it you and Mr. Taggert travel a lot?" She nodded. "On business?" Again the nod.

"So other than Columbus Day weekend and Thanksgiving, you hadn't seen Laney?"

Marta Taggert's expression was annoyed and suspicious. "I don't know what you're talking about. We hadn't seen Laney since we brought her up here in August. She came a week early to help with the new students' initiation. I told you. We've been very busy. Jack travels a lot and I go with him." Her eyes narrowed. "I know at Thanksgiving she went home with her friend Merri but I didn't hear anything about that other weekend. That's just the sort of thing I was saying to Mrs. Chapin. This place is supposed to keep track of their students and now you're telling me she was allowed to go off campus for a weekend and no one knows where she went?"

That wasn't what I'd said at all. I hadn't said a word about Laney going off campus either weekend. I'd only suggested I assumed she'd spent them with her parents.

I searched through the file, found what I wanted, and handed it to her. She stared down at the two pieces of paper in her hand. One was a photocopy of the sign-out cards the house parents were supposed to keep—the ones the school had gotten a bit lax about—signing Laney out to her parents for the Columbus Day weekend. The other was a handwritten note from Jack Taggert, asking that Laney be released for the weekend. She stared at the note, rereading it several times.

"You can see why I was confused," I said.

Her mouth opened and shut a few times like a beached fish. Finally she handed them back to me with shaking fingers. "I don't know anything about this," she said. "You'll have to ask Jack."

I delivered Marta Taggert into Dave Holdorf's capable hands, suggested some sherry might be in order, and went to ask Lori if Mr. Taggert was around. She shook her head, her ponytail bobbing. "Dorrie took him for a walk," she said. She looked out at the campus to see if she could spot them. "There they are now. Coming back across the circle." I joined her at the window. Dorrie was easy to spot. Although her coat was a demure and sensible gray tweed, she had a cheerful scarlet hat and scarf and matching red gloves. "She does that so she'll be easy to spot," Lori said. Beside her, Jack Taggert lumbered along like a tame bear.

"I like him," Lori said. "He's nice. He reminds me of my father."

"When they get back, will you ask him if he can give me a few minutes?"

"Sure," she said. "Do you need me to cancel someone to free up some time?"

I started to say no but the opportunity to postpone Curt Sawyer was more than I could resist. "Yes. Please. Can you reschedule Curt Sawyer for first thing in the morning?"

"Righto." Lori grinned impishly. "Sure you can take that so early in the day?"

"Better than at the end. I need to be bright-eyed and bushy-tailed to deal with him."

"That helps?" I shrugged. Lori laughed and picked up the phone and I went back to my office, my soul filled with longing for a sandwich. Unfortunately, I'd used my lunch hour meeting with Marta Taggert. For years I've meant to reform and start carrying something like multi-grain high-protein health food bars in my briefcase for food emergencies like this—something quick and nutritious and filling. My problem is that all those complete-meal diet bars and diet drinks taste like rodent droppings, or like I imagine rodent droppings would taste, so I never do it. As a result, I spend much of my life with headaches caused by lack of food. I could feel one coming on now.

I called Lori and asked if she could find me a Coke. Her reply was like water to a thirsty man. "Dorrie had the kitchen send over some sandwiches. I was just about to call and ask if you'd prefer turkey or tuna?"

"Tuna," I said, "unless it's on white bread."

"Nice, nutritious oatmeal," she said, "coming right up."

The sandwich and my next interviewee arrived together. In fact, he brought the sandwich. "Thought I'd save Lori the trip," he said, setting it down before me with a flourish. Through the industrial-strength plastic wrap, I could see thick sandwiches skewered with frilled toothpicks, carrot sticks, olives, and high-quality chips. I pushed away the greedy, drooling part of me that longed to devour the sandwich and concentrated on the man sitting before me. Chas Drucker, who had been Laney's advisor and her English teacher, was wearing a flat tweed cap dusted with snowflakes, a tan shearling jacket, and sturdy brown hiking boots whose water-shedding properties spoke of years of tenderly applied mink oil. He hung his cap carefully on one of the points of the chair back, unbuttoned his coat and unwound an ancient striped scarf, and crossed his legs, carefully drawing up his trouser legs.

I pegged him at somewhere between fifty and fifty-five. His wavy hair was graying and slightly too long. He had a manly cleft in his chin and a handsome face that was just beginning to sag. In a few years he'd begin to look raddled and the boyish hairdo would become foolish. For now, he remained a strikingly attractive man. I explained my mission and asked him to give me his view of Laney.

He bent forward, clasped his hands around his knee, and studied me thoughtfully. "You never met her?" His voice was deep and calm. I imagined its cadence rolling over decades of English classes. I shook my head. "That's too bad. She was a very unusual young woman. Gifted and rather misguided is how I'd describe her." He sat back as though that satisfied his obligation.

"I'm afraid I'm going to need a little more than that, Mr. Drucker," I said.

"Call me Chas. Please. Mr. Drucker sounds terribly formal and old. What is the purpose of all these questions about Laney, anyway?"

I'd already explained it and I was sure Dave Holdorf had, as well, but I also knew that after a sudden death, people close to the deceased were often in a state of shock. While they might seem to function rationally, they really were so distracted by their grief they had trouble focusing on things around them. This man had been her advisor as well as her teacher. If they are doing their jobs right, faculty advisors get very close to their students. I knew that that sort of attention was emphasized at Bucksport. It made Chas Drucker an important source of information. It also meant he was vulnerable and needed to be handled gently.

"As a faculty member," I said, "I know that you're aware of the impact of a student's death on a school like Bucksport. No one is callous about what happened to Laney Taggert. It's been a shocking and devastating experience for you, for all the faculty and staff as well as for the students. At the same time, from an administrative point of view, the situation has to be managed carefully to prevent a reactive outflux of students or a withdrawal of applicants for next year's class. I guess you'd describe me as the damage-control department. Mrs. Chapin has asked me to do an inventory of the procedures for ensuring student safety and well-being, a spot check, if you will, of whether the school took adequate care of Laney and whether things should be changed in the future."

His face had taken on an aggrieved, almost peevish look. I headed him off before he could say what he was thinking. "I know, at first hearing, that this sounds rather callous and self-serving, Mr. Drucker. But it's important to bear in mind that we have to consider the interests of the other two hundred fifty students at Bucksport. Their academic lives go on, of course, and they need stability and comfort, not upset and sensation. And then, too . . ." I hadn't been going to say this. It shouldn't have been necessary, but he still looked peevish and uncooperative. "Not only are the ongoing educational interests of the students an important consideration, but the livelihood of the faculty and staff depend on a well-regarded and economically healthy school."

He got the message. Damage control was essential to his job. He nodded thoughtfully.

"Along with an overall procedures audit, I'm trying to get a view of how Laney Taggert fit into the picture and to collect information about her activities on the day she disappeared. I'd like you to think of yourself as a camera.

Give me a wide-angle shot of Laney in the Bucksport community that gradually narrows down to a close-up of Laney herself and finally a shot of the last time you saw her."

"That was very eloquent," he said. "What's your background? Photography, fine arts?"

"Before I started working with independent schools, I was a newspaper reporter and a social worker. I like this better." I tucked back an annoying curl trying to wrap itself around my nose. "At Human Services we used to keep informal KBI ratings."

"What does KBI stand for?"

"Kids battered in. It got so depressing I could hardly bear to go to work in the morning."

"This is better?"

"No. This is the worst possible situation a private school can find itself in. Traumatic for everyone. But it does have to be dealt with." I could tell that Chas Drucker wished it didn't have to be. He didn't want to talk about Laney and he would go on making irrelevant conversation as long as I'd let him. "Was she a good student?"

He hesitated. "She had a good mind. She was clever. Quick. She took honors courses but she didn't like to apply herself. She'd gone to public schools until she came to us, as I'm sure you know, and she simply hadn't learned the habits of critical thinking. If all that was required was to regurgitate textbook and lecture materials, she did fine. If deeper analysis was called for, she sometimes floundered. Not," he added, "that she didn't have techniques for dealing with that, too."

"I don't know what you mean."

His brow furrowed and he looked at me suspiciously. "Surely everyone is telling you the same things. Laney Taggert was the most accomplished manipulator I've ever seen. It was a skill she'd perfected long before she came to us. If a teacher gave her a bad grade, she'd be in there pleading flu or cramps or depression or some reason why she should get a second chance. She was hard to resist."

"Did anyone ever resist her?"

He gave me a curious look, hesitating before he answered. "We were learning, but it was difficult. Her excuses, you see, were all things we might have accepted as reasons from some other student. With her, people were getting wise to the fact that she did it consistently. Once we became aware of the pattern, we went back and talked to her teachers at Ellanville. They confirmed that she'd been like this there, as well. I suppose she had to learn it to survive living with the lush and the lump."

"You mean her parents?"

"I see you've met them."

"I have."

"Well," he said, "I think deep down Laney desperately wanted to be loved and accepted by her mother. I hope this doesn't sound too much like second-rate psychology, but when you've worked with students as long as I have, you do begin to see patterns. Laney was very well defended. She was afraid to let people get close because she didn't want to be disappointed. But like any child—and they really are still children in a good many ways—she wanted to be known and loved. She'd settled for being admired. If she wanted your attention, she'd work hard to please, but she had no concept of working out of responsibility. I don't want you to get the wrong impression of Laney. If I let you think of her as sly, manipulative, and badly educated, you'd be missing the real Laney. She was quite a fascinating young woman. My analogy would be to a firefly."

"A firefly?" I said, wondering where he was going with this.

"Yes. She had a kind of magical illumination but it didn't come with any warmth. Hers was a cold, chemical brilliance. She had a knack for caricature that was both astonishing and terrible. She did devastating imitations of people."

"So I've heard. You were her advisor. Did you ever discuss these imitations with her?"

"Of course. I tried to tell her how hurtful they could be but she wouldn't listen to me. She just shrugged and said it was all in fun and she didn't understand how anyone could take it any other way." He shrugged. "It was one area where she felt successful and she wasn't willing to give that up."

"But people were upset, weren't they? Would you say that Laney made enemies through those imitations or is that putting it too strongly?"

He studied his knuckles and considered my question. "I hate to admit it but I'd have to say yes. She made some enemies. Or at least that she hurt some people rather badly and it made them quite angry at her."

"Angry enough to want to hurt her?"

He looked shocked. "Not the way you're suggesting," he said. "Bucksport is not that kind of community. We try to foster an environment of caring, communication, and responsibility. It wouldn't be consistent with the Bucksport ethic to strike out at someone physically because they'd hurt you with words."

"Even if you knew that words wouldn't work."

"No," he said, "not even then."

He wasn't going to budge and I didn't want to annoy him before I'd finished my questions even if he was being deliberately and unhelpfully naive. With some people I might have sighed and urged them to grow up, but I sensed that Chas Drucker took himself very seriously. Staying in the private school world all their lives sometimes allows adults to remain unnaturally naive and idealistic. "Had she seemed unusually depressed to you lately?"

"No."

"Did she tend to be a depressed young woman?"

"No." He wasn't even listening to my questions.

"Did Laney ever confide in you or consult you about her love life?"

"Her love life? The girl was only sixteen."

"And involved in a rather tempestuous relationship with Josh Meyer. You did know about that?"

"Well, of course, but she certainly didn't confide any of the details."

"She never mentioned their fights or asked you for advice?"

"I was her academic advisor," he said stiffly.

"Mr. Drucker, please. We're talking about a tragic death here. We both know that the role a student's advisor plays at a boarding school is not so limited. She never talked to you about relationships?" From the stubborn set of his jaw, I could see he wasn't going to cooperate.

"Who else on the faculty was she close to?"

"I really couldn't say."

Meaning he wouldn't say. He must have known. I changed the subject. "I understand that you normally had dinner with Laney and several other students?"

"Not exactly," he said. Now that he was annoyed, there was a prissy note in his voice that hadn't been there earlier. "I've been on the Bucksport faculty for about twenty-five years. Normally, a faculty member's responsibilities include coaching and dining hall duty. But seniority has its privileges. For years I lived in the dorms with my wife and family, serving as a house parent. Eventually we—my wife, Ellie, and I—graduated to a house on the campus but we still ate with the students. For the last few years, I haven't had any dining hall responsibilities. Much as I like the students, it has been nice to have quiet evening meals at home. I was just filling in last week for a faculty member who had to be away."

"Were you filling in on the night she disappeared?"

"I may have been the last person to see her," he said sadly.

"Can you tell me about that?"

"What's to tell? I was coming across the campus toward the dining hall and I ran into Laney. She said she wasn't feeling well and was going to skip dinner. She went her way and I went on to dinner."

"Was Mrs. Drucker with you?" I asked, hoping Ellie might have noticed something he didn't. He dashed my hopes with a terse no.

"What sort of illness was it? Did she tell you?"

"I have no idea," he said impatiently. "It was a five-second conversation."

"What time was it?"

He looked at his watch. "Almost two. I have to go. I've got a class."

"I meant when you met Laney."

"Around five, I think. I'm not sure."

"What time do you usually arrive for meals?"

"I told you. I don't usually arrive for meals."

I'd lost him. I made one last effort to get him back. "Did you notice what she was wearing?"

"Not really. What they all wear, I suppose. Some sort of jacket and a short skirt over those ugly leggings and clunky shoes. I really must go. If you have more questions you can call me." He reeled off a telephone number and stood up, concentrating on arranging his scarf. I could push and pry all I wanted but I wasn't going to get anything more.

"Thank you for taking the time to talk with me, Mr. Drucker." This time he didn't urge me to call him Chas. He just carefully arranged the scarf around his neck and the cap on his head, pulled on his gloves, and left. Was he too devastated by his student's death to talk about it or had he spent so many years in the rarefied atmosphere of the Bucksport School that any persistence was interpreted as undue pressure? I'd have to ask Dorrie what she thought.

I called Lori, who said Jack Taggert was around somewhere and she'd find him and send him to me. Then, like a hungry amoeba, I flowed around my sandwich and made it disappear. I'd had a very hard time ignoring it while Drucker was in the room. Talking with him had been like pulling teeth. I'd rather eat than pull teeth any day.

I was just licking the crumbs off my fingers when Jack Taggert came in. Lumbered in was more like it. He was dressed like a businessman but as he settled his bulk into the chair I was once again struck by how oddly his clothes went with his body. As if he were reading my mind, he grabbed his tie. "Marta says I ought to keep it on but I don't see what it has to do with being sorry about Laney. Do you mind if I take it off?"

. "Not at all, Mr. Taggert," I said. "Neckties have never made sense to me."

"Damned right!" he said, tugging at the knot with clumsy fingers. "I hate the damned things. Always have." He flung it over the arm of the chair. His face was wide and creased, the cheeks chapped, the whites of his eyes were red. He sat in the chair and stared at me and I don't think he saw me at all.

"I'm very sorry about your daughter, Mr. Taggert. It must be hard coming here and going through all this when you'd like to have a chance to be alone with your grief. I'll try not to take up too much of your time. . . ."

"I don't mind," he said, his voice harsh with the strain of controlling his feelings. "I'd like to talk about her. Everyone around here is so uncomfortable they barely mention her. Even to us, though that's why we're here. She wasn't a very nice girl but it was just a phase she was going through. She would have gotten over it." He put his hands over his face and started to cry. I got the box of tissues that has become part of my standard interviewing equipment, went around the desk, and knelt down beside him, pushing a handful of them into his hand. He gripped my hand so hard it hurt and held on tight. "Oh, God, I don't know what I'm going to do without her. I never wanted her away from me in the first place, her funny little laugh, the way she'd cock her head and tease me, those wonderful impressions she did . . . and now this."

He tried to bring himself under control but the tears

were there and they needed to come out. I couldn't visualize Marta putting her arms around him and comforting him but I knew a whole lot about what he was going through. About how life, with its too-fast pace and superficial expectations won't let people grieve, but hustles them past the moment the way you'd steer a child around something unsightly on the sidewalk. I ended up beside his chair with his head against me, gently stroking the stiff graying hair. He was a massive man and hard as a rock and right now that rock was being shaken by a succession of earthquakes.

It was ironic that I could comfort this stolid man when I hadn't been able to comfort Josh Meyer, but it made sense. Josh had that distrustful adolescent skittishness that made him difficult to approach, while Jack Taggert was just heartbreakingly sad.

Finally the tremors subsided and he lifted his head, embarrassed. "I'm sorry, Ms. Kozak. Awfully sorry. I don't know what came over me. I've never . . ."

"You don't have to apologize, Mr. Taggert. I lost my husband in an accident a few years ago. I know how it feels."

It was the right thing to say. He settled himself back in the chair, blew his nose, and raised his sad red eyes to meet mine. "How can I help you?"

I wanted to ask him lots of questions about Laney. He had a very different view of her, but I didn't think he was ready to spend a lot of time talking about her. I handed him the sign-out card and the note. "Your wife says she doesn't know anything about this. Did you write this note?" He nodded. "So only you spent the weekend with Laney? Mrs. Taggert wasn't with you?"

He shook his head and sat looking at me, hands folded in his lap on top of the papers, looking like a guilty child called to the principal's office. "I wasn't there either," he said in a gruff voice. "I just wrote the note for Laney."

"Do you know where she went that weekend?"

"No." He stopped, realized that it was not enough, and

tried to explain. "Laney didn't want to be at Bucksport. It was her mother's idea. Having Laney around made Marta very nervous, particularly since Laney became a teenager and got willful. They didn't get along. Probably they never got along. Marta has about as much maternal instinct as a clam. When Laney started getting into trouble at school, Marta couldn't deal with it and insisted on sending her away. I did what I could to stay in touch. We talked on the phone a lot. She even wrote me letters. I have all of them at work. In my desk."

"Columbus Day weekend?" I prompted.

"Oh, yeah." He shook his head as if he were trying to clear it. "She called me. Said she and a friend wanted to go off campus but she knew she wouldn't be allowed to leave unless it was with a parent. She asked me if I'd write the note. It all sounded perfectly innocent. A group of them were going down to Cape Cod to someone's beach house. There was going to be a college-age sister there as chaperon."

"So you knew it was going to be a mixed-sex group?"

"You make it sound bad," he protested. "It wasn't like that."

"What was it like? Can you give me names of some of the other kids who went so I can ask them about it?"

He thought for a minute, kneading his broad forehead with a big hand. "This is embarrassing. The only one I can remember was Merri. It was Merri's sister who was going to be the chaperon. I don't know what you think of me, but try to understand. We'd sent her away against her will. I couldn't deny her this favor that she asked for. I expect her boyfriend went along as well."

"Laney's boyfriend?" He nodded.

"Have you met him?"

"No," he said loudly, "and I hope I never do. I'm not sure I could control myself after what he did to Laney."

"You're sure he was the father of Laney's baby?"

He gave me an angry look. "She wouldn't have been promiscuous."

I asked a question that was really too pushy, but sometimes you have to be pushy, and Jack Taggert, for all his devotion to his daughter, hadn't given me much of an idea of how close their relationship was. "Did she discuss her sex life with you?"

"Of course not!" he said. "But I knew my daughter. She wouldn't have . . . look, I'd like to help you, but I can't do this . . . analyzing her like some casual acquaintance." He stopped talking and just sat staring at his hands.

I gave up, feeling a little guilty about what I'd asked. Jack Taggert's emotions were too stirred up. It was time to send him on his way and call it a day at Bucksport. Not that my day was over. When I called the office, there were sure to be half a dozen things that needed attention. "Thank you for talking to me, Mr. Taggert."

Relief that he was being dismissed was all over his face. He got up from the chair, stuffed the tie in his pocket, and grabbed another handful of tissues. "Never know when you're going to need these," he said, and shambled out, a great big weary man. He might not have known his daughter very well but he sure had loved her. It was some small comfort to think that the girl who had been described to me as cold, brilliant, and manipulative had had at least one person who simply loved her.

I finished my notes on what he'd told me and added them to the file. On the way out I stopped to ask Lori when I was going to be seeing Merri Naigler. "Tomorrow," she said, "right after you've finished bright-eyeing and bushy-tailing Curt Sawyer. Dorrie wanted to see you before you left but she's in a faculty meeting right now."

"Have her call me. I'll be at the office until seven, home by nine. She can call anytime." I gave her the cellular phone number since I didn't know where I'd be sleeping. I should have stayed longer and done more, but I was bone weary. Talking to sad and anxious people all day had taken a toll. Nothing about the matter was simple or easy. A night on the red-eye hadn't helped, and neither had the news about my condo. I wanted to go home and curl up with Andre and I didn't expect I'd get to do that.

"Tell me something, Thea. Do you ever have time for fun?"

"What's that?"

"Thought so," she said. "Now, when I get home, I've got Al. And Al is fun, that's why I married him. That and to get rid of my maiden name."

"Which was?"

"Snitz. I swore if I heard one more joke about someone getting in a Snitz I was going to court and changing it. Then I met Al."

"You're a lucky girl."

"Woman," she said. "We are very PC around here."

"And proud of it, I'll bet."

She took me by the shoulders, turned me around, and pushed me gently toward the door. "Go home, Thea, before you put your foot in it." I went.

CHAPTER 7

THE WORLD I was driving through was a riot of gay and gaudy Christmas lights and I was so far from feeling festive I almost snarled. Against my will, I was getting caught up in the story of Laney Taggert. I wanted to put her out of my mind, go home, and veg out in front of the TV. But Suzanne's spare room wasn't home, my condo was trashed, and home was in Maine, two hours away. I could go there, if I could summon the energy, but not yet. Dark might have fallen, but the day had hardly begun.

Back at my office, I found things in a state of orderly chaos. Magda was still conducting intense negotiations in Hungarian with someone. The repairman was back for the second time that day and the copier was still broken. I decided we'd had enough. When your solution to a problem only causes you more problems, it's time to send it packing. I nudged him out from under it with my toe, showed him the list of repair calls Sarah had prepared, and asked him who I needed to talk to to get rid of the thing. He gave me a name and number, and added, "You're doing the right thing, you know. This model has been a lemon from the get-go." Everyone brightened considerably when I announced that the machine was getting the hook.

I called Yanita, but she was out, so I left a message, and

I was elbow deep in correspondence when Sarah stuck her head in. "Almost forgot. Your mother called. She wants to be sure you're coming for Christmas dinner and wants to know if Andre is coming, too."

Christmas. Bah, humbug. The gaudy decorations, the trashed carols piped into every public place, the buying frenzy everyone got into, the delicious strain of mandatory family events. I wasn't really a curmudgeon. I loved listening to the *Messiah* and wrapping presents. I still got a flash of that powerful excitement on Christmas Eve that Santa would come and the world truly was infused with magic. I loved every sentimental story of good deeds and love discovered and impulsive generosity. I just didn't want to spend Christmas with my family.

Explaining my family is a long and complicated story. Before my sister Carrie died, I thought I had the world's greatest family. Since then, I've come to see all of us in a new light, and not a particularly favorable one. Last spring, my mother pressured me into helping out a friend of hers accused of murdering her husband. No matter what I did, my efforts didn't satisfy my mother. We ended up having a fight so major neither of us has gotten over it, though she pretends she has. The fight was at my brother Michael's engagement party—which I walked out of—and that made Michael and Sonia's wedding, in September, even more tense and difficult than their awful personalities had already assured it would be.

I wish I were a more forgiving person. I wish that with respect to my family I had a more generous and tolerant nature, but I don't. I've always been the fixer in my family, the one everyone has always turned to to make it right and to work things out. But somewhere along the line, even though I still find myself rescuing strays of the human variety and taking on lost causes, I've lost my charity toward my family. Yes, it's stubborn and perhaps wrongheaded. My second favorite cop in the world, after Andre, Dom Florio, calls me headstrong. But whatever you call it, I believe I'm the wronged party and it's up to my family, especially my mother, to make the first move. Something more substantial and personal than Christmas dinner, which can be conducted on the level of a family ritual.

Then, too, there was something else. I wanted to spend Christmas with my own family, that is, with Andre. I wanted to sit with him in our living room, looking at the lights on our own Christmas tree and holding hands in the peaceful darkness. But we hadn't even discussed Christmas yet. Maybe he was expecting to spend it with his own family, with or without me. The whole business depressed me. My idea of a great present would be a year without holidays.

Sarah cleared her throat to remind me that she was still standing there. "I don't know what to tell her," I said, knowing Sarah understood about my mother.

She grinned conspiratorially. "Next time she calls, I'll apologize for failing to give you the message. She thinks we're all bozos anyway. I can go on being forgetful as long as you want." She hesitated, not being one to intrude. "Look, Bobby told me about the condo. If there's anything I can do . . ."

"I think things are under control. The guys who cleaned up after the fire were coming today, and they're great."

She nodded. "Yeah. You told me about them. They sound fabulous. Wish I could get them to come to my house. Maybe I'll set a fire. . . ." She turned to go and then turned back. "I'm thinking of asking him to leave." I didn't need to ask who she meant. Sarah's husband has been like a blister on her heel for years, his criticism rubbing away her self-esteem until she is always spiritually sore and limping. "I'll wait until after Christmas, of course. But I'm afraid of how he'll take it, no matter when I do it. Oops, that damned phone . . ." She reached across the desk and picked it up. "Yanita Emery." She passed the phone to me and went out.

"Sorry to do this to you," Yanita said, "but how about

tonight?" In for a penny, in for a pound, I thought, and agreed to set aside an hour at six-thirty for a phone conference. She was an hour away, and a face-to-face wasn't necessary until we'd done preliminaries. Suzanne and the baby stopped to say good night, followed by Lisa, Magda, and Sarah. Bobby left without saying good-bye, which hurt my feelings. I spread out my papers and the phone rang.

Dorrie's voice was leaden with fatigue. "How's it going?" she asked.

"Slowly."

"Everyone cooperating?"

"After a fashion. Drucker wasn't very forthcoming."

"Any idea who was out there with Laney?"

"Not yet. You?"

"Not a clue," she said grimly. "I can't get it off my mind, the idea that someone knows something and won't tell us. I think I'm going to mention it at school meeting tomorrow. . . ."

"You run the risk of upsetting them."

"They're already upset. But I'd appreciate it if you could be there."

"What time?" I asked, feeling as though someone had just added another brick to my load.

"Eight. Look, I know you like to check in at the office, but can't that stuff wait, Thea? This is important."

I hoped my sigh was inaudible. I knew it was important. "Don't worry. I'll be there."

I did a few things that couldn't wait and then, realizing I could talk on the phone just as easily in the car as at the office, I called Andre to tell him I was coming, and headed north to Maine. I hoped he'd check his messages. I figured it was worth four hours of driving to spend the time with him. It wasn't worth it to spend the time alone. I was on the phone with Yanita for almost an hour, and ended up setting up another meeting, with the King administration and their lawyer, for the following evening.

For the rest of the trip, Laney Taggert was my only

companion. What was it her father had said? She wasn't very nice but it was just a stage she was going through. Now she'd never get past that stage. I pictured him sitting alone by his Christmas tree, weeping, Laney's wrapped presents by his feet, the only person I'd met so far who genuinely mourned her death. I could almost feel the wrench of those sobs in the emptiness of my car. Laugh and the world laughs with you, cry and you cry alone.

By the time I pulled into the driveway, I could barely keep my eyes open, and Andre's car wasn't there. All up and down the street, the houses gleamed with holiday cheer. Ours was just dark. I stumbled up the slippery steps, unlocked the door, and went in. It was cold and the air smelled of old fried eggs. I turned on a few lights, said hello to his breakfast dishes, turned up the thermostat, and called Andre. No one in the office knew where he was. I left word that I was home and dragged myself, my suitcase, and my ever-bulging briefcase up the stairs.

Half an hour later, I climbed out of a lukewarm bath into an icy room and decided that the heat wasn't working. I was prowling around the smelly, cobwebby basement with a flashlight, trying to find the gauge on the oil tank, when the phone rang. I stumbled upstairs, banging my shin, and squelched an armload of epithets as I grabbed the receiver. An unidentified voice that sounded a lot like Roland Proffit gave me a number where Andre could be found. I abandoned my heat-seeking mission and called, knowing, even before the phone was answered, what I was going to hear. I wasn't, and was, disappointed when it was blond, bubbly Amanda who answered the phone, the unmistakable sounds of a party behind her. "He's right here. I'll put him on."

With coplike precision he cut to the heart of things. "Where are you?"

"Home."

"Which home? Suzanne's?"

"Our home."

"Goddamn. Why didn't you tell me?"

"I tried. I called. I left messages. I thought they were always supposed to know where to find you. I think they're a hell of a lot better at knowing how not to find you." Damn. I didn't want to fight. Why was I doing this? "Are you coming back? There's no heat."

"I thought you were up to your ears in work and couldn't get away."

"I missed you." Idiot, I thought, just say you're on your way. I didn't add an extra four hours of driving to my life when I'm already dead tired so I could talk to you on the phone. I could have stayed in Massachusetts and done that.

He was talking, but not to me. To someone else. Explaining why he had to go. "Because the heat's not working." Not because he wanted to be with me, though it was silly of me to expect him to say that out loud.

I heard her reply, loud and clear. "Well, then I'd guess you'd better take that hot body home, handsome. Too bad. The party is just getting started."

"I'm on my way," he said. "Did you check the tank and see if we're out of oil?"

"Yes. No. Well, sort of."

"Well, check it," he said. "If it's empty, the fuel company number is on the wall by the phone." He hung up.

Now I was feeling distinctly snarly. I hate domestic crises. It's not that I'm helpless or timid. I live in a condo by choice so someone else can take care of such things because I'm busy. I'm busy and tired and now I was stone cold and the thought of going back to that nasty basement made my skin crawl. Boldly, I hefted my flashlight and set forth. The gauge, when I finally found it, was designed to be readable only to those under three feet tall who had long, narrow heads. When I finally managed to read it, it said empty. I called the emergency number, got someone who promised to come within the hour, washed the cobwebs off my face, combed them out of my hair, and went to bed, huddled beneath all the blankets I could find.

An hour later, I responded to feet on the steps with a joyous smile at my loved one's return, and received in return a delivery slip from the oil-blackened hand of a very surprised oil-truck driver. One good thing about the damned cold—I greeted him in a flannel gown and robe and not something skimpy and alluring. From an upstairs window, I watched the big truck lurch away down the street, a panorama of rear lights flashing. Watched a dusting of snow settle onto my car. Watched Christmas lights go off along the street. Watched with reddened nose and cold-stiffened hands as the rest of the world went to sleep.

Half an hour after that, as I lay there sleepless and abandoned, feeling homeless and wretched and wondering if Andre was in a ditch somewhere, he finally turned up, smelling ripely of smoke and alcohol. By then, on a scale of one to ten, my mood was well into the minus numbers. He came to bed warm and loving and said and did all the right things but I went to sleep feeling unsettled, unhappy, and unconnected. Lonely, even with company in the bed, and uncharacteristically pessimistic about the future.

My dreams were a rehash of all my Bucksport interviews, a confused melange of comments from which Laney Taggert emerged innocent, young, confused, sly, wily, manipulative, and ambitious. Not an easy read. Experience has taught me that when I dream about things I'm working on, I don't get restful sleep. I stumbled forth into the predawn darkness of another snowy morning feeling old and tired and not at all ready to face the day, not even fortified by the bowl of oatmeal my unusually attentive beau had produced without making eye contact. I think he was afraid, in the cold light of day—warmer, actually, than the dead of night, inside at least—that I would raise the subject of Amanda and her remark about his body.

The snowy drive didn't help. I arrived, neck stiff with tension, just as Dorrie was calling the all-school meeting to order. "Good morning," she greeted them, to a chorus of moans and groans. Adolescents don't like to get up in the morning any more than I do. "I know. I know. You're all tired. But soon you'll all be going home for eighteen days, and with luck, you'll be able to sleep late on many of them. You need the rest. I know it. We're all tired after the last few days. I know they've been very hard on all of you, just as I'm sure you realize that they've been very hard on us." There was a murmur of agreement.

"One of the reasons that Laney Taggert's loss has been so hard for all of us is that here at Bucksport we have a community, rather like our own small town of which we are all the residents. When a close community loses one of its members, the whole community suffers. The whole community grieves. When the death is unexplained, as is Laney's, there is also fear and uncertainty in the community. The other members worry about what happened, and it makes them uncertain about themselves. I know that some of you are worried that Laney's death was not an accident, that she was worried and unhappy and deliberately put herself in the way of danger."

Oh, no, Dorrie, I thought. You shouldn't do this. Why didn't you talk to me before you plunged ahead with this speech? It's only going to upset them more. If I could have plucked her out from behind her podium without making a scene, I would have done it.

"We have no reason to believe that that is what happened," she said. "We have no reason to believe that her death was anything other than an unfortunate accident. Now, I know how news travels around here. Just like in a small town, it's very hard to keep a secret. So I expect you all know about the woman some people are calling 'Dorrie's detective.' " She motioned for me to come up and join her. I went forward with leaden feet and a plastic smile, trying to keep my irritation off my face as I forcibly unclenched my teeth. "This is Thea Kozak," she said. "I've asked her to come in and look over our shoulders—us meaning all the adults, the dreaded grown-ups whose job it is to keep you all safe and cared for—to be sure we're doing for you what you have a right to expect from us. Ms. Kozak's job is to see if we're doing things right or tell us where we need to change. I'm introducing her to you because in a small community like this, it is better to know than conjecture and guess. If there's anything you think she should know, you should feel free to drop in and tell her. She's in the office right next to Mrs. Drucker's."

Dorrie cleared her throat and looked out at the rows of upturned faces. "One last thing. Part of being a member of a community like ours is taking responsibility for the well-being of the community. For its peace of mind." *Shut up, Dorrie,* I thought. *Quit while you're ahead. Don't say it.* "Now we have been told that there were two sets of footprints going down to the pond. . . ." She paused for effect as a ripple of realization ran through the students. "Which means that someone else was there, someone who has information about what happened. Maybe you're scared, or maybe you're feeling guilty because you couldn't help her, or maybe you had a fight and walked away, and now you're too shocked by the terrible thing that happened to come forward. But we need you to come forward. We need you to talk to us. We need to know. Not just me. Not just the faculty and the administration, but everyone here. So please . . ."

She gripped the podium and leaned toward them. "Please, if you were there, if you know something about what happened . . . for Laney's sake, for her parents' sakes, for all of our sakes, please come forward and tell us about it. I'm available. Thea's available. Your counselors and advisors are available. Get it off your chest. Come talk to us." She dropped her arms. "Thank you. Now, in accordance with our meeting procedures, the floor is yours. Is there anyone who wants to speak?"

Josh Meyer jumped to his feet and strode toward the front. I knew what was coming, and gritted my teeth again. This was all we needed. This disaster had definitely sidetracked Dorrie from her normal style of caution and control or she never would have set this in motion. And there was no sense in hiring me to give her advice if she wouldn't take it.

Josh replaced her at the podium with a graceful bow, and leaned out over it, draping his lanky body sinuously across the wood. He stared out at his schoolmates. "You all know who I am, so I guess I don't have to waste your time on introductions. Many of you even know why I'm here, which, to get right to the point, is Laney's death. You can forget that"—he waved his arms in the air, like a baseball ref declaring the runner out—"bullshit our esteemed headmistress just fed you." Dorrie stiffened beside me and I heard her moan.

"You all knew Laney, right? Not exactly an Eddie Bauerette, was she?" Josh the actor paused for his laugh. "She wouldn't have gone out to that pond at night unless she had to, right? And not to be too euphemistic about it, she was hardly the suicidal type. She might have wished some of us would drop dead, but never herself. In Laney's book, if someone had to die, it was someone else. What happened is that someone lured her out there, shoved her out on the ice, and walked away. Her death was no"—his voice took on a sneering tone—"unfortunate accident, as our fearless leaders so euphemistically put it. Ms. Margaret Delaney Taggert, late of the Bucksport School, was murdered, pure and simple."

He straightened up, slamming his fist down for emphasis, pausing dramatically as the sound echoed in the incredibly silent room. "And if anyone knows anything about it, they'd better speak up. We need to demand some answers!" He shook his head in disgust. "Unfortunate accident. And they wonder why our generation is cynical about truth." He walked off the stage, down the aisle, and out the door, slamming it behind him.

CHAPTER 8

SHE SAT BEHIND her desk with her head in her hands. "Why on earth did I do that?" she moaned.

"I wish you'd—"

"I know. I know. I know. You told me not to do it. I didn't listen. I thought it was the right thing to go directly to the students—"

"I don't believe it was a student that she met. All we can do now is pray that this doesn't get back to Chip Barrett and become front-page news."

"All we can do now is for you to find out what really happened, as quickly as possible."

"Do you think Josh Meyer is right?" Dorrie didn't answer. Her chair was turned away from me and she was staring out across the circle, where a mean gray sky was spitting snow. "What does Rocky think about Josh's theory?"

"Rocky thinks we should declare the whole thing an accident, send you home, and get back to business as usual. As for Josh, Rocky thinks he's a smart-assed troublemaker out to call attention to himself."

"He's a good actor," I replied.

"Yes, but is that all?" She swung around to face me. "Isn't it time for you to start?" Dorrie wasn't my child or my charge; she was my client and my boss. If she didn't want to discuss things, I couldn't make her. She turned back to the window. "Find out what happened."

I gathered up my stuff and went to work, feeling utterly unprepared to face Curt Sawyer.

Curt didn't seem to be doing much better. He huddled in the chair and glowered at me. His graying hair was cut so close to his narrow head that his ears looked like big pink cup handles. His nose was as red as Rudolph's from a combination of the chilly air and too many years of liberal drinking. His eyes were watery and it was clear he was fighting a cold. None of it did anything to improve his disposition. "This is all just a goddamned wild-goose chase," he said as he unbuttoned his jacket. "Dumb kid falls through the ice and the press and everybody else acts like it's the first time an accident's happened in the history of the world. Nobody kills themselves that way and there sure as hell wasn't no murderer out running around that night. Too darn cold."

"Did you know Laney Taggert, Curt?"

"Miserable little hoity-toity pain in the ass, she was."

"What's the basis for that assessment?"

"Huh?"

I forgot that subtlety doesn't work with Curt. "What made you decide she was a pain in the ass?"

He shrugged. "She just was. Most of 'em are. Arrives in my office with a list as long as her arm of stuff she wants done for the spring show and then it's, 'We'll need this, Mr. Sawyer, and this and that and that and can you have it done by Friday?' Not so much as a please. If their parents had spanked 'em more, maybe they'd 've learned some manners."

"Was the spring show the only time you dealt with Laney Taggert?"

"Don't I wish! Once she'd made my acquaintance she was in and out all the time, acting like I was her personal servant. 'Mr. Sawyer, the shower is dripping. Mr. Sawyer, the lightbulbs need changing. Mr. Sawyer, there isn't enough hot water.' If I wasn't there, she'd bug my staff.

Make 'em stop what they were doing and come and wait on her. Like some little princess or something."

"Was she unique?"

"Huh?"

"Was she the only student who bugged you like that? Was her behavior unusual?"

"There's a lot of 'em that are spoiled rotten but she was one of the worst."

"Is there any chance she was hanging around because she was interested in someone on your crew?"

Sawyer shifted uneasily in his chair. "My men," he said stiffly, "are trained to handle problems like that. They do not fraternize with the students."

"I'm glad to hear that, Curt, but what I asked was whether Laney Taggert had showed a special interest in anyone."

"You're talking through your hat, lady," he said, assuming a stubborn posture, arms folded firmly across his chest.

What I could see, even through my hat, was that Laney had been interested in one of his men, or one of his men had been interested in her and Curt knew it. He tugged at his ear and sucked his teeth and didn't answer. "Who was it, Curt? And what did you do about it?"

"I swatted that miserable cock-teasing little bitch on her adorable ass and told her to go play with kids her own age."

"And did she?"

He grunted something that sounded affirmative. "Did you talk to her dorm parents?"

Another grunt. I waited. Finally he said, "I talked to Kathy Donahue. She was about as responsive as a pet rock. Bland smiles and would you like some tea, Mr. Sawyer, and a brush-off along the lines of 'Wasn't it up to my man to discourage that.' "

"I get the picture. Let's switch to something else. What procedures do you use to test the safety of the ice and warn the students about it?"

"Enough," he said gruffly. "There's always a sign by the pond that says No Swimming and No Boating without Permission. They've got to sign the book in my office and get the boathouse key if they want to use the pond for that. Then when the weather gets cold we've got signs we put out that say Danger, Thin Ice. One of the guys checks the ice every day and if it ever does get thick enough for skating, which it usually doesn't, we'll post a sign with the skating rules. There are also announcements periodically at all-school meetings about the danger of going out on the ice. We tell 'em we'll let 'em know when the ice is safe for skating." He shrugged. "I don't know what more we can do except put a fence around the pond. And if we did, they'd climb over it."

"They probably would," I agreed. "Tell me about how the security service works. How many people do you have on campus at night?"

"Enough."

"Curt, don't start stonewalling me. This is important."

"There's never been an incident that suggests we aren't providing adequate security. Besides, I've been over all this with the chief. I don't see why we need to go over it again."

"Well, we do, Curt, because my job is to be sure that all the procedures for the protection of the students are adequate." After a few more rounds of verbal wrestling we reached a truce and Curt reluctantly gave me some of the details. It was a minimalist offering but I knew it was all I was going to get. As soon as the last phrases were out of his mouth he stood up and started buttoning his coat. "Not so fast, Curt," I said. "We're not done."

"I've got work to do," he said.

"This is part of your work. Do you patrol the woods paths on a regular basis?" He took a step toward the door. "That was a question, Curt."

He swung back toward me and the face he presented was distinctly unpleasant. "What difference does that make now?"

"Just answer the question, Curt." He stood there sullenly silent. "Do I need to bring Dorrie in to moderate this discussion? You know she asked me to do this."

"I don't have enough manpower to do all the things we're supposed to do. When the weather is warm it's even worse. I'm supposed to have guys checking behind every bush."

"I assume, then, for the record, that someone was supposed to check the woods path but didn't do so?"

Curt stared with interest at his shoes.

"Who was the guy who found Laney?"

"That crazy McTeague."

"He doesn't work at Bucksport?"

Curt shook his head vehemently. "No way. Guy's a nutcase, lives half a mile down the road. He just comes here to jog."

"Are there many joggers who use the path?"

"Not in the winter. Some of the students who like to stay in shape and a few hard cores like McTeague."

"Ever had any trouble between the students and joggers?"

He shrugged. "Once a jogger came in to complain that two of our boys had followed her and made suggestive remarks."

"What did you do about that?"

"Said I'd refer the problem to the dean of students . . . and advised her she might want to wear more clothes. All she had on were these skintight little shorts with half her butt hanging out and a little bra top with her nipples stickin' out like traffic signals. You ask me, it's a damned-fool thing to do to dress like that and then go running through a campus full of horny boys. That uptight asshole Van Deusen's always talkin' about this thing or that thing being an attractive nuisance. You ask me, that's just what that woman was."

Unreconstructed as Sawyer was, I was inclined to agree with him. I find myself casting disapproving glances at women—and men—who go around in public with every wrinkle and bulge of their anatomy outlined in tight, shiny fabric. "Joanne Perlin says one of your maintenance men saw a girl who might have been Laney heading off toward the jogging path around five-thirty on Friday. I need to talk to him. Can you find out who it was and call Lori to put him on my schedule?"

It wasn't a request, it was a polite command, but Curt's reaction didn't surprise me. "There's no more to it than that," he said. "He didn't know the girl. You've heard what he saw. There's no need to talk to him." Curt had talked himself into a foul mood and decided it was my fault.

"That's my decision, not yours, and I want to talk to him. Please arrange it." I had a pretty good idea that the man in question was the same one Laney had taken an interest in.

"It's not important," he said, and walked out.

"And the horse you rode in on," I muttered, making a rude gesture at his departing back. Dave or Dorrie could handle this. Curt was immune to charm and persuasion. The only thing that worked with him was authority and I didn't have it. Not that I'd tried charm or persuasion. I know better than to waste my time.

Conflict always whets my appetite and I was ready for breakfast. I was about to ask Lori if she could find me some food when there was a tentative knock on my door. I called a brisk "Come in" and it opened to reveal a vibrant pixie in a long red stocking cap, bulky red parka, red-and-black striped leggings, and shiny black boots. I half expected her to say "Ho ho ho, Merry Christmas," but all she did was shuck the parka, kick off the boots, and curl up in the chair, cozy as a kitten, and regard me with her shining black eyes.

"I'm Merri Naigler," she said. Her cheeks were pink, her curls were black and saucy and her smile infectious. I'd never seen a person better named. "Lori . . . I mean, Mrs. Leonard . . . said you wanted to talk to me. Is it about Laney?"

"Yes. My name is Thea Kozak. Were you at the meeting this morning?"

She shook her head. "My mom was having a cow about my not being dressed warmly. By the time I went back and changed, I'd missed it."

"I've been hired by the trustees to review the circumstances surrounding Laney Taggert's accident—the procedural things like sign-outs, student-faculty contacts, safety precautions, things like that. They want to make sure everything possible is being done to keep you all safe." We shook hands. Hers was small and warm.

"Oh, was it an accident? I'm so glad! I mean, I'm not glad about Laney being dead. She was my best friend and I don't know what I'm going to do now. I feel sort of lost without her." She hesitated, absently fingering a curl. "I mean I'm glad it was an accident. She'd been so moody lately, I was afraid she might have—" She stopped and shrugged. "You know . . . gone out on the pond on purpose." She stared down at her clasped hands. "And I'm sure you know what Josh is saying. . . ."

"I've spoken with Josh," I said. "But so far, we have no reason to think it was anything but an accident."

She gave me a grateful smile.

"I'm trying to get the best picture I can of what sort of person Laney Taggert was. You probably knew her better than anyone so your impressions are very important. I know it won't be easy for you to talk about her but I hope you'll try."

Her smile drooped a little. "I'm happy to cooperate and everything, but how will I know what you want to know?"

"Would it be easier if I asked you questions?"

"I think so. One thing I don't understand," Merri said quietly, "why do you have to know about Laney to figure out about the rules and stuff?"

"That's a good question," I told her. "I guess I didn't explain it well enough. It's not just rules per se, but all the things Bucksport does to keep track of people. Contacts with dorm parents, advisors, things like that, that tell us whether we know the students well enough or whether people can fall through the cracks." I watched her closely as I talked. She didn't look so merry anymore.

She nodded vigorously. "If Laney fell through a crack, it was because she wanted to." Then she clapped a hand over her mouth.

I definitely wanted to know more but I decided to work around to it gradually. "How long were you and Laney friends?"

"Ever since she came to Bucksport. We were both new kids. I started here last year when my parents moved to Sedgwick and she'd just transferred here so Laney and I were sort of natural to become friends. Sometimes it's not easy to make friends at a new place so I was especially glad to meet Laney and she was just as glad to meet me. At least, I think she was." She fingered the silver button covers on her white shirt. The shirt was big enough to have covered about three of her. "You could never be quite sure with Laney."

"You mean you couldn't really tell if she liked you?"

Merri wiggled uncomfortably. "I'm sure she liked me. We were friends. I just don't know if she liked me as much"— she hesitated—"as I liked her. I mean, you never knew exactly where you stood with Laney. She wasn't in the habit of telling the truth . . . no . . . that's not quite what I mean . . . Laney was . . ." She paused, reluctant to go on. Finally she said, "She was a manipulator of the truth. I think she got so in the habit of lying . . . mostly to her mother . . . if you ever met her mother, you'd understand . . . anyway, so she lied habitually about things even when she didn't need to. So it was like I knew she was my friend but then sometimes I couldn't be so sure, you know what I mean? There were people who didn't like her. You've probably already heard that. Unfortunately one of them was her roommate but then Genny's so damned stiff she doesn't like anybody who can't produce a pedigree going back to the *Mayflower* and whose family isn't rolling in money. Besides, Genny is a plodder and Laney was quick. Genny was so jealous she couldn't appreciate the fun things about Laney. No. Wait. I'm doing this all wrong!" she said. "You're going to get a totally negative impression of her."

She picked up her pack, dug through it, and handed me a picture. It showed Merri and Laney, identically dressed in black-and-white striped tops and tights and little black pleated skirts, holding up clumps of each other's hair as mustaches. "That's before I cut my hair," she said. "Laney was funny and crazy and she was a great friend. Very understanding. She could hear what I wasn't saying as well as what I was." She held out her hand and I gave her back the picture.

"Not that Laney was all sweetness and light." She lowered her voice and said in hushed tones, "She had a dark side, too."

"You make her sound like Darth Vader."

She nodded vigorously. "Well, it was kind of like that. I mean sometimes I really worried about her. She scared me."

"What do you mean? What sorts of things would she do that scared you?"

"Breaking the rules. I mean, you know that people sometimes say that rules were made to be broken? Well, Laney really believed that. She had a sort of desperate compulsion to break rules. Mostly little things like getting out after curfew or skipping gym or not doing her work and getting her teachers to excuse her. But she aspired to bigger things."

"Such as?"

Merri hesitated. "I'm not really sure I should tell you."

"You need to, if I'm going to understand her."

She studied her hands. "I guess you're right, only it seems sort of like I'm betraying her, saying bad things about her when she's not here to defend herself, you know what I mean?"

I nodded. "A very wise policeman once told me that

the dead have no right to privacy and I guess I believe that. At least I believe that's true in cases where the death is unexplained—"

"But you said it was an accident!" she interrupted.

"It probably was, Merri, but you know, don't you, that some of the students here are worried that it was suicide? You worried about that a little yourself, didn't you?" She nodded. "We need to reassure them and part of the process is being sure ourselves that Laney didn't have some reason to consider suicide. When we started talking you seemed relieved that her death was an accident so you must have had some reason to believe it might not be."

"Laney was pregnant."

"She told you that?"

Merri nodded. "That's why she was coming home with me for the weekend. She was going to get an abortion."

"Was she upset about the pregnancy? Is that why she might have considered suicide?"

"She needed money. For the abortion. She didn't dare ask her parents, not even her father, and he dotes on her. It had her very worried. And she was afraid of the procedure. She hated doctors and nurses and medical people generally."

"How was she planning to arrange this abortion?"

"Oh, it was all arranged," Merri said. "She'd called and made an appointment. We were going to tell my mom we wanted to go into the city shopping. She lets us do that. We go in and out on the train. She drops us off and then we call her when we're ready to be picked up. The hardest part was when she had to go to court. She had to cut school for that."

"Go to court?"

"Of course." The word "dummy" was implied in her tone. "You don't think a sixteen-year-old can just waltz in and have an abortion, do you? She had to get a judge to rule that she was old enough to consent on her own without telling her parents. That upset her so much she was up all night throwing up, the night before and the night after."

"Was she staying at your house?"

"Can't do that during the school week." There was that implied "dummy" again. "She was in the dorm." What were her dorm parents doing, I wondered, while this child was being violently ill?

"You weren't worried about complications or bleeding or Laney being incapacitated in some way?" It seemed very sad to me that these two young girls had been so innocent and unrealistic that they'd assumed they could incorporate an abortion into a day's shopping trip, despite the level of competence and ingenuity they'd shown in navigating the procedural hurdles. Where were all the grown-ups who were supposed to be paying attention?

"They said she'd be fine. Just to bring a friend," Merri said defensively.

"Who was the baby's father? Did she tell you?"

"No. That's one of those things I was telling you about. I mean, Laney wanting to break the rules. You know she had this boyfriend, Josh? Have you met him? He's gorgeous! Well, she was cheating on him. She also had another boyfriend. Someone more grown-up but she wouldn't tell me who he was. All she ever said was that if people knew who he was it would really tip the campus on its ear."

"You have no idea who it was?"

She shook her head. "None. Laney was having too much fun being mysterious about it. Well, I mean I did wonder if it might not be that new maintenance guy. The one who's kind of good-looking if you like them semi-evolved? I mean, there's probably nothing to it, but once I referred to him as Neanderthal and she had a fit." She shrugged. "I don't know if that was political correctness or improper interest. You never knew what she was going to get mad at. Anyway, Laney hung out around there a lot and I saw them talking together a few times. She and Josh had a fight about it. You could ask him what he thinks."

"As far as you know, Josh and this mystery man were the only two she'd slept with?"

Merri squirmed in her chair and made a face. "I don't know," she said. "She didn't tell me." She bent down and started putting on her boots. "I'm not particularly comfortable talking about sex. All I can say is that I wouldn't rule out the possibility there were several men." She said it with a tone of finality, as if she'd said all she was going to. But I wasn't finished.

"Do you know whether she tried to get money for the abortion from Josh or this other guy?"

"Why would she try to get it from Josh? It wasn't his." She started fidgeting with the fringe on her scarf.

"She told you it wasn't his?"

Merri stared at me coldly. "It wasn't."

"Would she have asked him if she was desperate?" She didn't answer. Maybe this wasn't my day. First Curt had clammed up and now Merri was doing the same thing. Maybe it was my breath but I didn't think so. What I thought was that there were things people didn't want me to know, maybe about Laney, maybe about themselves. I wasn't going to get anywhere by badgering people. I changed the subject. "Who did Laney confide in, besides you?"

"She wasn't much of a confider. Like I said, she liked having secrets."

"No one on the faculty?"

"Well, there was Mr. Drucker, he was her advisor, but she'd sort of gone off him. He lectured her too much. He was big on reforming her and Laney wasn't about to be reformed. Maybe Russ Hamlin? He directed her in a couple plays and I know she hung out down at the theater a lot. But I don't know if she talked to him. She never said much about him. You could usually tell who she was interested in by how much she said, or didn't say, about them."

"What about her dorm parents?"

"The ice queen and the dolt? You've got to be kidding. Mrs. Donahue is everything Laney ever loathed in a grown-up. And Bill is just Kathy's yes-man. They want everyone to be nice little boys and girls and talk in well-modulated voices and wear clothes that match. No sex, no skin, no sleaze." She giggled. "It's too bad Laney's dead. Her imitation of Kathy Donahue was to die for. I don't know how she did it but she'd sit there and carefully arrange the folds of an imaginary skirt, pick pills off her sweater, put on this sweet, blank look, and start saying sweet, dopey things in this soft, little-girl voice."

She broke off as something occurred to her. "Josh has it on videotape. Make him show it to you. She does Kathy, and Genny, and Ellie Drucker—" There was a crash in the next office and Merri jumped. "I'm pretty nervous these days, I guess. I've been talking to Carol Frank, she's one of the school counselors. She's good, too. Laney liked her, and Laney didn't like too many people." I made a note to put Carol Frank on my list.

I asked her about the Friday Laney had died. "Dean Perlin says that you and Laney were arguing after gym on Friday. What were you arguing about?"

"We weren't arguing," Merri said, "she was just in a bad mood because she didn't feel well. Being pregnant made her sick all the time. I told her it wasn't my fault and not to take it out on me."

"Merri, she told me you said that you and Laney were arguing and that when Laney didn't show up, you thought it was because she was sulking."

"I never said that."

"When Laney didn't show up, you went to her room to look for her?"

"Yeah. Genny was there. She said Laney had taken a bag with her earlier and she assumed that Laney had gone to meet me. I went back to the circle and Laney wasn't there so I gave up and left."

"Even though you knew Laney was counting on you to

help her get an abortion the next day? Weren't you worried?"

"That was her problem, wasn't it? I figured she'd show up later. We were going to meet a bunch of kids at the movies. I expected she'd show up then but she didn't. Josh was there and he was upset when she didn't show. She'd told him she was going to be there. I spent most of the movie calming him down." She shoved a stray lock of hair out of her face. "Look. Okay, so maybe I was a little mad at her for what she was doing to Josh. He didn't deserve it. So I told her that after gym and she said it was none of my business and wasn't it really that I wanted Josh for myself. I said I was just concerned about treating people fairly." There was a tearful note in her voice and the dark eyes were moist.

"She said fair, schmair, if I thought life was fair I was just a sucker. I said I'd rather be a sucker than a manipulative, two-timing bitch. She just gave me this odd look and said, Wasn't she lucky to have such a good, supportive friend, that she was really learning who meant what they said and who didn't, and she was sick of people trying to manipulate her feelings to get what they wanted from her. She said if this pregnancy business had taught her anything, it was that you couldn't trust anyone. Then she ran out of the locker room." She shrugged. "But I figured she'd get over it. She'd been weird all day. Sort of hysterical. Like she was high on something, you know."

"Did Laney use drugs?"

"I don't know. She never said she did. I never saw her doing them and she never offered me any. But she hung out with the theater crowd and they do a lot of drugs. So maybe."

"When I referred to Laney's death as an accident, you were relieved. What did you think had happened? From all you've said, it doesn't sound like Laney was very upset or depressed about her condition. It sounds like she was handling it. Is there something you haven't told me?"

"Not really," she said, her dark eyes fixed on my face. "I was afraid maybe she'd tried to get money from the baby's father and he killed her. Or that Josh killed her. He's got a wicked temper and he's hit her before. But I guess she wasn't killed, was she?" She shoved her arms into her coat and pulled on her boots.

"Columbus Day weekend," I said. "A bunch of you were going down to the Cape. Your sister was going to chaperon?" She nodded, edging toward the door. "Did Laney go with you?" She shook her head and edged a little more. "What did she do?"

She shrugged. "At the last minute, she said she couldn't go. Too much work. It was a lie, I think. She ruined the weekend. Josh was in a piss-poor mood and he spoiled things for everyone. That was Laney. She didn't care about other people's feelings one bit. She never thought about us." She left me staring at the spot where she'd been standing. One of Santa's elves, eh? Only if she worked for a very twisted Santa. Under the guise of not wanting to tell me anything, she'd painted a very unfavorable picture of her so-called best friend.

Everything about this business was harder than I'd anticipated—ugly death, difficult people, evasive answers. It had seemed so straightforward when I started—ask some questions, get some answers, and write it up in a report for Dorrie saying either that everything was hunky-dory and the school had behaved responsibly or that the situation revealed some problems with the system that ought to be corrected. My problem was that I couldn't eliminate the human factor. Yes, this was about the role of a boarding school in monitoring the lives of the students; it was also about a child who had died.

I couldn't keep things at an arm's length, the process wouldn't let me. The more I learned about Laney Taggert, the sadder the whole business seemed. Even her self-proclaimed "best friend" hadn't entirely liked or trusted her. It was awfully depressing to think that an attractive, bright young girl could die the way Laney had and leave behind such a legacy of distrust, uncertainty, and dislike. I checked my schedule. Next up—I'd come to think of them as batters—was Kathy Donahue, Laney's house-mother. I was hoping she'd have a more mature and com-passionate view of Laney, some insights that could help me put the others' comments in perspective.

Meanwhile, I had five minutes to myself and five hours' worth of stuff to do. I called work and spoke with Lisa. I wanted to get her going on the King problem. Then I put my head down on the desk. I know they say that we use only a tiny portion of our brain capacity, but mine felt full. Between Bucksport and King, I had too much work. Then there was Andre, Sarah's marriage, my trashed condo, the fact that Bobby was avoiding me, and the joyous holiday season with all that it entailed. Even with a clone, I didn't see how I was going to do it all.

If appearance was any criterion, Kathy Donahue was the perfect model of a grown-up prep school girl. Her straight blond hair was pulled back and secured with a demure pink bow. She was wearing a pale pink hand-knit sweater patterned with pastel flowers and a matching flowered skirt. In her ears were small pearls. Everything about her said neat and prim and perfect. She shook my hand briefly and sat cautiously on the edge of her seat, legs crossed at the ankles and hands folded on her knee. Her face was grave as she waited for my questions.

I went through my usual introduction, explained my mission, and began. "Were you Laney Taggert's house-mother all year?" She nodded. "What about last year?"

"Yes."

"Laney's mother says that Laney liked you very much and saw you as a substitute mother figure. Is that how you perceived the relationship?"

Kathy Donahue had to think about that. Finally she nodded. "I guess you could say that."

"What was she like?"

"Complicated."

"In what ways was she complicated?"

Kathy seemed annoyed by the question. "Complicated," she repeated. "Hard to understand."

"Did you feel that you didn't understand Laney?"

She shook her head quickly. "Oh, no." She was hoarding her words like precious jewels. I wondered how someone so silent and undemonstrative could be an effective house parent.

I tried to give her the benefit of the doubt. Maybe she just didn't understand. "Look," I said, "I'm trying to get a picture of Laney. Trying to understand what she was like, and I need your help. Didn't Dave Holdorf explain that?"

She nodded. A small, spare nod. I waited for more, for an expression of understanding, a description of Laney, or at least an explanation of her reticence, but nothing more came my way. Grief takes people in strange ways. I knew that. But Kathy Donahue didn't seem to be grieving. She seemed indifferent, cold, unwilling to get involved. "You were her housemother, supposed to stay in touch, have some contact with her every day. And you can't tell me anything about her?"

"She liked to read *Moby Dick*."

"Who were her friends?"

She shrugged. "Merri Naigler."

"Merri was her only friend?"

"And Josh. Josh Meyer. He was her boyfriend."

I tried asking the question a different way. "What about kids she hung around with? I understand she was part of the theater crowd." She nodded. "What I meant," I said, trying to keep my irritation from showing, "is who is in the theater crowd?"

"You'd have to ask someone who does theater, I guess."

After a few more questions and monosyllabic answers, I gave up. When Laney's mother had described Kathy Donahue as a second mother to Laney, she'd been right on the money. Kathy was as indifferent, oblivious, and self-involved as Laney's own mother. Even if I found nothing wrong procedurally with the Donahues' care of Laney, Dorrie and I needed to talk about the distinction between technical observance of procedures and genuine concern for students.

"According to Dean Perlin, students who are going away for the weekend have to complete a card and leave it with you. Is that right?"

She had picked up a fold of her skirt and was twisting it between her fingers. "That's right."

"Did Laney fill out a card for last Friday night?"

"I don't know. You'd have to ask my husband, Bill. I was sick last Friday."

"You and your husband never discussed it?"

"No."

"Even after Laney's body was discovered?" She didn't answer.

"Is there a particular place where the cards are kept?"

"Yes. Well, no. I mean, sometimes. That is, there's a place where they're supposed to go, but sometimes Bill and I are a little careless about getting them into the box." She was picking little pills off her sweater.

I didn't think she'd looked at me once since I started asking questions. "After the accident, did either of you look for a card?"

She shrugged. "Maybe Bill did."

"So, as far as you know, no one has looked for Laney's sign-out card, no one has asked you for it?" It seemed unlikely that this was the case, since they'd been so efficient about giving me the sign-out card for the Columbus Day weekend.

She abandoned her lint picking for a minute. "Oh, people asked. Dorrie wanted it. Maybe Bill gave it to her."

"But you don't remember?" I said, hearing the accusation in my voice. "You have no idea if you had one or what's happened to it?"

Kathy Donahue shrugged. "I've had a lot on my mind."

I wanted to shake her out of her dreamy complacency and make her acknowledge that Laney Taggert's death mattered. "Dean Perlin said that you were afraid Laney's death might have been your fault because you and Laney had had a conversation about how pretty the pond looked in the moonlight. Can you tell me about that conversation?"

Kathy Donahue looked at me for the first time. Her face was a perfect blank. "I don't remember saying that to Joanne. Laney and I had no such conversation. Laney had been kind of withdrawn lately. I'd tried to talk to her but she hadn't been responsive." I waited for more but that was all she said. She went back to picking lint off her sweater.

"Did Laney often go to Merri Naigler's for the weekend?"

"I think she went a few times."

"Did she usually sign out when she went to Merri's?"

She shrugged. "I don't remember."

"Do you remember her signing out for Columbus Day weekend?"

"No." I gave up. To answer these questions, I'd have to go back and look at the cards I did have.

"Genny Oakes said that she had asked for another roommate. Did you discuss that with Laney?"

"Of course. I was hoping Laney and Genny could work things out once Laney knew that Genny was unhappy, but it didn't seem to be working. Laney didn't care whether she stayed with Genny or not. It was just a bad match, that's all. It happens sometimes."

"What did Laney say when you told her that Genny wanted another roommate?"

Kathy Donahue gave me another one of her infuriating blank looks and gave the answer I expected. "I don't remember."

"Did she seem upset? Did she wonder why? Did you suggest the two of them try to work things about? What is the procedure for handling a roommate conflict?"

She shrugged as if she were enormously tired and I was keeping her from her nap. "I don't think she said anything. Laney was like that."

"Had Laney seemed unusually depressed lately?"

"No more than usual, Laney wasn't a very happy person." She hesitated and then added, "And she was mean and selfish." She sounded almost childish as she said it.

"Mean? In what way was she mean? To the other girls? To you?"

She shrugged. "She was just mean."

"What is the procedure for handling roommate conflicts?" I repeated. I wanted to shake her. If she was the type of caretaker Bucksport was offering the students they were in for a lot of trouble. She hadn't used the words but everything about her attitude said that frankly she didn't give a damn.

She sighed and plucked at an especially large piece of lint. "I already told you. They sign out on cards. We keep the cards in a box."

"I asked you," I said, unable to keep all my irritation out of my voice, "what the procedure is for handling roommate problems and a request to change roommates."

"Why do you want to know that?" she said, rousing for a minute from her trance, "Laney's dead. Genny doesn't have to worry about it anymore."

"Mrs. Donahue, have you been paying any attention to this conversation at all?"

"You don't have to yell at me," she said petulantly. "I can hear perfectly well. We were talking about Laney Taggert."

"No. I've been asking questions about Laney Taggert. You haven't been responding."

"I've been completely cooperative," she said, "and I don't have to sit here and take this from some nosy outsider who doesn't understand."

"I've been trying to understand. Maybe you need to explain it to me again. How do you feel about all this?"

"Tired," she said, getting up and slinging her purse

strap over her shoulder. "I'm going back to the dorm to lie down. Get Bill to help you." She walked out, leaving me staring after her in astonishment. This listless, uncaring woman seemed no more racked by guilt about Laney's death than a cat that's just killed a mouse. I couldn't picture her as Laney's substitute mother or as Josh Meyer's confidante. I'd spent much of the last seven years interviewing private school personnel and I'd rarely met someone as indifferent as Kathy Donahue.

CHAPTER 9

I LOOKED AT my list. Next up was Josh—an official visit this time—followed by Bill Donahue. Then I had to jump in my car and hightail it back to Route 128, swoop down around the south of the city, and meet with the King School folks, and then check out my condo. An hour here and an hour there. What the hell. I was queen of the road, even if thinking about it did make me weary. I yawned but that reminded me of the repellent Kathy Donahue. I snapped my mouth shut and stood up. Somewhere along the line I'd better bag a sandwich or I was going to be in poor shape to deal with the alleged sins of Denzel Ellis-Jackson. I took a break to freshen up and went to get some hot coffee and beg for food.

Lori and Ellie Drucker were standing by the coffee machine talking about a case in the local news where a teenage girl who was having an affair with her coach had taken her father's handgun and tried to kill the coach's wife. "It seems so unfair," Lori was saying. "If anyone deserved to be shot it was the husband."

Ellie shook her head vehemently. "I disagree. Why not the girl? If I'd been the wife, I would have shot her. She had no business messing with a married man."

"But he was the adult. She was just a kid. He's the one who ought to have exercised self-control," Lori began, "and anyway, I don't think the wife knew. The whole thing's a mess. What really offends me is that now probably all of them will get rich selling their stories."

"I don't know which is worse," Ellie mused. "The cases where the wife knows or where she doesn't. I think one of the worst situations is where the wife doesn't know but everyone else does and they're feeling sorry for her."

"It's time to bring back the stocks and the ducking stool," I suggested. "That guy was the girl's coach, wasn't he? There have always been cases of older men getting involved with young women, especially in the educational arena, because the opportunities are there—sex for grades, or adults taking advantage of student crushes or vulnerable students. It's an area where we've learned we can't cut the offending adults any slack. We need to enforce the obligation, as teachers and as adults acting in loco parentis, to retain the adult role and act responsibly and maturely for the benefit of the students. We stress it, schools stress it, the law stresses it, yet I've been in this business for seven years, and if I had a hundred dollars for every breach I've dealt with, I could retire. In some schools, it runs rampant."

I stopped, suddenly and uncomfortably aware that I'd climbed onto one of my own personal soap boxes. I was mortified to discover that I'd drawn a crowd. Worse than that, when I stopped, they began to clap. Abandoning my coffee-seeking mission, I tucked my soapbox under my arm and scurried for the security of my office, my face flaming, pausing only long enough to ask Lori if she could add Carol Frank to my list.

Ellie followed me down the hall. "Great speech," she said.

"I didn't mean to—"

"Don't worry about it. It was fine. They seem to be keeping you awfully busy, I've noticed. There's a continual parade of people in and out of there. It was never that busy when Ruthie was here. I don't suppose it should have been, though," she said, smiling, "since all Ruthie dealt with was numbers and you're dealing with people."

"I hope I'm not bothering you."

"Oh, no. Of course not. One good thing about these older buildings, they've got thick walls. See you later," she said, disappearing into her office.

My office door was slightly ajar and I assumed Josh had arrived early. I peeked in and saw Chip Barrett behind my desk, going through my open file. I grabbed a passing student and sent her down to Lori. "Tell her to get campus security over here pronto. Tell her Chip Barrett's in my office." Then I stepped into the room and shut the door loudly behind me. The little weasel was as guilty as a kid caught with a hand in the cookie jar but he didn't seem at all concerned. Actually, he wasn't all that little, he just seemed small because of his furtive posture. He looked like a rat about to scuttle down a hole with some stolen cheese.

"I was waiting for you," he said. "We've got a lot to talk about."

"If I had more time, we might have a talk about journalistic ethics and honesty, Mr. Barrett, but I've got a full schedule and you're not on it, so why don't you take my papers out of your pockets and put them back on the desk while we're waiting for security."

"Papers? What papers?" He tried to look innocent, standing there with bulging pockets. I suppose he occasionally fooled someone or he wouldn't bother.

"Don't waste my time, Barrett. I wasn't born yesterday."

He gave up the pose of maligned innocence, and stepped toward me, trying to look menacing. "Look, it's no big deal. I was just leaving anyway. Why don't you get out of my way, sister?"

"You've been watching too many old movies," I said, "and I'm not your sister."

He put an hand on my arm and tried to shove me out of the way but he wasn't used to pushing people around, at least not people who are bigger, and anyway I've been menaced by some of the best. Compared to them, he was a marshmallow. "Take your hand off me," I said loudly, startling him. "Unless you want to add assault and battery as well as theft to your list of offenses."

"Take it easy," he said, dropping his hand like he'd been burned. "I already told you. I didn't touch anything. I was just waiting for you."

"And going through my files. And I notice that your pockets crackle when you walk. I suppose that's just stuff you always carry with you?"

"That's right."

"You're pathetic, Mr. Barrett, you know that?"

"I'm a reporter," he said. "Getting stories in my job. And this is a big story. Pregnant preppie lured to death by unknown assailant. And that's just the tip of the iceberg, too. Just wait till you see how this thing unfolds." His face was greedy with anticipation.

Speaking of old movies, this was the man who knew too much, or at least had guessed too much. I wanted to knock him down and kneel on his chest until he revealed his sources but it wouldn't have been ladylike, and besides, I didn't want to confirm what he suspected. Instead I said, "You mean careless teen in accidental fall through ice, don't you?"

"I wasn't born yesterday either, Ms. Detective," he said. "What do they need you for if it's an accident? This is only getting hushed up because Ms. Dorrie Chapin and good old Chief Rocky are getting it on. Getting his 'rocks off' so to speak."

Chip Barrett epitomized everything I'd found abhorrent about newspaper reporting. He was a nasty-minded, malicious, scandalmongering son of a bitch. "I'm here to inventory the systems for keeping students safe and if necessary to suggest ways of making things safer."

"Yeah? You going to recommend a celibacy rule? Or have Curtie and the boys patrolling every bush? You're just window dressing. Everyone already knows what happened. That little honey was boffing some staffer until she got knocked up and then he killed her. You're just part of the cover-up, whether you know it or not." Behind me, heavy footsteps signaled the arrival of help. I stepped away from the door and Chip Barrett made a dash for it, running straight into Curt Sawyer's massive sidekick.

It was a repeat of the performance I'd seen the day before. Curt and his assistant seized Chip and prepared to eject him from the premises. "Wait," I said, "before he goes, I need to check his pockets." Barrett glared at me as I stuck my hand into his jacket pocket and pulled out a sheaf of my handwritten notes. In the other pocket I found the sign-out card and Jack Taggert's note. "Nice try, sleazeball. People like you help remind me why I gave up the newspaper profession."

"You were a reporter?"

"Until I got sick of scraping the shit off my shoes that people like you tracked in." I shut the door. At least I no longer needed coffee, thanks to my adrenaline surge. Before I could even catch my breath, Josh Meyer came hurtling through the door at the same speed as last time and tumbled into the chair as if he'd been flung there by an unseen hand. He brushed the hair back from his face, gave me a lopsided grin, and said, "Hi. I see you were under siege by the awful Barrett. You've got to watch him. He'll nibble away at you like a rodent until he gets what he wants."

"Well, I won this round. Or I think I did."

"Maybe you did and maybe you didn't. He's a very devious character. Steals anything that's not nailed down. I found him trying to get into my room and I hear that he tried to get into Laney's, too. Genny Oakes whacked him with her field hockey stick."

"Athletics can be excellent preparation for life, Josh."

"How many attackers have you beaten off with field hockey sticks?"

"Most of my attackers have been the sneak-up-on-you-and-hit-you-from-behind type, I'm afraid. The only thing that might have protected me was a football helmet and I can't go through life wearing one of those."

"I guess you're right. What's up?" He talked like we were old friends so I slipped into the same mode.

"Tell me about the last time you saw Laney."

"Saw physically or saw to talk to?"

"Laid eyes on."

"It was Friday." He stretched his legs out in front of him and folded his arms over his chest, getting comfortable for a chat. Today he was dressed for the weather. Jeans without holes. Sorrels. Heavyweight rugby shirt. "I was going over to the art studio to work on a painting. She was coming the other way. She was carrying a duffle bag so I assumed she was going to meet Merri. I said 'Hi,' she said 'Hi, I can't talk right now, I have to meet somebody.' Then she headed off away from the circle, which struck me as odd if she was going to meet Merri. I said, 'See you at the movie?' She said she'd be there, and that's the last time I ever saw her."

"What was she wearing?"

"A fancy pink, purple, and blue parka I'd never seen before but under it she had her regular Laney clothes."

"Which were?"

"Black leggings, black sweater and a long, weird skirt. Some sort of little-girlie shoes. She usually wore Doc Marten's."

"You didn't see her meet anyone?"

"Not really."

"Not really?"

"She stopped a minute to speak with someone, Mr. Drucker, I think, at least some faculty person, but only for a minute and then she walked on. I did see her pausing at the far side with someone but I couldn't see who it was. A woman, I think. Maybe Mrs. Drucker. I couldn't tell."

"You're looking better today."

"Yeah? Well, my dorm mom's been on my case, makin' me eat and all that crap. It kind of bugs me but mostly I don't mind. Yesterday she wouldn't let me go to class, she made me stay in bed all day." So her instincts had been the same as mine, and from all appearances, they'd been exactly right.

"Merri Naigler says she thinks Laney had another boyfriend. Do you know anything about that?" Now I was touching a sore spot. I had to go carefully or I'd lose the easy flow.

"She must have. Unless you believe in immaculate conception. I told you that the baby wasn't mine."

"You're absolutely certain the baby wasn't yours?"

"Look, I'm not stupid! I know how babies are made and I know how babies are not made, okay?"

"Any idea who this other guy was?"

"None. If I did, I'd kill him for doing that to her."

"Surely Laney also knew how babies are made?"

He folded his arms across his chest and regarded me as if I were a simpleton. "Like I told you the other day, Laney was real screwed up. She tried to be real sophisticated and stuff . . . and because she was smart, and because she was good at those imitations, a lot of people were intimidated by her and they thought she was cool and distant and very mature. But she wasn't. See, Laney really just wanted to be loved. To be approved of. To be important. To have her mother love her, if you want to get real psychological about it. Only her mother couldn't because her mother only loved herself. And her booze."

He sat up and leaned forward, wrapping his arms around his knees. Once again I had the impression of a boy in constant motion. Still, he was calmer today. "So Laney was sexually vulnerable," he said. "The sort of thing you read about in books. I mean, it was kind of a cliché, but clichés come from real life, right? She needed to believe it was a spontaneous act of love . . . even if we'd had to plan for days to find a time when we could sneak away and be together . . . so she couldn't deal with stuff like birth control. Between us that was okay. I knew that about her so I took care of things but some other guy might not have been so careful. Most guys just want to get it in there and bang! They don't care about what kind of risks they're exposing the girl to. Some other guy got to her and didn't bother to take precautions. It's criminal, especially if this guy was older. I mean, he should have known better but I can imagine the crap he gave her—all that stuff about it spoiling the sensation and ruining the intimacy. I wish I knew who it was," he said again. "I'd kill the bastard."

"No birth control is one hundred percent effective except abstinence," I reminded him.

He just rolled his eyes. "Give me a break, lady. Our generation has had more sex ed than the last ten generations put together." His smile was challenging. "They ever make you put a condom on a cucumber? After that, you always look at salads differently. I know it wasn't mine."

"What makes you think it was an older guy?"

He shrugged. "Stuff she said. You didn't know her, so you can't understand. She loved me even though she was cheating on me. I know it sounds crazy but your generation was different. We're not so possessive is what I mean. She wouldn't tell me who it was or anything but she kind of needed my support as a friend, you know what I mean?"

I wasn't quite sure I did. He made me feel as old as Methuselah when he talked about my generation, but he was right that we were more possessive. I also didn't believe he was as generous as he pretended to be. "Merri says that Laney was friendly with some guy who worked for maintenance and that you and Laney had a fight about it. Is that right?"

"Is what right?"

"That Laney was paying too much attention to some other guy and you two fought about it?"

"There was no specific guy. She just hung around there too much. I told her it was a dumb thing to do. They were working-class guys, trashy guys, and her hanging around them, dressed like she did, one of 'em might get the wrong idea."

"How did she react?"

"The way she always did when I tried to tell her something sensible, something for her own good. She told me to go—excuse the language but these are her words—fuck myself. She couldn't stand being told what to do."

"How did you react to that?"

"I got mad at her. We yelled at each other. She slapped me. I slapped her back. It's ironic, isn't it? Merri said I was being abusive for hitting Laney but no one would think she was being abusive for hitting me. She hit me a lot more than I hit her."

"But yours was a very physical relationship? The two of you did hit each other?"

"Yeah." There was tremor in his voice which reminded me that despite his charm and his candor, he was still a kid and none of this was easy for him.

"I heard you at the meeting this morning. You don't think her death was an accident?"

"I already told you. It was no accident and it was no suicide. Laney might not have been a very happy person but she was smart enough to know things would get better."

"Do you know how Laney was planning to pay for her abortion?"

He shook his head. "I offered her some money but she refused. Said she wouldn't take it from me. She was going to get it from the baby's father."

"And you have no idea who that was?"

"I already told you. No. Can't you stop asking? Why do you think she would tell me, of all people? She knew what I would do. I'm sure that you've heard she was cruel and heartless and loved to break rules. But she loved me, Ms. Kozak, I know she did. This other thing was just something she had to do. She didn't want it to hurt me. Don't you know how hard this is?" Josh Meyer, beautiful, rested, and in control, started to cry. I handed him my box of tissues and sat there watching him, feeling like the world's biggest heel, wanting to put my arms around him and comfort him, and knowing he'd resent it.

"Who, besides you, did Laney confide in?"

"Merri Naigler, sometimes, though Merri could be pretty judgmental. Occasionally to Nadia Soren. And that woman in the counseling office. Carol something. Laney really liked her."

"What about Kathy Donahue?"

"At first, maybe. But not recently. Laney said Kathy didn't like her. Kathy's been kind of weird lately."

"Do you know why?"

"Why Kathy didn't like Laney? Kathy likes good girls and Laney didn't fit the bill. Why Kathy has been weird? You'd have to ask Bill. Look, I'm going. I can't talk about this anymore, okay? You find out who did this and let me know. I'll take care of him." He staggered to his feet, fumbled for his things, and was gone as quickly as he'd come. It seemed as though everyone was in control of these interviews but me. I understood. These were emotionally trying for people who'd known Laney.

Once again I hadn't had a chance to ask about the mysterious Columbus Day weekend. One more person for my phonathon. Maybe it was just as well. What might be lacking because I wasn't having face-to-face contact might be compensated for by being able to ask everyone the same questions in rapid sequence. While I was at it, I thought I'd call and ask her advisor the same question. If he was close to Laney, she might have said something to him.

I was rubbing my forehead and wondering if I could afford to take a sick day when Dorrie stuck her head in the door. "Hi. How's it going?" she said. "You were great with the Taggerts yesterday."

"I'm beginning to wonder if there are any normal people left in the world," I said.

"Oh, come on. Is it that bad?" She had a please-don't-quit-on-me look on her face.

"No. Not really. Have you got a minute?"

"Of course." She settled herself in my chair and waited.

"What's the story with Kathy Donahue?"

"Is there a problem?"

"I think so. Something's going on with her. I have no idea what. When I interviewed her, she was practically catatonic. Acted like she didn't give a damn about Laney. Denied having conversations about Laney with Joanne Perlin. Wouldn't answer any of my questions. Didn't even seem to know what the procedures were for signing students out. Couldn't focus on why it was she'd taken more than six weeks to get around to resolving a roommate dispute between Laney and Genny. She was scary, Dorrie. I hope she's not an example of the kind of dorm parents you've got here."

"That's odd," she said. "Kathy Donahue is one of our most popular dorm parents. I know she's been sick. Maybe she'd taken too many decongestants or something. You know how spacey they can make you. But I'll double-check. I'll ask Joanne what's going on."

There wasn't anything I could put my finger on but I had the feeling that Dorrie wasn't telling the whole truth and it disturbed me. Maybe it was just the insidious effects of Chip Barrett's suggestion that there was something everyone else knew and I wasn't being told. If I kept on getting that sense, I'd have to confront Dorrie, but it was too soon for that. Her explanation was a perfectly reasonable one and she had offered to look into it instead of ignoring my concern.

"I'm getting an interesting and complicated picture of Laney Taggert. The rest is more of a mystery than anything else."

"What do you mean?"

"Some people think she was careless and had an accident, some think she might have been depressed. Josh and Chip Barrett are sure it's murder. Everyone is sure she had a lover other than Josh. Some older man. But everyone denies knowing who it might be, except it was someone on the staff."

"Oh, God, no!" Dorrie covered her face with her hands. "Who told you that? Kathy?"

I studied her, thinking her surprise didn't seem genuine. "That's what you wanted me to find out, isn't it? That's what this 'audit' is really about."

Dorrie shook her head. "I want the audit," she said firmly. "We need it for the trustees, for the parents, for our reputation. You won't find many flaws in our system. . . ." She hesitated. "The other thing? I want you to find out who was out there with her. You heard me this morning. It weighs on my mind . . . what kind of a community we are . . . when someone knows what happened and won't come forward. . . ."

"Do you think, because of the second set of tracks, that Laney was murdered?"

"It could have been an accident and the person who was with her panicked and ran. Especially if it was someone who shouldn't have been there with her."

"And you'd like to know who he was." Dorrie didn't reply. "What does Rocky think?"

"I told you. That there's no sense in stirring up trouble. That we should plump up the pillows and put some flowers on the coffee table and get on with life as usual."

"Even if a troubled sixteen-year-old has been murdered?"

"He thinks it was an accident, at least that's what he says. I'm not sure that's what he believes. He's still poking around but he's trying to be subtle about it."

I tried not to smile at the idea of Rocky being subtle. "Can you find out what she was wearing when they pulled her out of the pond?"

"Call him yourself. It's okay. He won't bite your head

off. And keep me posted." She gave me Rocky's number and left.

I looked at my watch. Bill Donahue was already late. I didn't want to be in the middle of a phone call when he arrived. I could call Rocky in the morning. I reviewed my files, made some notes to myself, and still Donahue hadn't appeared. I called Lori and asked if she could track him down. I was running out of time. I was about to give up and leave for my meeting with Yanita when a slight man in running clothes opened the door. "Bill Donahue?" I said.

He shook his head. "Rick McTeague," he said. "Actually, it's Thomas Rodrick McTeague. That's what it's going to say on the book jacket, anyway. If I ever get published."

The polite and conventional thing to say would have been, "Oh, so you're a writer?" but I'm not especially polite or conventional and my frustrating day had made me impatient. "What can I do for you, Mr. McTeague?"

"Rick, please," he said, settling himself into my chair. "I'm the one who found the body."

"You're the jogger."

"Right," he said, delighted to be recognized. "I didn't actually find the body. I just saw the pink glove and the hole in the ice and suspected something might be wrong so I jogged over to the building and grounds office and got them to call nine-one-one."

"You're the one who saw the second set of footprints?"

"That's me." He seemed to be taking far too much delight in being a part of such a sad business, but maybe nothing exciting ever happened in his life. I'd met people like that. They didn't mean to act inappropriately; they honestly didn't know how they were behaving."

"What brought you to me, Mr. McTeague?"

"Rick," he corrected. "I thought you might want to talk to me."

"That was very thoughtful of you."

"She only drowned because of the boat channel," he said.

"Oh?"

"Yes, you see, the pond has been silting up and bushes have been filling in. It was almost impossible to launch the boats anymore, so last summer they got permission to redredge the channel leading out from the dock to the open water. Ten feet in either direction and she could have touched bottom. Poor kid. If only she'd known that this needn't have happened. But when people are drowning, they panic and lose their sense of direction. I've been reading up on drowning," he said, "for the book I'm working on. It's a terrible way to die."

I gave in and uttered the words he was longing to hear. "So you're a writer, Rick?" He nodded eagerly. "What sort of books do you write?"

"Thrillers," he said. "I'm trying to create my own genre, actually. Sort of a counterculture bodice-buster romance and macho adventure story. Well, not quite like that. Something that will appeal to both men and women. My heroine, see, is this woman who has had a sex change operation. She used to be this real macho cop but he, I mean, she, always knew that there was a softer, more feminine person inside and finally that person just had to come out. Anyway, she nurtures this secret love for the man who used to be her partner. Of course, she isn't a cop anymore, she's a private detective. That's why I wanted to meet you."

"Excuse me?"

"Research," he said. "Fact-finding. When you're a writer, everything is grist for the mill, isn't it?"

"I'm afraid I'm still not following you. What does all this have to do with finding Laney Taggert's body?"

"Nothing. I wanted to meet you because you're a detective. I wanted to study you. You're not at all what I'd pictured, though. Josh said you were motherly and I was quite intrigued by the idea of a motherly detective. I guess I was picturing Miss Marple and not Jane Russell."

For a fleeting second I wondered if I'd drifted through some sort of a warp and landed in an asylum but when I looked around I was still in my office, seated in front of my notes and Rick McTeague was sitting in the bishop's chair, grinning with delight, showing yellowish teeth through the gap in his luxuriant facial hair. "How did you hear about me?" I asked.

"From Josh. I teach a creative writing class and he's in it." If they let this nutcase teach at Bucksport, things were in even worse shape than I thought. I made a note on my pad.

He must have read the confusion on my face. "It's not a regular course. That is, I'm not getting paid for it. I'm not on the faculty. It's a volunteer thing that I do. The kids like it and it's fun for me. I started it when I got laid off. I was a software engineer until my company went belly-up. It's not easy to get another job when you're in your fifties. I tried for a while but I couldn't stand the rejection. I'm too old to sit there all bright and eager while some know-nothing tears my career to shreds. Anyway, my company let me take early retirement so I have a pension and stuff and my wife works, so I decided to write."

You, I thought, and at least two thousand other laid-off mid-level managers in Massachusetts. It was scary to think of the number of trees that were dying to support this endeavor. "What did Josh tell you?"

"Oh, he really didn't tell me anything. Just mentioned you, that's all."

I had a few more questions for Rick McTeague and then I had to figure out how to get him out of my office. I was already running late. "Tell me about the second set of footprints."

"There's not much to tell. There were two distinct sets going out onto the ice and then one set going on alone to the hole. Out at the end they were sort of confused, like there had been a scuffle and then the single set was widely spaced, like someone was staggering. At least, that's how it looked to me. Of course, by the time the police and the fire department got through out there, the whole scene was so messed up you couldn't tell what had happened. It was fun to watch, though."

"Of course," I said, "all grist for the mill, right?"

I must not have kept the sarcasm out of my voice because he looked hurt, and said, "I didn't say I wasn't sorry about what happened to that poor girl, but just 'cause something's sad doesn't mean I can't learn from it." He got up and headed for the door.

"Don't get huffy, Rick. Remember, I spend whole days immersed in Laney Taggert's life. For me, her death is very sad."

"You're right," he said, pausing in his aggrieved exit. "Maybe I could take you out there and show you the scene. It would make it easier for you to understand what happened."

There was nothing I wanted less than a hike through the damp, muddy woods with someone as garrulous as Rick McTeague, but he was right. I might learn something. We agreed to meet the following afternoon. He left. I called Lori, told her I had to leave, and asked her to reschedule Bill Donahue whenever she reached him. I was looking forward to my meeting at the King School. Their problems might be serious but at least the people there were refreshingly normal, willing to answer questions, and inclined to tell the truth.

I was almost at the door when a big hand reached out and pulled me into a dark alcove. It was Chris, the hulking guy from grounds and buildings. Seen close up, he was just as Merri had described him—attractive in a primitive way. His behavior, however, was anything but attractive. "You've been bugging Curt Sawyer about wanting to talk to his workers," he said hoarsely, almost suffocating me with his hot onion breath. "How he runs things is none of your business. You lay off of him, if you know what's good for you." He shoved me roughly against the wall and disappeared through the door.

CHAPTER 10

I REALLY BURNED up the road getting out of there. Partly I drove fast because I was late but mostly I drove fast because I was mad. Anyone will tell you that's a stupid thing to do, even I knew it was a stupid thing to do, but I couldn't help it. I hate being threatened. It's supposed to intimidate me but such is my stubborn nature that it usually has the opposite effect. The Neanderthal Chris couldn't have drawn my attention to Curt Sawyer's workers any better if he'd painted a huge red sign and stuck it in the middle of the lawn. Once I got myself sufficiently under control so that I could keep the rage out of my voice, I called Lori on the car phone and asked her to get me a list of names, addresses, and social security numbers for all the employees in the maintenance and security departments. Methought so much objection suggested something rotten in Denmark. I planned to take the list to Rocky and have him do some checking.

However, right now my concern was with the King School. I took all my Bucksport issues and all my Bucksport questions and filed them away for tomorrow, shifting into gear to do a different, but just as difficult, form of damage control. Yanita Emery, Arleigh Davis, Denzel Ellis-Jackson, and Lisa were waiting for me in the trustees' room. It had once been the dining hall of the mansion that now housed the school. A vast paneled room with a painted ceiling, a fireplace big enough to roast an ox, and tall windows looking out onto the grounds. The last time I'd been in the room it had been spring. Now the only view was whiteness where lights hit the sparse snow. The one statue in the garden that I could see looked cold and depressed. Someone had put a scarf on it.

The people waiting for me at the long mahogany table didn't look very cheerful, either. Behind each of their cordial greetings I heard a plea for help. I introduced Lisa, a formality since she'd gotten there first and introduced herself, then took the voice-activated tape recorder out of my briefcase and set it on the table. Arleigh groaned. "Do you have to do that?"

"I always do. It helps me remember for later and it helps keep things on track. So, what's the story?"

"Denzel will tell you," Yanita said, inclining her elegant head in his direction. He gave her an aggrieved look. "Well, you're the only one who knows the whole story," she told him. "We've got to start somewhere. Emmett is supposed to be here. I don't know what can be keeping him."

Denzel stared at the tape recorder with unveiled hostility. "I'm not saying this for any record. Not even for you, Thea."

"Okay." I reached out and snapped it off. "Now talk."

We were interrupted by the arrival of the King School's lawyer. I'd forgotten to suggest including him but obviously Yanita and Arleigh were way ahead of me. "Sorry I'm late," he said as he hurried across the room. "Ran into a judge who liked the sound of her own voice. Total waste of time, too. Lecturing my client about social responsibility is like trying to box train a cockroach." He shrugged. "Maybe it made her feel better."

Emmett Hampton was one of Boston's senior black attorneys. A small, trim man with graying hair, wire-rimmed glasses, and a very expensive suit, he was known for his keen mind and his facile wit but his principal asset was his voice, a rich, deep rumble that he could play like an instrument. Because of its financial situation, his services to King were voluntary. The school couldn't have had a better volunteer.

He settled into his chair, wiped his glasses, and said, "I don't suppose you have any coffee around here?"

"I was sort of hoping for sandwiches, myself," I said.

"You're never going to learn to eat on a schedule like regular folks, are you?" Arleigh said. "But we anticipated that. We've got soup."

"Soup?" Emmett made a face.

Arleigh gave him a scathing look. "Soup and sandwiches. This isn't the Ritz, you know."

Emmett leaned back in his chair and fixed his sharp eyes on Denzel. "We're waiting."

His story, in brief, was that an attractive young black woman had come up to him after a talk, voiced support for what the King School was trying to do, described herself as an education graduate between jobs, and inquired about openings at the school. He had invited her to join some people he was meeting for drinks. They had all had drinks and dinner, enjoyed a lively conversation, and she had left after shaking his hand. He had urged her to contact Yanita if she was serious about a teaching position. Her story was that he had lured her back to his room after dinner on the pretext of giving her further information about the school and that once she was in his room he had tried to force her to have sex with him. She had obtained a lawyer and though no suit had been filed, they were pressuring the school for money to keep the incident quiet.

"The thing is," Denzel said, "that there was no incident. LaVonne was an attractive woman but I don't force myself on people. She was never even in my room."

"LaVonne?" I said, realizing it was the first time he'd used her name. "LaVonne what?"

"Rawlins," he said.

"Did any of the other people at dinner see you shake hands and see her leave?"

Denzel stared at the tabletop. "You'd better be answering her, my man," Arleigh Davis said. "If you won't even tell *us* the truth, we can't help you."

He raised his eyes. "Everyone else had left."

"And you're telling us the truth when you say you didn't ask her back to your room?" Arleigh Davis said. She was the only one of us who could ask him that question. Head of the school's board of trustees, Arleigh was forthright, sensible, and wise. She'd chosen Denzel knowing his faults as well as his virtues and hoped through prayers, diligence, and a shared sense of purpose to keep him on the higher ground. So far, through a combination of luck and discipline, he'd rewarded her faith. She leaned toward him now, her turbaned head jutting from her large body, her bright earrings jangling. "Well?"

He spread his hands in a gesture of resignation. "I'll admit I wanted to take her back to the room. But I didn't!"

"Did you ask her? After she'd approached you about a job?" Arleigh said fiercely. "We need to know."

He shook his head. "I came awfully close. I did tell her I was very attracted to her. . . ."

"Fool!" Arleigh said.

"Oh, Arleigh, can't you lay off!?" he said. "Don't you think I know what a fool I was? Sure I wanted to do all those things but the fact is that I didn't touch her, I didn't kiss her, I didn't ask her upstairs. Maybe if I had she wouldn't be doing this."

Arleigh put the palms of her hands together and looked piously toward the ceiling. "The power of the almighty cock, amen!" she said.

"Did she let you know, in any overt way, that she'd welcome such an invitation?" I asked.

"You could say that. She put her hand on my thigh and her chest was practically in my dinner."

"What did you do when she put her hand on your thigh?"

Denzel gave me his megawatt smile, the one that made it so easy to understand why a woman would put her hand on his thigh. "I returned it to her lap and suggested it was not a good idea to do that in a public place, especially as we hardly knew each other."

"Was that while your friends were still at the table?" He nodded. "Do you think any of them noticed?"

"Malcolm did, I'm sure, because he raised his eyebrows at me and shook his head. Then he sent his girlfriend off to the ladies' room with this girl. Maybe to talk some sense into her. I don't know."

"But we could ask him?"

"Sure. Or you could ask his girlfriend. Woman friend? Her name is Janet Beecham. I can get you a phone and address."

"You're going to have to get me a lot of phone numbers and addresses," I said.

"So what do we do now, Thea?" Yanita said. "Do we respond to her lawyer's letter?"

I wondered why they even needed me, if they had Emmett. I looked at him.

"You first," he said.

His deference made me nervous, but I've never been one to sit on my hands, so I waded in. "Emmett may disagree with me, and it's really his call, but I wouldn't answer that letter at all. At least not until you see further indications of their intent. Then I'd suggest a brief and dignified response expressing shock at this attempt to slander Denzel and concern about this poor troubled woman. What do you think, Emmett?"

"That's about right. I'd want to draft the letter, of course."

Everyone nodded and we moved on to discussing what other actions to take. We agreed that I would get my staff to interview everyone who was at the table and collect their versions of the evening. Denzel was going to rack his brain to recall as much as he could about the girl and we were going to try to do some background checking. I wasn't too hopeful, since all we had was her name and address and where she'd gone to college, but Denzel thought, if he tried, that he could remember where she said she'd worked, and if he couldn't, maybe Janet Beecham could since the two of them had done a lot of talking.

Just at the point when I thought I might faint from hunger, they wheeled in a cart and served food. It really was soup and sandwiches, and the sandwiches had real filling, not just a thin layer of vegetables, and the soup was rich and hearty. Perfect for a cold night. I tried to approach it without showing my desperation but Arleigh dug in without hesitation. "This is a lifesaver, Yanita," she said. "You were clever to think of it. I'm going out Christmas shopping now and I'll be able to stay out much longer since I won't get hungry."

"Mine's mostly done," Yanita said, "except for the wrapping. I get exhausted wrapping presents. Toward the end they get no ribbons and sometimes even no tags. I just scribble people's names on the wrapping. How about you, Thea? You done? I'm not even going to ask Denzel. I'll bet his momma does it all for him." It was clear that the two women he worked with were very annoyed with Denzel.

"You be wrong, bitch! And I don't want you talkin' 'bout my momma," Denzel said, and lapsed into an extended rant imitating some of the more challenging inner-city speech of the King students. I only got about one word out of three but Yanita, Arleigh, and Emmett were almost falling out of their chairs. I sat and drank my coffee, feeling very out of it and very, very white. I didn't venture to suggest that they were dissing this honky. Each of them had put up with plenty of feeling out of the mainstream themselves.

Arleigh left to do her shopping, Emmett went back to

his office, and Denzel went to make some phone calls. Lisa and I stayed behind with Yanita, working on a list of information that I wanted. "What do you think, Thea?" Yanita said. "Is he really just an innocent man?"

"That's not a term I'd ever use in connection with Denzel, but I think he's telling what my little sister used to call a 'most truth.' He probably couldn't help flirting a little but I believe he resisted her invitations and I'm sure he didn't take her back to his room." She nodded. She might be irritated with him for not using his common sense, but she believed him, too. He was too committed to the King School's mission to jeopardize it for an evening of pleasure.

Lisa nodded. "It will be interesting to see what we learn about LaVonne Rawlins." She stifled a yawn. "Tomorrow morning, bright and early, I'm on the case." She was actually eager to get to work, I could see.

There was something I had to get clear before things went any further. "You know that this isn't our usual sort of work—investigating a sexual harassment case outside the school environment. I'm not sure how much help we can be. If this becomes public, we can advise you on damage control and we've done enough personnel stuff so that if we can get the names of any schools where she's worked, Lisa's very good at talking with administrators and we can probably get some information about her. But if all you can come up with is a name and address, it may take a private detective to dig up information. We don't claim to be detectives and we don't want to be. I wouldn't even suggest trying that unless they become more insistent about their demands. Do you know Janet Beecham?"

Yanita smiled. "We uppity black women trying to make it in the academic world tend to stick together. Janet and I go back a long time. I introduced her to Malcolm. Were you wondering if she'd cooperate?"

Yanita was a petite, quiet woman but from the first I'd been impressed with her. She'd come to EDGE Consulting looking for a job when we fired an incompetent employee. Even though I'd really wanted to hire her, I'd sent her to the King School to be assistant headmistress because they'd needed her far more than I did. When I suggested sending her to King, she had briefly taken offense and thought I was giving her the runaround, based, it turned out, on a series of unpleasant experiences at other job interviews. Once she understood that I was trying to give her a better opportunity, she'd eagerly gone off to meet with Arleigh and Denzel and they'd grabbed her.

"Will she?"

"You can count on it."

"How are things going, anyway? Are you still happy here?" I asked.

"Very," she said. "Every day is a challenge but I feel like I'm finally doing something worth doing. Not many people can say that."

I felt a twinge of envy. I liked my job but there were times when I wondered if I shouldn't be considering alternative careers, especially when I'd been running too hard and too fast to meet deadlines. I didn't want to still be doing this when I was fifty. I wouldn't have the energy. On the other hand, there wasn't anything else I wanted to do. In the back of my mind, Andre's wild brown girls might dance, but their ma and pa had a bit of dancing to do ourselves before anything so serious could be considered.

For now, at least, I'd stay put and see where life took me. Right now, life was taking me in Arleigh's footsteps. Off to finish my Christmas shopping. I said good-bye to Yanita, got in my car, and headed north on 128 toward the mall and home.

I like going to the mall during the Christmas season about as much as I like stitches without an anesthetic. I'd done most of my shopping in San Francisco at a wonderful shop that carries Italian and Portuguese pottery. Feeling a bit like Mrs. Rockefeller, I'd sailed in with my list, bought beautiful platters and cups and bowls, laid down my credit card, and had everything packed and shipped. But there were a few people I couldn't give pottery to, like my dad and Andre and my brother Michael's awful wife, Sonia.

There aren't many people in this world that I seriously dislike, but in that category, Sonia is right up there at the top. She's mean and chronically dissatisfied and lazy and her influence on Michael, who already had tendencies toward being unpleasant, has not been salutary. The two of them have a relationship that is based on seeing who can make the other more miserable, a challenge since both of them are so good at it. Anyway, I knew I couldn't give Sonia pottery and while my first choice was a hair shirt and a case of itching powder, I was trying to be a good doobie and get into the generous spirit of the season.

One of the remaining legacies of a childhood spent trying to be the "good kid" is that I still fall into the trap of trying to please people who can't be pleased. A friend of mine describes herself as a "recovering good girl." It's an idea I can really relate to. Knowing that it was an exercise in futility, I nonetheless threw myself into the overlit, overcrowded, noisy mall, despite a looming headache and a weary body, to find the perfect present for Sonia. Along the way I managed to acquire an armload of stuff. An expensive, conservative tie and beautiful Ralph Lauren sweater for my father, a gorgeous Italian wool shawl for my mother, a pair of nifty lightweight snowshoes, a polar fleece pullover and a baseball glove—not the easiest thing to find in December—for Andre. I bought myself a glove, too, figuring he'd need someone to play catch with.

At last, burdened like a packhorse and ready to collapse, I found the perfect sweater for Sonia—an oversized pink cashmere in an argyle pattern of pale gray, pink, and yellow. It was on sale for a mere $225, more than I wanted to spend on the woman in a lifetime, but I was tired of looking and caring and thinking about it. At least, for that price, they were willing to wrap it for free.

The clerk even filled out a tag that gaily urged her to have the merriest of holidays.

As she attached the tag to the package, the clerk's weary eyes took in my bundles and bags and my own weary face. "May I make a suggestion?" she asked. I nodded glumly. "A few years ago, I decided to give myself a Christmas present every year. That way I can always be sure I get something I really want." I nodded again, more hesitantly. I don't like people who try to sell me things. "Well, anyway . . ." She was rushing now, afraid she'd offended me. "There's this sweater that would be really beautiful on you." She bent down so that her disembodied voice was rising from behind the counter. "I put it away for my daughter, but it would be better on you. It's the last one. . . ."

She opened a box and spread the sweater out on the counter. It was an oversized tunic style with a rolled turtle neck. Soft, soft mohair, in wide stripes ranging from brilliant turquoise to a deep forest green. "Take it," she urged. "It was made for you." It was and I did. She even wrapped it and affixed another tag wishing me a happy holiday.

The overwhelming proximity of so many holiday reminders forced me to think about my own holiday plans or lack of them. Tonight when I talked to Andre I'd see what he wanted to do. I didn't expect it was to spend Christmas with my family. What I didn't know was whether he was planning to spend it with me. He had to, didn't he? We lived together.

Despite a high level of carbon monoxide from all the cars prowling around looking for parking spaces, the outside air felt deliciously good after being inside. I trudged along through the slush, trying not to get run down or backed over, stowed my purchases in the trunk, and headed on up the highway. Eric Clapton proved to be a good antidote to saccharine Christmas carols and by the time I got home, I was in a pretty good mood.

Except, of course, that it wasn't home anymore. Home

was in Maine, with Andre, at least if home is where the heart is. If home is wherever you spend your time, then it was a toss-up between my office and my car. If home was where you kept your clothes, then my home was a suitcase. My good mood vanished, leaving me feeling depressed and homeless and confused.

It didn't help that, despite the cleaning company's heroic ministrations, the place looked bare and battered. Geoff, from the cleaning crew, had left a succinct message on the counter. Rugs and drapes had been taken away for cleaning; one chair had gone to be recovered. Several things were too damaged to be repaired. I called down a thousand curses on the head of Bobby's so-called friend, the prick, and picked up the receiver to check my voice mail.

CHAPTER 11

ACCORDING TO THE pleasant canned voice on our office voice mail, a lot of people had tried to reach out and touch me. There was a message from Dorrie, saying that she'd spoken with Kathy Donahue who had reported I was the one who'd been rude and impossible, but that Dorrie felt Kathy was behaving strangely and was looking into it. She asked me to stop by in the morning before I started interviewing. Next was a message from Rocky Miller asking if I'd give him a call at my convenience. Lori Leonard had called to say she'd have the list ready for me in the morning. Suzanne had called to remind me that we were all supposed to go out for dinner on Tuesday in lieu of an office Christmas party and I was supposed to get gifts for Sarah and Bobby.

"Yes, yes, I know all that," I said impatiently, realizing that during my blitz at the mall I'd forgotten to get something for Sarah. Bobby was getting a lovely big bowl to support his adventures into creative pasta. I supposed Sarah wouldn't be satisfied if I told her her present was that I was getting the copier replaced for the second time this year. I suspected she took a secret pleasure in yelling at the repairman. It kept her from biting her husband's head off.

The next call was from Andre and I must have been

feeling very lonely because despite the awkwardness of the night before, I listened to it twice. He told me that he expected to be working much of the night—the holiday season brings out people's homicidal tendencies—but to please call him at work because he missed me. It was nice to hear his voice. Sitting in the wreck of my lovely condo, I suddenly missed him terribly.

The last message was from my late husband's friend Larry, who looks after me on David's behalf by calling a few times a year and leaving jokes on my machine. I don't think I've spoken to him more than once since David died, he's kind of weird and shy, but the jokes are nice. And shy as he is, he's made the transition from my answering machine to voice mail. I think it's because the jokes are not communications but memorial acts.

Tonight's joke was, when a man is making love to a prostitute, his mistress, and his wife, what is each woman thinking? Well, the prostitute is thinking *Faster, faster,* the mistress is thinking *More, more!* and the wife, noticing that the ceiling needs paint, is thinking *Beige. Maybe I'll paint it beige.*

There was a call from my mother that I wasn't ready to return. Otherwise, the world had left me in peace. I kicked off my shoes, longing for bourbon and popcorn but the cupboards were bare. I settled down on my lovely leather couch for some mindless television. I couldn't find the remote and after ten minutes of fruitless searching, I concluded that the rat must have taken it. Channel surfing is no fun if you have to stand right beside the set to do it, so I settled for a colorized Rosie and Charlie heading downriver on the *African Queen.* I had no choice but to settle on Bogart and Hepburn. Even though I despised colorizing, I was definitely in the mood for a bit of love triumphing through adversity.

At least the little prick hadn't stolen my phone. Couldn't. It lived in my purse. I settled into the soft leather, remembering the first time Andre and I had tried it out, and dialed the number he'd left. No deep voice. No chance to flirt or even to tell him how much I missed him. Just a brusque, businesslike fellow who offered to take a message. Settling for secondhand romance, I remained glued to the screen until Charlie and Rosie were married and the *Louisa* blown up.

But when I turned off the TV and the silence and emptiness of the place enveloped me, Laney Taggert took over my head, foreshadowing another night of troubling dreams. Something I'd read recently urged people who had trouble sleeping to eat potatoes as their evening snack because they helped the body produce tryptophans or some chemical that helped induce sleep, but it was cold and late and the nearest grocery store was five miles away. I was too tired to drive ten miles for a damned potato, even if it would help me sleep. Maybe tomorrow I would lay in a supply of health-giving potatoes and other good things, like leafy green vegetables and foods rich in fiber.

Healthy eating is not much fun. The way things are going, soon we'll all be breakfasting on an amorphous bowl of multigrain somethings with no more than two tablespoons of blue milk from free-range cows, lunching on shaved carrots, sweet potatoes, and cruciferous vegetables with a splash of nutritionist-approved oils, unless we're supposed to rub the oils on our skins while we're eating. For afternoon snack it will be organic potatoes grown in soils high in zinc and magnesium and at dinner a minuscule portion of fish caught off Greenland where the waters aren't full of toxic chemicals, napped with a sauce of puréed fennel and kohlrabi, no salt, please, and some kasha and lentil salad with enough vegetables to be sure we've gotten our five servings, plus maybe a compote of dried prunes and other fruits to promote regularity unless we've been careful to ingest sufficient roughage in other ways. Just thinking about healthy food was enough to put me in a deep depression.

I shrouded myself in a voluminous flannel nightgown and fell into bed, which some kind person on Geoff's team had been kind enough to make. I was ready to fall into Morpheus's arms but not even potato power could have protected me from the workings of an agitated mind. My dreams were restless again. I spent the night racing through damp, fog-shrouded woods on the Bucksport campus, pursued by unseen predators, carrying Laney's bright nylon duffle bag. Ahead of me, chattering gaily, Rick McTeague the would-be novelist crashed his way through the underbrush, speculating endlessly on who might be chasing us and how they might intend to do away with us. His imaginings were vivid, graphic, and sick, and I couldn't get him out of my mind. Periodically, the hulking lout from buildings and grounds would grab me and shake me. I succeeded in drowning Rick McTeague and woke up with a dull and fuzzy head from a dream in which Denzel Ellis-Jackson was swimming in the icy pond while a woman in a tight sequined dress gyrated on the shore to Aretha Franklin's "Respect."

I put on my robe and went into the living room. It was a clear night and moonlight glinted off the snow and lay like silver frosting on the water. The world looked beautiful but it could be an ugly place. Look what happened to Laney Taggert. Even if my audit showed that generally those responsible crossed their t's and doted their i's, I couldn't shake the feeling that everyone had failed Laney, that they hadn't been listening. And that one of them had taken advantage of her in a forbidden way.

The phone rang. Andre. "Thea," he said, "I'm sorry to wake you. I couldn't wait. . . ."

I wanted to crawl into the phone and be transported across all those lonely miles. "It's okay. I was awake. Missing you . . ."

He made a small humming sound of agreement. "When are you coming home?"

"Friday, I hope. I hope. I hope. This thing at Bucksport is complicated and I have to talk to everyone before they break for Christmas . . . and then Denzel's gone and gotten himself into a scrape. . . ."

"Denzel?" he said sharply.

"I told you about it. The King School. Sexual harassment—"

"He's the guy you think is so good-looking?" He didn't wait for an answer. "Why don't you let Suzanne handle it?"

"We're all handling it. Besides, she's pretty overwhelmed with the baby and all."

"I thought we were supposed to be living together."

I made a frustrated gesture to the empty room. I wasn't the one who had avoided him much of the past two weeks. "Yeah, so did I. But I was home last night, and you weren't, and I called home tonight, and you weren't there. . . ." But this wasn't the conversation I wanted to have. "I miss you, too," I said. "You at work?"

"Yeah. You know how it is. The holiday season. All that pressure and expectation. People go snap and kill each other. . . ."

"I know what you mean. My mother keeps calling and asking if I'm coming for Christmas. No . . . if we're coming for Christmas . . ."

"My mother keeps asking the same thing."

"And?"

"I haven't called her back. What are we doing?"

There were loud voices behind him, yelling. People always seemed to be yelling around him. I wondered how he stood it. At least the people I deal with mostly whine. "Andre?" No answer.

I heard him speaking to someone and then he was back. "I don't believe this, Thea. Guy just used the first barrel of his shotgun on the Christmas tree and threatened to use the second on his wife. I'll call you as soon as I can."

I went cold all over and started shivering. Just as he wanted Suzanne to do the work so I could come home, I wanted someone else to go after the bozo with the gun so I'd have someone to come home to. "Andre . . . please . . .

be careful. Very, very careful. Call me as soon . . . as soon as you can."

"You'd better believe it."

After that I dozed a bit, in a restless kind of pre-exam anxiety, and started my day far too early feeling as if I'd been beaten about the head and shoulders and stuffed into a plastic bag.

The person most likely to succeed in curing plastic-bag syndrome was standing at the front of the aerobics studio in an adorable red-and-green holiday unitard, his smile as bright as the Christmas star. He wished me a cheerful good morning as I skulked off to my usual place in the corner. I was pleased to see I wasn't the only person in the room who wasn't cheerful in the morning. Across the room there was a guy who looked like he'd already dined on prunes and lemons, and the woman behind me kept making little low moaning sounds as we went through the warm-up. An hour later, weak-kneed and spit-shined, I was disgorged from the mouth of the health club like Jonah from the whale, my faith restored, ready to go into the world and do good work.

I found Dorrie at her desk, makeup flawless and every hair in place, signing Christmas cards. She looked up and smiled. "Want some coffee? I started some a few minutes ago. It ought to be ready." Over coffee, she reviewed my progress. "I told Rocky you had some questions. He said he'd call you."

"He did. Last night. I had a meeting and then I went shopping."

"This year I'm doing it all from catalogues," she said. "And having everything wrapped and sent. I'm not setting foot in a store. Except bookstores. I can't stay out of bookstores. Luckily they've given me a house here with hundreds of feet of shelf space. I'm filling it as fast as I can. Oh, speaking of books, I ran into Bill Donahue last night coming out of the library. I asked him about Kathy. He said her mother has been very sick and Kathy has been distracted by that. He promised to talk with her, so maybe tomorrow you can speak with her again and find her more cooperative."

"Thanks. I appreciate that. Their perspective is critical." I hesitated, not wanting to sound like a complainer, but decided the point was important. "You should know that he hasn't been helpful, either. He was supposed to see me yesterday and he didn't bother to show up. I need their cooperation. Not just on procedures, although that's important. They're the ones who ought to be able to tell me the most about Laney. About her moods. Who she hung around with. About her interesting habit of flouting the rules."

She frowned at that but didn't say anything. I moved on to the next item on my agenda. "Dorrie, something happened yesterday as I was leaving that was quite upsetting."

"What was it?" She spoke with the hesitation of someone who isn't sure she wants to hear any more bad news. I described my encounter with Chris from the maintenance department and my resulting decision to have the chief do a background check on all Sawyer's people. Her shoulders sank as she listened and her face took on a look I'd seen before at other schools when I delivered the news they were expecting and didn't want to hear. I called it the shoot-the-messenger look.

She sighed wearily. "I'm sorry that happened, Thea. You know I wouldn't have asked you to do this if I'd thought there was any risk to you. Curt Sawyer is supposed to do a check on all his people before he hires them, but we both know Curt. I'd rather he didn't know about it, though, the check, I mean, unless something turns up."

I was disappointed even though it was the reaction I'd expected. To me it was simple—if he threatened one person and got away with it, what was to keep him from doing it again? I could sympathize with her position, though. She didn't want to rock an already unsteady boat.

"Of course. Also, I need to be able to lock my office door. You heard what happened yesterday, didn't you?"

"You mean Chip Barrett?" I nodded. "He didn't take anything, did he?" she asked anxiously.

"He tried to. I caught him before he could get away. He said something upsetting, though, before he left."

"He's always saying upsetting things. That's part of his technique. To be so controversial people will correct him and give him the information he wants or to get people so mad they blurt things out they don't mean to say. I wouldn't pay attention to anything he said. You used to be a reporter. I should think you'd be used to that."

"I'm sure you're right but I'd like to tell you what he said—"

"Why don't I tell you what I think he said?" she suggested. "He said that everyone knows what really happened here, which is that a pregnant student was murdered, but the whole thing is being hushed up because Rocky and I are lovers."

I was astonished. It was almost word for word what Barrett had said to me. "How did you know?"

"He tried the same line on me. And on Rocky. And on Dave. And who knows how many other people."

"But how did he know Laney was pregnant?"

Dorrie looked troubled. "I wish I knew. It's not information available to the public. We've tried to keep him off campus but he keeps showing up. Some of the students know about the pregnancy, how could they not with Marta Taggert bellowing it all over the place like a wounded cow. He probably heard it from one of them, unless he goaded Curt into telling. I could see that happening." She changed the subject. "Any idea who the father of the baby was? Was it Josh?"

I figured we might as well get this one out on the table, too, even though I wasn't done with my interviewing. "We may have a real problem here. He says no. He and Merri both say she had another lover, Merri says an older man, though older to these kids could be nineteen, but neither of them know who it was. Or so they say. Except to suggest that it was someone who works here. I keep getting the sense that everyone is holding things back, that there's a lot they're not telling me. . . ."

"Maybe I was overly optimistic, thinking they'd talk to you," Dorrie said, "but I had to try it. Rocky thinks I'm just trying to prove I can do anything. To prove I can handle this better than he could."

"Do you care what Rocky thinks?"

She gave me a cool look. "You know the answer to that. Anyway, he's wrong. I'm doing it because it's my job and because I can imagine how he'd approach things. I still wish you were coming up with more, though. Any clues about who might have gone out there with her?"

I shook my head. "Is there anyone who thinks there were two people out there besides Rick McTeague?"

"So you've met our local author?"

"He came to see me yesterday."

"And you thought he'd never leave, right? I wish someone other than Rick had noticed the footprints. He's hardly a credible source. He starts out reasonable enough but then he gets sidetracked onto one of his crazy ideas and he's off into never-never land. The problem is that everyone else arrived there with a specific purpose—to rescue someone from the pond—they weren't there to observe what might have happened."

"Wait a minute," I said, "what about the police? Were there any cops at the scene?"

"Of course."

"Well, they're trained to observe. What did they see?"

"I don't know," she said. "I never thought to ask. Do you want me to ask Rocky?"

I didn't think Dorrie was that dumb and wondered if she was letting her relationship with Rocky interfere with the performance of her job. Still, I offered her an out. "I have to call him anyway. I'll ask him then."

"How are we doing otherwise," she asked, glad to drop

the subject even though she'd brought it up, "are our procedures working?"

"I'll know better when I get some straight answers from Bill and Kathy Donahue. But if they're any example of your dorm parents, then you'd better start looking over Warren Winslow's shoulder. . . ."

"Thea, I resent that," Dorrie interrupted. "One person has a bad day and another misses an appointment and on the basis of that you conclude that my houseparents are failures."

"Hold on, Dorrie. That's not what I said. Remember, you and Dave made up the list and it was up to you and Dave to impress upon people the importance of these interviews. Furthermore, Bill and Kathy Donahue aren't just any dorm parents. They are the dorm parents in charge of the dorm where Laney Taggert lived and they are the dorm parents charged with paying attention to her mental and physical state and ensuring her personal safety. The only thing of any substance that Kathy was able to tell me was that they were very lax about keeping track of the sign-out cards. If this thing comes to litigation, a vague 'I don't know, you'll have to ask Bill' isn't going to reflect very well on Bucksport, is it?"

Dorrie had been standing, her hands on the desk, looking for a minute as though she wanted to jump across it and pick a fight, but she sank slowly back into her chair and rubbed her forehead. "I'm sorry I snapped at you, Thea. I'm under a lot of pressure here." She smiled ruefully. "I'm supposed to be able to handle it, aren't I?"

She was trying to change the subject but I was too concerned about the turn things had taken to let it drop. "I think we need to be clear about what you want me to do here, Dorrie. If you want a true picture of what's going on I can continue with the project. If you want a whitewash, if you want someone to find that everything was nice and proper and everyone was scrupulously careful and did things right, I can send you a bill for the work I've done and recommend someone else for the job."

"Thea, please. Take it easy. We both understand what you're supposed to do—exactly what you're doing. Of course I don't want a whitewash. You don't need to jump all over me because I was a little protective of my staff."

"And you don't need to jump all over me because I was a little critical of your staff."

Dorrie held out her hand. "You know what I want you to do, Thea. I want to know if there's any reason to think someone killed Laney Taggert. It's just hard for me to face it, that's all. I believe it was a tragic accident. I just don't want to find out later that I missed something obvious. In particular, since we're into truth-telling here, I don't want Rocky to be able to come back and throw it in my face, okay?" she said. "Truce?"

"Truce," I agreed.

We shook hands, both smiling again, and then Dorrie went back to signing cards and I went along to my office, thinking that Dorrie had entirely avoided the issue of the baby's father being someone on the Bucksport staff. I didn't think she was entirely surprised, though. When she'd asked me to take on the project, I'd known there were several unspoken questions behind the obvious one.

I met Lori in the hall, her nose bright red from the cold, her arms loaded with mail, and followed her back to her office to get the list of Sawyer's people and my day's schedule. "Who's up for today?" I said.

"It's not as bad as yesterday," she said. "You've got Russ Hamlin, her drama coach; Carol Frank, one of our school counselors—you asked for her, remember?—and Bill Donahue, who promises he'll make it this time. Then lunch and the long break you asked for, then I've scheduled Nadia Soren, another of her friends, and Curt Sawyer asked me to put one of his people, a guy called Chris Fuller, on the list." The guy who'd threatened me was named Chris. I quickly scanned the list to see if he had several employees named Chris, but Fuller was the only one. My concern must have shown because Lori said, "Thea, is something wrong?"

"I was just thinking about yesterday. Could you ask Curt to have someone put a lock on my door?"

"No more Chip Barretts, eh?"

"That's right."

"He's a horrible person," she said. "My neighbor had a child badly burned in a fire. He came to talk to her, practically forced his way in, and while she was crying he stole a picture of the child and used it in the paper. Did you get coffee?"

I got a fresh cup and went to work. The dreary little cubicle was beginning to feel like home. I had a sweater on the rack, a pair of shoes under the desk, and several unwashed coffee cups sitting around. That was about all it took to establish me. All that was missing was a liquor bottle in the desk drawer and I wasn't about to add that. In 1930s' detective stories it seems just right but I can't drink during the day and expect to get any work done.

I'd gotten off to a nice early start and still had about twenty minutes before the first victim appeared. I checked my school directory and called Chas Drucker.

The voice that answered sounded teenaged and bored. I asked for Drucker and heard her calling, "Dad, phone," loudly, several times. Finally she came back on the line and asked, "Who's calling?"

I identified myself, and added, "Tell him I'm the consultant working on the procedures audit."

I heard her shout again, "It's Theo Kotchick, some auditing consultant." Boy, I thought, that ought to really bring him running. It didn't, but after I'd cooled my heels a while she came back on the line. "I'm sorry," she said, "we don't accept telephone solicitations."

"This is not a solicitation," I said coldly, before she could hang up. "Please listen carefully and try to give an accurate message to your father. My name is Thea Kozak. I'm a consultant working with Dorrie Chapin on Laney Taggert's accident and it is important that I speak with him."

"Why didn't you say so?" the voice asked. It was slightly nasal and just offensive enough to infuriate.

Again I cooled my heels, taking advantage of the opportunity to drink my coffee before it was cool, too. I could have pushed back my cuticles and manicured my nails in the time it took Drucker to finally come on the line. "Sorry," he said, "Angie misheard you the first time. What can I do for you?"

"Just a quick question, Mr. Drucker . . ." I waited for him to say "Chas," which he did. He was feeling friendly again this morning. "Chas. Laney Taggert signed out to her parents for the Columbus Day weekend but she didn't spend the weekend with them. I was wondering if she might have said something to you about her plans."

"Not that I recall." He cleared his throat explosively into the receiver. "Sometimes she treated me like her father confessor and other times she was like a clam. Anyway, I don't remember her saying anything about that weekend and I couldn't tell you whether she stayed on campus because I wasn't around. That was parents' weekend at my son's college. Roger is at Cornell. Sorry I couldn't help you and please feel free to ask other questions as they come up." He hung up before I could ask anything else.

I called Genny Oakes, a call that involved many rings, a hurried girlish voice that agreed to check and see if she was around, and finally Genny herself on the phone, sounding breathless. I identified myself and asked if she knew what Laney had done on Columbus Day weekend. "I don't know. I went off with my parents that weekend to look at colleges. But she was supposed to go to the beach with Merri and a bunch of other kids. I assumed she did. I saw her packing and she came back after I did on Monday night. There was one odd thing, though, come to think of it. She packed a couple dresses and her best shoes. I remember thinking that was odd stuff to take to the beach. Sorry I can't help you more." Today Genny was behaving better, being the polite, well-brought-up girl she was supposed to be. I thanked her and disconnected.

My mind was beginning to follow the same course Josh's had except that where he believed I needed to find out who had fathered the baby, I thought I needed to find out who she'd spent the weekend with. If my calculations were right, they were the same person. I tried to call Josh but he wasn't there so I popped out to Lori's desk to ask if she could track him down and send him to me later. "I've got a message for you. Two messages, actually. Rick McTeague called and says he'll have to cancel for this afternoon. He's blocking out a scene in his living room and doesn't want to break his concentration. Bet you're heartbroken, aren't you? Well, don't think you're going to have time on your hands because Rocky Miller says he can see you at one, and when Rocky says he can see you, what he really means is that you'd better be there."

"Gee, thanks, Lori. Got my weekend planned, too?"

She turned her back on me and tapped a key, bringing up a sea of figures on her monitor. "I'm strictly eight-thirty to five, Monday through Friday. What you do on weekends is your business. But if you want my opinion, I hope you've got a hot date." Lori has joined the ranks of people who want to marry me off. People like my mother and Suzanne who think I'd be happier if I were married. I don't know where they get the idea I'm unhappy. I'm too busy to be unhappy.

"I do have a hot date," I told her, and went back to my cubicle to wait for Russ Hamlin. When he came in, the thought flashed across my mind that if I were Laney Taggert and I'd wanted to have an affair with an older man, Russ Hamlin would have been a great choice. He was small, too short for me, since I tend to be heightist, but beautifully put together and he moved with a sort of balletic grace. He had a healthy, outdoorsy tan, dark, wavy hair in a rock-star layer cut that fell to his shoulders and slightly elfin eyebrows. His whole face was as mobile as his body, his smile was inviting and his eyes were bright and brown. I have a soft spot for brown eyes.

He settled himself in the chair, bathed me in the warmth of his smile, and blew me right out of my chair. "Dorrie's instructions are that we're to be open, candid, and cooperative, so here goes," he said. "I was in love with Laney Taggert but I don't think she ever knew it, clever as she was. And I never laid a hand on her. Not to touch her, no matter how much I wanted to, never to have sex with her and certainly never to kill her. Having such a brilliant light extinguished is like a knife in my heart. She was a sad, lost, magical young woman."

"You forgot to say 'Any questions?' " I told him, half expecting him to be offended.

He nodded. "You're right. Do you have any questions?"

"I'm afraid I'm rather astonished at your forthrightness."

"People often are," he said. "Most of us waver and prevaricate so. I decided long ago that I would carry one of the lessons of the theater over into my own life. When you're acting you need to be able to let yourself go and feel what the characters are feeling, to immerse yourself in it, yet in the rest of life we all keep our feelings in. I decided not to do that. As a result, I tend to speak my mind rather more freely than most. But," he leaned toward me, his brown eyes fixed on my face, his whole being engaged in compelling me to believe him, "I can hide my feelings when I need to, I have to, working with teenagers, they're both hyperperceptive and hypersensitive."

"You've got to tell me more about this, Mr. Hamlin. You can't just drop a bombshell like that and then retreat."

"I could, actually," he said, "but I've chosen to cooperate with you even though I resent the intrusion into my privacy because I want the man who seduced her found just as much as Dorrie does."

"So you don't think it was an accident?"

His lip curled with scorn. "Oh, please. Do I look like I was born yesterday?" He looked as though he was born about five to ten years before the time I was born but he could have been younger or older. I wasn't a great guesser of ages. "It was no accident. Someone wanted her dead."

"Why?"

"Why was it no accident? Because of who she was, what she was. Laney wasn't the type to go out into the woods in the dark on her own. She was brave in company, she drew courage from her audiences, but she was kind of timid on her own. Besides, she was hardly a nature lover. I'm sure Kathy Donahue has told you her nutty story about beauty and the moon. . . ." He broke off with a satisfied nod. "I see that she has." I didn't bother to tell him I'd heard it elsewhere. I didn't want to interrupt the flow. "That wasn't a recent conversation. I told Kathy she was all wet—kind of an awkward expression under the circumstances, isn't it—but that's just Kathy feeling guilty. She had been ignoring Laney. Kathy's basically a very selfish woman." Once again I was struck by how much people will tell you. I didn't even know why this guy had been sent to me but I was fascinated by the stuff he was saying.

"What about suicide?"

He shook his head vehemently. "No way! Laney wasn't the suicidal type. She had ambition. She had plans. She was just biding her time until she was out from under her mother's thumb and then she was really going to break out. All the nickel-and-dime badness she was indulging in at Bucksport was just a rehearsal for the life she planned. If she had any role model it had to be Madonna. You know what was odd, though? Her favorite book was *Moby Dick*. I never could understand that." He was fun to watch, more like a storyteller than a conversationalist. He put his whole self into his narrative, supporting it with his expressions, his hand movements, his body language, his intense, luminous eyes.

"She tried to explain it to me once—something about singularity of vision and personal quests and having to put what you need to do personally above the interests of the people around you even if it seems selfish and even cruel. It was pure Laney and it didn't sound much like what I remembered about the book. Of course, I probably just read the trot anyway, but it would have given me the benefit of what some great thinker had concluded. All I remember is something about what you took away depended on what you brought to the book—and maybe that explains Laney's reaction. So anyway," he said, spreading his hands in an apologetic gesture, "you must be wondering how this answers your question. The short answer is she had a lot to live for, loads of ambition, and a finely developed ability to be selfish when her own interests demanded it. That doesn't sound like a suicidal nature, does it?"

"I've heard she was depressed."

"Have you met her family?" he asked, glancing at the door and lowering his voice. "Have you met her roommate, Miss Hockey Stick?" I nodded. "Well, that accounts for some of it. Besides, it's quite normal for adolescents to be depressed, particularly the ones who find the systems set up to control and protect them unwieldy and confining. Laney was born to be a grown-up, you see. She chafed at the confinements of adolescence. All those grown-ups clucking and tut-tutting and putting their heads together to decide what was good for her without listening to a word she had to say. No wonder she was so determined to beat the system. And then there was her delicate condition."

"She told you?"

"That wasn't the sort of thing Laney would share. Josh told me."

"Before or after the accident?"

"Before."

I needed to ask more about this, but questioning him about how he'd handled the information in his role as teacher might stop the conversation. I decided to defer the lecture on responsibility. It was Dorrie's job anyway.

"You said you were in love with Laney. Tell me about that."

"I've confessed to the feeling," he said, placing his hand mockingly over his heart. "I prefer to keep the details to myself. It should suffice for your purposes that I never acted on it."

"You are close to Josh as well?" He nodded. "Could he have been responsible for Laney's death?"

"I'm sure there are times when he wanted to be," Hamlin said, "but that would have been too bold a move for Josh. He's more the spin-around-in-his-own-space-like-a-dervish type. He can work himself into quite a frenzy but underneath he's a decent, polite kid who was brought up to be nice to others. He and Laney had a volatile and very physical relationship that frankly did sometimes come to blows, but I think it was really a form of theater. They were acting out their emotions, testing the limits to which they could take them, rather like boxing in a padded room where you know you can't get seriously hurt. No, I can't see him as a killer. He would have dithered about too long to ever get around to it. If he'd taken Laney out to the pond they would have skirmished for a few rounds, gotten themselves all stirred up, and then come back and hopped into bed. At least, that's how I see it." He grinned at me and folded his hands like an obedient schoolboy. "Next question?"

"Do you know where Laney went over Columbus Day weekend?"

"Is that when we think the love child was conceived?"

"Maybe. Do you know?"

"I know where she was supposed to go. To the beach, with Merri and Josh and a bunch of the kids. Merri's older sister was going along to provide an adult presence. As I heard the story, at the last minute, Laney said she couldn't go because she had too much work to do. The rest of them went, though, and that led to an interesting complication. I hear that Laney's so-called best friend, Merri, got her hands on Josh and had herself quite a good time comforting the poor bereft lad." That was consistent with what I'd observed, so I wasn't too shocked.

"Do you know if Laney did stay on campus?"

"No."

"No, you don't know, or no, she didn't?"

"That sounds like Gilbert and Sullivan."

Russ Hamlin's gossipy, theatrical cheerfulness was beginning to wear on me. He was a beautiful creature until he opened his mouth. Then he was a fascinating raconteur for a while but his flippancy about a girl who had died was inappropriate and even a bit ugly. This was true despite the fact that he was providing a wealth of useful information. He loved to gossip, too, I could tell. His self-selected role was gadfly and troublemaker and he obviously found it great fun.

"Do you know of anyone who might have wanted to hurt Laney?"

His smile was sly as he peered at me under lowered lids. "You've talked with Kathy? So you know about her troubles?"

"What troubles?"

The smile grew, if possible, slyer and more insinuating. He resembled a faun, or was it a satyr, I never could keep them straight. I knew before he answered that I was going to get another of his coy refusals. "If she didn't tell you, I certainly can't. Maybe you need to ask her."

"Ask her what?" I couldn't keep the impatience out of my voice even though I knew it would please him. He obviously thrived on the disapproval of others. No wonder he'd been attracted to Laney. Loving her had been like looking in a mirror.

"How she felt about Laney's delicate condition. And then there's Merri the loyal friend. Other than that, who knows? She hung around with the grounds and buildings crew a lot. Probably atavistic memories of daddy the workman or something. Wish I could help you more but alas, I was not her confidant. Things were fevered between us. She wanted me to be attracted to her, of course. Her power over men was the only power she thought she had. I'm afraid my influence tended to stir her up. I don't regret it, though. When Laney was stirred up, her performances were brilliant. I have a video of one of our workshops, Laney as Ophelia—who knew then how prophetic that was?—and she's marvelous. I'd be glad to show it to you sometime." He rose from the chair with enviable grace. "Duty calls," he said.

"Who was her confidant?"

His face twisted with distaste as he said, "Drucker."

"Do you think there was anything between them?"

"You've got to be kidding. Drucker? That dried-up old . . . never mind, forget I said that. No. I don't think so. No way. Besides, Ellie keeps him tied to her apron strings. Even if he'd wanted to stray he'd never have a chance. Living on a campus like this is like living in a small town, and Ellie is the all-knowing, all-seeing, omnipresent wife. Kind as can be, but I'd hate to be married to her."

"Were there other guys besides Josh? Students, I mean?"

"A lot of guys were interested. How could they help it, with that Julia Roberts face and that"——he kissed his fingertips and waved them in the air—"that delicious little body. And she could be anything! The ultimate fantasy dream girl. As sexy or sedate as she needed to be— madonna, whore, schoolgirl, nun, sophisticate. You name it and in the blink of any eye, she could be it. It was unnerving in one so young."

"Do you know of any particular other guys—her age or otherwise?" I persisted.

He shook his head. "It's been lovely chatting with you, but alas, duty calls. If you have a chance, do visit our theater. We're quite state-of-the-art, you know."

"Just one more question. What did you mean when you said Kathy had been neglecting Laney?"

"That's a question for Kathy, isn't it?" he said. "Along

with the possibility that Kathy might have been neglecting Bill, and Bill might have turned to Laney . . . but I do doubt that. Bill's awfully straitlaced. More the drool-but-not-touch type." He sketched a mocking bow and departed.

I stared at the closed door for a minute and then made a flurry of notes, trying to get down all the questions he'd provoked before I forgot them. After seven years of this, I knew that some of the people attracted to teaching in private schools were pretty unusual, but Russ Hamlin was right up there in the all-time quirky top ten.

CHAPTER 12

MY CHAT WITH Russ Hamlin had left me tired. I already had a page of things to follow up on from earlier interviews and he'd given me a second page all by himself. It was only midmorning, and I was ready to go home to bed. Instead I called my office, attended to some business, and then I treated myself to a refreshing trip down the hall to the ladies' room where I gave my skin a spritz of Evian water and let my hair go free. It was one of those days when it felt too long and too heavy. On such days I have to stay very busy because I want to go into a salon and get it all chopped off. I'm like a modern day Samson; I'm afraid if I lose my hair I'll lose my strength.

When I got back, a man was waiting for me. He was large and had a broad, pleasant face with deep smile lines around his eyes. "Carol got tied up so we switched places," he said, offering his hand. "I'm Bill Donahue." I shook his hand and got immediately to my questions, quickly discovering that his pleasant look was misleading. His manner, at least in response to me, was glum; his answers, while more responsive than his wife's had been, were definitely on the laconic side. He addressed all his replies to the folded hands in his lap.

The more I talked, the more glum and taciturn he became. I managed to establish that each student had a sign-out card, that there was a sign-out box where cards were kept, that it sat on a desk in their living room and that all the students knew what to do when they wanted to sign out, and that unless a student had been unreliable, sign-out worked on an honor system. Beyond that, he had little to offer. I asked if Laney had been considered unreliable. He said yes, and no, and sometimes. I asked what they did about sign-out for unreliable students. He said they paid more attention. I asked how they went about that. He scratched his head and finally said he guessed they kept the card out of the box and the student had to come to them to get it.

We seemed to be getting warmer, so I asked him if they'd kept Laney's card out of the box. He couldn't remember. I asked if Laney had come to them on Friday to sign out to go to Merri's house. He said he couldn't remember. I asked if he'd been around on Friday afternoon. He said he couldn't remember. It felt like putting together a particularly frustrating jigsaw puzzle. After fifteen minutes of struggling to draw out his grudgingly measured words I lost my temper. "Does it bother you at all that Laney Taggert is dead?"

His head shot up and he stared at me in surprise. "Of course it does. Kathy and I were very fond of Laney."

"Then why won't you talk to me about her? Why are you both making this so hard?"

He hunched his big shoulders together defensively. "Kathy warned me you'd be like this," he said. "She said she couldn't understand why Dorrie had hired such an insensitive person for such a sensitive job. Now I see what she meant."

"Did Dave Holdorf explain to you what I'm supposed to be doing here?"

"Yes," he said, his lower lip thrust out like a sullen child, "to review our procedures for keeping track of students."

"I'm also supposed to put together a picture of her last day. And to get a sense of Laney as a person, to see whether anything suggests her death might not have been an accident—"

"Of course it was an accident," he interrupted. "She went out there with her head in the clouds, probably imagining some romantic role or other—Laney was like that, she tended to live inside her own head—got herself out on the ice, and she just fell through. That's all. There's no great mystery about it."

"Maybe there is and maybe there isn't, Mr. Donahue. You knew Laney pretty well. Why do you think she was out on the ice when she was supposed to be going home for the weekend with Merri Naigler? And why wasn't she in bed if she told Chas Drucker that she was too sick to go to dinner?"

"Beats me," he said. "Probably she was working on some scheme. You know how Laney was. Always playing both ends against the middle—"

"No, Mr. Donahue, I *don't* know how Laney was. That's what I'd like you to tell me. You've just told me two very contradictory things about her." He gave me a puzzled look. "First you said she was very dreamy and probably just wandered onto the pond. Then you said she was probably working on some scheme. Which was she, Mr. Donahue? Dreamy and distracted, or scheming and worldly?" Donahue made no effort to answer the question. Just sat in infuriating silence, watching his interlaced fingers. Waiting, I suppose, for me to give up and send him on his way. Check him off my list. Yep. Saw that one. Nice guy, that Bill Donahue, if you like sullen lumps of clay. But he'd misjudged his audience. I always want to grab people who refuse to answer a direct question, particularly a reasonable one, and shake them.

"It was dark, Mr. Donahue. She was way out in the woods and she wasn't wearing boots, and you have no ideas about what she might have been doing there?" He shook his head. "You said she was probably working on some scheme. Can you suggest a scheme that would have led her into the woods on a dark winter night when she was supposed to go home with a girlfriend because she was planning to have an abortion the next day?"

He sat up straighter in his chair. "Who told you that?"

"Who told me what?"

"That she was pregnant."

"Don't you watch TV, Mr. Donahue? When there's an unexplained death, they usually do an autopsy. Didn't you know she was pregnant?"

"Maybe she told Kathy." He looked anxiously at his watch and then at the window. Maybe wondering if he should jump out.

"Did anyone ever find her overnight bag?" I asked.

"I don't know."

"When was the last time you saw Laney?"

"Sometime on Friday," he said. "We try to see all the students at least twice a day and make some sort of significant contact at least one of those times. You know, just to check in, see how things are going."

"When on Friday? And do you remember what you talked about?"

He shifted restlessly in the chair. "I don't remember. Sometime in the morning I think. I asked her what she was doing for the weekend. She said she was going to Merri's. I think I said 'Don't forget to sign out' or something like that, and she said she always did."

"So her card was in the box?"

He made a helpless gesture. "I told you. I don't remember."

"Did you ever find her sign-out card for Friday?"

"I don't know. Did you ask Kathy?"

"She said to ask you."

He looked at his watch again. "Well, I'm sorry, Ms. Kozak, but we each have more important things to do than to chase after pieces of paper."

"You don't consider sign-out cards important? What if there was an emergency?"

"I didn't mean that." His whole face and posture reminded me of an angry dog about to snarl and strike.

I held out my arm for him to bite. "Then what did you mean?"

"Kathy's been having health problems. We've been distracted. . . ." He trailed off without explaining.

"Based on your impressions of Laney, do you have any reason to think her death might have been a suicide?"

"None at all. That's a crazy idea. Who told you that?"

"No one. I'm just trying to rule it out as a possibility. You know that in a suggestible community like this a suicide presents a very real risk of copycat behavior."

"Of course I know that. But no one thinks Laney killed herself. If they don't think it was an accident, they think she was—" He stopped abruptly.

"They think she was what?"

"Nothing," he said. "I'm sorry. I've got to go. I can't talk about this. It's too upsetting."

He headed for the door but I beat him to it. If it had been a gun fight, he would have been the loser. "What is it, Mr. Donahue? What are you and your wife hiding from me?"

"Nothing. We aren't trying to hide anything. I don't know where you got that idea." He looked frantically around, trying to find another exit, then shouldered me aside and escaped, confirming my impression that something was terribly wrong. I closed my eyes and for a few self-indulgent seconds I wished that Andre Lemieux would come galloping up in his fat, funny-looking government-issue Chevy and take me away from all this. Carry me off to that California hillside where we would raise solemn-faced brown-eyed boys and tanned and willful girls and live happily ever after.

Carol Frank was a blessed relief after the men who'd come before her. My first impression of a dumpy, middle-aged woman vanished as soon as she'd crossed from the door to the chair and I could see her face. She wore shapeless clothes and had curly, shoulder-length gray hair that still looked girlish and she had the face of a girl. Not just any girl, either, but a girl you wanted to be your best friend. She glowed with a comfortable warmth and happiness and an overall aura of goodness. No wonder the students were willing to confide in her. If I hadn't had a job to do, I would have tucked my feet under me and confided in her myself.

She considered my questions carefully, answered them fully and was genuinely sorry there wasn't more she could do to help. She was also genuinely sorry there wasn't something she could have done to help Laney. "She was a very complicated girl, Ms. Kozak. A real challenge to understand. A real challenge to help. Sometimes she was astonishingly mature and clearheaded, other times she seemed years younger than sixteen and terribly vulnerable, lost, and needy."

"How does a student get referred to you?"

She smiled. "There are lots of different ways. Sometimes an advisory will notice a student needs a little help, sometimes a dorm parent. A lot of times they refer themselves."

"How do they do that?"

"It was Dorrie's idea. She said maybe it would be a little expensive but it was an experiment she wanted to try. She has one of us available a few hours a week and the students can just sign themselves up."

"On a sign-up sheet? Isn't that awfully public?"

"It would be, if they used their own names, but they just have codes. One day last week I saw Zorro, Killer Angel, the Weasel, and Black Bart's girl. Laney was Moby Dick."

"Why did she come to you?"

"She was struggling with her relationships. Particularly with her roommate. They didn't get along very well and Laney needed help deciding whether to try and salvage the relationship or give up and move into a single room by herself. I think she was a little afraid of being alone and of having failed at such a basic relationship. She was also struggling in her relationship with Josh. It was, as I'm sure you've heard, very intense. So intense that it frightened her. She was an emotional girl. People have probably told you about her imitations? Well, that was an outlet for her emotions. Not always a very successful one, since she seemed to be especially good at offending people, but necessary. Laney liked to be in charge. Like her mother, she was very controlling. She couldn't control Josh and it scared her."

Carol Frank pulled some sensible glasses out of a pocket and put them on. "I think I should tell you that I asked Peter Van Deusen whether it was all right to tell you these things. I wasn't sure how confidentiality applied once a person is . . . was . . . dead. He said I should tell you whatever you wanted to know."

I was so grateful to her for making this easy that I could have hugged her. "Was Laney afraid of Josh?"

"She was more afraid of herself."

"How do you mean? Afraid she might be considering suicide?"

"Oh, no, not like that. She was afraid of her impulses. Of how powerful her desires were, of wanting her own way too much. We were working on understanding the difference between wanting something but recognizing you couldn't or shouldn't have it and wanting something and having to make it yours or you'll die. In short, we were working on impulse control."

"Do you know whether there were any other men in Laney's life besides Josh? Men she was intimate with?"

She hesitated briefly and then gave me an apologetic smile. "Keeping people's secrets gets to be such a habit that I find it hard to share them. I know I'm supposed to be open with you but I can't completely shake the notion that I ought to protect her privacy."

"I understand how you feel. When my sister was killed and the police interviewed me, I felt exactly the same way. It seemed wrong to reveal personal and intimate things about her to total strangers. But if there was foul play involved in Laney's death, it isn't her privacy you're protecting, it's the killer."

She stared at me wide-eyed, her hands gripping the arms of the chair with white-knuckle intensity. "Foul play? Killer? I thought you were doing a procedures audit. I thought you were just checking to be sure that we were taking care of our students . . . checking on our counseling function . . . to see if we were available . . . I mean accessible . . . giving them the necessary attention. And . . . and maybe, knowing the effect a suicide can have in a community like this, making sure she wasn't suicidal. Which she wasn't."

It was then that I realized I'd completely abandoned the idea that Laney's death might have been an accident and was almost as certain that it hadn't been suicide. Too many people were acting too strangely and too many people had told me she wasn't the suicidal type. "I'm sorry," I said. "I didn't mean to shock you. There's no evidence that it was anything other than an accident, but since she was pregnant—"

"Pregnant! Yes, she was, poor child. Is that why you were asking about other men? Oh, of course it was. Because Josh wasn't the father, was he? The question does come up then, doesn't it? I suppose you do need to know, then, don't you? I don't remember their names, though I have them in my notes. We'd mostly been talking about Josh. We'd only begun to talk about others. . . ."

"Others? There was more than one?"

She ran a hand distractedly through her hair. "I . . . this is . . . I mean I'm not ready to . . . I wasn't expecting . . . this makes things a little more complicated. . . ." Her sweet face was terribly distressed. "I was comfortable talking to you about Laney, and even about Josh, since their relationship is pretty much public knowledge . . . but this stuff about other men . . . that brings other people into it. Other people whose privacy matters, too. I'm just not sure how I ought to handle it. This is such a tight-knit . . . there are academic reputations . . . unless it really matters . . ." She stopped and looked at me, hoping for some direction.

"What if Laney Taggert was murdered?" I asked.

"I think I'd better talk to Peter Van Deusen again before I say anything more."

All I could do was stare at her in astonishment. I felt like Wile E. Coyote. Every time I got close to that damned Roadrunner, I fell off a cliff or someone slammed a door in my face. How could this nice, smart woman be so dumb? Talk about a lack of impulse control. I wanted to jump over the desk and shake her until she told me what I wanted to know.

"Ms. Frank . . . Carol . . . you have names in your notes?" Reluctantly, she nodded. "Don't you realize how important your information may be? This isn't something to play games about."

"I am not playing games," she said quietly. "I just need time to consider the implications of what I may be saying."

"Excuse me." Lori Leonard stuck her head around the door. "I'm sorry to interrupt but we have a student over at the infirmary crying uncontrollably and she won't talk to anyone except you, Carol."

"I'm sorry," she said, "I have to go. I know this is important to you. Let me think about it and talk to Peter. Maybe we can talk again later." She struggled into her coat and hurried out.

Lori handed me a plate shrouded in plastic wrap. "You'd better hurry up and eat this if you don't want to keep Rocky waiting."

I had a visions of myself as a prisoner in a cell, being brought my meals so that I'd never have to leave it. The stuffy little office lent itself to that kind of imagining. Well, I thought as I unwrapped my lunch, it had come just in time. I didn't have time to stop and get something and I was hungry enough to forage for wild nuts and berries. I took a huge bite. The sandwich had some strange flavor I couldn't identify. One of those nouvelle or nouveau combinations of tuna fish with something crunchy and slightly off-flavored. I'm as culinarily inventive as the next guy but this particular combination didn't appeal to me. I wrapped up the rest of it and stuffed it in my briefcase. Maybe later, when I'd gone from hungry to ravenous, it would be more appealing.

I called the office to bring Suzanne, who hadn't been in earlier, up-to-date about the King School's problem and the necessity for a new copier. Then I gathered up all my papers—they hadn't come and installed a lock yet and I wasn't leaving anything for Chip Barrett or like-minded nosy types to find—made sure I had the list I wanted to give Rocky, and drove into Sedgwick. It was only about three miles, but halfway there I ran into some road repairs that were being handled by the Keystone Kops. A bunch of warmly bundled men, surrounded by pale green trucks with the Sedgwick logo, were watching a cheerful yellow backhoe maul a portion of the street. The police officer detailed to direct traffic was watching also, with the avid interest of a small boy watching big equipment. Occasionally, one of the workmen would say something and he'd laugh. The result was that no traffic was moving in either direction.

Finally the car in front of me, impatient with the delay, sounded its horn and began to edge by. The useless cop abandoned his merry companions, stopped the car, and wasted more of my time checking the driver's license and registration. Finally I lost patience, got out of my car, and went up to him. "Excuse me, Officer," I said, "but I'm already ten minutes late for a meeting with Chief Miller. Any idea how much longer this delay is going to be, because I called him on my car phone a while ago and told him where I was and that I expected to be there momentarily." It was a lie. No way had I called Rocky, but I hoped that if he thought his chief knew he was causing long delays, he might be motivated to get the traffic moving.

It worked. He tossed the license and registration at the man he'd stopped and ordered him to move along. I moved right along behind him down the gracious main street. Following Rocky's instructions, I turned left on Maple Street, passed the library, and beyond it I turned in and parked in front of a brick building clearly labeled Sedgwick Police. The outside door let me into a small entry with yellowish cinder-block walls. On one side was a large window looking into what must have been a communications center. In the center of the larger window was a small opening that looked like the teller's window at an all-night gas station.

A man in uniform came to the window and asked if he could help me. "I'm here to see Chief Miller," I said. "My name is Thea Kozak."

He picked up a phone, spoke into it briefly, and came back to the window. "He'll be right out."

I paced the small room restlessly. Maybe it was too many hours of sitting or something, but I felt incredibly agitated. It couldn't have been because I was anxious about meeting with the chief, because I wasn't. I was puzzling about that when a door opened and Rocky beckoned for me to follow him. "Would you like a tour of the station?" he said. "It's brand-new. State-of-the-art. We're very proud of it."

"I'd like that," I said, which was true. We citizens rarely get to see the insides of police stations except under the most unpleasant circumstances. It would be fun to have a VIP tour. "But I can't today. I've got more people to see this afternoon."

"My office is this way," he said, leading me down a hall. He sounded a little sulky, as if in rejecting his offer, I'd rejected him. Obviously the station meant a lot to him. Along the way, he couldn't resist giving me a minitour. "That area where you checked in is our communications center. State-of-the-art, one of the best in the state. On the right is the records room. That room there is the supervisor's, behind it is a locker room and along back there are the cells. Here," he grabbed my arm and steered me through a large room where several people seemed to be doing clerical duties. "Through there is the training room, and here's my office. I hear they're keeping you busy." He went behind the desk and I sat down in a comfortable blue chair. Sitting. Just like I'd been doing all week. The only difference was that I was in the interview chair. I tried to remember what else I wanted to discuss, besides the list, but I couldn't seem to focus on the purpose of my visit. I felt the way I'd felt in high school just before a basketball game—the same keyed-up anxiety that meant I couldn't sit still. I got up and started walking around the room, looking at the things on his bookshelf and on his walls.

"What I wanted to see you about was to get a progress report, see how things are going," he said. "After the buildup Dorrie gave you, I half expected you to arrive with a killer tied onto your roof." Even on his best behavior he still couldn't resist a little jibe or two.

"Something strange is going on out there, Chief," I said, "but I haven't figured out what it is yet. I don't think Laney Taggert's death was an accident."

"Is that right?" he said. "Maybe you should tell me why you think that and let me take it from here. Is that what you wanted to see me about?"

"I'm not quite at that point yet. I'm still collecting information." My hands seemed to belong to someone else. They kept picking things up and putting them down. I straightened a picture, twitched at the curtains. He was looking at me like I'd lost my mind, and I couldn't blame him. My body seemed compelled to keep moving. "There were a couple things, Chief. First, what was Laney Taggert wearing when they pulled her out of the pond?"

He nodded. "Mm-hmm. I can tell you that. I'll have to look it up. What else?"

"Was the duffle bag she was carrying ever found?"

His eyebrows went up at that. "I don't think it was," he said. "Next?"

"You've heard about the second set of footprints, right?" He nodded. I wanted to finish the question but suddenly I had this terrible pain in my stomach. It felt like the beginnings of a flu. I willed it away and it went, but before I could relax the pain was back and getting worse. Now that I was paying attention, I also noticed that the light seemed too bright. Rocky was staring at my eyes. "Why are you staring at me?" I bent forward, folded my hands over my stomach, and waited for the pain to pass.

"Your pupils are dilated. Are you all right?" he said, starting to get up.

"Just a little pain. It'll pass in a minute," I said, waving him away. I hate to be fussed over. It makes me claustrophobic. I tried to distract myself by continuing with my questions. "I was wondering if the first officer on the scene might have noticed those tracks as well. I was hoping I could talk to—" This time the pain was so sharp it brought tears to my eyes. I barely had time to get out the word "him" before another one hit. He came out from behind his desk, put an arm around me and steered me back to the chair. I tried to master my body so that I could go on talking but it felt as though an animal inside of me was trying to claw its way out.

"What's wrong?" he said, bending over me.

"Nothing serious," I gasped. "I keep . . . having these . . . strange pains. . . ." Behind the pain, a wave of nausea was rising. I tried to force it back down until I'd finished what I had to say. I managed, with many pauses, to get out a half-coherent account of being cornered and threatened by the guy named Chris. "I have a list of Curt Sawyer's people here. I was hoping . . ." The bile was rising in my throat. ". . . you could run a . . . check on them. . . ." I stopped, panting.

The pains just kept getting worse and worse and I was getting scared. I tried to bend over and get the list out of my briefcase, ended up out of the chair and on my knees on the floor. The pain was constant now, steady and terrible and I had to make an effort not to scream. I had the list halfway out when it became clear that I was going to be sick and there was no time for the niceties of the ladies' room. "Quick, your wastebasket!" I said in a strangled voice.

Luckily Rocky was a man of action. He didn't quibble or try to convince me that I should wait. He grabbed the wastebasket, dumped the papers out and shoved it toward me. It arrived just in time. Afterward I felt better just long enough to grab the list and hand it to him before the pains came back. This time they were so awful I didn't even try to pretend I wasn't in agony. I just curled up in a ball on the floor, tears running down my face, and waited to be sick again.

But this wasn't like any sickness I'd ever experienced. When I was sick again, I didn't feel any better and the cramps just kept getting worse. On top of that, I felt like a giant hand was squeezing my chest. "Rocky. I can't breathe." I was wheezing like an ancient elevator. I was lucky this had happened to me here instead of while I was sitting in my car waiting to get past the road work. At least here I was in the presence of someone familiar with emergencies. I was engaging in every-cloud-has-a-silver-lining thinking, but I was scared.

I heard him pick up the phone. "This is the chief," he said. "There's a woman in my office being violently ill and in respiratory distress. I need an ambulance and some EMTs." He knelt down beside me. "Do you know what's the matter with you?"

"Some weird flu?"

"I don't think so. Maybe food poisoning? What did you have for lunch?"

All I heard clearly was the word "poison." "That's it," I mumbled. "Poisoned. I've been poisoned. The funny-tasting sandwich. In my briefcase. Don't throw it away." An elephant was standing on my chest. A huge, stubborn elephant that wouldn't move aside and let me breathe. I had to throw up again and now I felt the first stirrings of the corollary to vomiting as the giant hand moved below my stomach and started squeezing. It's funny how modest one can be, even in the face of death. I might have been willing to throw up in Rocky's wastebasket, but I wasn't going to lift my skirt and sit on it.

I grabbed the chair and hauled myself to my feet. "Bathroom," I said. It took as much energy and effort to say that one word as to prepare and give a thirty-minute speech to the American Association of Independent Schools.

"Just relax," he said, patting my arm, "the ambulance will be here in a minute."

"Bathroom," I repeated, trying to convey a sense of urgency and decisiveness. If he didn't act soon, I would have to cast modesty aside. Letting go of the chair, I staggered toward the door.

"Here," he said, opening another door. His friendly demeanor had changed back to the more familiar irritation but I didn't care. All I focused on was the fact that the man had his own private loo. He grabbed my arm and steered me toward it. I staggered in, shut the door, and all hell broke loose. When I had myself under control again, I leaned wearily against the wall, gasping for breath. The pains were unrelenting and I was dizzy from all the vomiting. I stared at myself in the mirror. I was a peculiar shade of ashen gray, my eyes were streaming, and the pupils were huge. I heard a commotion that signaled the arrival of my saviors. On unsteady legs I went to meet them.

As they strapped me onto the stretcher I saw Rocky standing there, holding the sandwich, a strange look on his face. I tried to sit up, to push away the oxygen they were trying to give me, to tell him again that there might be something in it, but they were wheeling me out. I fought them, got the mask off and said, "Don't throw it away!"

"I won't," he said. I realized that he was putting it in an evidence bag. The animal in my stomach was trying to get out to attack the elephant on my chest and I was sure I had never felt more awful. This time I knew that I was going to die and at the same time afraid that I might not die and would have to live with this pain forever. I couldn't stand being strapped down and despite my failing breath I fought to make them release me.

The ambulance wasn't going fast enough. I tried to tell them to hurry but you need breath to speak and I didn't have any breath, not even with the oxygen. I'd been pulled underwater once as a child and held there while my lungs grew desperate for oxygen. I felt like that now. Surrounded by air and unable to breathe. The mask made me claustrophobic but even if I'd wanted to take it off, I couldn't. My arms and legs were twitching and restless rather than obedient. I kept seeing Rocky but I didn't know whether he was in my imagination or in the ambulance or whether we'd arrived at the hospital. Because I had no breath I couldn't tell them I hated emergency rooms. I couldn't tell Rocky that no one must let Andre know about this. He mustn't know, mustn't be scared by seeing me in a hospital bed again. Hadn't he just been through enough? Hadn't I promised I'd stay out of dangerous situations? Ha. I was a walking magnet for catastrophe.

If I had retained any doubt that what had happened to Laney was an accident, it was all dispelled now. Someone had killed Laney and now they were killing me to keep me from finding out why.

People were bending over me, doing things to me, trying to stick things down my throat. I tried to fight them off and on its own my body was writhing and jerking like Linda Blair in *The Exorcist*. If I ever got out of here alive, I'd never be able to hold my head up on the streets of Sedgwick again. I could hear Rocky's voice, talking to someone, and heard the word "poison" very clearly. "Poison" and "plant" and "sandwich." Two people held my arm and someone stuck a needle into me.

A peculiar lassitude overtook me, flowed through me like honey, thick and slow, easing the pressure in my lungs. I started to drift, to watch the strange fuzzy shapes of the lights, the odd misshapen heads that floated above me. Voices became background, a steady hum of high- and low-pitched tones. I stopped caring about the awful things they were doing. Stopped being embarrassed about throwing up on everyone. Stopped caring if I lived or died. I imagined someone else sitting in my chair back in my little room at the Bucksport School, trying to find out what had happened to Thea Kozak.

CHAPTER 13

WAKING UP WAS no picnic. I felt like I'd been trampled by a whole herd of cattle. All my muscles ached. My chest felt like I'd coughed for a week and busted all my ribs. My stomach seemed to have stopped a few punches and I knew what that felt like because I have stopped a few, which is not something every woman can say. I tried to remember what had happened. I'd gotten a bad case of flu, that was it. So bad I couldn't even remember coming home and going to bed. In the dim light, my room looked funny. While I was sleeping someone had come in and rearranged the furniture and my bed had shrunk. Maybe it was that rotten little prick of a tenant. Maybe I still had a fever and was delirious. Once I got some water and took some aspirin things would seem better.

I pushed back the covers and sat up. I felt odd and light-headed so I rested at the edge of the bed before getting up. What was going on here? My reindeer sheets were gone, my soft old nightgown was gone, and someone had taped plastic tubes to my hand. As I tugged at them impatiently, there was a stabbing pain in the back of my hand, but finally they came loose and a big metal pole tipped over and crashed onto the floor at my feet.

Dizzy and confused, I sat back down and stared at

the blood that oozed out from under the tape. It ran across my hand and slowly down my bare leg. My nightgown was short, a thin cotton with a faded blue print. I didn't own anything like it. I'm no fashion plate but I'd never buy something this ugly. I got up and made my way slowly across the room, tripping once on the plastic tubing and once on the metal pole, heading for the light switch. Someone had moved that, too. I opened the door and cowered back from the bright fluorescent lights. I wasn't in Maine or in my condominium. It looked like a hospital corridor and I thought, what the hell, I spend enough time in places like this that I could call them home. I just needed to know the name of my current temporary residence. Eventually my keen memory would return and fill in the blanks.

I braced a noodle-weak arm against the door frame for support and leaned out. A uniformed policeman was sitting in a chair by the door. "Where am I?" I asked him, knowing I sounded like a cliché from the movies. "What's going on?"

He stared at me as if I were the undead come to get him, whirled on his heel, and headed off down the hall. "I'll get the nurse," he called back over his shoulder.

Suddenly the word "poison" flashed onto my mental screen and everything came racing back—the stuff I needed to remember and the stuff I didn't want to, like crouching on Rocky Miller's floor throwing up in his wastebasket. A nurse was coming down the hall toward me, a vision in crisp white, trailed by the cowardly cop. I knew before she even opened her mouth that she was going to yell at me—part of the hospital ethic is to infantalize adults—and that I didn't want to hear it. I cut her off with a question of my own. "Where is the nearest phone?"

"You're not making any phone calls, dear, you're going right back to bed. You've just been through a terrible time. You need to rest."

"You're right," I said, "I need rest. And water. And something to kill this pain. Right after this phone call." She didn't know what to do with me. People as sick as I was were supposed to be docile. Hospitals always expect it; I always disappoint them. "You have a phone right by your bed," she said, "and what have you done to your hand?"

I looked down at the little drops of blood dripping off my fingers. "I was disoriented. I must have pulled it off. I'm sorry."

"Well, we'd better take care of that right away." She began to herd me back toward the bed, persistent as a sheep dog, clucking over the scattered tubing and the overturned IV pole. While she was clucking, I picked up the phone and called Dorrie. My watch said it was almost seven but she was still in her office.

"Dorrie, it's Thea—"

She cut me off before I could continue. "Thea? My God! I'm *so* sorry about what happened. How are you? Aren't you supposed to be resting?"

"I'm supposed to be dead. Fortunately, I have a habit of not doing what I'm supposed to."

"I'm on my way over there," she said, "we need to talk. I'm not sure you should continue with this, after what happened."

"Later, Dorrie. That's not what I called about. Listen, this is important. Does Carol Frank live on campus?"

"No. She has an office here but she lives in town. Why?"

"I think she's in danger." It sounded absurdly dramatic, even to me, but I persisted. People getting drowned and poisoned was dramatic. I didn't want anyone else added to the casualty list. "We were interrupted today before I could find out what she knows, but Laney Taggert told her some things that might help us identify Laney's killer—"

"You're sure that she was killed, then?"

"If I had any doubts, they were dispelled this afternoon."

"What makes you so sure?"

"Please, Dorrie . . . not now . . . I feel like I've been marched over by a platoon of marines. You've got to find her and warn her. And tell Rocky she needs protection. Right now! Don't waste time arguing with me. It may be a matter of life and death. And as soon as you've done that, will you come and get me out of here? I can't stay. I've got to go home. . . ."

"Okay, okay, I'll do it," Dorrie said.

"Call me as soon as you've talked to her. I need to know that she's all right. And someone needs to go to her office and get Laney's file. Right now. Tonight. If the killer hasn't already taken it." Dorrie started in with her questions again but I'd used up my energy. I said a quick good-bye as the trembling hand holding the phone collapsed into my lap and the receiver slipped out of my fingers. I stared weakly at it, hearing Dorrie's faint voice talking to my foot, too exhausted to do anything about it. "Can you hang that up, please?"

The nurse picked it up, realized that Dorrie was still talking, and explained that I couldn't talk anymore. Then she cradled the phone, tucked me back in, and repaired the IV line. She was gentle enough but the peevish expression on her face said more clearly than words that she disapproved of my behavior. Nurses like their patients quiet and grateful. Rather like my mother. It was just like being at home.

"I'm thirsty," I said.

She poured me some water and the sound of the ice tinkling into the glass made me dizzy with anticipation. She popped in a straw and held the glass so I could drink. I sucked greedily at the straw until the icy water hit my stomach; I could feel it recoil in shock. Every muscle in my body tensed in anticipation. At that point I would have preferred open-heart surgery performed with a knife and fork to throwing up again. Even though I was still thirsty, I stopped drinking.

"It's too cold," I said. "It hurts. Do you have any tea?"

"I might be able to find some," she said doubtfully. "Do you need anything else?" She wanted the answer to be no.

"Blankets," I said. She left to find some and I huddled in the bed, trembling and miserable. The icy water had left me shaking, unless it was getting out of bed, unless it was just the whole experience. All I knew was that I was shivering. Now that the lights were on, I could see how stark and utilitarian my room was. I was all alone in a strange hospital in a strange town. I felt awful and nobody cared and I was too sick and weak to take myself home.

Maybe it meant that I was a better detective than I knew, since I'd obviously done something so threatening that the murderer wanted me out of the picture, but I didn't feel fine or clever or even have any idea what I'd done. I knew what I wanted to do, though—die. Put myself out of my misery. I was just too stubborn to give anyone else that satisfaction. I curled up in a ball and buried my head in my pillow. My hair smelled awful, my face needed washing. I wanted to brush my teeth but I couldn't have made my arm go up and down and I was too big to have someone do it for me. And I hurt! Oh, God, did I hurt.

I stayed curled up in my ball, feeling extremely sorry for myself, while the nurse came and put blankets over me, tucking them in quietly and efficiently, fed me some tiny colorless pills from a little pleated paper cup, lowered the lights again, and went away. There were things I needed to think about, things that needed to be done. I wasn't sure Dorrie had appreciated the urgency of my message. If I could have gotten out of bed I would have gone and found Carol Frank myself. Found her and asked her my questions. But I couldn't do it. Frustrating as my weakness was, I couldn't fight it. Gradually I got warmer and a dizzying lethargy crept over me until I fell into a dreamless sleep. I woke to the sound of voices and foot steps out in the hall. The door opened with a burst of light and Dorrie, Rocky, and another uniformed policeman came in, followed by the nurse. The nurse attempted to hush them with all the gusto of a burnt-out schoolteacher.

Rocky snapped on the lights, stormed up to my bed, and bellowed at me, "What's all this about Carol Frank? And who gave you that sandwich? I said you couldn't handle the job and now you damned near got yourself killed!" He stood over me, his face pink, his blond hair awry, breathing heavily and glaring.

The sudden glare of light felt like a physical assault but I managed to respond using my best Miss Manners technique. "Thank you for your kind expression of concern about my welfare. I'm doing much better, thank you." He just stared at me in openmouthed astonishment while behind him Dorrie struggled to repress a smile. "Would you please go away now?" Being bullied always brings out the sweetest side of my nature.

"I'm not going anywhere until you tell me everything you know," he said.

"Hope you've got lots of time, then," I said. "Where shall we start? Recipes? Poetry? Statistical methods? Interviewing techniques?" His face got redder and with his boyish looks he reminded me of a furious child. I decided not to start a fight. I didn't have the energy. "I'm sorry about your wastebasket," I said.

"Forget about the goddamned wastebasket," he said. "Why did you eat that sandwich?"

What a stupid question. "Because I was hungry!" It was supposed to sound defiant but it came out sounding pathetic. I'd expended all my energy on my first sentence. On a good day, Rocky's belligerence didn't bother me, but I was weak, dizzy, and bleary from sleep. Being sick always leaves me feeble, and this time I'd been sick and pumped and purged and drugged and I had no fight left in me at all. Despite the fact that I am the toughest kid on the block and I know that big kids don't cry, as Rocky Miller stood over me yelling, I started to cry. "Go away," I said. I pulled the covers over my head.

Through the covers I heard Dorrie's voice. "Now you see why I didn't want your department to do the interviewing?"

"I don't know what you're talking about," he said.

"I'm talking about bullying people. I'm talking about tailoring your style to the situation. I'm talking about what you just did. You're forgetting something very important here. Thea isn't some criminal you're trying to get a confession from, Rocky. She's a victim. Someone tried to kill her today. But instead of acting sympathetic and protective, instead of saying, 'I know you've been through a horrible time but I need to ask you a few questions,' you're standing there yelling at her. Why shouldn't she have eaten a sandwich? I have one sent to her every day."

"Well, I didn't know that."

"Because you didn't ask—"

"Dammit, Dorrie, will you let me handle this?"

"How would you like it if you were sick in bed and someone came and yelled at you?" she said.

"It's happened," he said.

"Oh, spare me the macho bullshit, Rocky! You aren't listening."

I pulled off the covers. I was still crying but it wasn't something I could control. Let him think I was a weakling and a wimp. I didn't care. Through my tears, I stared past him at Dorrie and asked the question that was uppermost in my mind. "Did you find Carol?"

She shook her head. "She was out. I left a message on her machine and Rocky has someone watching the house."

"What about the file?"

"Gone. When I got to her office, it looked like a tornado had gone through it. I only hope she has it with her. Someone went through your office, too. I don't know if they took anything—"

"There was nothing to take. I had all my papers with me." So much I wanted to tell them and I could barely speak. My throat felt scratchy and my mouth was dry. Everything took too much effort. Every word was too hard. I closed my eyes, shutting out the sight of Rocky's angry face and Dorrie's worried one.

"Goddammit, you can't go back to sleep now!" Rocky said. I think he would have shaken me if Dorrie hadn't been there. "We need to know everything you know. This isn't some simple consulting thing anymore. This is attempted murder! Let's start with the sandwich—"

"It never was a simple consulting thing," I muttered.

"Can't you see she's exhausted?" Dorrie said.

"This is police business," he said. "After she answers my questions she can settle down for a nice, long sleep." He pulled up a chair and sat down, while his underling fetched a second chair from somewhere and sat down behind him, notebook ready. It was clear that whatever the reason, whether it was because I'd had the nerve to collapse in his office or just because I'd had the nerve to get involved in the first place, Rocky Miller was cutting me no slack.

I wasn't surprised. It wasn't even the first time I'd had to deal with obnoxious cops while I was helpless in a hospital bed. Once it had even been Andre. So I mentally girded myself for battle, a pathetic little David in a flimsy johnny against a healthy and belligerent Goliath. I didn't have a slingshot but I could always just close my eyes and refuse to open them. "Dorrie, could you find me some tea, please." She nodded and left the room, glad to escape a situation where she'd felt helpless. Dorrie doesn't like feeling helpless any more than I do.

The nurse was still hovering in the background, obviously intimidated by the presence of the police chief. "Nurse," I said, "could I have a few minutes alone with you?"

It took her a minute to grasp my meaning but then she timidly cleared the room. "Would you like the bedpan?"

she asked as the door closed behind Rocky and his minion.

"I do have a bathroom, don't I?"

"Yes, but . . ." she began.

I sat up slowly and swung my legs over the side of the bed. Long white rubber noodles between me and the floor. "If you could help me . . ." She shook her head. Probably she rarely had to deal with as many strong-willed people as she'd seen tonight. She propelled my IV pole and gave me her arm and soon I was back in bed, propped up on the pillows, ready to receive company. Then she ushered Rocky back in and, with the restorative help of the tea Dorrie brought, I tried to tell him everything I knew. The problem was that all I could tell him were my questions, my suspicions, the paths I'd decided I needed to explore.

Once we ended our battle of wills and he saw that I was willing to cooperate, he calmed down. And I tried hard to cooperate, since I didn't like the idea of someone trying to kill me any more than he did. It took a tremendous effort to stay coherent, to keep my thoughts organized, even to speak. He was a strange man. The more we talked, the gentler he became. Soon he was helping me drink my tea, smoothing the hair back from my face, patting my hand.

"I tried to call your boyfriend, but I couldn't find him," he said. "I figured he'd want to know."

"Oh no!" I said, sitting up. "He can't know! I hope you didn't leave a message."

"I don't understand," he said. "I would think you'd want him with you at a time like this."

"I do want him with me." My voice had faded to a whisper and exhaustion lay on me like a lead apron. "But I don't want to worry him. Not now. He's had enough death and near-death in his life recently. Besides, I promised him I'd stay away from anything dangerous." Maybe it was cowardly of me, cowering before Andre's imagined disapproval like this. It wasn't that I was ready to let him run my life. He'd tried that before and I'd had to back him off. He knew me well enough to know that I had to do what I had to do. But this would have been the third time he'd found me in the hospital and I wasn't sure he could take it. I wanted to explain that to Rocky, to make him promise that he wouldn't do anything rash, but my eyelids were coming down and they were too heavy to lift. "Promise you won't call him," I said.

He patted my hand. "You get some rest. I'll see you in the morning." He pulled up the covers, turned off the light, and left me alone. I wanted to stay awake a little longer and think through what had happened, but I couldn't. My thoughts were little spots of light spinning around in a huge black centrifuge. They spun out to the sides, became a bright, circular blur, and then spun away into space, while I fell down into the whirling black center. I stayed there for a long time.

CHAPTER 14

I WAS HAVING a lovely dream. I was home in my wonderful sleigh bed, cuddled up next to Andre. In the dream I was going to sleep until noon, take a long hot bath and then Andre was going to fix me breakfast. Though I often had extremely vivid dreams they were not normally this pleasant. Usually I dreamed about work and my dreams were peopled by the difficult characters I dealt with during the day. Sometimes my sister, Carrie, would still appear in my dreams. At first it was always the way she'd looked in the police photos of the murder scene, but lately that image had been fading and I could see Carrie as she'd been when she was alive.

I turned over, looking for a more comfortable position, and my sore muscles were quick to protest. I moaned and lay still. In my dream, Andre put an arm around me and pulled me close. I snuggled into his warmth. He was so real I could feel his breath on my neck. So real that I felt safe. "Don't let them get me," I said.

"I won't let anyone hurt you." Dreams can be very sensuous experiences. When he said that I could practically feel the rumble of his voice through his body. Even in my debilitated state I felt my body responding. Just thinking about him does that to me. Then I slipped into a heavier sleep, a sleep too deep even for dreams.

Sometime in the middle of the night I heard the sound of the door opening. I sprang upright, gasping, and sat staring at the slice of light the door admitted. Andre put a comforting arm around me. "It's okay, Thea," he said, "it's just the cop on duty, checking on you. Your bodyguard."

"I thought you were my bodyguard."

"Looked like the job was taken."

"You're not a dream?" I said.

"Some people think I am. There was this girl once who—"

"I don't want to hear it, Lemieux," I said. "Just shut up and hold me."

"Anytime." He kissed me and he didn't even seem to mind that I hadn't brushed my teeth. I had managed a little mouthwash in honor of the police chief. It was one of those kisses that starts out saying "Glad to see you", and progresses rapidly to breathless passion. When we finally came up for air, he said, "Just wanted you to know that I'm glad you're alive."

"We've got to stop meeting like this."

"You're telling me?" he said. "We spend more time in hospitals than some doctors."

"And have less fun, too. At least we don't have to do the paperwork."

"I'm giving you a nurse's kit for Christmas."

"If I can't be a doctor, I won't play."

"Oho," he said. "The girl wants to play doctor."

"Woman," I said.

"You want to play woman?"

"Please," I said, putting a hand over his mouth. "Please, please, please don't make me laugh. You know what stomach muscles feel like after you've been poisoned? You know what chest muscles feel like when you've been struggling to breathe?"

He put a hand on a very personal part of my body. "You know what Theadora Kozak feels like when she's too weak to resist?" I yawned. "I'm not sure I've ever had a woman respond to me that way," he said.

"Don't take it personally. I'm not at my best. Another time I'm sure desire would course through me like waves of lava from an active volcano."

"I love it when you talk dirty."

"That's not dirty. That's poetic. Did you bring anything to eat?"

"Sorry. In my haste to reach your side I forgot to stop at Dunkin' Donuts."

"I forgive you. I wonder if the cafeteria here is open at night. If they even have a cafeteria."

"Don't ask me to go and get you something."

"Why not? Afraid it would be bad for me? Nothing could be worse than hospital food. Cold wet cereal. Soggy toast. Congealed overcooked eggs. Coffee without caffeine. Flat ginger ale. Warm juice."

"You're telling me?" he said. "I had a couple weeks of it, remember?"

"How could I forget? I lost eight pounds hanging around there myself, worrying about you."

He nuzzled the top of my head with his chin. "I'm not going to get you something because I'm not leaving you. Even though you are in serious need of a shower and shampoo, ma'am, I am sticking to you like glue."

A few hours ago I'd felt all alone in the world, longing for someone to come and take care of me. Now I had someone. And I was afraid I was losing some of my protective shell because I wasn't bristling at the notion of being watched over, I was enjoying it. I didn't want him to leave. "Hospitals should have room service, like hotels. Champagne and fresh dressings to Room three-oh-two. Chicken salad on rye and Demerol to two ten. Maybe my bodyguard could go?"

"I can ask. He seems to have been very intimidated by his boss. He may be afraid to leave."

"Tell him you promise to keep me safe."

"I do. I do," he said. He went to the door and spoke briefly with someone I couldn't see.

Alone in the bed, even for only a minute, I felt bereft.

When he came back and reported success, I burrowed into his woolly sweater and clung to him. "Don't leave me again," I said.

He pulled me close. "So, something finally scared the indomitable Thea Kozak," he said.

"It's not the first time," I told his chest. "I'll get over it."

"I know you will. You are too brave and too stubborn to stay intimidated for long."

"I'm sorry."

"Don't be."

"Did Rocky call you?"

"Everyone called me."

"What do you mean?" Morpheus was reaching for me and I was ready to tumble back into his arms, but first I needed to know what Andre meant.

"Rocky. Dorrie. Suzanne. They all said you'd be furious if you knew they'd called. I half expected your mother to call, but I don't think she knows you're here."

"She doesn't. And don't you dare call her. Not even if I relapse and it looks like I'm going to die. I'm going to sleep now. Wake me when the food comes." I closed my eyes and drifted away. A while later he woke me up and spooned chicken soup into my mouth like I was a baby bird. I think I thanked him. I don't remember. Then he tucked me in and I went back to sleep. Sometime around the crack of dawn a nurse woke me to establish for the record that I was still alive. That's one of the things hospitals do best—disturbing you whenever you try to rest in order to help you get better. So far this place had been better than most. She and Andre eyed each other warily but didn't exchange words.

The next exciting event in the life of Thea Kozak, girl detective, was the arrival of a bona fide physician. She was small, sandy-haired, freckled, and totally without a bedside manner. She had a plastic name tag on her chest identifying her as Dr. Banter. Hell of a name for a person who looked as though she'd eaten bird gravel for breakfast. She asked me how I was feeling, agreed that it was perfectly normal that I should feel awful, informed me that I'd had a very close call, and lectured me sternly about the dangers of ingesting wild plants without sufficient knowledge of their danger. "You're not the first person to mistake water hemlock for ginseng but it's a dangerous mistake," she said.

Across the room, Andre was standing by the window, his arms folded, his face impassive. It was only from his eyes that I could read his amusement as he watched to see what I would do. "Excuse me?" I said in my best affronted matron's voice.

"It was a stupid thing to do," she said.

"You should save that lecture for the person who put the stuff in my sandwich," I said.

Now it was her turn to be puzzled. "I'm sorry. I'm afraid I'm not following you," she said. She snapped my chart shut. "You'll be fine. Just get plenty of rest. Fluids. Eat lightly for the next few days. You may experience some residual anxiety and restlessness from traces of the chemical still in your body. Maybe you can get your boyfriend," she nodded in Andre's direction, "to make you some soup. You can leave as soon as the police chief has had a chance to talk to you." It was the way she said "police chief" that explained it all. She didn't have the story straight but her abrasiveness wasn't really directed at me. I was just another warm body laid out for her tender ministrations. Maybe she had had something going with Rocky and it hadn't gone well.

"From what I've seen," I told her, "he's no loss."

She stared at me. "How did you—"

"And for the record, Doctor, I was poisoned. Someone put that stuff in my food to try and kill me. I don't know whether you like to keep track of things like that or not, but it's bad form to lecture a poisoning victim about carelessness, don't you think, particularly in an age when we don't use personal tasters?" She didn't know what to say, so she didn't say anything, just turned on her heel and left.

"My, my, my," Andre said. "Aren't you in a sweet mood this morning."

"If I have ever said or done anything to mislead you into thinking I'm sweet, I apologize. And while I'm apologizing, I also apologize for being here and for dragging you away from work in the middle of the night and for getting poisoned. I honestly didn't think I was in any danger . . . I promised to be careful and I was careful. . . ."

"Hey, hey, hold it," he said. "You don't owe me any apologies."

I stared down at the ugly blue-and-white garment I was wearing. I was feeling weepy again. I knew it was only weakness. I was not turning into some soft, sweet, dependent woman just because this guy was being nice to me. I was just glad the guy was here. "How are you?" I said. His face was finally healed. He looked good. No. He looked better than good. He looked almost cheerful. As cheerful as a guy with an impassive face can look. A guy who's just had two brushes with death, has just lost a good friend, and who has a significant other who keeps getting into awful scrapes. Now that I know him well, I read his eyes. He can shut them down if he wants to. He has a terrifying ability to lock emotion off his face but today he wasn't doing that.

"I'm fine," he said. "Hungry, though. Once we get you out of here we are heading straight for the nearest diner and I am going to eat two lumberjack specials."

"This isn't exactly diner territory, Lemieux. If the houses and cars are any indication, around here they go for presentation rather than substance. Besides, you'll get fat."

"And then you won't love me?"

"And then you'll break the bed. I'll always love you, thick or thin. Anyway, I can't go anywhere until I've had a shower. And I don't have any clothes."

"Break the bed, huh? Now, there's a challenge. Once you're back on your feet that's exactly what we'll do."

"We're going to break the bed standing up?"

He nodded approvingly. "You bet. Meanwhile, I can help you with the shower," he said, leering and twirling an imaginary mustache.

"Fine. First I have to get rid of this." I held out my hand, which was still attached to tubes and bottles. I rang for the nurse, who came, protested briefly, and finally liberated my hand. I also persuaded her to give me another one of the detestable johnnys to wear like a robe so I didn't have to do the clutch and shuffle if I wanted to get out of bed. Some hospitals—and I spoke from a wealth of experience—even gave out robes these days.

I was sitting on the edge of the bed, gathering strength for the long trek across the room, when Rocky burst on the scene, shouting as usual. "Now they've broken into your car," he said. "Right there at the police station. Makes me look like an idiot. What did you have in there that someone might have wanted to steal?"

A word popped into my head. Bombastic. That was it. It wasn't that Rocky was perpetually angry, he just had a bombastic style. "My briefcase, I suppose. I hope you have it?"

"Of course I have it. Who's this?"

"My bodyguard. My personal bodyguard. Detective Andre Lemieux, this is Sedgwick Police Chief Rocky Miller."

Andre grabbed Rocky's hand and pumped it. "Thanks for calling me, Chief. She's a handful but I'd hate to lose her." Over Rocky's shoulder he made a face at me. Andre knows exactly how I feel about references that fall into the "little woman" or "my girl" category. He was doing it on purpose. He says I'm cute when I have steam coming out my ears. I'm like the woman in *Bull Durham*. I think cute is for baby ducks and kittens, not grown women.

It was clear that I wasn't going to get my shower for a while so I got back under the covers and waited while they went through the rituals of male bonding. It was worse in this case, of course, because they also had to do "cop bonding." These guys have a real affinity for each other. They'll even tolerate a complete asshole if he's a fellow cop. Or so I claim. Andre says I'm wrong but I say the evidence is all on my side.

When they'd gone through an appropriate amount of ritual, Rocky turned his attention back to me. "So, Thea, how are you feeling?"

"Like I've been worked over with a rubber hose. The doctor said it was something called water hemlock? Then she lectured me on being careless with wild plants as if I'd gone crawling through some swamp to find the thing and then eaten it voluntarily." I don't suffer fools gladly and my time in hospital emergency rooms has caused me to relegate most doctors to that category. They tend to treat me like a steak, which offends my dignity even if I did feel a little bit like a Swiss steak after it's been pounded.

"Laura?" he said. "She didn't mean anything by it. She's just not a very happy person."

"I gathered. Did you find Carol Frank?"

He shook his head. "She never came home."

Just a few words and I was dumped off the raft of happiness I shared with Andre and back into the murky world of Bucksport's problems. It felt like someone had dumped ice water on me. A chill spread through my body. I knew, with a certainty I couldn't explain, that he never would find her. Not alive, anyway. "And she isn't coming home, either," I said. "She's dead. Because she came to talk to me."

"We don't know that," Rocky said.

"*I* do."

He gave me a funny look. "What did she tell you?"

"We went over it all last night, Chief. She didn't tell me anything new. She was unsure about patient confidentiality, particularly where other living people were also involved. When we got to the part about who Laney might have slept with, other than Josh, she got nervous and thought she ought to consult school counsel again. We were just beginning to negotiate that delicate subject when she was called away to deal with a student emergency. She was supposed to get back to me after I came to see you, but, as you know, I never went back to Bucksport. Did you check on those grounds and buildings employees yet?"

"I've got someone checking this morning. Meanwhile, we need to figure out why someone wanted to kill you. I talked to that guy, Chris Fuller—the one who threatened you—but he was home sick all day yesterday, according to his girlfriend and his mother. A peculiar menage."

At that point the cop at the door ushered Dorrie in. She was carefully dressed and made up, as always, but the strain was beginning to show. She looked every year of her age and more. She came straight to me and took my hand. "I'm so sorry, Thea. This is all my fault. I should have let Rocky handle this. It's all falling apart anyway. Maybe if I hadn't tried to keep things quiet none of this would have happened." Her voice shaking, she broke off and stared at Andre. "Detective. I'm sorry. I didn't mean to ignore you." They shook hands and she immediately switched her attention back to me. "This is an awful thing to ask, after what you've been through, but can you come out to Bucksport today? If you're well enough, I mean. Peter's coming, and Curt. We need to talk about where to go from here. Rocky and I've been discussing it. We think if you keep on . . . talking to people . . . maybe the killer will . . . oh, God, how can I ask you this?"

She turned on the chief. "Rocky. This is a stupid idea. We can't ask her to come back . . . to . . . to put herself in danger again. It's inhuman! I can't believe I listened to you for even a minute, that I even considered asking Thea to risk her life to protect the reputation of a school. This whole business must be affecting my judgment." She hunched forward and buried her head in her hands, the picture of mortification.

"She'll be perfectly safe. I'll have an officer watching her every minute," he said.

"You arrogant bastard!" Andre said. "First you don't want Thea involved because she's just a woman and can't handle it, and now you want to use her as bait? I guess people don't matter to you, is that it? Whatever works to solve the case? Well, you can forget it. There's no way she's setting foot on that campus again. Not if you surround her with an entire army."

"Oh, she can handle it. She told me so. Said she'd probably solved more murders than I have. If she hadn't been so sure of herself, none of this might have happened. If she and Dorrie hadn't been so sure of themselves . . . if they'd just let me handle it in the first place—"

"You would have swept it under the rug, let that girl's killer walk away, and preened smugly about your low crime rate," Andre said.

I watched them openmouthed, thinking it was really a very short leap from macho bonding to bulls in rut, each of them equally certain they knew what was right.

"You thought it was an accident," Dorrie began. "You would have let the killer get away."

"And that would have been the end of it."

"You can't know that," she said.

"If you hadn't brought her in to stir things up, everything would have been fine," he interrupted.

I took a deep breath—a breath that reminded me of what I'd just been through in no uncertain terms—and plunged in, cutting her off. "Hold it, all of you! Rocky, you said treating it as an accident would be the end of it. The end of what? A problem for Dorrie? A troublesome investigation for Rocky? What about the victim here? What about Delany Taggert? Doesn't she matter?"

I thought about Laney's father, Jack, saw his anguished face, the big hunched shoulders, the dejected slump of his body, and heard him tell me that while his daughter hadn't been very likable, it was just a phase she was going through. I heard the love in his voice. Her father had loved her and so, in his own frenetic way, had Josh Meyer. Screwed up and manipulative though she might have been, she couldn't be discarded like an old tissue. If we in the education business had any basic duty at all, it was to remember that each of our students mattered, and to treat them that way. It was Dorrie's concern about doing things right, about taking all the necessary steps to oversee and protect the students, that had brought me in in the first place.

I wasn't sure what she wanted, or what she and Rocky meant by using me as bait, but I had enough concerns of my own that I wasn't ready to quit and walk away. Because I knew so much about it. Because I hate it when someone tries to intimidate me and scare me away. Stubbornness is one of my acknowledged character flaws. I saw this as *my* job because I'd begun it. Things were terribly wrong at Bucksport. I needed to finish gathering my data and to have a serious discussion about the results with Dorrie and her staff. Not without a cop at my side, though. I'd learned my lesson.

"No one seems to be thinking about Laney," I repeated.

"Of course we are," Dorrie said with undisguised irritation. "If you leave us, we'll still muddle along on our own and we'll get the thing done. I'm sure we're capable of getting to the bottom of this."

I thought about Bill and Kathy Donahue, still in charge of a dorm full of students, and Dorrie's ignorance of the serious nature and extent of their neglect, including Laney's long unresolved roommate conflict. I thought about Carol Frank's remark regarding Laney's promiscuity and the unaccounted-for weekend, the suggestions, increasingly plausible in light of Carol's reaction, that Laney's secret lover had been someone on the Bucksport faculty, and wondered how diligent Dorrie would be in pursuing the facts. So there was still my job to be done—a job I had by now invested a lot of myself in.

Then there was the other side. Wasn't this only a small

piece of my life? Andre didn't want me to go back to a place where I might be unsafe and he'd have to worry. He didn't want to have to go through the agony of seeing me sick or hurt anymore. I looked at him, painfully conscious of his opinion of what I should do, and of the wonderful comfort I'd derived from his presence by my side. He wasn't going to like what I was about to say. I only hoped I could make him understand. "I've got to go back. I can't leave the job half done. Dorrie needs me."

Andre's expression didn't change but his eyes were angry. I put a hand on his arm. "You know how it is, Andre. It's the same for you. I can't let someone try to kill me and walk away from it."

He pulled his arm away and held it stiffly by his side. "That's exactly what you should do," he said. "That's what a person with any sense would do. It's time to hand this over to professionals."

We might have been alone in the room for all the difference Rocky and Dorrie made. Our eyes were locked. This wasn't really a conversation about what I was going to do next. It was about the nature of our relationship. About control and respect and giving each other space and supporting each other's work and all the things we struggled with. About the difference between caring and control. About how much space you can give someone else and still get what you need from the relationship. About not just loving each other but respecting what we each did and understanding the demands it placed on us. About what you can give up for love and what you can't.

Twice lately I'd had to live with the heart-stopping fear that he was in danger and risking death because of his job. It had focused my love and my fears very clearly, but it had never occurred to me to suggest he quit and find something safe to do. Being a cop was what he did. Would he give me the same understanding?

I didn't know how he was going to react. At the moment when I needed him most I was taking a position that might drive him away. He couldn't help feeling protective. He didn't want to lose me, couldn't bear to see me hurt. I'd already put him through a lot of that and now I was asking for more. "If you were in the middle of something and things got rough, you wouldn't walk away. You'd seize it in your teeth like a pit bull and hang on until the thing was solved," I said.

"But I'm a cop," he said. "It's my job. It's Rocky's job. Let him do it. Please, Thea . . ." His voice sank almost to a whisper. "Do you remember what you said when we were in San Francisco? About David. About letting yourself care about someone. About not being able to stand the pain of losing someone again?" He waited until I acknowledged that I remembered. "Well, it goes both ways. This is the third time I've stood by your hospital bed and waited to see if you'd be okay."

"The first time you thought you were waiting to question a careless drunk—"

"Twice, then. Look, this isn't about keeping score. I just can't stand the idea of losing you. I can't go through this. It's not that I want some sweet little stay-at-home woman. I just can't take this . . . this terrible fear that one of these days I'm going to get a call and find you dead! You're not even a cop. You're a consultant to all these nice private schools. I don't understand how you keep getting into these situations. You want a lot of slack, I'll give you a lot of slack. I don't complain when you work too hard or are away a couple nights a week or fall asleep over dinner. All I'm asking is that when things get too dangerous you back off and let the professionals take over. Is that too much to ask?"

Andre angry is something to behold and he was angrier than I'd ever seen him. His sallow skin was flushed, his eyes narrowed, his mouth a thin, hard line. I was panting from the intensity of my own feeling. Every breath hurt like hell and I was clutching my stomach, hoping I wouldn't be sick again. I loved this man and I knew that what he was asking was reasonable. I also knew there was no way I could make him understand that this wasn't just a job anymore. It was personal. Someone had tried to kill me. If I was going to let them intimidate me, if I was going to give up and go home and be safe because things had gotten scary, then I might as well just give up and become the sweet little housewife that part of Andre wanted.

And then there was Laney. She might have been difficult and dishonest and manipulative but she had also been a confused, needy, vulnerable kid. Someone had used her—even if she'd been the initiator or seducer, adults are still responsible for protecting kids—and thrown her away. Somebody had to stand up for her.

"Please, Thea," he said. "Please do this for me. Look, in case this is why you think you have to stick with it, Laney's not Carrie. You don't have to be the champion of every lost soul in the world just because you couldn't save your sister."

"This isn't about Carrie. It's about me."

"You didn't even know the girl."

"You don't know your victims. Does that mean you don't care?"

"It's different. I'm a cop. It's my job. Finding out who killed Delaney Taggert isn't your job." He was yelling at me now.

"Someone tried to kill me because I'm getting too close."

"My point exactly. That's why I'm asking you to give this up!"

My mother says I've always been too stubborn for my own good. That I make things unnecessarily hard on myself because of a misguided sense of right and wrong. She spent years trying to instill by example, coercion, and sometimes physical force, a docile, ladylike nature in me. It didn't work. I'm still stubborn, pigheaded, determined, and absolutely convinced that I have to do what I believe is right, even if it has the effect of cutting off my nose to spite my face. Knowing what I knew and feeling what I felt, I couldn't fold my tent and slink away, not even for love.

"I can't quit," I said. "Please don't ask me to."

"I already did," he said. "I guess that's no, isn't it? I was being too romantic, wasn't I, thinking you might choose what I wanted instead of your almighty principles? You'd risk your life for some dead girl you never even knew but you won't do anything for me. Okay. I get the message. I understand. You've got to do what you've got to do. No one is going to get their hooks into you, tell you what to do or tie you down, are they?"

"It would be different if I was a cop, right?" I interrupted. "Then if I said I just had to do this you'd understand? Then it would be okay for me to have to do something even if it was dangerous? Then it would be all right for me to be mad that someone had considered me expendable!"

He picked up his small gym bag from the floor at the foot of my bed. "Maybe the late, sainted David Kozak was lucky. He died before he had a chance to find out who you really are. Or maybe you would have done this for him?" His angry gaze swept from me to Rocky and Dorrie, uncomfortable witnesses to the scene. "If something happens to her, please don't call me, okay? I don't want to know. You don't even have to bother to drive to Maine, Thea. I'll pack your stuff and ship it. You really weren't living there anyway."

He left. I went after him, unable to let him leave like that. I followed him down the corridor, using the wall for support. "Andre, wait. . . ." He turned and waited, a hopeful look on his face. "Can't we talk about this? I'll be very careful. I won't take any chances. . . ."

I watched him close down again. "I was hoping you were going to say you'd changed your mind. There's nothing else to talk about." He turned and walked away.

I leaned against the wall, watching his broad back

moving away from me. My fingers had danced along that rigid spine, knew every inch of that skin. I wished I could rush after him and give him what he wanted. *Please,* I thought, *please turn around and look back at me.* A door closed behind him and he was gone.

CHAPTER 15

IT'S NOT ANATOMICALLY correct to describe the heart as breaking. That's fiction. What was real was the incredible pain I felt, watching him walk away, like being slowly gutted with a dull knife. Like my spirit screaming for him to change his mind and come back. As the poet said, "I could not love thee, dear, so much, Loved I not honor more." It was small consolation right now.

I found the nearest bathroom, threw up, and dragged myself back to my room. Dorrie and Rocky were standing there, looking like guilty children. "I'm sorry, Thea," Dorrie said. "I had no idea . . . I never would have suggested it if I knew it would cause this much trouble for you. Has he gone?"

"He's gone." My own words. They reverberated through my body like echoes in an empty room. Confirmed what had just happened. If I lived that long, I was going to be sitting alone on Christmas Day with two baseball gloves and no one to play with. By choice. Because a woman's gotta do what a woman's gotta do. I couldn't stand up any longer. I got back into bed. I would have pulled the covers over my head and shrieked, but I wasn't alone.

"Look," Rocky said, "you don't have to do this. You

don't wanna ruin your life just because of some consulting job. That's a good man you've got there—"

"I know that."

"Not worth losing over some dead teenager—"

"Oh, shut up. Both of you. You've got what you wanted. I'll come out there, like I said. I'll work with you and we'll keep on plugging until we've licked this thing, but right now I need to be alone for a while. Please." I was weak and shaking and the tears behind my eyes were pressing and I was holding on to control so hard it hurt. They just stood and stared at me helplessly. Infuriatingly stupid and kind, though neither of them was stupid and Rocky wasn't normally kind. "Go away! Go find me some clothes. Some food. Shampoo." I buried my face in my pillow and refused to look at them. I'd stood my ground. Gotten my own way. I was just terribly sad.

"Come on, Rocky, out!" Dorrie ordered. At the door she paused. "Suzanne called. She's coming over with some clothes. We'll go find you some breakfast."

"Real food," I said. "Not hospital stuff." At last they went away and left me in peace. I lay in my bed and rested, eyes closed, the picture of the docile patient, but my mind was racing on to the job ahead. That was my nature. When David died, I took refuge in work. I could always do it again. I wrapped some emotional strings around my shattered spirit and took stock of the physical plant. I still felt absolutely awful. There were occasional flutters of yesterday's anxiety and my entire digestive system was wrecked but being able to breathe without feeling as if I was drowning was such a miracle all the rest paled in comparison. The idea that my own body could try to drown me, the memory of strangling when I was surrounded by breathable air, still terrified me.

The fancy medical term for it was pulmonary edema—fluids leaking back through the alveoli and pooling in the lungs. It had felt to me like a rising tide and I'd been helpless before it. Breathing, struggling, gasping for air, the tide kept on coming in. I don't like being helpless and last night I'd been helpless because of the workings of my own body. Like Laney, I'd been drowning. The experience had left me with a connection to Laney Taggert I hadn't had before. The flash of recognition I'd had in Rocky's office stayed with me.

I'd seen Laney drowning in that murky pond as clearly as if I'd been there. That was part of why I couldn't just walk away from this thing. I'd spent a week getting to know Laney. Talking about her, thinking about her, reading about her, and then her killer had given me the final push—trying to make me die like her. Inadvertently, instead of killing me or scaring me off, the killer had bonded me with Laney and left me furious. No one was going to kill us and get away with it.

Meanwhile, I was hungry and dirty and cold and tired enough to go back to sleep. Cold from the shock of knowing that someone on the Bucksport campus was a killer who would kill again and again to avoid discovery. Chilled at the thought of the pleasant, normal, caring woman Carol Frank had been, now dead because she'd been Laney Taggert's counselor. And I had no doubt that she was dead. Why had the killer waited so long? What had I said or done, and to whom, that had triggered the attack on me and Carol's disappearance?

I went back through yesterday's itinerary. What had I done? Gotten the list from Lori. Made some phone calls. Talked with Russ Hamlin. An enigmatic character. If this were a novel and not real life, he'd be my prime suspect. He was too confiding and too provocative. Or Bill Donahue, so closed and defensive, so righteous and judgmental. What did he have to hide? Carol had been a welcome relief after the two of them. I tried to recall who had brought me the sandwich but I couldn't remember. Carol and I had been talking and then Lori had interrupted us to tell Carol there was an emergency. Had she handed me the sandwich then?

Why had the killer waited a week to go after Carol?

And why go after her at all? How could the killer have known Carol was coming to talk to me? Had he not known about Laney's visits to Carol Frank? Assumed that the records were confidential? That made me wonder who knew that Carol Frank had consulted with the school's attorneys about confidentiality and whether it was relevant. More questions for Dorrie.

At that point Suzanne finally arrived with my clothes, looking perfectly pulled together and disgustingly healthy. She made me feel more tired and hungrier and dirtier than ever. "If you weren't my partner," she announced, "I'd fire you. I cannot keep finding you in hospitals like this. You know I hate hospitals."

"While I love them, right?"

"Paul sends his love," she said. "He wants to know if you need blood?"

"Not this time."

She marched up to the bed and bent to kiss me. "Whew!" she said, straightening up. "You are a mess. I think this is the first time in months I haven't been jealous of you. Sorry I took so long but just as I was leaving, Junior blew his breakfast all over me. I've been up since five. The kid is definitely a morning person. I've already read *Pat the Bunny* and *Goodnight Moon* five times each. You really want a socially useful job, write some new children's books. Most of them are awful."

She started pulling things out of the bag and put them on the bed. "Here's a robe, some underwear, toiletries. I brought a nightgown in case they wouldn't let you go but I guess you don't need that. I'll put them in the bathroom. You've got to take a shower." She hurried off to arrange things, still not letting me get a word in. She was almost as hard to live with as I was. Stubborn, used to having her own way, and a confirmed workaholic. That's why we made such good partners.

"Guess I'll take that shower now."

But Suzanne wasn't quite ready to let me go. "Where's Andre?" she asked.

"He was here," I said, "but he got into a fit of male protectiveness. We had a disagreement and he left."

"Meaning," my partner said, "that he told you to leave the whole Bucksport fiasco to the proper authorities and you said no one was going to try and kill you and get away with it, right?"

"That was part of it."

She held the back of her hand to her forehead and closed her eyes. "Don't tell me," she said. "Let me guess. You also said you had a job to do and it wasn't finished."

"You know me too well."

"I was afraid that might happen."

"What? That I'd be stubborn or he'd walk out?"

"Yes," she said.

I shrugged, elaborately casual, only awakening the pain-carrying nerves in about a third of my body. "Anyway, thanks for calling him. Until he stalked out in high dudgeon it was nice to have him around."

"He'll stalk back in," she said. "I'm sure he will."

"I'm not so sure," I said. "I think he gets enough violence and death at work. He doesn't need it in his personal life. This time he'll probably go find one of those nice, docile, stay-at-home women that most of his friends have married. The kind he always says he doesn't want and always wishes I was. Or a nice tough female cop who is allowed to get into trouble." I remembered Andre at the hotel in San Francisco. Thought of the solemn boys and the wayward girls running around on our mountaintop. Took a deep breath and packed all those feelings away for another time. They hurt too much. I wasn't ready to contemplate what I'd given up.

I glided with leviathan grace across the room and into the bathroom. Alone in the sterile, sanitized cubicle, I struggled out of the johnnies, dropped the detestable things onto the floor, and gave my sore, miserable body up to the mercies of hot water and soap. I managed to get myself reasonably clean and wash my hair but there was no way I could hold my arms up long enough to comb out the tangles.

I leaned against the sink, staring at my underwear. Putting it on seemed an almost insurmountable obstacle in my feeble state. Someone knocked on the door.

"Need any help?" Suzanne asked.

"In a minute." I put on the underwear and robe and then sat on the toilet seat while she combed out my hair. Suzanne was much gentler than my mother. Not once did she complain that she was going to cut it all off if I didn't hold still. But what it reminded me of was not my mother. It was a night at the Florios, when Rosie had combed my hair. When I'd talked with Andre on the phone and woken the next morning to find him in terrible danger. Other people's lives were never like this. Suzanne dressed me while I obediently stooped and turned and bent to order.

"You're more fun than a Barbie doll," she said. I didn't know how to respond to that. A few minutes later I emerged from the bathroom a whole new woman. Elegant in black stirrup pants, a long red-and-black tunic sweater, and shiny black tooled-leather cowboy boots that Suzanne just knew I needed. Every man's dream girl, as long as I didn't open my mouth. As long as I was, as my great-grandmother used to say, "biddable." It meant docile and willing to take direction.

Rocky, who had returned during my ablutions, stared and whistled. "I can't believe it. Yesterday you almost died and today you look like a million dollars."

"It just goes to show that you can't keep a good woman down, Chief."

"I guess not. Dorrie's gone on ahead. I'll drive you out to Bucksport when you're ready. We've got someone coming to fix your car window. Should be ready by noon."

"I'll drive her," Suzanne said. I could have hugged her. I far preferred her company to Rocky's.

Fortified by a breakfast that only slightly defied the advice of my caring doctor—Rocky and Dorrie having recognized, though I had not, that my stomach wasn't ready for serious eating—I went back to Bucksport to go to work. I should have gone home to bed but my poisoning and Carol Frank's disappearance had changed everything. I felt a sense of urgency I hadn't felt before, when my main goal had been the competent completion of a professional task. I didn't go without trepidation. Not to a place where someone had gone to great lengths to kill me in a terrible way. I tried to tell myself that it was like getting back on a horse after being thrown, but as I walked down the long, echoing corridor from the front door to Dorrie's office, I was trembling.

Lori was hunched over her desk, staring intently at her screen. She jumped up when I came in. "Oh, God! Thea, I'm so sorry. I mean, it was me that brought you the sandwich but you know I wouldn't . . . I mean, never in a million years would I do something to hurt you . . . I had no idea . . . I found it on my desk and just assumed food services had sent it. . . ." Her voice trailed off and she just stood there, looking ashamed. "You do believe me, don't you?"

I tried to reassure her but she was feeling too guilty to accept reassurance, guilty and shocked. Everyone's foundations had been rocked by the past week. She followed me into Dorrie's office. It was the same cast of characters who had been there on Sunday. Dave Holdorf, looking pale and subdued, Curt Sawyer, peevish behind his red face and redder nose, Peter Van Deusen, and Rocky and Dorrie, as well as a new face, a balding, rounded man whose feet didn't reach the floor and who sat with his hands clasped over his stomach and smiled at us all anxiously. Lori hovered in the background, too restless to keep still, looking terrified. Everyone else accepted her offer of coffee, but much as I wanted it, I knew my stomach wasn't ready for an acid infusion, so I asked for tea. "Just water and a tea bag, no foreign substances," I said, trying to lighten things up. My jest fell flat.

"Okay," Dorrie said, "everyone knows what has happened. Yesterday someone tried to poison Thea by putting water hemlock in her sandwich. Luckily, she only ate a few bites, otherwise she wouldn't be with us today. Also, Carol Frank is missing. Yesterday, in her interview with Thea, Carol admitted she had some potentially important information concerning Laney Taggert's relationships. She wanted to consult Peter before she revealed them. They were interrupted by a student crisis and now both Carol and her records concerning Laney have disappeared."

She indicated the quiet stranger. "This is Dr. Tuff from our science department. He is with us in case anyone has questions about water hemlock. And this is Suzanne Merritt, Thea's partner, who is here to advise us on public relations issues."

"The PR is simple," Curt Sawyer said, "we just keep Chip Barrett off the campus. As for what happened to Thea, why the heck does anyone need to know about that anyway? If I'd been sick all over the police chief's office, I sure as heck wouldn't want anyone to know about it."

"Thank you, Curt," Dorrie said. "I'm sure we can rely on you to keep Barrett away. In fact, you'd better go and attend to that now."

"Maybe we should just give him a little of that . . . what did you call it . . . water hemlock?"

Dorrie ignored the comment. "Also, we need a lock for Thea's door and a new lock on Carol's office, and you'd better send someone over there to do some clearing up. Jeannie Duncan is over there trying to make sense of the records but drawers have been pulled out and cabinets overturned."

"None of my guys are file clerks, Dorrie. You know that."

She folded her arms and gave him a look that would have wilted a more sensitive person. "Just for the heavy lifting. Real guy stuff," she said sarcastically. "Maybe you haven't realized it, Curt, but we're in the middle of a tough situation here. The way we're going to get through it is cooperation. Working together. This isn't a question of whether something is guy stuff or girl stuff or in someone's job description. There are things that need to be done." Her voice was calm and level but I could hear the anger simmering behind it.

Curt got up and stomped to the door. "Oh, spare me the touchy-feely stuff," he said. "And," he pointed at Rocky, "tell your boyfriend to stop nosing around my people. It makes 'em nervous."

We all stared in astonishment at the closed door. "Peter," Dorrie said decisively, "I've had it with him. Figure out how we can fire him without bringing the MCAD, EEOC, ADEA, or any other tenderhearted cluster of initials down on us. Now, Rocky . . . you and Dave and Thea figure out how you want to proceed today. Peter and I are going to meet with Suzanne." She rubbed her forehead wearily. "I just have to hope we're going to find Carol Frank alive." Everyone nodded. We all wanted that to happen. No one was optimistic though no one seemed as sure as I that she was dead.

"Before we go, I have a question for Peter," I said. "I understand Carol Frank consulted you about the appropriateness of discussing Laney Taggert with me?" He nodded. "How did you communicate?" He looked puzzled. "I mean, did you speak on the phone? In person? Was there any written communication?"

"She phoned me. We spoke briefly and then I did some research and faxed a letter stating my opinion that it was all right for her to reveal her conversations with Laney to you."

"Did you send the fax to Carol?"

"No. To Dorrie. Why?"

"I'm trying to figure out what triggered the killer to go after Carol and the counseling office records almost a week later instead of right away. Lori, do you remember when it came in?"

"Sometime yesterday morning. I went over to the dining hall to deliver some things for Dorrie and when I came back it was on my desk. I don't know who took it off the machine but we're pretty informal around here. If something needs to be done, anyone might do it."

"How long was it sitting on your desk?"

She shrugged. "Maybe half an hour, maybe a little less. I'm not sure."

"I took it off the machine," Dave said, "and put it on Lori's desk."

"Even though it was a sensitive communication from your attorney, you didn't put it in a folder or cover it in some way? You just left it there for everyone to see?"

"This is a school," he said defensively. "I'm not used to living like someone is always looking over my shoulder." His hurt look said much more than his words.

"I'm sorry, Dave. It was a natural mistake. I'm just trying to find out who might have seen it. Something happened that got the killer worried—about me and about Carol."

The phone rang. Lori answered it quietly and then looked at Rocky. "It's your office," she said.

"I'll take it at your desk," he said. We waited in silence, one shared, unspoken thought filling the room. When he came back, we watched him as expectantly as hungry pets watch the food dish. "I've got some more bad news, I'm afraid," he said. We waited for him to tell us that Carol Frank had been found. Instead, he said, "We finished running the check on Curt Sawyer's people . . . that list you gave me yesterday, Thea. I'm not surprised that Chris Fuller, the guy who threatened you, didn't want anyone looking at him too closely. He's got a criminal record."

"That damned Curt Sawyer!" Dorrie said. "What did this guy Fuller do?"

"Rape of a minor under fourteen. Indecent assault. Assault and battery. He got the job because he's Uncle Curtie's nephew."

"Just the sort of person you want to have access to a

whole campus full of teenage girls," Peter Van Deusen said.

The pencil Dorrie was holding between her fingers snapped, the two pieces dropping unnoticed onto the desk. "If Chip Barrett gets his hands on this, we might as well all slit out throats," she said. "There's not enough damage control in the entire world."

We all sat in stunned silence as a day that had begun bleak and terrible got worse. "There's more," Rocky said. "My guys went out to his house to talk to him. He's disappeared."

CHAPTER 16

DAVE AND ROCKY and I adjourned to Dave's office to plan my day. Now that we knew more about Chris Fuller, there were a lot of specific questions I wanted to ask about him. I also wanted to get to the bottom of Bill and Kathy Donahue's strange behavior, talk with Josh one more time, and see if there weren't some things Chas Drucker wasn't telling me, since Russ Hamlin had told me he was Laney's confidant. I told Dave who I wanted to see and he shook his head.

"But these are people you've already talked to."

"That's why I need to talk to them again, Dave. They're the ones who knew her best. You might as well put Russ Hamlin on the list, too."

"They aren't going to like it, especially Bill and Kathy. She's really taken a dislike to you."

"Good thing this isn't a popularity contest, Dave." Dave hadn't looked well since I arrived and today he looked terrible. There were ugly dark circles under his eyes and he'd cut himself shaving more than once. "I'm sorry. I don't mean to sound so harsh. I don't want to upset people any more than you do, but we've got a crisis on our hands."

"I know. Believe me, I know," he said, and went to confer with Lori about setting up appointments, leaving me alone with Rocky. Rocky had a lot of questions of his own for each of them but we agreed that questioning them together would not be a good idea.

As soon as Dave was gone, Rocky started to talk. I guess my determination to go on after such a close call had convinced him, in a way that nothing else could, that I was tough enough to handle the job. "You sure you're okay? Sure you can handle this?" he asked.

"You sound like my father, you know that? You also know the answer to your own questions. No, I'm not okay and no, I'm not sure I can handle this, but what choice do I have? This isn't optional, like a lunch date, this is life and death. Including my own. What am I going to do, go home and crawl into bed and let someone else handle this? Somebody wants me dead, too, remember. How do I know they won't try again? Maybe the murderer makes house calls." I said it lightly but it reminded me, as I said it, of a midnight intruder who not so long ago had dropped a gruesome hunting knife on my back deck. Bad guys do make house calls. And car calls. And hospital visits. In my experience, the safest place to be was at work.

"Very funny. Now, I'll have a uniformed officer watching your door at all times. Not right outside. That would spook people. And if you go anywhere, even to the ladies' room, you let him know. I will personally check your lunch and I guarantee there will be no exotic additives."

"Soup would be nice."

"Soup it is, then. Straight from the can." He hesitated. "Thea . . . you know this is dangerous—" I started to say something but he held up a hand. "No. Wait. Let me finish. I know you're brave or you wouldn't have come back here today. I also know you're stubborn, or you wouldn't have let Andre go. Just listen to Uncle Rocky for a few minutes, okay? We're letting you go on asking questions because that's what Dorrie wants and because we hope it may smoke out the bad guys. That doesn't mean I like it or that I've changed my mind that this is police business. So please, do your job without doing anything foolish. I don't want you wandering off somewhere to play Thea Kozak, girl detective, do you hear me? No wild-goose chases. No heroics. None. Nada. You hear me? If the murderer shows up or calls you and invites you to tea, or to a stroll by the pond, or to a private viewing of Carol Frank's body, call us. Let the police handle it. I don't want to have to explain to Detective Andre Lemieux how I let something happen to you—"

"He *said* he didn't want to know," I interrupted.

"In a pig's eye. You two were made for each other. Forty, fifty years from now you're still going to be having cataclysmic fights. He'll be back or"—he shrugged—"or you'll go after him. Meanwhile, I've gotta see that nothing happens to you."

"Right," I agreed. "Very important thing, protecting another cop's woman. Something you'd better take very seriously." Andre would have found me very cute.

"Oh, don't get your dander up. You know what I mean."

"Sure. I know what you mean." I changed the subject to another of my peeves. "You didn't even believe Laney Taggert was murdered."

"Not at first, no. Now I'm just trying to keep more people from getting killed. Look, I've gotta go to work." Rocky's face was red but he was keeping his temper. "The guy who's watching you this morning is Joe Hennessey. Officer Joe Hennessey. He's a nice guy. Don't give him a hard time just 'cuz you're peeved with me, okay? You might even want to talk with him. He was the first officer on the scene when they found Laney Taggert's body. I'm going to go look for Carol, or at least her car. And we're checking the pond for that duffle bag. See if you can get someone to tell you where Laney went Columbus Day weekend. If we can find the place, maybe we can find the guy."

"I've tried. No one knows."

"Someone knows—the person she went away with. And Carol Frank. I'd bet a hundred dollars that they're not the only ones. Never knew a teenage girl who could keep her mouth shut." He levered himself up out of his chair and headed for the door, his mind already on his next task.

"Rocky?" He hesitated, half turned toward me. "What about Merri Naigler? Do you think she's in danger?"

"Does she know something?"

"I think so. Laney was her best friend. They'd arranged the abortion together. Laney was supposed to be staying with her that weekend."

"I'll talk to her mother," he said, and left, leaving me feeling as dissatisfied as if the waiter had cleared away my dinner when it was only half-eaten. At least today we'd fenced with blunt swords. A few more decades and we'd be downright civil.

Outside the window, a brilliant sun was trying hard to melt the snow that had fallen overnight. A noisy group of students in bright jackets were sculpting an elaborate creature in the circle. In the background there was the ugly scraping sound of shovels on asphalt. I heaved myself up—and heaved was the right word, my body was doing nothing easily today—and went to my office, lugging my briefcase with me. The first thing I did was take out my notes from interviewing Carol Frank and reread them, hoping I'd find something I'd missed.

There was a knock on the door. I expected either Lori or Dave, but it was Ellie Drucker, carrying a steaming mug, her face solemn and concerned. "I am terribly sorry, dear," she said. "I heard about your awful accident. This is peppermint tea to help settle your stomach." My hesitation must have shown on my face because she quickly added, "I don't blame you for being skeptical, after yesterday. I brought the bag from home this morning and I just made the tea myself two minutes ago with Lori Leonard as a witness." She set the mug in front of me and sat down on the edge of the chair. "I can't believe what's happening. Bucksport has always been such a wonderful place . . . it's been home for Chas and me for almost twenty-five years, and now, suddenly, it seems like danger is lurking behind every bush. Do you think they're going to catch this person?"

"I hope so." The tea smelled delicious. I thanked her for bringing it and was about to take a sip when the phone rang. It was Lori, ready to review the day's schedule.

"I won't keep you," Ellie said, rising swiftly from the chair. She was very agile, despite her weight. She left so quietly I almost didn't hear her go but maybe that was because I was distracted by what Lori had to tell me.

"You can see Kathy and Bill right now," she said, "but they'd like you to come to them because Kathy isn't feeling very well. After that you can see Russ Hamlin down in the green room—he's going to be there all morning—and I haven't found Chas Drucker yet but I left a message with his daughter, Angie. She says he's out running some errands and should be back soon. I can call you over at Bill and Kathy's and let you know when I've heard from him, okay?" Yeah, right. I felt really sorry for Kathy Donahue. No one should have to go outside on a winter day when they aren't feeling well.

"That's fine, Lori. Can you call Kathy and Bill and tell them I'm on my way?"

I opened the door and summoned Officer Hennessey, who was gazing longingly out the window. "Wish you were playing in the snow, Officer?" I said.

"With my kids," he said. "They love making snow forts and my wife hates going out in the cold."

"They can't go out by themselves?"

He shook his head. "Jed is four and Caitlin is three. They need a grown-up just to roll the balls. . . ."

"I'm sorry. I wish you could be with them. You're going to get bored out of your mind today, I'm afraid."

"Better bored than the alternative," he said grimly. "I've been a cop eight years. It doesn't get any easier, seeing what people will do to each other."

"You were there when they found Laney Taggert?" I picked up my coat and started struggling into it. He quickly grabbed it and helped.

"We going somewhere?"

"Over to Oakley Hall and then over to the Stannard Theater building. You need to tell somebody?"

He already had a radio out and was giving the information to someone back at police central. His leather jacket creaked like a saddle when he shoved the radio back and picked up my briefcase. "Ready," he said. "Is there someplace where we're going that I can loiter inconspicuously?"

"There's no place on this campus where *you* can be inconspicuous, Officer. You'll just have to hang around the halls and get stared at."

He shrugged. "I'm used to it. You'd be amazed at the way people stare at us."

No, I wouldn't, I thought. I was used to it, too. His remark brought to mind my brother Michael's nasty inquiry about whether I'd gotten over my obsession with guys in uniforms. They'd all met Andre several times and yet no one in my family seemed to have noticed that he didn't wear a uniform. Michael could be such a jerk. I wouldn't mind missing Christmas with Michael and his wife, Sonia, even if it meant, as it now appeared, that I'd be playing catch by myself on the beach. Maybe listening to "Rockin' Around the Christmas Tree" on my portable tape recorder. Maybe I'd just spend the day in bed. Maybe I'd give myself a festive bottle of bourbon and drink the whole thing.

He cleared his throat as a tactful attempt to recall me to the present. "The chief said you were interested in what it was like when they found her?"

"That's right." The sun off the snow was blindingly bright. I had to squint to see. My sunglasses were in the car and the car was back in town, hopefully even now receiving the tender ministrations of a glass installer. I'm hard on cars, hard on clothes, hard on men. One tough gal. Phooey. Today I felt as tender as a marshmallow.

"I was the first one on the scene, about ten minutes after we got the call from Sawyer's people. Sawyer and a couple other guys were out on the ice. I approached them, determined that there was someone under the ice, or at least, some brightly colored cloth under the ice, and that the person, assuming it was a person, could not be reached without equipment, which I didn't have. I radioed that information to dispatch, who informed me that EMTs and the fire department were en route to the scene. Within ten or twelve minutes the firefighters were there with grappling hooks. They were able to retrieve the victim, and the paramedics started trying to revive her."

"They tried to revive her, even though she'd been missing all night?"

"No one knew that. It's standard procedure. People can be revived after significant periods of time underwater, you know. We didn't learn until later that she'd been missing all night." He hesitated, reluctant to say any more.

"What was she wearing?"

"A heavy jacket, very bright, lots of colors. You know the type, all the kids have 'em. That's probably what killed her, her jacket got waterlogged and pulled her down. A long skirt, black tights. No shoes. Maybe she'd kicked them off."

"No hat?"

"No hat. That coat and skirt made her look big, but she was just a little bitty thing. Poor kid."

I liked Hennessey a lot. He had a refreshing openness unlike everyone else, who saw Laney's death as the beginning of their own problems. He simply seemed sorry she was dead. "Did you find a duffel bag anywhere around?"

"No. They're looking for it in the pond this morning."

"Rick McTeague says when he passed the pond that

there were two sets of footprints going out to the ice and one set coming back. Did you see those footprints?"

"I wish I had. You've got to understand . . . when Sawyer's people went out there . . . when I went out there . . . when the EMTs and firefighters went out there . . . we were all trying to save somebody. I don't recall seeing two sets of prints . . . but it would have been hard. Sawyer's people had tramped all over the place by the time I got there. You've also got to realize . . . I guess I can tell you this, we're all on the same side here . . . McTeague is kind of a nutcase. Guy I know had the brakes fail on his car. He slammed into a tree and McTeague shows up at the hospital and asks him all these questions about what it felt like to be out of control and know he was going to crash. The man is sick. McTeague, I mean, not my friend. Even went and took pictures of the car and the tree."

I agreed with Officer Hennessey. It was sick. It was exactly the sort of thing my fellow reporters used to do. On the other hand, I wished McTeague had taken pictures of the footprints. They would have been enormously helpful to us now. "If that bag is in the pond, how will you find it?"

"Grappling hooks, just like we found her."

"Did anyone look through her room?"

"After we heard she was pregnant. Didn't find anything. We asked her roommate if anything was missing but she didn't seem to know. I got the impression she didn't like the dead girl much."

The conversation brought us to the doors of Oakley Hall, a nice, sturdy, Georgian building with a slightly battered, lived-in quality. There was a big plastic-draped hump of bikes on the porch, a few pairs of cross-country skis leaning against the walls, and just inside, a small array of shoes and boots lined the walls. Straight ahead was a staircase and the sound of feet and voices echoed down to us. We went past the staircase and I knocked on the Donahues' door. Across the hall there was a lounge with a television set, several couches, and a piano. "I'll wait in here," Hennessey said, handing me my briefcase.

Bill Donahue opened the door, a sour, wary look on his face. "I'm going to tell you right now," he said, "that you aren't to do or say anything which will upset my wife."

"I'm not sure I can do that, Mr. Donahue," I said. "This is about murder and attempted murder. Those are inherently upsetting topics. Are you going to let me in or should I go and get Chief Miller and let him ask the questions?"

Reluctantly he stepped aside and let me in. Kathy Donahue was sitting across the room in a rocking chair, her feet on a hassock, wrapped in a soft pink mohair throw. Obviously she believed pink was her color. Her hair needed washing and was held back by a cheap plastic headband. She didn't get up, extend a hand, or say hello. She just sat and stared at me, her lips set in a thin line. "Now what do you want?" she demanded.

I looked around for a movable chair. There were none nearby and I was too tired myself to do this interview standing up. Bill Donahue, his arms folded over his chest, stood behind his wife and matched his glare to hers. Ignoring their determined hostility, I said, "I'm afraid I'm not very well myself today. Could you get me a chair?" He responded grudgingly but was too polite to refuse a direct request. He went into the other room and came back with a faded director's chair, which he shoved in my direction. I sat down, took my notes of their previous interviews out, and went to war.

"Other than Merri, who were Laney's friends?"

They looked at each other as though the question puzzled them. Kathy shrugged. "The theater crowd," Bill said.

I had had that answer before. "Can you give me some names?"

"Maybe Nadia?" Bill suggested.

"Nadia Soren?" He nodded.

"Anyone else?" This time they both shrugged.

"Where did Laney Taggert go on Columbus Day week-end?"

"To the beach," Bill said.

"I don't know," Kathy said.

"She filled out a card and attached a note from her father. Did she go away with her parents?"

"I don't know," Kathy said. "I guess she did."

"Her father says she didn't. Was she here on campus?"

"No," Bill said, "she went to the beach."

"How do you know?"

He shrugged rudely. "They all did. A whole bunch of them."

"If you knew that, then why did Laney go through the elaborate charade of getting the note from her father?"

"They all did," Bill said again. "We couldn't let them go off with some teenaged older sister."

"But you did."

"On paper, I mean," he said lamely. This was something else besides sign-out cards they were getting lax about. I made a note for my report, holding back the follow-up questions that jumped to mind—questions I'd have to ask as part of my job. I didn't want to alienate them yet.

"Laney's mother said that her daughter was very fond of you, Kathy. That you were her confidante. Did Laney tell you that she was pregnant?"

"No!" They both said together.

"You didn't notice anything unusual about her? She wasn't unusually tired, didn't have morning sickness, anything like that?" Again a collective no. "None of the other girls suggested to you that Laney might be pregnant?" They shook their heads. "What about Josh?"

Kathy turned and looked back over her shoulder at Bill. He shook his head. She looked back at me, her lips pressed firmly together, and said nothing.

"So it was Josh who told you she was pregnant?"

"Why would he do that?" Bill Donahue asked.

"So you did know she was pregnant. Did you talk to her about it?"

"That's none of your business," Bill said.

"That's precisely my business. Did she come to you to find out what she should do?"

"She didn't want her parents to find out," Bill said. "We told her to go see Carol Frank."

"We told her about a good maternity home," Kathy said. "She didn't want to keep the baby."

"Was it Carol who advised her about the procedure for obtaining an abortion?" Neither of them responded.

"Whose baby was it?"

"We don't know," Bill said. "We don't know anything that can help you figure out what happened to Laney. Now, please, go away and leave us alone."

"Did you know that Laney was planning to have an abortion? Did she tell you? Did Josh tell you?" Once again they stonewalled me with their collective silence. There was no sense in holding back for fear I might offend them into not cooperating. They had no intention of cooperating. "What did Russ Hamlin mean when he said Kathy had been neglecting Laney Taggert because of her own troubles? Is that what you're afraid of? That someone will accuse you of neglecting her? It's a little late to worry about that now. This is no time to be thinking of yourselves. We need to know what happened."

"Our troubles are none of your business. Russ Hamlin is nothing but a rabble-rousing gossip who doesn't know enough to keep things to himself," Bill said. "Go away and leave us alone."

But Kathy was determined to defend herself. "I was *not* neglecting Laney, I just couldn't stand to have her around," Kathy said, "knowing that that careless little girl could do what I've tried and tried and can't do! Why can't you go away and leave me alone? Leave both of us alone. We didn't kill her. We just didn't want her to have that abortion—"

"Kathy, be quiet!" Bill said. "This is none of their business. This is private. Personal. It doesn't have anything to do with Laney's death."

"The two of you are having fertility problems?" I said.

"Infertility problems," Bill said in a loud voice. "We have been tested and prodded and drugged and scraped. We spend half our lives taking our temperatures. Our sex life is a joke. We might as well be making love on an examining table there are so many people looking over our shoulders. I've been intimate with a test tube so many times I feel like an adulterer every time I see one. We are devoting all of our emotional energy to trying to have a baby and then Laney comes waltzing in one day and says she's pregnant, can we tell her where she can get an abortion?"

Kathy buried her face in her hands and refused to look at me but Bill, despite having cautioned Kathy not to talk, suddenly had a lot to say. He went on talking, his voice rising. "We explained our situation. Asked her to consider having the baby and giving it to us. Kathy's parents have plenty of money. We could have sent her somewhere, supported her, given her anything she needed. She laughed in our faces. Laney could be very cruel. She said she was sorry about our troubles but she wasn't about to ruin her life and her figure having a baby at seventeen just so she could give it to us." He broke off, his voice quivering with emotion, and put his arms around his wife.

"So you started ignoring her because it was too painful to deal with her?"

"We tried to talk to Josh," Kathy said in a barely audible voice. "We assumed the baby was his and we thought he might have some influence over her. He didn't even know that she was pregnant. They had a terrible fight about it. He was extremely upset by the news. But I don't think he killed Laney. Despite what she did to him, he still loved her."

"What about you? Did you know Laney was planning to have an abortion last weekend?"

"Yes. I tried to talk her out of it. She wouldn't listen."

"So the two of you, even though you knew that a child—and Laney Taggert was still a child—a child under your care was going off on her own to have an abortion, didn't do anything to help her or make sure that she would be safe? You were willing to let her go into the city on the train and have an abortion? With no thought for the consequences?"

"Don't you understand?" Bill Donahue roared, leaping toward me and grabbing me by the arm. "Are you an idiot? She was killing a baby!" He pulled me out of my chair and propelled me across the room. "We didn't want to help her. We wanted to kill her!"

At that moment, Officer Hennessey opened the door. "Is there a problem in here?" he asked. It was the understatement of the decade.

CHAPTER 17

OFFICER HENNESSEY WAS an experienced cop. It showed in his timing, which was perfect, and in the cool, careful way he surveyed the scene when he arrived. His quick eyes took in my staggering progress toward the door, Bill Donahue's aggressive stance, and Kathy's furious face. He stepped quickly forward, took the briefcase from me, and kept the door open. "Finished?" he said.

"You bet." I exited with all the dignity I could muster and then collapsed against the wall, stunned by the emotional firestorm I'd just come through. I was in no shape to be shoved around, but that wasn't what bothered me. What bothered me was how unbalanced their personal tragedy had made the Donahues and how readily the community had closed around them and protected them, protection that gave them access to and responsibility for vulnerable students when they no longer had any emotional energy to spare for anyone but themselves. I assumed it had been done with the best of intentions, faculty communities being so close, but sacrificing a dormful of students to the Donahues' personal crisis represented a serious lapse of judgment. It was something Peter Van Deusen needed to know about.

"Guy got a little upset with you," Hennessey said.

"I'm afraid I bring that out in people sometimes. I have a habit of asking the wrong questions."

"Or the right ones," he said, grabbing my arm. "Just through here is a little kitchen with plenty of tea bags. I think you could use a cup right about now, couldn't you?" He got me settled at a little table with a cup of steaming tea, sat down across from me with his own mug of coffee, and said, "Want to tell me what happened in there?"

"Are you supposed to debrief me?"

He shook his head. "Just thought you might want to talk about it. You looked a little shook up when you came out."

"You can say that again. I think Donahue wanted to dismember me. He may look like a big teddy bear, but he is one angry man!" I'm a great one for keeping things to myself, but after yesterday, it didn't seem like a bad idea to share what I had learned. Just in case someone did kill me, it wouldn't hurt to have a second person who knew what I knew. While my tea cooled, I told him what had happened. He was a good listener, quiet and watchful. Obviously Rocky didn't hire men in his own image, for which I was grateful. I wasn't up for bombastic explosions and difficult questions today.

The warm tea had a soothing effect. I could have put my head down on the table and gone to sleep, but it was time to see Russ Hamlin and then others. I had a long way to go before I could sleep. A long way. "Thanks for the tea," I said, "it was kind of you."

"You sound surprised. Are the police not supposed to be kind?"

"That's mostly been my experience." It would take all my fingers and some toes to count the number of times a cop, including Andre, has yelled at me or badgered me or tried to keep me from doing what I had to do because I was woman and needed protecting.

"Well," he said with a rueful smile, "I guess we'll have to change all that."

I pondered that statement as we crossed the campus to the Stannard Theater and got someone to direct us to the green room. I was never a theater person myself, too private for public exhibitions, but Joe Hennessey was, or had been. On our way down the stairs to the bowels of the building, he explained that the green room is where the actors wait. As we walked through the darkened, deserted halls, I was glad I had Hennessey with me. I kept expecting someone to jump out of a doorway and bop me on the head.

Eventually we came to a door with Green Room stenciled on it in black letters. As Hennessey opened the door we could hear the sound of angry voices. Most of the room was dark but the center, where an open space surrounded a miniature stage, was brightly lit. Russ Hamlin, dramatic in head-to-toe black, stood with his hands on his hips, glaring up at the hulking figure of Bill Donahue. They hadn't heard us come in. Hennessey shut the door quietly and we faded back against the wall and watched the scene unfold.

"You gossiping little faggot!" Donahue yelled. For such a mild-looking man, he sure seemed to yell a lot. "Why did you have to tell that bitch about Kathy? It wasn't any of her business."

Hamlin spread his arms wide, a stage-gesture protestation of innocence, executed a graceful half-turn, and walked a few steps away. "You've got it all wrong, Bill. I *didn't* tell her about Kathy. She asked me some things about Kathy and all I said was she'd have to ask Kathy those questions directly. What's wrong with that?"

"Liar!" Donahue said. In the bright light I could see little flecks of spit fly out when he spoke. I half expected him to say "Liar, liar, pants on fire," he sounded so childish, but he didn't. "She says you told her that Kathy had been neglecting Laney." He took a menacing step toward Hamlin and I felt Hennessey shift beside me, poised to intervene if necessary. "Why did you tell her that?"

Hamlin danced away again, calling back provocatively, "Well, it was the truth, wasn't it?" He'd reached the edge of the small stage. He placed his hands on the edge of it and leapt gracefully up, standing so that he was now taller than Donahue.

"She doesn't need to know everything about our lives just because one of our students died. It's not her business—"

"You're wrong, Bill. Let's see . . . now, what was it Dave Holdorf said to me when he asked me to go and meet with her? Oh, yes . . . that she was checking out our procedures for keeping track of the students and ensuring their safety to be sure Laney didn't fall through the cracks somehow. That's just what happened to her, wasn't it? Poor little Laney fell through the cracks while you and Kathy were agonizing about your inability to reproduce." He glided away across the stage. "Seems to me that that was precisely her business."

"That big cow! I can't believe Dorrie hired her. She has no tact and she doesn't understand anything about private schools. She's no good with people. Just because Laney got careless and fell through the ice and drowned is no excuse to turn our private lives inside out." I felt Hennessey's hand on my shoulder, restraining me, though he didn't really need to. I wasn't about to go charging up and interrupt the conversation just because Bill Donahue didn't find me smart or attractive. People never like you when you're threatening to them.

"Where have you been, Donahue? On the moon?" Hamlin's voice was heavy with scorn and disbelief. "Laney's death was no accident. Nor was the attempt to poison Dorrie's consultant. And now Carol Frank is missing. You look surprised, Bill. What's the matter, too busy cozying up to a test tube to pay attention to what's going on? It's all over the campus." He backed away from Donahue, his hand on his chest. "Oh, I get it. You and Kathy did her in because she wouldn't sign over the kid and now you're playing innocent, is that it?"

"You bastard!" Bill Donahue jumped up on the stage

himself, landing with an awkward thump and clambering to his feet. As he jumped up, Hamlin jumped down.

"I'm no bastard," he said. "I'm a perfect blend of both my parents and we can trace ourselves to back before the *Mayflower.* Why don't you go home and have sex or something? I'm trying to work."

"Well, at least we know it wasn't your baby, don't we? Your kind doesn't reproduce. You probably did her in yourself because you were so jealous that Josh was interested in her instead of you."

"My, my," Hamlin said, marching back and forth with his hands on his hips as he stared up at Bill Donahue, "do I detect a bit of homophobia there? You're assuming that just because I'm small and graceful and interested in theater, I must be gay, right? It might surprise you to know that it was Laney I was in love with and not Josh." He clapped his hands together, imitating a small child's delight. "It does surprise you, doesn't it? I can see it all over your face. You really don't know much about people, do you, except in that narrow-minded, black-and-white student council president sort of way. Unlike you and your greedy, self-centered little wife, I knew it would be bad for Laney to have a baby at seventeen." There was a stool beside him. He sat down on it, twining his legs around the rungs, seeming remarkably unafraid of Donahue's looming anger.

"Kathy isn't greedy," Donahue insisted. "She's sad. She couldn't see—neither of us could see—why it didn't make sense for Laney to have the baby and give it to us. . . ."

"No, I suppose you couldn't see that, could you? Did she ask you for money?"

Donahue shook his head angrily. "She knew better than to ask us to finance the murder of a baby."

"She never asked me," Hamlin said sadly. "And I would have been so glad to help. Do you have any idea who the father was?" He sounded hopeful.

"Of course not!"

"So it wasn't you? You didn't get sick of those test tubes and jump at the chance to stick it into a real woman?"

Donahue kicked furiously at the stool, sending it over with a crash, but Hamlin, lithe as a cat, landed on his feet and danced away a few steps. "Look, this is really stupid, you know, us fighting like this. Our real goal ought to be to find Laney's killer. Isn't that right, Ms. Kozak?" He spun around in our direction, threw his arms wide, and bowed slightly.

I walked toward the light with Hennessey trailing after me. Bill Donahue stood on the brightly lit stage, pounding one fist into another. All his body language said how clearly he wanted to hit Hamlin, and probably me, as well. Instead he slammed a fist into the black wall beside him, punching a hole in the black-painted cardboard. "Oh, cut it out, Bill," Hamlin said. "We're still using that." Donahue vented his anger by punching a few more holes and then stormed out without another word.

"Bravo," I said, the sound of my clapping hands echoing in the empty room. "Quite a performance."

He sketched a brief bow. "Thank you, thank you. Always do better with an audience, of course."

"You knew we were there?"

"I didn't hear you come in," he said, "but I have sort of a sixth sense for when I'm being watched. I felt you out there. Who's this?" He pointed at Hennessey. "Your bodyguard?"

"That's right," I said, introducing Hennessey. "Don't you think I need one?"

"I'm beginning to think I need one, too. Donahue is pretty mad at me."

"You were pretty hard on him. Are you two usually like this?"

"Bill's okay most of the time. Big, affable Boy Scout type. It's this reproduction thing. The frantic pursuit of that mystical union between egg and sperm has made both of them nutty as fruitcakes. Kathy spends half her time weeping or reclining like an invalid and Bill's touchy as hell. They used to be sort of a fun couple before they became obsessed with ovulation. Their egg, their temperature, their sperm. I will spare you the clinical details but believe me, I've heard them. I know more about what can go wrong with the human reproductive system than a biologist." He shook his head sadly.

"Pardon me for saying this, but it's gotten so bad, and I've heard so much, that sometimes I go to take a leak and I stare down at the thing in my hand and I say, 'Well, John Thomas, what nasty little secrets are you harboring?' Look, you two want to sit down? There are chairs over here." He led us to some battered folding chairs, dropping into one and waiting for us to join him. I didn't mind sitting. I was having a little trouble focusing anyway. Visions of big, soft beds kept getting in the way. He crossed his legs and smiled, his good humor apparently intact despite what had seemed to me a dangerously provocative encounter. But I'd forgotten. Being provocative was his style. "Now," he said, "what can I do for you?"

"Yesterday when we were talking I asked if you knew where Laney went on Columbus Day weekend. We talked a lot about where she didn't go, but it was only after you'd left that I realized you never answered me when I asked if you knew where she did go. Do you?"

"I was hoping you'd miss that."

"Why?" Hennessey and I said together.

"What are you two, Siamese twins?" he said.

"Why?" I repeated.

"Because it was supposed to be a secret and I hate to tell secrets."

Like hell. He just liked to get the most mileage possible out of each revelation. It was more fun that way. "Where did she go?"

"You won't give up until I tell you, will you?" I shook my head. "Okay. She went to a country inn with a man."

"What inn?" I said.

"What man?" Hennessey said.

Hamlin just shrugged. "She didn't tell me. I don't think she knew. I mean I don't think she knew what inn it was. I'm sure she knew who the man was, but all she'd tell me was that he was someone she'd met here on the campus and everyone would be very upset if they knew what she was up to. She was very excited about her illicit little enterprise, but not so excited she lost her discretion. She said if people knew they'd gone away together, the man could get into a lot of trouble and would probably lose his job. She hinted that he'd been in trouble before."

"Was she in love with this man?" I said.

"Maybe, but I don't think so. I think she just got off on the fact that it was forbidden. That was the way she was. Laney loved breaking rules."

"I'm surprised she decided to have an abortion, then. Having out-of-wedlock babies is a good way to break the rules. And it sure is something parents can't control," I said.

Hamlin shook his head vehemently. "Laney wasn't a fool, Ms. Kozak. And she wasn't the type to cut off her nose to spite her face. She had no interest in doing something which would mess up her plans for the future. According to Josh, she was very angry when she discovered she was pregnant. He says she swore she would make the man pay." He shifted restlessly in his chair. This conversation wasn't exciting enough to hold his interest. "By pay, I think she meant literally, as in cough up the money for the abortion, not that she meant to get some kind of revenge. But who knows? She could be pretty mean sometimes. Really, I wish I could help you more but that's all I know. And I do have a lot of work. . . ."

He trailed off hopefully, set his folded hands on his thighs like a good little boy, and sat watching us, the signal that it was time for us to leave. His performance was done. Except his audience wasn't finished.

"She never said anything that gave you an idea of the man's identity?"

"No. Never. And I was very curious, too. I tried to get her to tell me but she knew I wanted to know and that made keeping it from me all the more fun." He cocked his head sideways and grinned at us in a way that must have been adorable when he was younger, and now verged on pathetic, showing, as it did, the wrinkles on his neck and the loose skin at the jawline. The Pirate King in his middle years. "She did say something once, just to tease me."

"Which was . . ."

"She looked up at the sky one day and said it was just the color of his eyes. And that is absolutely all I can tell you." This time he stood up and ushered us to the door. "Do you think you can find your own way out?"

"Easily," I said, "we left a trail of crumbs."

"Then you should be fine, unless the rodents have eaten them. You certainly don't have to worry about maintenance cleaning them up. Sawyer's people all believe it's someone else's job." Hennessey held the door for me again, making me think he must have had a very nice mother to have learned such good manners, unless it was only that I was looking as feeble as I felt and he was afraid I'd collapse before his tour of duty ended, getting him into trouble with the irascible Rocky. Whatever the reason for it, I was grateful for the strong arm that helped me up the stairs and guided me back across the campus. Normally I might have bristled at the implication that I couldn't take care of myself, but not today. Today I understood all too clearly the meaning of the expression "the spirit is willing, but the flesh is weak."

He delivered me not to my office but to Dorrie's, where we found Dorrie and Rocky, Curt Sawyer, and another uniformed officer I hadn't met, standing around staring into a green plastic trash bag. Rocky greeted me with his characteristic friendliness. "How the hell did *you* know about this?"

"I don't even know what *'this'* is, Rocky, but you can assume it's because I'm such a good detective." He really brought out the brat in me. "Have you found Carol?" I teetered past them and dumped myself onto the couch, curling into a ball as I watched the others with tired eyes. I felt like sucking my thumb, but as my mother told me often, big girls don't, so I supposed that big women, or cows, as Bill Donahue had called me, don't either. I noticed that Rocky was wearing latex gloves, giving his hands a pale white, eerie look, like they were swathed in condoms, as he plunged them into the bag and held up a dripping purple duffel.

"We found it in the pond," he said. Maybe it was because things had been going so, wrong, but to have one thing go right made me feel very happy. Officer Hennessey was beaming at me as though I were his own personal discovery, and even Dorrie seemed excited. "Probably nothing in here that's useful," Rocky said. "But we'll see what the lab turns up."

"There has to be!" I insisted.

He lowered the duffel back into the trash bag and started to close off the top. "Hey, wait a minute," Dorrie said. "You mean you're not even going to look inside?"

"We'll inventory the stuff back at the station and then send whatever's appropriate on to the lab—"

"No way," Dorrie said. I was so surprised I sat up. "No way," she repeated, "that that bag is leaving this office until I know what's in it." She planted her hands on her hips and gave him a hard, level stare. I'd seen tougher men than Rocky quail before it—I'd seen CEOs of multimillion-dollar corporations lower their eyes and say "Yes, ma'am" like chastened schoolboys.

"For Christ's sake, Dorrie!" he exploded. "Will you just for once let me do my job?"

"If it weren't for Thea, you wouldn't have found it. Now let us see."

It sounded childish but I understood the impulse. It felt like it was "our" find and we were all entitled to know.

Rocky puffed up his cheeks and let the air out slowly. His face was terribly red. "It's against procedure. I should be letting the lab do this," he said, "but I suppose there's

no harm in taking a peek before we turn it over to them."
He removed the duffel again, unzipped it, and spread out
the contents on the trash bag. The officer, whose name
tag said Liam Nance, made a list of the items as they appeared. It was not an exciting collection. A change of
clothes, heavy sweater, toiletries, nightgown, a package
of sanitary pads, a tape player and some tapes, some sodden cigarettes and matches, and a copy of *Moby Dick*.
Laney Taggert had packed lightly for her final journey.

I don't know what I was expecting, but I was disappointed. I laid my head on the arm of the couch. My eyelids were slowly sliding down when Rocky suddenly
turned to me and shot out one of his loud questions.
"Okay, detective. What did you learn this morning, anyway? Anything to make the day worthwhile?"

"Not much," I muttered. "Kathy and Bill Donahue
were upset with Laney because they are having fertility
problems and they wanted her baby. They tried to talk her
out of getting an abortion and apparently were so furious
with her when she wouldn't change her plans that they refused to have anything more to do with her. I don't know
if goes any farther than that—"

I would have gone on, but Rocky had turned on Dorrie.
"Did you know anything about this?"

She had the grace to look embarrassed. She should
have. If she knew about their troubles and hadn't kept an
eye on the situation, then she'd deliberately abandoned
Laney Taggert to their less than tender ministrations. She
nodded. "I knew they were seeing a fertility specialist.
I'm ashamed to say I didn't realize it had become such an
obsession that it affected their performance. But I should
have been told. That's why we have Rita and Warren. I've
been concentrating on admissions and fund-raising and
the financial morass that Wingate left me. But I have no
excuse, really. . . ." She picked up the phone. "Lori? Is
Dave still around? Good. Can you send him in, please."

"Okay," Rocky said, "we're looking into that. What
else?"

"There was an older man she was involved with. Someone here on the campus. She spent Columbus Day weekend with him at some country inn. And Russ Hamlin says the man had blue eyes."

"Well, that certainly narrows the field, doesn't it? All we have to do is investigate the whereabouts of every blue-eyed man on the faculty and staff and every country inn in New England. Or maybe New England and New York? Canada? Why the heck did the girl have to be so secretive? Why couldn't she have left us a diary or confided in a friend?"

"Because she didn't want us to know! And because she didn't have many friends. Her best friends were Merri Naigler and Josh Meyer. And Merri had her eyes on Josh," I said. "Laney Taggert wasn't an outgoing, confiding sort of person. She'd spent her life evading her controlling mother. She'd learned to be deceptive. Not many people keep diaries anyway, Rocky. If Laney had kept a diary, her mother would have read it." In the center of the room, Laney's sodden belongings were accumulating little pools of water.

"All right, smarty-pants," Rocky said, "so how would you find out where she went?"

"Was that supposed to be a compliment? You've finally noticed that I'm smart? Or have you noticed my pants?"

"Okay, Okay. I know you're smart," he said, grudgingly.

I snuggled deeper into the soft velour of the couch. I did want to be helpful, even to someone rude enough to call me smarty-pants—this business was bringing out the childishness in everyone—but I was terribly tired. I needed a little rest before I went back to work. "Talk to Merri again," I suggested. "Or Genny. Or that other friend I was supposed to see yesterday . . . I forget her name . . . something like a Russian gymnast . . . that's it . . . Nadia something. Go through her things again. See if you can find a business card, matchbook, shampoo or soap or stationery, anything to identify the inn."

I let myself drift away, let the hum of their voices become just a background. I was only dimly aware that Rocky had gone back to the pile and was looking at things again. "Matchbook," he said, picking it up and examining it. "Right. Here it is, folks, the clue we've been looking for. New England Tractor Trailer School."

"Jerk," I whispered.

He picked up the soggy copy of *Moby Dick* and tried to thumb through it, muttering a running commentary to himself as he did so. "Goddamned thing's like a sponge. What's this? Sales slip for toothpaste. Dentist appointment. Maybe her dentist has blue eyes? This book is a frigging filing cabinet. Index card. Shopping list. A note from someone. Wait. Wait!" The second "wait" was loud enough to wake the dead, or at least, to wake me.

"Keep it down over there," I said. "Some of us are trying to sleep."

"Not anymore you're not," he said, waving a soggy piece of paper around, "we've got work to do."

"Let George do it," I said, closing my eyes again.

"I don't know who the hell George is," Rocky said, "but here's the name of the inn. It's called the Monadnock Valley House and it's in Oxton."

I knew I ought to be excited. It was a big break for us, but hot on the heels of the discovery my mind started generating a list of questions as long as my arm. "Wake me in an hour," I said.

The last thing I heard before I exited through the soft, dark doors of sleep was Rocky's querulous voice. "Can you believe this? How can she go to sleep at a time like this?" I didn't bother to wake up and tell him that sleep was one of the things I do best.

CHAPTER 18

THEY WERE KIND. They let me sleep. Some caring soul even found a blanket and covered me. It must have been a madhouse in Dorrie's office with all that was going on, but I slept through it, curled up on my couch, dreaming. I was dreaming that my brother, Michael, and two of his awful friends were chasing me around the yard, catching up with me from time to time and shaking me roughly and calling me a wimp, then backing off and attacking again. After one particularly rough shake I gave up on dreaming and opened my eyes. I was always willing to do a lot to get away from Michael. Even with my eyes open the shaking went on. Lori Leonard was bending over me, trying to wake me up.

"Cut it out," I mumbled sleepily.

She jumped back like she'd been bitten. "Sorry. I've been trying for about five minutes and I couldn't wake you up. I was getting really scared." She backed slowly away. "You aren't going to go back to sleep on me, are you?" I shook my head. "Good, 'cuz everyone is looking for you. You've had three phone calls from your office . . . someone named Lisa? She's desperate to talk with you. Guess you're not the only workaholic there, huh? And your lunch is here. Josh came by. I told him to come back in half an hour. Nadia Soren has already left school. She's traveling somewhere with her parents. I'll see if I can track her down if you want. I'll just tell Officer Hennessey you're awake. He's been fretting like a new mother." She was gone in a swish of skirt, her ponytail flying out behind her.

I sat up and tried to wake myself a little more, stupefied from sleep. The cording on the edge of the couch had left a groove in my cheek and my hair had gone completely wild. I swung my feet to the floor and stared at the ugly traces of salt on my spiffy black boots. It didn't matter. I wasn't here because I was a fashion plate, nor to be a dress-for-success role model. They liked me for my mind. Lori came back with a tray and Officer Hennessey and swore on a stack of imaginary Bibles that she'd carried the soup from the cafeteria herself. I ate my soup while he filled me in on what I'd missed.

Laney's picture had been sent to the Oxton police, who'd carried it to the Monadnock Valley House. People there had recognized the picture but no one could give a good description of her companion, except that he was older. But older than Laney meant pretty much everyone, since she hadn't been an old-looking sixteen. "Nobody takes responsibility for anything these days," Hennessey said. "Why'd they let him check in with a sixteen-year-old anyway? We've got a copy of the register for that weekend. I expect it won't surprise you to learn that there are no familiar names on the list."

"No one remembered anything about the guy?"

"Nothing. Or at least, nothing they're willing to share with us. Maybe they're afraid they'll get into trouble." He seemed to have fallen into a funk. He'd been fine when I went to sleep.

"What's the matter, Hennessey? Rocky yell at you?"

He smiled sheepishly. "He yells at everyone."

"That can't be very good for morale."

"We get along. He's got a good heart. It's not easy having an unsolved murder in a small town. People expect a lot from him."

"About the guy she was with. Laney, I mean. There's handwriting. And pictures," I suggested.

"Sure, if we knew whose writing to compare it to. Or whose pictures to show them."

"You could start with the usual suspects," I suggested. He looked blank. Obviously not a *Casablanca* fan. "I mean the people we know she was regularly involved with." The idea seemed to cheer him up. Maybe he could share it with Rocky and gain some points.

"His temper's gonna be a lot worse when they find Carol Frank. They haven't found her yet?" He shook his head. "What about her car?"

"That was never missing," he said. "It was parked behind the gym in the visitors' lot. She called security, said it was broken down and that someone would be coming to tow it."

"To a garage?"

He nodded. "Look," he said, "this thing may be blown all out of proportion. It may be that nothing has happened to Carol Frank. Rocky says she was training to be a mediator and that involves a lot of two- and three-day training courses. Maybe that's what she's doing."

"Right before Christmas? And without telling anyone?"

He shrugged. "She usually isn't at Bucksport on Thursdays. There was no need to tell anyone. She's a grown-up."

But I had snapped at the idea of Carol's car the way a snapping turtle, with its very simple brain, snaps at something and won't let go. Hennessey was still talking, explaining why we shouldn't assume anything had happened to Carol and I was thinking "Car, car, car."

When he paused for breath, I said, "What about the mess in her office? And the missing file?"

"Mischief?" he suggested, but he didn't sound as though he believed it.

"Where is the car now? Has it been towed? Did anyone look in the trunk?"

"I don't know," he said. He was staring at me like I had egg on my face.

"Don't look at me like that. People are always being found in their own trunks. Maybe our murderer isn't very sophisticated, despite the hemlock." I got up and grabbed my coat. He went on staring at me. "Come on, let's get over there and take a look." He still didn't move. "Okay," I said, "I'll go by myself." I knew that would move him. He was my bodyguard. He had to go with me.

As we sailed past Lori's desk, I blurted out a string of messages. "Save the soup. If he comes back, don't let Josh get away. And if Lisa calls again, tell her I'll call her back as soon as I can." It was windier outside, and colder. I started buttoning my coat and pulled up my scarf to cover my face, looking around for my car, which was supposed to have been delivered.

"Hold on," Hennessey said, stopping beside a salt-crusted cruiser. "I'll drive."

"I've got heated seats."

"How were you planning to open the trunk? Your fingernails?"

"You carry burglarious tools?"

"I carry cop tools."

"You're right." I reached for the handle, but he was there before me. "You must be a wonderful husband," I said.

"My wife didn't think so. A lot of women don't like being married to a cop. The hours, the worry, it gets to them." He backed deftly out of the space, spun around, and wound through a maze of buildings to the back exit.

"Do you know where it was towed?" I asked, but we were already moving. We pulled into a Texaco station and parked behind a black Volvo. Hennessey disappeared inside and returned a minute later with keys dangling from his hand. No need for cop tools.

"Look," I said, "no one goes away for a conference and leaves their keys behind." We approached the car cautiously, moving much more slowly than we'd left Dorrie's office, afraid of what we might find. Someone had written Wash Mc in the dirt on the car's side. I wondered if Carol Frank had children and if so, what they would do now. There had been no mention of a husband.

Hennessey pulled on his thick leather gloves, took the keys, and walked to the rear of the car. I turned my back, not ready to see what I was sure was there. The sun was warm on my back, the heat absorbed by my dark coat, but I was facing into the wind and it blew sharp pellets of ice into my eyes and ears and down my neck. Behind me, I heard the grate of the key in the lock and then the sound of the trunk lid bouncing up, followed by Hennessey's loud exclamation. I turned and looked. He'd pulled out what looked like a big piece of carpeting and was pulling back some clear plastic. Underneath, curled up on her side, was Carol Frank.

I'd solved a few mysteries in my time. I'd seen horrible pictures of bodies and heard ugly descriptions of bodies and gone to the victims' funerals, but I'd never seen an actual dead body like this before. She didn't look peaceful. I wouldn't have expected her to. She wouldn't have wanted to die like this, stuffed into the trunk of her car, disposed of like unwanted goods. Yesterday she'd sat in my office looking so warm and vital and understanding that I had wanted to confide in her myself. Now her healthy pink skin was a waxy gray. Her bloody face was grimacing, the one visible eye open and slightly bulging, her long curly hair matted with blood.

A couple guys from the garage had gathered and were talking noisily and pointing as they jockeyed for a better view. I turned away from the ugly sight in the car's trunk and stared out across the street. Children playing, shovels scraping, a few plow trucks plying their trade. Cars passing, their tires hissing through the slush. It all looked so normal. I wanted to scream, to shake the skies at the unfairness of it, at the shocking evil that had done this to such a good woman, but I had no voice.

Big black spots danced before my eyes, spots that got

bigger and bigger until all I was seeing was black. Swirling, tipping, tilting black and I was in the middle of it, spinning, off balance, falling. Fainting, just like the weak, helpless female I refused to be.

Andre had his arms around me, holding me tightly so that I was breathing through the scent of his detergent and his soap, my face buried in his hard chest. But as my confusion faded and the dizziness receded, I knew it wasn't Andre. It was Hennessey. I'd been engaging in wishful thinking, avoiding the reality of what was only a few feet away. Avoiding the awful face of death.

I had no one to blame but myself. I'd insisted on staying on the job, on being here. I'd demanded that Hennessey come with me and open the trunk. The price of my willfulness was that now I had to face what we'd found. I wasn't going to hear about Carol Frank's death through a phone call or even Rocky's raucous shout; I wasn't going to read about it on paper. I was always going to have the awful picture of her in my mind, embedded there as deeply as if it had been branded.

"Come on," Hennessey said, "let's get you into the car. I've got to call this in." I didn't want him to take away those comforting arms. I wanted to linger a little longer where it felt safe, but duty called. He dropped his embrace, put one arm firmly around my shoulders and steered me to the car. "None of you touch anything!" he told the small crowd. "This is a crime scene."

What he reported on the radio was so disguised in codes and euphemisms that if I'd been listening on a scanner I would have had no idea what he was talking about, though I knew that scanner aficionados did. I thought about Dorrie and what a nightmare all this was for her. Knew there was no way to keep this one out of the papers. Wondered what on earth we could do for damage control now. Was it any better that this body had been found off campus, even if it had been conveniently towed there?

Luckily the school was closing for Christmas vacation

in a few days. Maybe the best thing to do would be to close now and send everyone home. I wasn't sure. I needed to talk to Suzanne and get some input from psychologists about whether it would be better to keep them together in the face of tragedy or send them back to their families. The psychologist who knew the students best wasn't going to be able to help us now.

The problem was, so many of them came from dysfunctional families. For many of the students, Bucksport played a vital in-loco-parentis role, with the dorm parents closer to the students than their own families. Except for Bill and Kathy Donahue. Maybe they had been, once, but now they were so isolated by their lack of a biological child that they were neglecting all their existing children.

I was shivering, chilled to the bone even though I'd only been outside for a few minutes. I knew it was shock and not cold. My hands were like ice and my heart was pounding. I could hear my own pulse whooshing in my ears. I no longer felt like I might pass out but I was still light-headed and weak. Hennessey started up the car and turned the heat on full blast. At that moment, I couldn't have gotten too much heat. "As soon as they get here, I'll take you back," he said.

"She is dead, isn't she?"

"Yes. I know this is a shock. The first body always is. I wish you hadn't had to see her . . . like that." He reached over and took my hand. His own was almost as cold as mine. His fingers traced the faint line of scars across my wrist and he looked at me curiously.

"It's not what you think," I said. "Someone tried to kill me."

"An odd method to choose."

"It was supposed to look like a suicide. I'd rather not talk about it, especially not right now." I rested my head against the seat and closed my eyes. There were no words for what I was feeling. Nothing in life prepares us for moments like this. It shouldn't. The only kind of preparation would be some kind of desensitizing, something to get us even more used to violence and death than the media already has, and the world doesn't need any more of that. "Was she married?"

"Divorced."

"Children?"

"Pretty well grown-up, I think."

"So she lived alone? And the killer must have known that and counted on no one missing her for a while. It's so cruel! Not just the killing but to dump her here, to leave her to rot in her trunk like that, as if she wasn't a person at all but just a—a—thing." My voice was shaking and I knew I was going to cry. I'd had a hard twenty-four hours. I'm big on control but all the lids that I kept on my feelings had been jarred and now they came popping off. All my fear and pain and weariness and shock and sorrow and awareness of the loneliness I was going to feel without Andre came flying out like the troubles from Pandora's box.

When Rocky came screeching up beside us and threw open the door, he found me sobbing like a lost child in Hennessey's arms, and for some unexplainable reason, he didn't bluster or yell, just handed me his handkerchief and took Hennessey off to debrief him. I used the time alone to get myself back under control. I would have powdered my nose, but it would have taken a lot more than powder to subdue it. I looked like Rudolf. Anyway, my limited supply of cosmetics was back in Dorrie's office in my briefcase. The best I could do was find an elastic to tie back my hair, which was clinging to my wet cheeks and making me crazy. By the time Hennessey came back, I was once again a poised professional. With my blotchy face and shaking hands, I looked like a professional druggie, but there wasn't anything I could do.

We left a crowd of blue-clad men standing around Carol's trunk and drove back to the administration building. Hennessey pulled in, reached past me, and opened the door. "You're not staying?" I said.

"Can't. Got to get back. I shouldn't have left in the first

place and neither should you. Being the first ones at a crime scene and all. The ADA will probably chew my ass but I didn't want to keep you there. It only gets worse, the longer you stay around."

"But someone is trying to kill me, too."

His eyes were pleading with me to forgive him. Nice eyes, too. A kind of greenish brown. I was slipping slowly into spinsterhood, just as my mother always said. Too busy working to notice the world around me. I'd just spent four hours with this guy and even trembled in his arms, and I hadn't ever noticed what he looked like. "I'd stay if I could," he said. "The chief's sending someone over. It shouldn't be long. Just don't eat or drink anything, okay?"

He meant it as a joke, but today my sense of humor was a little bit dull and I didn't smile. I didn't want another baby-sitter; I liked the one I had. I got out of the car and plodded up the steps, feeling unreasonably aggrieved and abandoned. I half expected someone to launch a huge stone at me from the upper reaches, or jump at me from the shadows, but no one did, and I reached my office without incident. Josh was sitting in the chair, his arms wrapped tightly around his body, looking young and fragile and needy. His head jerked my way as I came in. "Lori let me in," he said. "I hope that's okay." He took in my blotchy face and bedraggled appearance. "You've found Mrs. Frank, haven't you?"

"I'm afraid so."

"She's dead." It wasn't a question. He buried his face in his hands and his poor, bony shoulders began to heave. I got some tissues from the desk, knelt beside him and pressed them into his hand. He grabbed my hand and held on, clinging to me as if I was a lifeline. With my other hand I rubbed his back, the vibrations of his sorrow traveling up my arm and straight to my heart. He was so thin it made me want to cry right along with him. When he was calmer I called Lori and asked if she could bring us both some tea. The peppermint tea Ellie had brought me was still on the desk but it was cold. I set it in the corner of the bookcase, thinking I might nuke it later. Even cold, it smelled soothing.

Over tea, we got down to business. I apologized for dragging him back again. "I'm not trying to harass you. I just keep hoping someone will come up with a clue that will tell us who the other man was. Is there anything Laney said, anything at all, that might help us identify him?"

He shook his head, a slow, helpless gesture. "Why do you keep asking me? Don't you see? I was the last person she'd tell. She was afraid I might do something violent. And I would have, too. If he hadn't done what he did, she'd still be alive. Did you ask Merri?"

"She says she doesn't know."

"She might be lying. Merri is neither as sweet nor as innocent as she appears."

"So I hear." His eyebrows went up but he didn't ask what I'd heard. "Josh, is there anyone else I could talk to that she might have confided in?"

"I don't think so. I wish I could help. Are more people going to get killed? I guess it doesn't matter. I'm not staying around to see. My dad wants me to come home. He's coming to get me Saturday morning. Sure took a lot to get him to take an interest. I used to think I'd have to be dying before he'd notice. I guess other people dying is enough. I know that sounds awful but you haven't met my dad. A man born with a telephone connected to his ear. He even has a fax in his car, just so he won't miss anything, but I've been in five plays and he hasn't made it to a single one."

"Next time you're in a play, call me," I said. "I'd love to come and see you perform."

"You already have," he said. "I'm a pretty good actor, too. Can I go?"

"Of course." He left. And I sat in my chair staring at the closed door, pondering his last remark and hoping I hadn't been conned. No one had a better motive for killing Laney than Josh did . . . except for the baby's father. And we had only Josh's word that it wasn't his. But wasn't his Friday evening accounted for? And wasn't that Rocky's problem, not mine? My staring and pondering were interrupted by the phone.

"Thea? It's Lori. You have a call. She didn't give her name but I think it's that woman from your office who's been trying to reach you. She's on ninety-two."

I pressed the button and said "Hello?"

"Are you Dorrie's consultant? The one that called about Columbus Day weekend?" It was a girl's voice, young and full of emotion, but whether it was anger or distress, I couldn't tell. She sounded vaguely familiar.

"Yes. Who's this?"

"It's Angie. Angie Drucker. I heard my dad telling you that he was at Cornell for my brother's parents' weekend. My dad, the jerk who just grounded me when the coolest concert of the year is happening? Well, he was lying. My mom and I went but he didn't go. He said he had too much work to do to take the time off." She disconnected before I could say anything.

CHAPTER 19

I RUSHED DOWN the hall and into Lori's office, almost knocking over Ellie Drucker, who was standing in the hall. She stared at me in total surprise as I went by, a sort of openmouthed what-are-you-doing-here surprise, an expression that didn't flatter her wide, shiny face. Perhaps, having seen me earlier, she hadn't expected me to still be working, or perhaps the vigor of my movements astonished her. It was certainly true that I'd been moving very slowly earlier. Poor woman. If it turned out that the folks at the Monadnock Valley House recognized her husband, she was in for some unhappy times.

Lori was fluttering solicitously around a distinguished-looking older man in an expensive suit, collecting his hat and coat and offering him coffee. He turned toward the door when I came in, obviously expecting Dorrie. His craggy, rough-handsome face was familiar from many years reading the business section of the paper. Oliver Caldwell Dawes, CEO of the Dawes Company and chairman of the Bucksport board of trustees. He stared at me for a moment, tapped his forehead lightly, and held out his hand. "Thea Kozak, right?"

"What a good memory you have, Mr. Dawes. I'm flattered."

"I don't imagine many men forget you once they've

met you," he said. It was the kind of flattering courtesy that older men can still get away with and younger men have to use very carefully now that we're in the age of political correctness and a sexual harassment suit lurks behind every encounter. It was silly and it was trivial, but after the last twenty-four hours, the idea that anyone could even claim to find me attractive was very pleasant.

"I'll be with you in a minute, Thea," Lori said, obviously flustered at being left in charge under such difficult circumstances. She ushered Oliver Dawes into Dorrie's office, where several of the other trustees were waiting, closed the door behind him, and leaned against it, rubbing her forehead with both hands. "There isn't enough extra-strength painkiller in the world to handle this headache. I can't even remember how he said he'd like his coffee, and I've been fixing him coffee almost every week for two years."

"Black. One sugar," I said.

She gave me a faint smile. "Thanks. And what can I do for you?"

"Got any pictures of Chas Drucker around?"

"Not here, but I'm sure there are lots of them in the yearbook office. Or you could just look in last year's yearbook. Or any yearbook for the last twenty-five years. There's a bunch of 'em over there on the shelf. What's the matter? Seen so many people you've forgotten who's who? Or do I mean whom? I know this is an educational institution, but if you ask me, the word 'whom' is for the birds. It never sounds right even when it is." Good old Lori. Still cheerful even if it was a forced cheerfulness. She was a peach of a secretary in a time when good secretaries were hard to find. She fixed the coffee and carried it into the other room.

I got the most recent yearbook and thumbed through it. There were several good pictures of Drucker. There were also pictures of Josh, of course, and Russ Hamlin, and even a picture of the now-vanished Chris Fuller, smiling a predatory smile and looking primitive and virile and dangerous as he bent forward over the handle of the shovel he was holding. It was the perfect thing to show to people at the Monadnock Valley House. No need even to point out Drucker, just let them browse and see if anyone picked him out.

I was impatient for Rocky to get back so I could share what I'd learned. I had no idea how long he might be tied up dealing with Carol. I thought of getting in my car and driving to the inn myself, but a couple things held me back. First, I had no car. Rocky had said he was going to get it repaired and have it ready this afternoon, but I hadn't seen it out there and now he was busy with more important things. Second, I didn't want to take a chance on tainting the identification. A very coplike phrase. Maybe I'd been in this business too long. It needed to be done by someone who knew how to do it properly.

Lori came bustling back, shaking her head. "We are in the midst of a catastrophe here," she said, "and they want tea and sandwiches. Someday, just once before I die, I want to be the person who gets to be waited on. I am supposed to be at home right now getting lots of lovely little snacks and desserts ready for a bunch of our friends. Twenty-five people coming at seven and I've done nothing. Al is happy to help, but he's a man who needs direction. I know it sounds heartless, but I don't care if even more people get killed, I'm out of here at four." She picked up the phone, called the dining service, and explained her need for sandwiches and cookies. Whoever she spoke to was very understanding and she came away from the phone smiling.

"The people Dorrie has hired are so nice! They never say it can't be done, they just do it. The last person in charge over there thought it was too much trouble to put out cocktail napkins with the hors d'oeuvres."

"Are you really in trouble with your own hors d'oeuvres? Because I've got some great quick and dirty recipes."

"I am. I was just going to go to the market and hope for

inspiration," she said, sitting down and picking up her pen. "Shoot."

Maybe it was callous of both of us, when Carol Frank and Laney Taggert were both brutally dead, to sit and exchange recipes, but life goes on. And anyway, I had to keep my mind moving or the image of Carol would come back to haunt me. "Hope you don't mind cream cheese. It's the staff of life."

"Not at all."

"Get some smoked trout, about half a pound. You have a food processor?" She nodded. "Okay, you mix it with a package of cream cheese, horseradish, and lemon juice. Thin it with some half-and-half if it's too thick. Great on crackers. It's also wonderful on cucumber slices. Use the English kind, they don't have those big seeds. Next, a can of crab, another package of cream cheese, a little lemon juice, and a teaspoon or two of curry, mix it together in the food processor, put it in a dish and bake for about twenty-five minutes." I dictated while she scribbled frantically.

"Now, everyone is impressed by piles of food. Doesn't have to be special, just has to be massive. So get a couple pounds of shrimp, pile 'em on a platter on a bed of lettuce, use a green pepper filled with cocktail sauce in the middle and lots of lemon wedges. Do the same with a platter of raw veggies. Use sugar snap peas, red, yellow, and orange peppers, those ready-peeled baby carrots, cauliflower, and broccoli. Hollow out a small red cabbage and a small green cabbage, fill one with ranch dressing and one with honey mustard dressing. Belgian endive. Separate it into spears, fill the big end with herbed cheese, arrange on a tray like flower petals and sprinkle with sprouts."

"Stop," she said, "this is great but you're making me hungry. But how do you know all this? You never entertain. You're always at work. I know you are."

"I used to have a life once. And my mom is the world's greatest cook. Don't forget little smoky sausages and

Swedish meatballs with a dish of mustard. Don't forget toothpicks."

She wrote it down. "So you're what people are talking about when they say 'get a life,' is that right?"

"This is a good life, too. Keeps me out of trouble."

She regarded me skeptically. "Excuse me," she said, "but that's bullshit. If you wanted to stay out of trouble you wouldn't be sitting here right now, would you?"

"It's my job," I said. I got up, tucking the yearbook under my arm.

"I've offended you, haven't I?" she said.

"No. I just don't want to start feeling sorry for myself. It's too easy to fall into it, especially when I'm tired like this, and it gets me nowhere. Good luck with the food. As for dessert, it's too late to suggest you get your guests to bring it . . . you can remember that for next time. Just hit a bakery. The stuff doesn't always taste that great, but for appearance it can't be beat. And people get so excited being given a choice of goodies. A cheesecake. Something dense and chocolate. A plate of elegant cookies."

"Thanks, Thea," she said. "You're wonderful."

"Let me know when Rocky shows up, will you please?" I avoided responding to the compliment. I never know how to take them.

I didn't have time to sit and ponder, because as soon as I was back in my office, Ellie Drucker came in with another cup of tea. Maybe it was just me anticipating the sorrow she had ahead, but I thought she looked older and wider and utterly worn out. She was wearing a coat and gloves and had a canvas tote bag slung over her shoulder. "Thought I'd try again," she said. "I know you never got to drink your last one, with all the running around you've been doing. Isn't it just terrible about poor Carol! I can't imagine anyone wanting to hurt such a nice person. Or why? I mean, if Delaney Taggert was involved with some man, what did that have to do with Carol?"

I didn't know what Rocky might want to be open about and what he might want to keep secret, so I didn't explain our theories to Ellie. It seemed a little unfair, since she was about to be mixed up in it anyway if my suspicions about her husband checked out, but it wasn't my call. She lingered at the edge of my desk, waiting for something. Maybe it was an answer to her question. "Maybe Laney had been seeing Carol."

"That wouldn't make any difference," she said. "Those things are all confidential."

"Of course." She shot me a strange look and went on standing there, perhaps waiting for compliments on the tea. I tried to take a sip, but it was too hot, so I just pretended. "Delicious. Thank you."

Her smile was too quick and too grateful. Maybe she was one of those perpetual givers who rarely get enough thanks. She seemed to be playing the role of mother to everyone. "Glad you like it. Well, I'm off. Got to check on Lori and see how she's holding up and then it's off to the market. Dinner party tonight. I'm afraid it won't be very cheerful, not after the news about Carol. She was a great friend of ours. I wonder if I should cancel?" She shook her head. She wasn't talking to me, anyway. "No. People will need a chance to talk. Will I see you tomorrow?"

"I guess that depends on what happens."

"Yes," she said, an odd expression on her face, "I suppose it does." I wondered, as the door closed behind her, whether she had her own suspicions about her husband. I began pulling out my files. As I did, my elbow caught the cup and the hot minty tea went everywhere. I grabbed some tissues and mopped it up. Looked as though I was batting zero in the soothing beverage department. Maybe the fates didn't want me to be soothed. The silver lining to this cloud was that I hadn't had time to spread out any papers.

At that point, the phone rang. Lisa had finally caught up with me. "Thea?" She sounded breathless. "Sorry," she panted, "I had to run upstairs and lock myself in the bathroom with the portable phone. Baby-sitter finked out on me. Christmas shopping, I suppose. That child has been wrapped around my leg all afternoon, chanting a steady Mommy do this, Mommy do that, until I thought I was going to scream. I love her more than anything, I truly do, but I was feeling suffocated. When that husband of mine came through the door, I practically threw her into his arms and ran up here. Listen to me, will you? Someone tries to kill you and here I am babbling on about my troubles. Excuse me. . . ."

I could hear her talking softly to someone. "No, sweetie, Mommy needs some privacy for a while. Yes, Mommy will be out soon and we'll go play snow. Yes. Yes, baby, a great big snowman. You tell Daddy to help you with your snowsuit. Mmm-hhm. Yes. I think Daddy should help, too. Yes. He does know how to roll snowballs but he can't do it in his suit. Tell him that's the rule. Okay. Bye-bye. Tell Daddy the pink mittens."

A long sigh and then she was back on the line. "Are you still there? Did you hear? Can you believe she's not sure her father knows how to make a snowman? There's division of labor for you. Daddies wear suits and go to work. Mommies wear suits and go to work and do everything else too and know how to make snowmen, make food, do laundry, change babies—"

"I hear you. Maybe you need to be out of town for a weekend. Let the two of them rough it together. I can arrange it." Lisa worked for us before the baby came and then planned to stay home, but quickly found that being a stay-at-home mom didn't suit her temperament, especially when her mother-in-law started dropping in every day to be sure that the baby was being cared for properly. When she asked if she could come back part-time, Suzanne and I jumped for joy. It was a great arrangement for everyone, but Lisa still grumbled about her husband's failure to do his share.

"Going out of town won't help. He'll just take Charlotte to his mother's."

"It might help *you.*"

"I never thought of that."

I would have been happy to just sit and chat, but despite my nap, I was fading fast. If Rocky didn't show up soon, I'd find someone else to get me to my car, and then I was going to crawl home and sleep for twelve hours. "What's up?"

"Good news, I think, about the King School and our friend Denzel's problem."

I closed my eyes and tried to shift my mind to a different venue and set of problems. "You have no idea how badly I need some good news."

"Oh, I think I do," she said. "It's not just you, either. Everyone's at the breaking point. Sarah's sour as curdled milk, Magda's barely speaking English, and even Bobby, our little ray of sunshine, is sunk in gloom. Soon as you can, you've got to come back here and fix things."

I didn't bother to ask why me. I've been the designated fixer since birth. "As soon as I can," I agreed. "Meanwhile, the good news?"

"I got some useful leads about LaVonne Rawlins from Janet Beecham. I guess LaVonne talked to Janet pretty freely while they were in the ladies' room. From the amount Janet learned, they must have been in there a long time. Anyway, LaVonne used to work at an elementary school in Nashua, New Hampshire. I tracked down the assistant principal and here's the story. While she was there, she accused one of her fellow faculty members of sexually assaulting her. Sound familiar? Poor guy was arraigned and charged and everything, only it turned out that there was a witness who was able to prove her story was improbable. The charges were dropped and she resigned."

"You talk to the guy?"

"Not yet, he wasn't home, but I caught up with him this morning. He could meet us for breakfast tomorrow."

"Us?"

"I assumed you'd want to be there."

She'd assumed correctly, of course. Normally, I would

have insisted on attending an interview that might be vital to the success of a project for one of our clients, it was just that I'd been hoping to sleep late in the morning and get some rest before coming back to Bucksport. "What time?"

"Eight-thirty."

"In Nashua?" She murmured an assent. "Shit!"

"Did you just say what I think you said?"

"I did."

"Look, you don't have to come. I'm perfectly capable of doing it myself, I just thought—"

"You thought right. Will you drive?"

"You'd rather go in the bucket of bolts?" She meant her aging Ford.

"My car. You drive."

"Yippee! I love driving around in a bright red turbo Saab with a sunroof. Makes me feel young again."

"Lucky you. I'm not sure anything is ever going to make me feel young again. We found another body this afternoon. I don't think there are enough damage-control measures in the universe to handle this situation. Too bad schools can't get enrollment insurance."

"I thought the tuition was nonrefundable."

"It is. I'm thinking about next year."

"Just a minute," Lisa said, "did you say that you found a body . . . you mean you personally, not just someone on the campus?"

"That's right."

"Maybe it's time EDGE got our own staff psychologist. After that last case . . . your mother . . . Thea . . . I don't know . . . it can't be easy . . . all that psychological battering? Are you seeing someone?"

"I'm a great believer in self-help. Not everyone is a good candidate for therapy, Lisa. When people sit and stare at me with kindly eyes and sincere faces and ask me in gentle voices how I feel about things, I want to scream, and when I ask the psychologists how the system is supposed to work to make me feel better and they counter by asking me why I'm asking the question, I want to yell back in their faces that I'm asking because I want to know the answer. I guess I'm too result oriented for the process to work. I tend to go for the therapeutic Jack Daniels and a good long walk on the beach. And work. I can always lose myself in work."

"That's the risk, isn't it? That you'll lose yourself." Before I could form a suitable response, she'd rushed on. "Just don't be so proud and stubborn that you won't ask for help if you need it. I'll be there at seven-thirty, okay?"

"It's not okay, but I'll cope."

The door burst open with Rocky's characteristic entrance, a loud "Lori says you wanted me. What is it now?"

"Oops, a tornado just swirled in the door. I've got to go, Lisa. Have fun making the snowman. See you in the morning." I shifted my attention to Rocky. "Angie Drucker called me. Chas Drucker's daughter. She says that Drucker was lying when he said he was at Cornell visiting his son for parents' weekend. Columbus Day weekend. He didn't go, he stayed here." I patted the yearbook. "There are lots of pictures of him in here. Also pictures of Josh, of that guy Chris Fuller, who's missing, of Bill Donahue, of Hamlin, all the guys we know she was close to. Get someone to show it to the folks at the inn. See if anyone IDs Drucker."

"Can't leave you alone for a minute, can I, before you come up with another little bombshell. I'm half surprised someone hasn't thrown themselves at your feet and confessed."

"Maybe tomorrow. Except I'm coming in late, so if you get here early, they can confess to you instead. Can I get my car now? I need to go home."

"Unlike the rest of us," he said dryly.

"That's not fair, Rocky. You didn't get poisoned, or spend last night in the hospital, or find your first dead body—"

"Thought you were just one tough gal out to show us

cops that no one could stop you when you had to do what you had to do."

"Don't rub it in, Rocky, okay? You want me to stay around? I'll be happy to. Just say the word. Who's next? Line 'em up, march 'em in. I'm ready. . . ."

"Forget it," he said. "Dorrie and your partner, Suzanne, are tied up with the trustees. I've got my men out beating the bushes. I can't think of anything we need you for right now. I can't send you up to the inn. I need an officer for that. You can go. Young Hennessey's waiting downstairs to drive you to your car. And don't you go messing with that boy's head, you hear? He's had a hard day."

"Unlike the rest of us," I said, handing him back his own line. "And what's that remark supposed to mean, anyway? You think I'm going to use him up and then bite his head off? You think I'm some sort of wicked femme fatale? Andre and I have our differences, yes, but it's not one-sided. He's not some poor abused man. What would you have done if you'd been me?"

"I would have walked out, just like he did."

"You weren't listening. I said what would you have done if you were *me!* Me, not Andre. If your woman— that sounds nice and primitive, doesn't it—if your woman had said, 'Don't go back out there, Rocky. It's dangerous. Let someone else do it, stay here with me where you'll be safe and I won't have to worry about you,' what would you have done?"

"I'm a cop," he said.

"Right. And I'm tired. See you later." I threw the yearbook at him and picked up my coat.

"Hey, take it easy!" he said, coming over to help.

I jerked away. "I can do it myself." I grabbed my briefcase and stomped out the door.

Rocky followed me, an amused expression on his face. "Hey," he called, "how did you know she was in the trunk?"

"I watch too much television." There's nothing like a burst of anger when you're tired. It carried me down the hall, out the door, and all the way to Hennessey's cruiser. I got in and slammed the door.

"Guess I'm not the only one the chief's yelled at today," he said.

"Bingo," I said, and that's all I said as the cruiser crept slowly along the sinuous road that led us out of the campus. Around us, even though the early winter darkness had fallen, groups of happy campers were out enjoying the snow, oblivious, as yet, to the fact that another tragedy had occurred.

CHAPTER 20

THE SNOW THAT the bright sun and road salt had melted earlier had crept back across the road as black ice, making the last ten miles tough going. I made it mostly on willpower. Remembering my empty cupboards and refrigerator, I forced myself to stop and lay in some basic supplies. Coffee, bread, milk, bagels, cereal, juice, mayo and canned tuna, tea and soup, cheese and crackers, salted nuts, white wine, bourbon and bubble bath. The bubble bath was a bribe. Only the thought of climbing into a steamy tub enabled me to force myself back into the car and out onto the skittery roads again.

By the time I got home, weariness lay on me like a lead apron but I did a quick survey of the parking lot before I crawled to my door. I wasn't in the mood for any more nasty surprises and I knew that bad guys sometimes did come calling. If you live in a place for a while, the cars become familiar. You start to think of your neighbors, in this anonymous world, as the gray Taurus or the shiny black Blazer. I'd been gone six months but the cars hadn't changed. Both Taurus and Blazer were home tonight. So was the little two-Geo family, a small, trim, cheerful couple who never failed to say hello, though I didn't know their names. Two days ago, getting into her car,

Mrs. Geo had been looking a little rounder. Someday soon they might need a bigger car. Mr. El Dorado, of the shiny, perpetually suntanned dome, who wore loose-fitting sport shirts to hide his bulging gut, was out. Someone was entertaining. I could tell, because the visitors' spots were all taken. A mostly upscale crowd. Nothing moved. No one seemed to be lurking in the cars, so I made a dash for my door.

My condo looked as bruised as I felt. I knew Geoff was coming back to paint and fix the scratches but for now my once-lovely place showed how kicked around and mistreated it had been. The damage gave it an ugly, temporary look that made it feel even less like home. The prick had broken lamps and failed to replace lightbulbs, so the corners of the room were dark, and, to my weary, wary senses, somehow sinister and threatening.

It was foolish, I know. None of the people whose tragedies had touched me had ever lived here, none of them had even been here, and yet the place felt dark and sad and heavy with loss. I suppose I carried it with me. And then there was the loss that touched me most, the loss of Andre, a living, vibrant person, a person who *had* lived here. We'd made love in every room, even outside on the deck, and we'd fed and stroked and cared for each other here and shown each other pieces of our souls. It wasn't just my body that hurt. The tightness in my chest reminded me of last night, but this time it was the poison of feelings suppressed that caused the pain.

I fixed myself a hot bath liberally laced with foaming blue bath salts, poured a generous measure of bourbon over a few ice cubes, and settled in for some hydrotherapy. My stomach was reluctant to accept the drink. It longed for tea and soup but they would induce neither sleep nor numbness. The normally comforting swirl of the sweet, warming alcohol jarred my still-fragile system and my stomach gave a few unsettling hops before it decided to accept what it was being given. It was only once

I was sure that it was quiescent that I was able to relax and enjoy my bath. Then I enjoyed it so much I almost fell asleep in the tub.

They say the Eskimos, or Inuit, as we now say to be politically correct, have two hundred words for snow. It's probably a myth, but it is true that if you live with something very closely you do tend to dwell on it. I lay in the tub and tried to count the number of words I knew for the state of being tired. There were the obvious ones like exhausted and weary, which I certainly was, but also less usual ones, like enervated and lethargic and languid and debilitated, all of which I also was. Too bad I didn't have a thesaurus right by the tub, I could have looked up more if I hadn't been too spent to bother. Or, if I'd only had some energy, I could have moved on to words for pain and found some elegant or unique ways to describe all the sore, miserable aches left from my night in the emergency room or profound ways to describe the emptiness I felt recalling Andre's retreating back.

I might easily have slipped silently under the water and drowned, but through the trance induced by the warmth, good old Jack, and my exhaustion, I heard a peculiar buzzing sound that changed to a bang and then a buzz and a bang. It took a while for my stupefied mind to recognize that someone was ringing the doorbell and pounding on my door. And that whoever it was, they weren't going to give up and go away. Unless I wanted to disturb all my neighbors, and I was walking a very fine line with them already, I knew I'd better go and answer the door. Or at least look and see who was there. I would only open it to someone I knew personally.

Reluctantly I abandoned the tub, pulled on some underwear and a robe, and padded on my still-wet feet to the door. Joe Hennessey was standing there looking frantic. "Are you okay?" he demanded. "I was afraid something had happened to you."

"The only thing that's happened to me is that you got me out of the tub, where I was having a wonderful, relaxing time, so that you wouldn't disturb all my neighbors and make them call the police."

He looked like a kid who'd been scolded. He even had the grace to blush. "I'm sorry," he said. "I was worried about you."

"You were worried about me? Or Rocky was?" I asked, stepping aside so he could come in. "I'm a grown-up. I can take care of myself."

"Carol Frank was a grown-up, too," he reminded me, looking for something to wipe his feet on.

The mat was gone, though. Stolen or ruined by the prick. "Don't worry about it," I said, as he bent to take off his shoes. Mother Hennessey must have been something, unless it was his wife.

He set his shoes neatly by the door and headed for the living room, talking as he did. "I was with Rocky when he told her kids what had happened. So he could show me how it was done. We don't have murders in Sedgwick, you see. Turns out they were younger than I thought. Just got home from college today. I have to tell you. It was harder than finding her." His eyes were taking in my place. The furniture, pictures, books. The peculiar gaps. The mottled walls where Geoff and his crew had patched but not yet painted. They came to rest on the Jack Daniels bottle and his face got hopeful. "Could I have some of that?"

"I thought cops weren't allowed to drink on duty."

"For medicinal purposes," he said, dropping wearily onto the couch.

He looked as if he needed it. I thought about the day he'd had, the day we'd both had, and headed for the kitchen to get another glass. A few of them had survived my tenant. "Those poor kids. I know what it's like for them. Is their father with them?"

"He is. What do you mean, you know what it's like for them? How can you know?"

He sounded aggrieved, as though I weren't taking his painful experience seriously enough. Most of the men I know aren't much for confessing pain and weakness, but when they do, they expect me to treat it very seriously. I put in some ice, poured him a drink, and made another one for myself. It was a dumb thing to do, I didn't need another one, but I felt like it. I was ignoring the fact that I was drinking on an empty stomach. Always a dangerous thing to do. "I know because my sister was murdered," I said.

He almost dropped his drink. "I'm sorry," he said. "I didn't know."

"You couldn't have. You want something to eat?" In my house, it's either a feast or a famine. When I'm busy, I forget to eat, forget to shop, forget to sleep. Then when things calm down I buy out the stores and stuff my refrigerator so full things rot. But I hadn't been living here, the prick had, so it was a good thing I'd gone to the store. I opened the can of mixed nuts, put the cheese and crackers on a tray, put my old friend Jack on the tray as well, and carried it into the living room.

Hennessey was staring at the wall. "What happened here?" he asked.

"The prick wrecked the place," I said.

"The prick?" he said, wrinkling his nose at the unlady-like word. "That your ex?"

I shook my head. Hennessey was a nice guy but I wasn't up to small talk. Or big talk. Or any talk. I needed to crawl into bed, pound my pillow, and weep. The only good thing about having him here was that the shadows in the corners had retreated a bit and I didn't feel quite so surrounded by death and destruction. "I don't have an ex. I have a late." I told him about my awful tenant. "If I ever find him, I'm not bothering with a lawsuit. I'm going to chop him up and feed him to the seagulls."

"You shouldn't have told me that," he said.

"Why, because now you'll have to report me?"

"Nah. Because now I want to help."

I didn't want to think about the prick, so I changed the

subject. "Were you just supposed to check up on me or are you here to baby-sit?"

"Baby-sit."

"Chief Rocky said, 'Get your ass out there and keep an eye on that troublesome broad, I don't want any more bodies on my hands,' right?"

"That's right. As soon as we finished up with the Frank kids, he turns to me and he says, 'Now you get your ass over to Thea Kozak's house. I'm not having any more murders on my hands.' So here I am. Your own personal bodyguard."

"He could have asked if I wanted protection." The alcohol made me hungry and I was scarfing down salted nuts at a frantic pace. To be fair, I passed the dish to Joe. He took a handful and put the dish down on his side of the table. I suspected he hadn't had any time for dinner either. Between us we'd reduced the cheese to a mouse-sized bite.

"The chief's not much for asking other people's opinions," Hennessey said. He stared at his empty glass longingly. "Mind if I have another?"

"Help yourself." My mother raised me to be a good hostess, but I was too tired to even pretend tonight. I let him get his own drink and declined his offer to pour another one for me. I was already numb from exhaustion and alcohol. Dead on my feet. Too tired to argue that I didn't want a bodyguard, to insist that I wanted to be alone. It didn't matter, really, whether he stayed or left, in terms of his intruding on my life. I was going straight to bed and when I woke up I was getting dressed and going to New Hampshire with Lisa. As soon as my head hit the pillow I was going to be in sleepyland.

He was studying my bookshelves. In the soft lamplight he looked young, even though there were bits of gray in his dark curly hair and mustache. His uniform needed pressing and he needed a shave. I could tell that he found the literary assortment peculiar. "Most of those were gifts," I said. "I keep . . . kept . . . my favorites in Maine. And the music is at work. That's where I spend most of my time."

"So I've heard," he said. "Why do you do that?"

"Do what? Work all the time? I like to work."

"That right?" He reached out and poured himself another drink and I didn't try to stop him. I wasn't his mother. The couch leather creaked softly under his weight. He leaned back against the cushions, folded his arms over his chest and stared at me, or, more particularly, at the spot where my robe was gaping. "What if this guy . . . Andre, is it? . . . that you've been seeing . . . the one who ran out on you . . . what if he showed up with an armload of flowers and got down on his knees and begged you to marry him? What would you say? Thanks, but no, I want to go on working?"

I set my own drink down with a shaky hand. "Look, Officer Hennessey—"

"Joe."

"Look, Joe, I don't mean to be rude or anything, but my relationship with Andre Lemieux is none of your business."

He smiled and picked up his drink again. "Whatever you say, but I'd never walk out on you like that. Leaving you alone when you're in danger."

"But you were sent here, like an assignment. You aren't here because . . . oh, forget it. . . ." I didn't want to talk about Andre, not even tangentially. I didn't want to talk at all. I wanted to sleep. I pushed myself out of my chair and onto unsteady feet.

"I'll show you where the guest room is and then I'm going to bed." He followed me down the short hall to the spare room I had used as a guest room and office. "There are sheets on the bed, and the bathroom is here. I don't know if the towels are clean. I've only been back in this place for one-day. I'll be in there," I pointed to my door.

Hennessey had a strange look on his face. He leaned forward until he was close enough so that I could feel the heat of his body, but he didn't touch me. "I wish I could stay with you," he said.

A man with his eye on the main chance, this Hennessey. He probably spent the rest of his time figuring out how he could replace Rocky. His timing was exquisite. I was seven steps beyond exhausted, two sheets to the wind, and recently and very publicly abandoned by my boyfriend. Primed to fall into his arms. "Thanks for the offer, Joe, but no. I'm a one-man woman, I'm not ready to write off Andre yet."

"The man's a fool to leave you like that," he said urgently. "But look, that's not what I meant. . . ." He touched his forehead with his hand, an embarrassed gesture. "I only wanted . . . I mean, nothing has to happen. Just let me be there. Let me hold you. . . ." There was an edge of loneliness in his voice, a hint of desperation. I looked at his face. There wasn't a trace of a leer or of lust. He looked a little scared and sort of sad as well as terribly embarrassed. "I'm sorry. I'm not saying this right. . . . It looks like I'm coming onto you when that isn't what I mean at all. Carol was . . . that is, it was . . . she was . . . the first murder victim I've found. You know how you felt there in the car, when you were shocked and scared and you cried? Well, that's how I felt, too, sort of."

He ran a tentative hand through his hair as he searched for the words to explain. "I mean, I could handle it, right? I'm supposed to be able to. That's what I'm trained for. It made me feel good that I was able to comfort you. Strong and powerful, you know. The cop who can handle the crime scene and comfort people, the whole thing. Taking pride in how I was calm and in control, feeling superior to you, feeling sorry for you because you couldn't take it and I could because I was the professional."

I was leaning against the door frame as I listened, and I was so tired my legs were trembling. He put out a hand and steadied me as I started to slip. Steadied me and turned me, and with an arm around my shoulders, led me toward my bed. He was still talking, and there was an urgent need in his voice that I understood. It wasn't just in his words but in his posture and his tone.

"It was only later, when I was driving here, that I realized how much I needed comforting myself." He hesitated. "That's what I'm trying to say here. That seeing something like that, and seeing her kids and their grief, and just thinking about everything that's happened . . . about pulling that poor kid out of the pond . . . it's all so sad and awful and I needed to . . . what? . . . affirm life? Cling to something good and warm and caring. Like today in the car. That wasn't a man-woman thing. It wasn't about sex. It was about two people helping each other through their pain and fear and shock. . . ."

My mind was so bleary I could barely follow him, but it sounded right. Either he was being surprisingly honest or else he was a wonderful actor. "I wasn't coming onto you because you're attractive," he said, "even though it's true, or because your boyfriend just left so, so I thought you might be an easy mark. . . ." He seated me gently on the edge of the bed and began pulling down the covers. His voice had become so quiet I could barely hear him. "I don't want to be alone tonight, that's all. I just need someone to hold me and reassure me and tell me that things will be all right. I'm sorry if I offended you. I didn't mean to."

Too weary to argue, and because I have a soft spot for strong men in pain, I reached out and took his hand. "We're just sleeping together, understand? No sex."

"Just sleep," he agreed. "No sex."

I put on one of my voluminous, comfortable flannel nightgowns. Joe stripped down to his underwear. We met in the middle of the big bed, nestled together like two spoons, and I was almost instantly asleep, falling endlessly down into a soft velvety blackness. Joe was a man of his word. He kept his hands to himself and let me sleep.

I slept heavily at first but then what I'd feared when I looked into the dark corners of my home, and what I'd drunk the bourbon to avoid, happened. I began to dream and they were not sweet dreams. I was walking down the path through the woods leading to the pond on the Bucksport campus. There were leaves on the trees, as there had been the one time I walked there, but the pond was frozen over and the path was an ugly wallow of much-trodden snow and mud. I was barefoot and in my nightgown and I walked along slowly, studying the ground, looking for footprints.

It was dusk. Light was fading rapidly under the trees. Behind me a branch snapped sharply. I turned and looked around, standing silently in the path, listening for sounds, but I could hear nothing except water dripping off trees and the too-loud sound of my own breathing. I walked slowly down the path toward the pond, the mud sucking at my feet. Behind me a branch snapped again, and this time, when I listened, I could hear the sound of footsteps. "Hello?" I called. "Hello? Who's there?" No one answered. In my sleep, I curled up into a tight, defensive ball.

At the edge of the pond I found what I'd been looking for. Undisturbed footsteps. I knelt down to examine them more closely. The two sets of footprints Rick McTeague had told me about. There was a commotion behind me, the thudding of heavy feet, as a gigantic dark shape rushed up and grabbed me. I was lifted high off the ground and carried out onto the ice, which crackled and thudded beneath our combined weight ominously. "Let me go! Put me down!" I screamed as I struggled but my captor's grip was like iron.

Ahead of us, two wet, dripping figures rose up out of the pond, shattering the ice as they rose. Chunks of broken ice flew in all directions, skittering and clattering across the frozen surface. Laney Taggert and Carol Frank stood suspended in air, surrounded by clouds of rising white steam, their faces dead white and silent with glazed, sunken eyes, their arms extended toward me, their fingers beckoning. I felt myself being lifted higher and higher and then suddenly I was catapulted through the air. I flew straight at them, a long, helpless, slow-motion drift through the misty air and then, when I should have struck them, my breath held tight against the horror of contact with those ghastly dead beckoning things, I passed right through, the only sensation not of contact but of clinging wetness and intense cold.

I hit the ice with a bone-jarring crash and it broke beneath me, dumping me into the frigid water. Then Laney and Carol were with me, their icy fingers more tangible now as they grabbed the folds of my nightgown and pulled me down, down, down into the dark water. I tried to fight them, but although they seemed to be solid when they grasped at me, when I struck out at them, my hands passed through them as if they were smoke. They were killing me and there was nothing I could do to get free. All the terror I'd experienced last night when I couldn't breathe came back. I thrashed at them, flailing frantically, trying to fight my way to the surface for air.

Screaming and sobbing, I gradually became aware that someone was holding me, stroking me, speaking to me in a calm voice. "Thea, take it easy. It's only a dream. You're okay. You're okay. No one is going to hurt you." The voice went on speaking, repeating calming things, and the hands went on stroking, but it was a long time before I was calm. A long, long time before the dark images left me and I trusted that I could breathe again. And all that time, he was calm, kind, and steady, being calm for me when I couldn't be for myself. As my eyes gradually adjusted to the dark and I could see his face, I saw that his so-perfect control was achieved through serious effort. His face was strained and as I slowly relaxed and became aware of my surroundings, I realized that our bodies were pressed tightly together and his was signaling very clearly that along with being two souls in need of care and comfort, we were undeniably a man and woman in bed together.

My feelings were scattered to all the points of the compass. One part of me wanted to exorcise those vivid ghosts who had been dragging me down into the murky pond by the very present immediacy of sex. I craved the heat, the sensation, the release. I wanted those hands that were stroking my back so steadily, so chastely, to be more impulsive, to wander, to take liberties. Going along with that impulse, another part of me, angry and defiant, wanted to flaunt my personal freedom and sleep with Hennessey as a sort of in-your-face gesture to Andre, who had abandoned me. I had no obligation, so my thinking went, to be faithful to someone who'd walked out on me. Still another part, the clearheaded, rational me, argued that you don't throw away the possibility of a fulfilling long-term relationship for a few minutes of self-indulgent pleasure.

Nature does not want us to be rational. She likes to defeat us, to render us helpless, to show us our animal nature, mocking us with our inability to control the elements, the climate, the winds, the weather, and sometimes even ourselves, and nature almost had her way. Hennessey's hands did stray, as of course they had to, he was no saint and, like me, he was needy as hell. And I didn't say "Why la, goodness me, sirrah, methinks thee doth overreach thyself" when my body responded with an involuntary wave of desire that ran through my clenched muscles, spreading through me the way a boat's wake spreads across the surface of a pond, a roaring, primitive chanting. *I want. I want. I want.*

What had Rocky said? Don't mess with the boy's head? Was I supposed to be the big kid and look after him, too? Thea the always-responsible? Thea the good. Thea the fixer. My chest was heaving and my body went on chanting *I want, I want, I want.* Oh, God, did I want! Like the good doobie that I was, I mustered enough control to say no. Gently, kindly, and regretfully, but no. It wasn't easy. It's never easy to pull back from the brink, to remove those seeking, pleasuring hands that I want, want, wanted, needed so much. But we did it. Well, okay, so I

did for Hennessey what I'd done a few times for my high
school boyfriend and what my girlfriends and I had pondered endlessly, wondering if technically it was a sex act.
Whatever the technicalities were, it put an exhausted
Hennessey to sleep and eventually my own tide of feeling
ebbed and I dropped into the deep, dreamless, restful
sleep that I needed. No one came to my door and no one
called me on the phone. I was hauled up on a safe little is-
land of sleep in the turbulent sea of life.

CHAPTER 21

JOE HENNESSEY DIDN'T even stir when the alarm went off. His face was half buried in the pillow and with his tousled hair and flushed face he looked like a little boy. I tucked the covers up around his neck and padded quietly to the kitchen, started the coffee, and then took a shower. Afterward, I wiped the steam off the mirror and peered curiously at my reflection. I didn't bother to ask if I was the fairest one of all. I was just glad I didn't break the glass. It didn't take an expert to tell me what I needed, just that glance in the glass said it all. I needed rest, sun, food, vitamins, moisturizers, conditioners, a little color in my face.

"Phooey on you," I told the mirror. The weatherman said it was going to be sunny and warming, which was good news. I needed a little sunshine in my life. I put on a long, black wool skirt, a peach-colored turtleneck, and a cozy flowered cardigan, wiped the salt off my cowboy boots and pulled them on, and put a bagel in the toaster. I was about to wake Hennessey when the phone rang. I barely had time to finish my hello before Rocky began to roar.

"Good work, detective," he said. "The desk clerk at the Monadnock Valley House positively ID'ed Drucker. We're off to talk to him this morning. Feel kinda sorry about it, though. I've always liked the guy. You'd better take it easy today . . . I didn't mean anything with what I said yesterday afternoon. I was edgy, that's all. Put Hennessey on."

"I'll see if he's awake."

"He damn well better be. Boy's supposed to be on duty."

"He's not a boy, Rocky." He harrumphed but didn't say anything more.

I asked him to wait, poured a cup of coffee, and went into the bedroom to wake Joe. He came slowly to consciousness, grabbing at the coffee like a lifeline and staring at the unfamiliar room with bleary, puzzled eyes. I had to tell him twice before he understood that Rocky was on the phone. Then he set down the coffee, rolled over, and picked up the phone. I left him to talk in privacy.

I went back to the kitchen, smeared cream cheese on the bagel, and added a bowl of cereal. I was hungry enough to eat a horse. It was true that Lisa and I were meeting someone for breakfast, but that was over an hour from now. In the past two days, I hadn't had many meals and they hadn't been substantial. I sat on my stool, eating and raising my caffeine level, watching the sun dancing on the water. It was pretty, as always, but it didn't do a thing for my gray·mood. I heard the shower run briefly and then Hennessey appeared, buttoning his shirt.

"The cupboard's pretty bare," I said. "I can do bagels or toast and cereal and juice."

"Toast and cereal would be fine," he said, "and more coffee, if you have it." He sat down at the table with his back to me, staring out at the water.

"Is something wrong?"

His shoulders went up and down but he didn't say anything.

"Hennessey, is something wrong?"

"Joe," he said without turning, "my name is Joe."

I stuck two slices in the toaster and poured a bowl of

cereal, sliding it and the milk in front of him. "Do we have to play twenty questions?"

He still didn't answer. I buttered his toast, carried the plate to the table, and sat across from him. "Talk to me, Joe."

He raised his eyes from the plate. He looked like someone who'd just lost his last friend. "I'm not feeling too good about last night."

"Because we didn't have sex? Or almost had sex? Or because you didn't sit outside my door like a faithful watchdog?" I said.

He shrugged unhelpfully. "Mixing business and pleasure."

"Two people caring for each other is wrong?" If he'd known me better he would have recognized the warning note in my voice. "I thought it was nice, myself, after that awful day—"

"I shouldn't have. We shouldn't have. . . ." he said.

"Shouldn't have what?" I said. "You're the one who suggested it. When I had that nightmare, I was very glad you were there." He didn't answer, just stared out the window, looking upset. I was getting annoyed with Joe Hennessey and I didn't want to get dragged down into the morass of his depression. If he was going to feel this guilty because he'd spent a night in my bed, he shouldn't have done it. We weren't children. We were both old enough to be responsible for our acts. "Eat your breakfast," I said. "I've got an eight-thirty appointment."

"Appointment?"

"Yes, appointment. In New Hampshire. For another client. Another job."

He shook his head. "I don't know about that. I'll have to check with Rocky."

"Forget it. I don't need Rocky running my life and I don't need you along. Someone from my office is picking me up. The bad guys aren't going to know where to find me. I'll be back around noon. If you and Rocky think I need a baby-sitter, you can come back then. Or," I said, being meaner than I should have been because he'd hurt my feelings about last night, "maybe Rocky should send someone else."

He opened his mouth but didn't get to answer because the phone rang. My mother had just read the morning papers and was charging full speed ahead with all her warnings and anxieties about the dangerous life I insisted on leading. I should have anticipated it, but my mind had been on other things. Life and death things.

"You have no idea how many phone calls I had to make to find you," she said. "You can't imagine how surprised I was when Suzanne told me you'd moved back into your condo." I groaned aloud. "Does that mean you and Andre have broken up?"

I wouldn't give her the satisfaction of knowing things were bad between us. I just said no.

She gave an elaborate maternal sigh. "Another murder. I just don't how much more of this I can stand, Theadora," she said, "you know that I was in to Dr. Barbour just last week and he's a bit concerned about my heart. My heart, Thea, and you know how dangerous stress can be to a person with a heart condition."

What could I say? "Look, Mom, you don't need to worry. I'm being very careful. In fact, I have a policeman here with me right now."

"Well, but Thea, a boyfriend . . . well, it's not the same as real police protection." I had no idea what she meant by that; Andre was as real as cops got, but before I could tell her that it wasn't Andre, she was babbling on. "That reminds me. I've called you several times about Christmas. I assume that secretary of yours has been giving you the messages. Now, I don't like to nag, you know how I hate to nag, but I need to know so I can plan. Is Andre coming with you?"

I settled for "I don't know," squelching a rude urge to tell her she could buy an extra half pound of meat and take her chances. It wasn't her fault Andre and I were fighting, and Hennessey and I were fighting. I was just a belligerent little thing. Couldn't get along with anyone. "We've been so busy we haven't had time to discuss it."

"Well, discuss it with him, dear, won't you please? Right now. I can wait a few minutes. Or you could call me back."

"Andre's not here. It's one of the Sedgwick police. Someone to watch over me." She made me so crazy. In another minute I'd be singing Cole Porter.

"Well, can't you call him and then call me back?"

Rather than trying to explain the complexities of the situation, which really weren't any of her business, and because I knew she'd gloat if Andre disappeared from the picture—she'd never quite approved of her daughter being involved with a cop, anyway—I agreed that I'd talk to Andre later in the day and call her back. I didn't have time to reach the table before the phone rang again. A woman's voice, high, querulous, and unfamiliar. She asked if Joe Hennessey was there. I agreed that he was and asked if she'd like to speak with him.

"No," she said, "just give him a message. Tell him that Maureen called. He's supposed to have the kids today and I've got plans. Tell him if he's not here by nine I'm leaving them at the station and after that it's up to him." She disconnected before I could say anything.

Joe Hennessey was watching me glumly from the table. "Was that Maureen?"

"Yes. She says you're supposed to have the kids today and that if you aren't there by nine she's leaving them at the station."

He threw his spoon into his empty bowl with a clatter and checked his watch. At least, I noticed, he hadn't been too upset to eat. "What time are you being picked up?"

"Seven-thirty." The doorbell rang. "Right now," I said, and went to let Lisa in.

She took off her silly pom-pomed ski hat and set it on the chest in the entry, then shook out her hair. "Whew!" she said. "I almost didn't make it. That hus-band of mine must have been in tune-out mode when I told him I had to leave early for work this morning, because he got up, got dressed, ate his breakfast, and was about to sashay off to the office with his briefcase when he noticed I was about to sashay off with my briefcase. We looked like one of those working couples from the TV commercial where they're both about to go to work and forget the baby sitting there in its chair. Anyway, he puffed himself all up like a self-important toad and said he was sorry but he had to go to work early, it was important."

"Is he still among the living?" I asked.

"The walking wounded. I took your advice. I said that despite our agreement to share the work, I'd taken Charlotte to day care every day for the past four weeks, that I'd called him at work especially to remind him I had to leave early today, that it was his turn and if he couldn't do it, then maybe he should call his mother. Then I unwound Charlotte from my leg, wound her around his, and left, and let me tell you, I feel like I've just broken out of jail!" Her eyes drifted past me and noticed Hennessey, standing by the table.

"Lisa, this is Joe Hennessey, my uh . . . bodyguard." Like the true professional that she was, Lisa stepped past me and shook Joe's hand and kept her face from showing anything but bland courtesy. I gave up on my breakfast and went to the closet to get my jacket. "How cold is it?"

"Nice," she said.

I grabbed my black leather jacket with the politically incorrect, animal-unfriendly fur lining, which was my favorite piece of clothing in the whole world and a gift from my husband, David. The Mace that lived in my pocket clinked gently against the little handheld alarm that always lived there, courtesy of Andre Lemieux, and the closest I'd ever come to carrying a weapon. In Massachusetts you need a permit to buy Mace, and all the policemen who liked to look out for me had made sure I was permitted up to my earlobes. I probably could have legally carried a grenade launcher, but they were too big to fit in my pockets.

A little bit of song flitted through my mind as I turned to say good-bye to Hennessey. A song that went something like, "Good-bye Joe, me gotta go, me oh my oh. . . ." Knowing he was already in a glum and put-upon frame of mind, I was kind enough not to sing it. All I said was, "'Bye, Joe. I'll be back in Sedgwick around twelve."

He should have demanded my itinerary, perhaps even come with me, but he was now on the daddy track, trying to get home in time to stop Maureen from humiliating him by dumping his kids at the station. He barely registered my departure. It was a supremely poor ending to our night of comfort and kindness and reminded me of why it was that as one grew older, the idea of one-night stands became increasingly less appealing. Invariably they were more trouble than they were worth. Not that I had much experience with one-night stands. I was relatively inexperienced when I met David, having been made shy and cautious by an adolescence burdened by a large chest and boys who had trouble seeing the person behind it, and my one-night stand with David had lasted for two glorious years.

I grabbed a hat and gloves, having been well trained by my mother never to go out in the winter without all the proper gear, just in case something happened to the car and I had to walk, and Lisa and I left. I was also very good about wearing clean underwear. Not once in my innumerable trips to the emergency room had I embarrassed my mother by having holes in my underwear, only holes in my body.

The guest spots were empty again, except for a battered Datsun that distinctly lowered the tone of the neighborhood. Probably belonged to one of my neighbor's college-age kids home for the holidays. I handed Lisa my keys and she slid happily behind the wheel. "What's with the sullen hunk?" she said.

I wasn't surprised. You don't hire someone because they're good at reading people and then expect them not to use their talents. "The chief was afraid someone might try to kill me again. He sent Hennessey along as a baby-sitter."

"And?"

"The two of us discovered a body together yesterday. And last night we shared a couple drinks, and he was supposed to stick around and make sure I was safe. . . ."

"And Andre just walked out on you. And you were bone tired and Joe Hennessey happens to be a handsome hunk of a man, so . . ."

"So you're almost right. One thing almost did lead to another. It's funny, though, I never really noticed what he looked like."

"I wouldn't tell him that. Almost, huh? So how do you feel today? Disappointed or pleased with yourself?"

"I'm fine. Maybe I'm getting more masculine in my approach or something, but it didn't bother me. It was Hennessey who got upset. I guess glum, sensitive, brooding guys just aren't my type."

"It could be Irish guilt," she said. "The madonna/whore complex. Now that he's spent the night with you he doesn't know where to put you . . . he's either got to head toward marriage or assume you're a slut, which he knows you're not, so he doesn't know what to do. It never occurs to them that they're sluts, so they just get glum and confused."

"Sounds like an ad hominem fallacy to me. I think it's more likely he thought he should have stayed up and kept watch instead of sleeping."

She shrugged airily. "Well, I won't try to force the theory on you, but remember, I'm the one who went to a Catholic college. But tell me honestly, it really doesn't bother you to have jumped into bed with a stranger like that? Okay, I know I'm being too nosy. You don't have to answer. Maybe, after four years of absolute monogamy and motherhood, I'm dying for a little vicarious adventure."

"But nothing happened. We came close but you know me . . . the queen of self-control."

"You slept in the same bed?" I nodded. "And nothing happened?"

"That's right."

"Nothing?"

"Nothing."

She made a face. "I'm heartbroken. I always wanted to be just like you when I grew up, but now I don't know. How could you pass up such an extraordinary opportunity to get completely carried away?" I just shrugged and that was the end of it. We were in Nashua in what seemed like no time at all and Lisa handed me her carefully written directions to the restaurant where we were going to meet Greg Jenner.

We told the waitress we were meeting someone and she said, "He's already here," and led us to a booth at the back where a slight man huddled glumly over a cup of coffee. I let Lisa take the lead, since she'd made the contact, and she greeted him warmly as we slid onto the bench facing him.

"We really appreciate your willingness to do this, Greg," she said, "I know it must be very unpleasant for you to relive the experience."

"You can say that again," he said. He had thick dark hair and hazel eyes and while he wasn't conventionally handsome, he had nice features that with a little animation would have been attractive. Instead he had a beaten-down air that was painful to see. "For about two weeks there, until that desk man got back from vacation and told his version of things, I thought I was watching my whole life go down the toilet over a piece of ass I didn't even get. When you called, I almost said no to you. I'd put all that behind me and didn't want to think about it again. But I couldn't let her get away with doing it to someone else, you know? Not knowing what I went through."

"Would you tell us the story again?" I said.

He shrugged. "Guess I might as well."

The waitress came and filled our cups and asked if we'd like to order. Lisa and Greg ordered little breakfasts, but I got the Lumberjack's Special—two eggs, bacon, toast and home fries, with orange juice and coffee and three buttermilk pancakes. I was betting I could eat every single bite, too. As soon as she left, he told us the story.

"I made the mistake of assuming she was helpless," he began. "She was a new teacher and she seemed so shaky and insecure that I felt sorry for her. She came to me pretty often for advice and I made the time to talk to her. And she was fun, you know, kind of cheerful and flirty and it made me feel good to be helping her." He spread his hands wide. "I used to be Mr. Nice Guy. Ask anyone who knew me then. I liked to help people. LaVonne changed all that. I don't know . . . I guess I'll never know . . . whether she genuinely misconstrued my help as something more, or whether she's just really screwed up. I guess what Lisa tells me about what she's trying to do to your client suggests she's just screwed up. It's too bad. She could have been a good teacher, too." He shook his head sadly.

"Anyway, on what the police kept referring to as 'the night in question,' I'd stayed late to get some work done. My wife had taken the girls to visit her parents for the weekend so I didn't have to rush home. I was in the classroom trying to get a head start on a bunch of worksheets when LaVonne came in in tears. The principal had audited her class that day and things had gotten a little out of control and since it was her first year and she was a probationary employee, she was afraid she'd really blown it. I stopped what I was doing and tried to reassure her. Told her all the usual stuff. That the principal understood how things were for a new teacher. That classrooms often get out of control when there are outsiders observing. That I was sure she was doing a fine job. All that stuff."

He stopped talking while the waitress delivered our food and then there was a lull in his narrative while he ate. Lisa made some small talk about his daughters, told him about Charlotte, and gently lifted his spirits, which had been sinking visibly while he talked. He ate quickly and efficiently and got back to his story, obviously in a hurry to be finished. I didn't blame him. I'd had my share of run-ins with the police and I knew how infuriated and helpless you felt when they didn't believe what you were telling them. Despite our system of assuming a person is innocent until proven guilty, you don't feel as though you have any rights or any protection when the police are treating you like the scum of the earth. I told him so and he smiled for the first time.

"Exactly," he said. "I've never felt so helpless. So anyway, LaVonne asked if I'd have a drink with her. She said she really needed one and she hated to drink alone. I figured what the hell, just because I was married didn't mean I could never again in my life be seen with a woman who wasn't my wife . . . I mean, I knew Lynne would understand. She was marvelous through the whole thing. Never doubted me for a second." He stopped and looked at me. "Are you married?"

"I was. He died."

"I'm sorry," he said, and he sounded as if he meant it.

I felt the beginnings of a real righteous anger toward LaVonne Rawlins. Whatever her own personal problems, she'd sure done a number on Greg Jenner. She'd taken a nice and generous man and hurt him so that he no longer dared to be spontaneous, so that he was afraid to be kind. Now she was trying to do the same thing to Denzel. Denzel was a different kind of man and the harm would be more to his professional status, but in the end, it would hurt him personally as well.

"We went to the bar at the Mountaingate Inn. I had a drink, I think she had two or three, but probably only two. A couple times while we were sitting there, LaVonne had put her hand on my thigh and once she brushed her breast against my shoulder. I was getting kind of nervous, wondering how I was going to handle her, so I said I had to be getting home. We'd come in separate cars and the quickest way out was down the motel corridor and out a door. As we went down the hall, she stumbled. I grabbed her arm to steady her and she tried to kiss me. I asked her not to, reminded her that I was married. Then she slapped me and ran out. I got in my car and drove home and didn't think any more about it until two cops came to my door the next day and arrested me for sexual assault. The next few days were hell on earth."

"Would you be willing to repeat all this on videotape?" I asked.

"I'd rather not," he said.

"I know. And I understand. I was just trying to think of a way to persuade her lawyer to back off without the necessity for you to have to see her again. If we could get your story on tape and copies of the police and court records, I think we could do that."

He was silent for a while, cradling his coffee in his hands and not looking at either of us. Finally he raised his eyes. "Okay," he said. "I'll do it."

After I paid for breakfast we separated. Lisa and Greg left in Greg's car with the video camera to go the school to tape his statement. I went to the Nashua Police Department to see if I could get any information. I knew that there was a wide variety of responses I might meet. Some police departments are user-friendly and believe in treating citizens decently; some operate like paramilitary organizations and refuse to give out records and information even if people are entitled to get them. There was no way I was entitled to stuff about Greg, even though he'd given me a handwritten note with his permission, so I was praying for user-friendly.

Although lately it had seemed like I was rather unlucky, today was my lucky day. The senior officer on duty was gentlemanly, polite, and bored out of his mind. He was happy to be interrupted by an attractive woman who was begging for a few minutes of his valuable time.

He also remembered Greg Jenner's case very well and recognized the damage that it had done. He was outraged to hear that LaVonne was trying the same thing again and glad to do what he could to help me out. I left with copies of LaVonne's interview, Greg's interview, and the desk clerk's interview and his promise to send me copies of the court documents as soon as he could get them. I also left with a warm feeling in my heart for those cops who elevate justice over rules.

I followed Greg's directions to the school and found Lisa standing alone by the door, soaking up some sun and reading a paperback book. She shut it and shoved it into her briefcase. We traded places and before she backed up, we slapped palms in a celebratory gesture of solidarity. Things were looking better all the time for Denzel Ellis-Jackson. As long as I didn't think about the Bucksport School, it was a fine day.

"You done good," I said.

"I am feeling rather proud of myself," she said. "Now all we need to do is finesse this just right."

"I think we can let Emmett do that." Emmett was a superb blend of the courtly and the crafty and he would play this like a poker hand. I closed my eyes and let Lisa drive me home.

CHAPTER 22

LISA AND I put the tape she'd made in my VCR and reviewed it. We both thought Greg Jenner came across very well. Then she left, taking the tape and the interview records I'd finagled to give to Emmett Hampton. I called the office. Things were quiet. Checked my voice mail. Lots of messages but no one wanted me for anything urgent, no one desperately wanted anything from me. No excuse to avoid going back to Bucksport. No call from the one person I wanted to hear from. This time it was up to me.

My listless, purposeless state didn't last long. I'm not the relaxed type. I called Suzanne, learned from Paul that she was out at Bucksport, and called her there. She sounded almost cheerful when she came on the phone. "Hi, partner," she said, "how'd it go this morning?"

"Very well, I think. The guy she dug up in New Hampshire is great. Very similar circumstances. Emmett and the rest of them are going to be very pleased. Lisa's going to do some more prowling around. I think she loves this detective stuff. She can't wait to go and talk to the people at the hotel."

"The folks at King already think you walk on water, Thea."

"Not me. Us."

"You are too modest for words. Well, we're doing pretty well out here, too, considering the circumstances. Coincidental with yesterday's nasty discovery, last night there was an ammonia leak at the skating rink and a water pipe broke in one of the dorms. I won't comment on whether these disasters were the result of natural causes other than to say that for once Curt Sawyer was a help rather than a hindrance. The whole campus had to be temporarily evacuated because of the ammonia and Dorrie is using it as an excuse to send everyone home early." She sighed.

"Today we've got a group of grumpy, tired trustees calling the parents and telling them to come and get their kids. I don't have to tell you what a headache it is. You know this place is Dysfunction Junction. We could use a full-time travel agent just to rearrange the flight schedules because Suzi can't go to Daddy in Santa Barbara yet because he and his third wife aren't back from Hawaii, and little Jerry wasn't supposed to arrive until next Saturday 'cuz Mummy's redoing his suite in a style more suited to his mature status. Probably putting in a minibar and an armoire stocked with designer condoms. But it's good for me. Keeps me from thinking about whether my own kid really is adjusting happily to life with Marion. She seems too good to be true. How are you doing?"

"Other than Bucksport, you mean? I'm teetering on the verge of the holiday blues. My mother wants to know if Andre is coming for Christmas dinner. I'm beginning to wish I could just skip the whole holiday season this year. Go to sleep on December twenty-fourth and wake up on January second. Once I've unpacked and done some laundry. I've been living out of a suitcase so long I feel like a traveling salesperson." I checked my watch. "If I hit the road now, I'll be there in less than an hour."

"You kill me, Thea," she said. "Most people look forward to the holidays."

"Most people lie. Besides, maybe most people haven't just had their homes trashed, their lovers walk out on them, topped like the cherry on a sundae by finding a body in a trunk. Most people live less eventful lives."

"You're whining," she said.

I'm lucky to have such a sympathetic partner. "True," I agreed. "All I want for Christmas is for the killer to be caught. I can't stop thinking about Carol Frank and Laney Taggert. I'd love to have my mind back."

"I know," she said. "I understand. I've got to go do some hand-holding. I'll see you when you get here." There was a pause, and then she said, "Did you eat?" My partner knows me too well.

"The biggest damned lumberjill breakfast you ever saw."

For all that she chides me for being too serious, Suzanne is even worse, but the "lumberjill" brought a genuine laugh. I unpacked the bag I'd taken to San Francisco. Less than a week ago and it felt like years. I felt silly and sad as I put away all the bits of frilly lingerie and the silk paisley bathrobe. I wondered how Andre was doing and whether our split had sent him back into his depression. The last thing out of the suitcase was one of his shirts I'd brought home to sew a button on. I buried my face in it, put it on, and inhaled his scent. I spent a full five minutes being a sentimental fool before I took off the shirt, threw it into the laundry bin with the rest of my things, and headed for Bucksport, giving the parking lot a quick once-over as I left. El Dorado was gone but now the rusty junker was in his spot with the hood up and one door open. Someone was lying underneath it with only his feet sticking out. Very reassuring. It didn't seem likely that I was being stalked by a car repair junkie.

I was only a couple miles down the road when the phone rang. My ESP told me it was going to be Rocky, so I braced myself for a boom of sound. I was right. His voice filled the car, more irascible than ever. "Okay, Sherlock," he said, "Drucker's got ironclad alibis for both murders. The night Laney Taggert was killed he was at dinner with a whole table of students and then went with

them, on a bus, to the movies and then out for ice cream."
He sounded as if it were somehow my fault.

"What about Friday?"

"Friday afternoon he went to the dentist and did some
errands . . . and he had time-dated receipts for the things
he bought . . . you'd think he was expecting me to ask . . .
then he and Ellie had dinner with a friend from out of
town and then he attended a lecture on Henry David
Thoreau's relevance to the nineties at the Unitarian
Church, had an Irish coffee at the pub and the friend
came back to spend the night. Have you got any more
bright ideas?"

I felt like I'd been physically assaulted. If Drucker
wasn't the killer, we were right back at square one, and
no, I didn't have any more bright ideas. Somehow, bright
ideas and murder didn't seem to go together. "What
about Chris Fuller? Or Josh? Aren't they still viable candidates? Anyway, Rocky"—I put on my sweetest voice—
"you're the cop. I'm just a lame-brained girl consultant.
How should I know?" Unnecessary, maybe, but I was annoyed that he, who'd been so ready to dismiss me, now
seemed to think we were a team.

"We're looking into it," he growled. "Call me if you do
get any ideas." He hung up.

I mentally reviewed my interviews. If the students
were going home, was there anyone I still needed to talk
to? Nadia Soren, the one Josh said Laney might have
confided in, had gone home. I'd never caught up with her.
The guy from grounds and buildings was missing. I'd
learned about all I was going to learn about procedures,
all that was left was the report. I wasn't even sure why I
was going back, except that I felt that I had to be there.
That maybe if I was there, something would happen or
something would change. Like someone coming up to
me and confessing.

I was tired and grouchy and I felt like a failure at work,
with men, in life. Lisa's coup this morning was the only
bright spot in an otherwise unendingly dim existence.

Why had I been such a fool as to let Hennessey into my bed? Why did I stubbornly cling to a job where I had nothing to offer? Then I mentally kicked myself. I had a lot to offer. Dorrie hadn't hired me to solve a murder, she'd hired me to do a procedures audit. If I accomplished nothing else, I could get rid of the Donahues and Chas Drucker, selfish adults who had preyed upon the vulnerabilities of the students in their care. I slammed my foot down on the pedal and the car responded so promptly I almost rear-ended the car in front of me.

As usual, my arch nemesis, the phone, continued to interrupt me. This time my ESP supplied no advance information, and when I said hello, a voice on the other end hit me with such a barrage of speech I couldn't process a word. "Excuse me," I said, "but you've got to slow down. I'm not catching anything you're saying."

"It's me, Rick McTeague. You remember. The writer." His voice was high and excited, like a record speeded up. "We were going to go over the murder scene but then I got hung up. I'm terribly sorry but when the creative juices are flowing I just have to go with them. All part of being a writer, I'm afraid. The characters just speak through me and I have to let them. Now I hear there's been another murder and you found the body. You must tell me all about it. Very important, that firsthand-experience stuff. Lends a real authentic touch to the work."

The wash of words rolled me around like a body caught by a wave. When I finally came up for air I cut off the flow. "Mr. McTeague, please, you've got to slow down or I'm not going to be able to follow you. We're in traffic."

"Rick," he said. "Please call me Rick. I'm sorry. I do tend to run on when I'm excited, but you see I am excited. I've just remembered something important that I didn't tell you the other day. Something very important."

"What is it, Rick?"

He laughed, the high-pitched bray of an agitated donkey. "I'm not telling," he said coyly, "but I'm willing to trade."

"What do you mean, you're willing to trade? This isn't a game. Two people have been murdered."

"I know. That's why I want to trade. My story for yours."

"I don't understand."

"Of course you do. I want you to tell me all about finding Carol Frank and in return I'll tell you what I just remembered about the murder scene. It's a fair deal."

"It's a sick deal and you know it. If you have information about Laney Taggert's death you ought to call Chief Miller right now and share it with him."

"I don't think so," he said. "They were not very nice when they questioned me. Miller and his people insist on treating me like a nutcase instead of respecting me for the author that I am." There was a protracted silence on his end. Silence to me at least. I could hear him talking to someone.

"Rick? Rick? Are you there?" I said. I jammed on the brakes and swerved around a Chevette doing fifty in the fast lane. Chevettes are the Pinto's first cousins. The people who drive them are always too small to see over the steering wheel and holding the wheel with a death grip. They also have the most annoying habits of anyone on the road. Always in the high-speed lanes. Always slowing down. Fearful as bunnies, they will brake for a snowflake. Someday I'm going to get my own APC and start driving right over them.

There was the clattering sound of the phone being dropped and then picked up again. "Ms. Kozak? Are you still there? Sorry. I got distracted by an idea and when I have an idea, I immediately write it down before I lose it. Many writers carry three-by-five cards for that purpose but not me. I'm high-tech. I carry a tape recorder. You wouldn't believe how people stare at me. One insensitive soul even asked me to leave a meeting. Just because I was dictating. Can you believe that?"

I could believe that the world was full of people as disgusted and astonished by Rick McTeague's sick, oblivious, self-centered personality as I was. But what I said was, "What did you remember?"

He gave another braying laugh. "Oh, no. Don't think you can trick me. Remember, I spend my life thinking up ways for people to trick each other. You know the deal. Now it's up to you. But remember"—his voice dropped so low I could barely hear it—"I won't tell anyone else."

I figured as soon as I got him off the phone I'd call Rocky and sic him onto McTeague but the bastard read my mind. Or maybe I was just so influenced by his sleaziness that I was beginning to think like him. "Won't do you any good to call the chief, either. I won't tell him anything. Not even if they pistol-whip me or stick my ass in jail. I've been wondering what it's like to be pistol-whipped or nightsticked or hit with a blackjack. It's not the kind of experience a law-abiding citizen gets to have. And I've always wanted to be in jail. The hard mattresses, uncivilized company, exposed toilets, leering guards—"

"Has anyone ever told you that you're sick, McTeague? That you need professional help?"

But Rick McTeague wasn't receiving messages. The man was a one-way street; there was no back-and-forth. "I'm trying to get professional help," he said. "Your help. I'll be at the beginning of the path in forty-five minutes. That should give you enough time. Wear rubber boots if you have 'em. That path is a real mess. And if you don't show, well, that's your choice, but I thought you wanted to solve the case."

"That's Chief Miller," I began, "he's the one—" But McTeague just laughed and hung up on me.

Anyone who has lived through more than one New England winter never leaves home without foul-weather gear in their car. I had my Bean boots. I had a hat and gloves. I had a heavy sweater. And I had time to get there. I checked to see that I still had the Mace and the alarm. I didn't expect I'd need them but it was reassuring to have them along. McTeague didn't seem dangerous, unless I was at risk of being talked to death, but once I'd learned what he had to share, I might give him a blast of Mace just so he could have the experience.

Just to be safe, as I'd promised Andre, I called Rocky to tell him what I was doing, but no one knew where to find him. Time was short, so I called Curt Sawyer, who could be found, and told him what was going on. After a bit of bluster, he agreed that maybe someone could keep watch and stay out of sight. Someone to watch over me. I wove my way down 128 through four lanes of sluggish traffic, wondering, idly, whether promises made to a guy who's deserted you are still in force.

McTeague was waiting for me, wearing his idea of what a detective wears to revisit the scene of the crime—a belted tan raincoat, faded brown fedora, and a plaid Burberry scarf. The oversized raincoat ballooned out around his thin frame like a dress and the hat was too big for his head. The ensemble was finished with green Wellington boots and a sturdy walking stick. I half expected him to produce a pipe and make me wait while he lit it, but he didn't. I reminded myself to be grateful for little things. We were almost at the shortest day of the year and I had no desire to be trudging through the woods in the dark.

"You made good time," he said. "I was afraid you'd be late and I have another appointment."

"With whom?"

"Josh Meyer. I called him after I spoke to you. Professor Hamlin said the poor kid was feeling a little down so I said I'd pick him up and take him out for dinner. His dad's coming tomorrow, you know. They don't get along."

"Are you going to tell Josh your big secret, too?"

He shrugged. "I might. He has an interest in this case, too, you know. He loved that girl even though she was seeing Drucker."

I stopped dead, staring at him. "You knew about Drucker? And you didn't tell anyone?"

He shrugged again, trying to be elaborately casual, but his delight in putting one over on us was too obvious. "No one asked."

If there hadn't already been enough death on the campus, I would have strangled him on the spot. "How did you know about Drucker?"

He gave me that horrible, infuriating smile again. "Something I heard. After you," he said, waving toward the path. I set off, trying to ignore my anxiety about setting off into the woods with a weird man who was carrying a big stick. Our feet were incredibly noisy on the path, especially his. The rubber made thick squelching sounds as he stomped through the mud. It had been a warm day and the warm air on the cold snow had created a rising mist so that it looked as though we were setting off into a bowl of dry ice. Too much like my dream for comfort. All around us little waves of mist were floating up among the black tree trunks. We might have been in one of Tolkien's living forests.

"Well, we're off," he said cheerfully. "So tell me about the poisoning."

"That wasn't part of the deal."

"Well, I'm changing the deal."

There was no sense in arguing with him. He wasn't susceptible to reason and he was as thick-skinned as an armadillo. I gave him a brief description of my ordeal and waited for the questions that were bound to follow. He wanted to know everything about the symptoms, my reactions, the reactions of people around me, and all the while we were tramping deeper and deeper into the woods and it was getting darker and foggier and colder and my skin was beginning to crawl.

Finally I stopped, turned around, and confronted him. "I don't believe you have anything to tell me. This is just a trick to pump me for details and I'll bet you don't have the faintest idea how unpleasant it is for me to have to face that experience again. This isn't simply something you can make happen to a character in your book! It really happened. I was poisoned. If I'd eaten that sandwich I would have died. And Laney Taggert and Carol Frank did die. It's not just a matter of turning the pages, McTeague. It happened." I'd had enough. It was stupid of me to have come out here at all and I was ending the stupidity right now.

A look of something like panic swept over his face and he raised his walking stick. It looked like he was going to hit me. I covered my head with my hands, dashed past him, and started running. "Wait!" he yelled, charging after me. "We're almost there. Come back. I'll tell you. I promise I will."

I stopped a safe distance away and looked back, not knowing whether to believe him or not, and wondered why Sawyer's carefully placed man hadn't jumped out of the bushes by now. McTeague was standing in the center of the path, shoulders slumped, and hat pulled low, the picture of dejection. Little patches of mist obscured his feet. "I mean it," he said. "No more games. This is no time to quit; we're almost there."

"Okay," I called, my voice distorted by the damp air, "but you have to promise no more questions about the poison."

We turned and retraced our steps. This time I stayed farther away from him. "It's just around that bend," he said, hurrying so that he was beside me. He was panting a little, which seemed odd for a regular jogger, but maybe it was an effort to keep the boots on his feet or his hat on his head. He looked ridiculous but given his overall lack of self-awareness, he probably had a magic mirror at home that told him he was the reincarnation of Dash Hammett. He grabbed my arm and steered me to a little rise looking down toward the pond.

"Picture the scene," he whispered. "Early morning, the first light just filtering into the sky with the promise of a clear, bright day. Temperature around thirty. A few inches of fresh snow on the ground. I was pounding along, feeling the physical rush from my exertion, exhilarated that I was fifty-four and my body still ran like a finely tuned machine." His voice rose as he spoke. "I was all alone in the world, the only tracks disturbing the snow were my own. I was free to imagine that I was the only inhabitant." The trail before us dipped down to a spot where the brush at the edge of the pond had been cleared away, then rose again and disappeared into the trees.

"I was coming from that direction," he said, pointing toward the other rise. "I broke out of the trees and suddenly there were other footprints. Naturally I noticed them." He grabbed my arm again and tried to pull me down the slope.

"I don't like being grabbed," I said, shaking him off.

"I'm interested in footprints," he said as we walked down to the edge of the ice, "aren't you?" I just shrugged. "Okay, let me set the scene for you." He pointed back the way we'd come. "Two sets of footprints coming from that way, down to the edge of the ice here, where we're standing. They paused here—I could tell from the way the area was trampled—and then went out onto the ice together, out to about here." Once again he grabbed my arm and tugged me forward. Once again I shook him off.

The ice between my feet gave an ominous crack and I made an involuntary startled sound. "It's okay," he said, "you're perfectly safe. The ice is plenty thick now. It's been below freezing for more than a week, until yesterday. Ice just makes those sounds as it expands and contracts." I felt a little foolish. I knew lakes did that. I was just a bit shaky, given the circumstances. "Now, about here," he drew a line in the snow with his foot, "the footprints showed signs of a struggle."

The pond around us showed all sorts of signs of a struggle, no doubt the product of yesterday's search for the missing duffle bag. In fact just ahead of us was a large black patch of thin, snow-free ice. He stared at it for a moment, a puzzled look on his face. "Yeah," he said, "the single set of staggering footprints led to a hole just like that . . . well, not exactly like that. It was smaller. And I could see a pink glove under the ice." He leaned forward and peered at the ice as though expecting to see another pink glove. "Looks like someone made a new hole. I wonder why."

"The police made a new hole. Yesterday," I said.

"Why?" he asked eagerly.

"I know but I'm not telling," I said, feeling as if I were eight years old and arguing with my brother Michael, "until you tell me something."

"You're learning," he said, nodding approvingly. "Okay, I guess I've played around long enough. Now, the footprints came out to about here and then, as I said, the one set went staggering on alone, like this—" He gave me a tremendous shove that sent me staggering forward toward the thin black ice. To avoid it, I hurled myself sideways, landing with a bone-jarring crash on the ice.

I was up and after him before he'd stopped laughing, fueled by fury at my stupidity for coming out here with him and his mean-spirited craziness. I still didn't think he was the killer but he could have just accidentally killed me by his stupid playacting and it probably wouldn't have bothered him a bit. I wrenched his walking stick away from him and whacked him with it. He fell back, cringing, and I whacked him again."

Where in hell was my police protection, anyway? "Okay, McTeague," I said, "the game's over. Now tell me what you brought me out here for and then get the hell out of here before I hit you again."

"Go ahead and hit me," he said, a shaky defiance in his voice. "I've never been beaten up by a woman."

"Well, don't flatter yourself that this counts for anything," I said. "If I really wanted to do some harm, I'd aim for your head, wouldn't I?" I swung the stick again, this time landing it on his thigh. He whined and clutched at his leg. "Now tell."

"It's about the footprints," he said quickly. "What was unusual about them."

Playing games was so natural for him that he couldn't

resist. He stopped there and grinned up at me. "You want to guess what it was?"

I swung the stick so it passed within inches of his head. "I said no more games."

"Okay, okay, control yourself," he said. "What was unusual about the footprints was that they were both small. Unless the person who met Laney Taggert and brought her out here was a man with tiny feet, Laney Taggert was killed by a woman."

I threw McTeague's stick out onto the patch of thin ice where it broke a hole and fell through. "You bitch!" he roared, getting to his feet and charging toward me. "That was my special stick."

I'd had enough of boys and their special sticks growing up with Michael. McTeague had made the mistake of confusing me with a character from his book. Probably the transsexual police officer in love with her former partner. Poor guy. He was in for a rude surprise. I pulled the Mace out of my pocket and gave Rick McTeague a generous opportunity to savor a new experience. I left him on his knees on the ice, groaning and wailing and pawing at his face like a bear fighting off bees, and walked back to my car.

On my way back, I saw no sign of Sawyer's man. By the time I reached my car, I was shaking with the realization that probably, Sawyer being the arrogant, slipshod asshole that he was, there hadn't been anyone there and I'd just been the biggest damned fool on the planet.

CHAPTER 23

THERE WAS A Sedgwick police car parked beside mine, the light flashing, and, as always happens when there's a police car, curiosity had drawn a small crowd of students to see what was going on. As I emerged from the woods, Joe Hennessey detached himself from the crowd and hurried down the path toward me. When I was in range, he greeted me with a blast that made it clear he'd been too long under the influence of Chief Rocky Miller. "Just what the hell do you think you're doing?" were the first words out of a mouth that not so long ago had been trying to be intimately attached to mine.

The curious students trailed behind him like a gaggle of baby ducks. "Not here, Joe," I said, furious with him for showing so little discretion in front of them. "At my office."

He tried to block my way. "Not so fast, Thea," he said. "First tell me what you're doing out here?"

"Officer Hennessey," I said loudly, and then lowered my voice so that he had to lean forward to hear me. "We are busting our butts out here to keep things calm on this campus. If you insist on standing here and shouting at me like you are some medieval lout and I am your wench, I will refuse to say another word to you or Rocky or anyone in the Sedgwick Police Department, you understand? And I have some very important words to say, too."

The skin around his mouth and eyes was tight and pale with anger but he wheeled without a word, stormed back to his car, and drove away without running over a single student. I stayed behind a minute to reassure the students. "It's all right," I said. "Just a security thing. The police are supposed to keep an eye on unfamiliar cars on campus and Officer Hennessey didn't realize this was mine." They probably didn't know me from Adam but the key was to act as though I belonged. If I said I did, they'd accept it. It seemed to work.

"Jeez," one lanky boy said, "my dad's coming tomorrow to pick me up. He gonna get the hairy-eyeball treatment, too?"

"Hairy eyeball?" a girl said, giving him the full benefit of her mocking grin. "Chad, that is so lame!"

"Yeah?" he said. "So what would you call it?"

"Police harassment," she said. "It's the pits. Ever since Laney died, this place has been crawling with cops. I half expect one to crawl out of the toilet every time I flush."

The others chimed in with their own versions of the intrusive police presence on campus—exactly what Dorrie and I had tried so hard to avoid—and I left them to it, reassured to see that the country was turning out another generation of young people with a healthy respect for the police. I got in the car and drove to the administration building. Hennessey's car was there but he was nowhere to be seen. Maybe he'd gone to tell on me and bring Rocky down on me as well. Which was fine. I didn't mind telling the story once instead of twice. My body, which was still feeling abused, thought it was bedtime.

I turned the corner and saw Dorrie, Rocky, and Suzanne striding purposefully toward me and I could see that I had a long way to go before I slept. They came at me like a flying wedge, caught me up in their midst, and swept me back down the hall to Dorrie's office. Seated and with the door securely closed behind us, I stared out at the now-dark campus and braced myself for Rocky's attack.

It was Suzanne, my partner and my friend, who attacked. "I know you are impulsive," she said. "And I know that while the rest of us have outgrown our illusions of immortality, you still cling to yours, but I've always assumed that you aren't a fool. Now I'm beginning to wonder."

They sat like a parole board, Suzanne, Dorrie, Rocky, and Hennessey, and stared at me like I was an incomprehensible and slightly dangerous object. I didn't understand why they were upset. "What's going on here?" I said. "What is it that I'm supposed to have done that has you all upset?"

"Stayed out of telephone reach all day when no one knew where you were," Rocky said. "Left your house without telling anyone where you were going. Went into the woods by yourself when you know there's a killer on the campus—"

"Suzanne knew where I was all morning. I was working, just like I am now. I called her. I talked with her and we agreed to talk again later. Officer Hennessey knew, too." I glared at both of them. Suzanne, at least, had the grace to look a little embarrassed but Hennessey just stared through me. I didn't share the insight his behavior gave me with the rest of the group, but I realized that one of the reasons I'd overlooked against the one-night stand is wondering how the other person will look to you the next day. We hadn't even had a one-night stand and he still looked like a handsome sack of manure.

"No one told me I was supposed to be reporting my whereabouts. Not that it would have done any good anyway. If I called in and said I was at home and then the killer came, broke in, and killed me, how am I supposed to have been helped? It won't matter a tinker's damn to me how soon my body is found, once I'm already dead. What I don't understand, Rocky—" This time I focused my anger on him. It was pretty powerful anger, too, the concentrated result of being poisoned, Andre's departure, the outrageous Rick McTeague playfully shoving me toward a hole in the ice, and now the combined arrogance of the people who were supposed to be my colleagues, sitting around engaging in the sort of tut-tutting, mindless criticism that has roused me to anger ever since elementary school. "What makes no sense to me, Rocky, is why it was important for me to have a policeman with me all night but not important for me to have police protection today. Especially since you haven't caught the killer. Were you just trying to give poor Hennessey a recreational opportunity?" That brought Hennessey halfway out of his chair, his pale face red. Rocky the Powerful quelled him with a look and came back to staring at me. His own face was just as red, his pale, protruding eyes narrowed with rage.

"Now, just come down off your high horse and listen for a minute, Sherlock," he said. "You know full well that it was stupid of you to drive over here and go out into the woods alone, without calling us and letting us know. Without taking someone with you—"

If the man called me Sherlock one more time I was going to do something unladylike. "I resent being called stupid, Rocky. If this had been left up to you, Laney Taggert's death would have been filed as an accident."

"And Carol Frank might not be dead," he said.

"You can't blame me for that. I told you to find her, to warn her. And I didn't go into the woods alone. I tried to call you, Rocky. They couldn't find you so I left a message, and then I called Curt Sawyer, told him what was going on, and he said he'd have a man out there watching the whole time." I didn't bother to share my suspicion that Curt had done nothing of the sort. "Where is Curt, anyway?" Rocky shrugged.

I didn't know if the body had a limited supply of adrenaline, but I might be about to find out. My temper, already so sorely tried by Rick McTeague, was sizzling like a Fourth of July rocket. "I don't know where you guys get off thinking that you're so superior, sitting around looking at me like I'm something that came in on a shoe when we're all supposed to be working together, but I do know this. I'm not a little kid who's going to sit here and be chastised by all the wise grown-ups."

The change in temperature after the outside was making my nose run. I took a tissue out of my pocket, swiped at it angrily, and went on. "You're all upset with me because you think I did something impulsive and dangerous. Of course, you're right. I should have stayed home and finished the laundry instead of meeting Rick McTeague and walking the murder scene. But if I hadn't done that"—I stood up and walked to the door—"I wouldn't have learned something that may turn out to be crucial to the case. McTeague says that both sets of footprints were small. He says it's extremely likely that Laney Taggert was killed by a woman. Now all you have to do, Chief, is find her." I walked out, slamming the door behind me.

I didn't know if they'd come after me or sit around and talk about me but instead of going out to my car, I went down the hall, trying doors. My office was locked, but they'd look there anyway. The door to Ellie Drucker's office was open and there was a desk light on, so I ducked in there and slid under the desk. Sitting there listening to the faint sounds of footsteps in the hall, I realized how childish I was being and how hilarious the situation really was, especially since I'd just told them I wasn't a child.

It had all the excitement of a game of hide-and-seek when it's played at night, and was just as meaningful, in the great scheme of things. From my hiding place, I heard them unlock the door and go into my office. Rocky and Hennessey. I was surprised at how clearly I could hear what they were saying. The walls didn't seem thin. It made me realize what a quiet neighbor Ellie was. I never heard any sounds from her office. By the time they'd finished looking in my office, which took a while considering that the place was no bigger than a closet and there was no place to hide, and I heard their footsteps heading off down the hall, my limbs were cramped and I was more than ready to come out from under the desk.

Beyond the pool of light from the desk lamp, the room was dark, but there was a strange light coming from the bookcase. I moved some books and discovered a small, jagged hole in the wall. That explained why I'd been able to hear Rocky and Hennessey so clearly. Had our positions been reversed, with Ellie the one who had a constant parade of people in and out of her office, I would have found the noise distracting. She must be a more concentrated worker than I. Knowing how hard it was to get Curt Sawyer to fix things, I wasn't surprised the hole existed. No wonder she'd stacked thick books in front of it.

I went back to Dorrie's office and found her and Suzanne head-to-head in soft conversation. They didn't seem surprised to see me. "I'm sorry," Suzanne said. "I don't know what came over me."

"You were scared," I said. "When you fear for another person's safety, that fear often comes out as anger."

She nodded. "You're right. I'm still sorry. Seven years we've been a team. You'd think I'd know better."

"Me, too," Dorrie said. "We're letting this whole awful business make us very uncivilized. Want some coffee or tea?"

I sat down on the couch, glad to take a load off my feet. "Tea would be nice. Twenty-four hours of sleep would be nice."

Dorrie brought me my tea and sank back into her chair. She looked more discouraged than I'd ever seen her. "A woman," she said, shaking her head sadly. "I don't even like to think about who it might be. . ."

"Or a man with very small feet," Suzanne said. "It's not a laughing matter but it is comical thinking about Chief Rocky lining up all the suspects and measuring their feet. When this is over we can collaborate on a true crime book and call it *The Cinderella Murders*."

"We may have to, after this," I said, "we may never work in this business again."

"That's not funny," Dorrie said and started to laugh.

We were punchy from fatigue, sinking into a kind of hysterical humor as we sat around together and played verbal Ping-Pong with the idea that our only clue was small feet. "You don't think McTeague might have made it up, do you?" Dorrie said.

I shrugged. "Who can tell—the guy is a serious nutcase—but why?"

"Then why didn't he tell Rocky?"

"Because Rocky didn't treat him with respect. You know what else he knew?" There was an expectant silence. "He knew that Laney's secret lover was Chas Drucker."

"What is the world coming to," Dorrie asked, clasping her head between her hands, "when people withhold important clues to murder because they don't like the way the police are treating them? Whatever happened to civic responsibility?"

"You should know better than most people," Suzanne said. "Schools don't teach civics anymore. Rosa Parks and Martin Luther King but not the Civil War. American Indians . . . excuse me . . . Native Americans, the influences of the Iroquois Confederation on the Constitution, maybe, but not the Constitution, or the Bill of Rights, or anything that suggests there's a moral component to life or any sort of responsibility to other people, or communities, or to the country. We've got an ahistorical country with no morals and an inflated sense of rights and entitlements."

"Whew!" I said, "you're beginning to sound like me."

"Ought to occasionally, after seven years." Suzanne patted her hair into place. She looked exhausted after her long stint calming and coping with Dorrie's trustees. "But it's not just you, Thea. Paul's kids are always saying as a justification for not doing things that it's a free country. Honestly, it makes my blood boil! They hate it but I always ask them just what they think that expression means and how much freedom costs."

Dorrie got up and started putting coffee cups onto a tray. "It's been a long day, ladies, what do you say we call it quits and reconvene in the morning?"

"Fine by me," Suzanne said, suppressing an enormous yawn. "I don't seem to have the energy I used to."

"Don't worry," Dorrie said, "in about eighteen years, when Junior leaves for college, you'll feel energetic again."

"Speaking of responsibility," I interrupted, "have you fired Drucker yet?" Dorrie wouldn't meet my eye. "I know it's Christmas, Dorrie, but you can't wait. With all that's going on, it's bound to come out, and things will look that much worse if you've sat on a serious breach of faculty ethics."

"But Thea," she said, "Christmas . . . his kids are home. . . ."

"He lost his holiday exemption when he took a Bucksport student away for Columbus Day weekend and got her pregnant."

"We don't know that he's the father."

"It's easy enough to check," I said, "with DNA. Are you saying it's all right for a faculty member to have sex with a student as long as he or she took precautions?"

"Of course not. It's just that he's been here for twenty-five years . . . and there's Ellie to think about. All that free time she's given, all those hundreds, maybe thousands of hours, and their kids . . . their son home from college . . ."

"It was his daughter who turned him in," I reminded her. "But I think you're losing sight of the issue here. Before all hell broke loose, or, more accurately, when only half of hell had broken loose, anticipating problems with Laney's parents and perhaps other parents, you hired me to do a procedures audit and advise you whether Bucksport was doing everything it could and/or should for the physical and emotional well-being of the students. Well, I did it, and I found some problems. . . ."

Dorrie didn't seem to be paying any attention to my pompous little speech. She was fiddling with the snazzy gold buttons on her jacket. "Dorrie," I said, trying to get her attention. "I think you should seriously consider firing Bill and Kathy Donahue as well."

"Oh, not now, Thea," she said wearily. "I've got more pressing things to worry about, with two hundred plus sets of irate parents and upset kids. Write a report. When things calm down, we can talk about what to do for the long term. . . ."

Someone in the doorway cleared her throat. Ellie Drucker was standing there with a sheaf of papers. "I think I've got all but four taken care of," she said. "I'm still waiting for call-backs on them. I gave them my home number so I think I'll head out now, unless there's something else you needed?"

"No, Ellie. You've done plenty. I don't know how I would have managed without you." She shot me a look, somewhere between please-try-to-understand and put-a-cork-in-it. Ellie turned and plodded away. I was disappointed with Dorrie's lack of courage and her failure to understand that she could protect herself and Bucksport from some of the fallout by acting swiftly and decisively to cut her negligent troublemakers loose. I dropped the subject, reminding myself that it was Dorrie's job, not mine. Meeting Suzanne's eyes across the room, I saw she was thinking the same thing.

Rocky came roaring back, greeted my return with predictable grumpiness, and then I left, taking Suzanne with me. Despite his tirade about my living dangerously, Rocky didn't insist that I take a cop with me, and Hennessey was nowhere around. On the way out I picked up an envelope from my temporary mail slot and shoved it into my briefcase.

When I dropped Suzanne off, Paul insisted that I come in, and he hovered over both of us while we ate big bowls of soup, a thick Italian bean soup with pasta. Paul was a good cook and we were both starving. In the background,

Ellie's niece played quietly with the baby, eliciting a series of joyous baby giggles. It was the one good thing to come out of my work at Bucksport. I wondered how she'd feel when she found out that Suzanne and I were partly responsible for getting her uncle fired.

I left Suzanne to her domestic bliss and drove home feeling lonely and sorry for myself. The gay holiday lights didn't help. I felt sour and mean and seething with frustration. Once or twice driving up Route 128 I was sure I saw the silver Datsun, but rusty old silver cars are common as cheese. I felt even more uneasy when I got back and the car wasn't in the parking lot, but I checked every few minutes for a while and it didn't show up.

There was no message from Andre. I gave up my pretense of being a tough guy and called him. He wasn't home. He also wasn't at work, if they were telling the truth, and no one admitted to knowing where I might find him. I left a series of messages that I had called, including one on our answering machine. "Hi," I said. "This is the woman who was willing to undress in front of the entire state of Maine just to try and save your life. You could at least call me."

I went into the living room to kick the cat. Not a real cat. A horrible, fluffy white stuffed cat with gooey blue glass eyes, gift from a guy named Steve whom I'd rather forget. When I do remember him, it isn't with affection, and then I go and kick the cat. Today I remembered Andre instead, but I still kicked the cat. The sight of that wad of ugly fake fur flying through the air was enormously satisfying.

Then, my spirits revived, I pulled the mysterious envelope out of my briefcase and opened it. It had come through campus mail, I could tell, because it had only my name and Metcalfe Hall written on it. Inside were photocopies of Carol Frank's file notes from her interviews with Laney Taggert with a handwritten note attached. Under the black script announcing a message from the desk of Carol Frank she had scribbled, "When we spoke, I was thinking of Bucksport and its public image but after reading them over, I can't justify keeping them confidential to protect the reputations of those who were so willing to take advantage of a troubled teenager. Other girls may have been affected and future students need protection. It occurs to me that these records may become of interest to Laney's killer, once it becomes known that I've spoken with you. I'm taking my copy with me. Having a second one out there seems like a good idea. Maybe these will help. I'll catch up with you as soon as I can."

With trembling hands, I carried the papers over to the couch and started to read. Despite her murderer's efforts, Carol had gotten through.

CHAPTER 24

I BLESSED CAROL Frank for having neat penman-
ship. If someone had tried to read my notes they would
have ended up with a migraine headache and the information that on the xtesost fo setsiht, Suzy fixtiror dhe
gone fisheihe. Even I sometimes have trouble with my
writing. The only person who can always read it is Sarah.
But I had no problem learning that Laney had made several visits to Carol Frank, freely discussed the men she
was sleeping with, and had been equally open about her
plans to have an abortion. I made myself read slowly,
carefully, and in chronological order even though I
wanted to rush through to see why they were so important to Laney's killer.

Going slowly and carefully didn't do me any good. If I
was expecting a new and fuller range of Laney Taggert's
conquests, I was going to be disappointed. Carol's notes
confirmed that Laney had slept with Chas Drucker and
Josh, which I already knew. About Drucker she'd observed, "He's both demanding and inept about sex, as
though he usually has to fight for it and hasn't any notion
that it's supposed to be a reciprocal act." Noting that, "If
I'd had to sleep with someone that fat, maybe I'd learn to
just hop on and hop off, too."

She'd also slept with Chris Fuller, but only once, and,

as she'd told Carol and Carol had written it down with quotation marks, "The guy's a troglodyte and who needs that?" True, Fuller was missing, which made him an interesting prospect, but he was a great, hulking guy and couldn't possibly have little feet. If possession of little feet was one of the vital criteria, we were no better off than before, unless Fuller had a jealous wife.

"Dammit, Carol," I told the unresponsive pages, "is that all you have to tell me? Someone killed you for that? Or was it because of what you knew?" But Carol would never be able to answer. I went back to the notes. I could see why she'd been hesitant to share them. Though clearly from Laney's point of view, and therefore to be taken with some grains of salt, there was a wealth of stuff about the Bucksport School staff that cast it in an unfavorable light. There was certainly damning stuff about the Donahues, stuff that, had I been them, I never would have wanted to have read, as well as the sad observation that had they only been nicer to her, had they only treated her as a valuable person they cared about, she might even have considered having the baby. But they had treated her like a nasty, miserable container.

Scathing criticism about her roommate, noisy, nosy, unsympathetic, and judgmental Genny and her frustration that Kathy and Bill wouldn't do anything to resolve the situation. All part of Laney's overall feeling that she had no control over her life, that she was always being manipulated.

At the same time, Laney had been a keen observer of the people around her, aware of a lot more about them than they gave her credit for. About Josh's friendship with Russ Hamlin, for example, Laney had observed that Hamlin basked in the admiration without really reciprocating the feelings. Professor Hamlin, Laney had noted, had the hots for her, though he thought she couldn't see it. As Laney had put it to Carol Frank, "How could I not notice he touched me every chance he got? Was I supposed to not notice his erection when he leaned against my leg to fix my makeup?" Laney had said, "Professor Hamlin would do anything for me, I'm sure, and so I have to always be very careful not to ask for anything." The notes continued Carol's own observations, expressing concern that the faculty needed reminders about their responsibility to the students. She had been distressed that Laney felt she had to protect her professors.

I got up again and kicked the cat, working up a pretty good sweat beating on the poor stuffed thing, then I kicked it into the corner and started pacing. Okay, I told myself, if it was a woman, who are the candidates? Who, whether because of her pregnancy or for some other reason, might have wanted Laney Taggert dead? I was pacing the floor and trying to juggle all the candidates in my brain when the phone rang. I grabbed it and said a fast hello.

It was my dad. "I'm sitting here working on my Christmas list. Tomorrow's the day your mom and I are going shopping, and I wondered if there was something special that you wanted." Every December they spent a day in the city shopping, usually on Newbury Street, had an early dinner, and went to a play. They'd been doing it since I was a little girl. I used to beg to be taken along but they always said no. It was a personal, grown-up thing. When we were little, Michael and I, and then Michael and Carrie and I, used to spend hours going through catalogs and making up our Christmas lists. Now, faced with the same decision, I couldn't think of anything I wanted, except to have the murderer caught, to be working on safe and simple projects, and to get a phone call from Andre, none of which my father could give me.

"Surprise me," I said, "I love surprises. Maybe a small painting? The only good one I have is that one Michael did."

"Okay, honey," he said, "we'll surprise you. Now, what about that young man of yours . . . Andre . . . I'd like to get something for him, too, since he'll be here with you. Any suggestions?"

It looked like a case of not-to-decide-is-to-decide. I'd refused to call and tell them my plans so they'd gone ahead and planned for me. "I don't know if he's coming," I said.

Dad hasn't been the town's best lawyer all these years without developing a strong instinct for what's unsaid. "Trouble, huh? Well, don't worry. You two will work it out. You've had fights before. Just tell me what he likes to drink. I'll pick up a big bottle and then if he doesn't come we can always drink it ourselves."

"Bourbon would be fine." He didn't need me in this conversation. He was doing just fine on his own. "Dad," I began, and then I hesitated. I sort of wanted his advice but it went against my strict policy of not involving him in my life.

It was too late to turn back, though, he'd read all the nuances in my voice. I have to be prepared if I'm going to fool him. "What is it, Thea? Is something bothering you?"

I shaded the truth a little and asked my question. "I've got this position to fill and a really diverse bunch of candidates. None of them are a perfect match. How do I choose?"

"You know what to do," he said in that condescending voice that I hadn't even realized was condescending until we'd differed as adults. As I child, I'd just thought that was how dads talked. "You make yourself a chart. Put the characteristics you need for the job across the top, then see which candidate fulfills the most needs. That's the one to hire. It's so logical, honey, that I'm surprised you even had to ask."

Don't worry, I thought to myself, *I won't make the same mistake twice.* "Thanks, Dad," I said. "Have fun tomorrow."

"We will. See you on Christmas day. Your mother wants you to bring that wonderful plum chutney you make. It goes so well with the turkey." He hung up without even waiting for my reply. Good, that meant I hadn't ever actually committed to going, had I?

I grabbed a pad of paper and a pencil to make a chart but before I'd even started drawing lines on the page I knew I didn't have to. My own phrase leapt back into my head. "Unless he had a jealous wife." Ellie Drucker, jolly, helpful omnipresent Ellie Drucker. Big body. Small feet.

Suddenly I was as awake as a person could be. How could I have missed something so obvious? Like the purloined letter, I hadn't seen what was right before my eyes. I had made the mistake of assuming she couldn't be the murderer because she was so nice. Psychologists tell us all the time that murderers, particularly passion killers, are often quite nice people. Hastily I reread Carol's notes. According to what she'd told Carol, Laney Taggert had asked Drucker for the money she needed to have an abortion and been upset by Drucker's response that he wanted to help her but didn't see how he could because his wife controlled the money.

I could hear Ellie Drucker's voice as clearly as a bell. She was standing by the coffee machine, chatting with Lori about the teenager who'd shot her married lover's wife. "If I'd been the wife," she'd said, "I would have shot that girl dead. Youth is no excuse for messing with a married man. Sometimes I think kids these days haven't got any morals at all." Then Lori had said, "Not me, boy, I would have shot the husband," and then Ellie and Lori had digressed on a long discussion of morals and who was at fault and why they'd shoot one or the other of the culprits, which I'd abandoned to go back to work. Poor hardworking, long-suffering cheated-on Ellie Drucker, the woman I'd been feeling so sorry for.

That hole in her office wall was no defect lingering for lack of repair, it was there so she could listen in on my conversations. No wonder I never heard anything from her office. She was down on her hands and knees listening at the hole. If it hadn't been so dreadful it would have been comical to think of her crouching there with her vast rump in the air, listening to everything that was said in my office.

With a shudder, I remembered the peppermint tea she'd brought me, her surprise when I was still around after the first cup, the way she lingered while she waited for me to drink the second. Invisible because she was always around, it would have been easy for her to doctor my sandwich. What had someone told me? Ellie did all the gardens, was quite an expert when it came to plants, knew the botany of the campus intimately. Dr. Tuff had even suggested she might know where someone could find water hemlock. And Carol, who thought of her as a friend, would never have been nervous at her approach.

To be fair, I considered the rest of my suspects. For every name I thought up I could come up with a dozen reasons why they couldn't be the one. Genny Oakes, for example. Killing two people seemed like a pretty extreme way to get rid of an unwanted roommate, even one who'd hurt your feelings badly, and the same went for Merri Naigler. It was pretty dramatic to kill someone because you wanted her boyfriend. In neither case could I see any reason to kill Carol Frank. Laney's mother might be thoroughly unlikable, but she seemed too upset by what people would think. That left me with Kathy Donahue.

I went back over Carol's notes. Yes, Laney had mentioned Sarah and Merri and Kathy. She'd even said that Kathy was trying to talk her out of an abortion, being cruel and making her feel abandoned. But that wasn't enough to make Kathy kill Carol Frank, was it? Could she have feared that Carol might get her fired? I didn't know. And there seemed to be no reason for any of them to want to kill me. What could Carol and I possibly know that would get us killed? Nothing except the truth about Chas Drucker.

I ran to the phone and called the Sedgwick police station. The person who answered the phone informed me that the chief was temporarily unreachable and they would have him call me as soon as they could. Not wanting to harm Bucksport by a public declaration about the Druckers, I left the message that I had some urgent information about Laney Taggert's death and asked that Rocky call me as soon as possible.

Then I tried the Bucksport switchboard and was informed that Dorrie wasn't to be disturbed and I could leave a message. Angry, I disconnected and called Dorrie at home but all I got was her machine. Once again I left a message, feeling frustrated and angry and invisible. After a minute, I tried again but all I got was the machine. The powers that be had taken the night off.

I sat and stared at the phone, frustrated by my inability to do anything. I got up and paced the room. Kicked the cat. Called Dorrie again. Got the machine again. Paced some more, seething with frustration and anxiety. Of all the times for everyone to go AWOL! All the pacing and worry was exhausting. I sat on the couch and stared out at the water, wishing there were something I could do.

Then the paranoid thought hit me that if I could figure things out, so could they. That maybe they knew and didn't want to act. Maybe no one was responding to my calls because they didn't want to hear what I had to say. Maybe once they'd known about Chas and Laney, and about the small feet, they'd been faster adders than I was and had already put two and two together. Maybe even now they were huddled together, pondering what to do, and they didn't want me to be part of the discussion.

I knew Dorrie was not happy with the way I was unearthing skeletons on her campus. Maybe at first she'd thought she wanted to find a killer but she certainly didn't want all this dirty linen aired in public. So far I'd turned up problems with Kathy and Bill Donahue, a faculty member who'd impregnated a student, a physical-plant employee with a history of sexually abusing young girls, and now I wanted to tell her that another valued employee was a murderer. Maybe she didn't want to hear it.

Maybe she'd never expected me to succeed. By now I was quite sure that Dorrie had hired me to solve her murder and not just to do a systems assessment, but it wouldn't be the first time someone had hired me to do a job and then been surprised when I did it. Dorrie was an excellent administrator and she genuinely believed in acting for the well-being of her students but her loyalty was to the institution—an institution that my discoveries threatened to seriously damage or destroy. Maybe I was wrong. Not about Ellie but about Dorrie. Maybe she, maybe all of them, didn't want me to find the killer just as they hadn't wanted me to know the truth about Kathy Donahue. Maybe they all knew what was going on and I was, as Chip Barrett had said, just window dressing.

I got up and started pacing around the room. On my third pass I stumbled over the cat. "No one," I said loudly, kicking the cat in a tumbling arc over the sofa, "hires me to be a fall guy or a fool." I kicked it again, and its gooney blue eyes caught the light as it flipped, giving it a surprised look. But surely they couldn't have all been in on a plot to kill me. That would be too much to believe. Maybe the conspiracy was just to protect Ellie. Maybe she knew she didn't have to worry, that they would cover things up and she would never be discovered. If that was the case, Dorrie must be mighty mad at me right now. Her token investigator actually solving the crime? And then again, maybe I was being paranoid and there was no plot and all of this suspicion was the product of an exhausted, overstimulated mind.

While I was still steaming and stewing, the phone rang again. There was only one person I knew who might be calling. Andre. Eagerly I picked up the phone. "Thea Kozak?" asked an unfamiliar voice.

"Yes."

"This is Ellie Drucker. I'm sorry to disturb you at such an awful time but I know you've been working on this murder business for Dorrie . . . that is, I know you know about my husband and . . . and that girl . . . and I've been sitting here thinking . . . and well, I need to talk to you. If you'd be willing . . . right away . . . if you could come here?" She stopped, breathless. Her normally pleasant and controlled voice sounded forced and staggering as though she were teetering on the brink of control.

There was only one reason for her to call me—to try to lure me there so she could finally kill me off. The suspicion flitted briefly through my mind that Dorrie had called and set me up. But I dismissed it just as quickly. However much her interests might seem different from mine, Dorrie wanted the killing stopped. She wanted her campus safe and orderly again. But right now my problem wasn't Dorrie, it was what to do about Ellie Drucker. There was no way I was delivering myself into the hands of a double murderer. "I'm sorry, Ellie," I said, "but I'm exhausted. I'll be happy to talk with you in the morning."

"I don't think you understand," she said, her speech once again hesitant and strange. "I know you think I did it. I heard you talking with Dorrie today and I know you were in my office, that you know I've been listening to your conversations. I don't know how to convince you, before you splash it all over the papers and ruin what little I've got left, which is my own self-respect, that I'm innocent. I'd never have killed that girl—" She was panting, as if she'd just run up several flights of stairs. "Look," she gasped, desperation in her voice, "just sit down and talk with me. Give me a chance to tell you my side of the story . . . then you can do what you want. I hate to ask you to come here . . . I know I should come to you but I'm . . . I'm not well. It's one of the penalties of being fat. . . ."

Another panting silence. I pictured her trying to get her breath back so she could speak. "I expect, being the nice, thorough little investigator that you are, that you've already called the police, and probably Dorrie, too. Have you?"

Stunned, I muttered "No," meaning that I hadn't reached anyone.

Before I could explain, she said, "Good. Before you jump in and destroy whatever bits of my life you haven't already smashed in your do-gooder zeal, I figure that you owe me this at least—give me the courtesy of coming here and listening to what I've got to say. I'll be waiting for you."

"Ellie, are you crazy? I'm not coming to your house, knowing what I know."

"What you think you know. Before you decide, you should know—" She broke off, her voice shaking, sounding like she was about to cry. "Josh is here. He wants to see you. Alone. If you don't come, I can't vouch for . . . for what might happen. . . ." She hesitated. There was a long pause, a pause during which I felt myself shaken to the bone. "You do understand what I'm trying to say, don't you?"

I thought I did. That damn fool Rick McTeague had told Josh his theory about the small feet and Josh, remembering he had seen Ellie Drucker crossing the quad right after Laney, had put two and two together and gone to see Ellie. Heaven only knew what she'd done to him, that poor boy who'd already been through so much. He was getting more than an education at the Bucksport School. Now he was caught like a fly in her spiderweb. "Perfectly," I said. "I'll be there in an hour. Is Josh all right?" She smashed down the phone.

I stood there, stunned, listening to a buzzing line. I needed help. I called Dorrie again, got the machine again, and knowing my voice was laden with impotent fury, told her what was going on and what I was going to do. I hung up without knowing whether I could count on her. Yes, I knew she was stressed and exhausted, and needed rest, but she'd picked a hell of a bad time to take the night off. I tried Rocky and got the same message. I'd have to wait until the chief called in. I told them it was an emergency, but I hung up without any confidence that the urgency of my message would be conveyed.

I might be big and brave and impulsive but this was one case where I had no interest in being the Lone Ranger and no certainty that anyone would be there to back me up. I called my friend Dom Florio, my second-favorite cop. I had met him when my friend Eve's mother was murdered. He'd cornered me at the funeral and tried to pump me for information about the family. Although I was reluctant to be his spy, as the matter unraveled, Dom and I ended up spending a lot of time together. He and his wife, Rosie, were everything my parents weren't, and we'd sort of adopted each other. Dom was a good man to know in a crisis and as far as I was concerned, that's what I was in. Besides, being a cop, he was used to being disturbed at night.

The phone only rang twice before he answered, sounding as calm and awake as if he'd just been sitting by the phone instead of sleeping. "Florio," he said.

"Dom, it's Thea Kozak," I said.

"Oh, no!" he groaned. "Now what's the matter?"

"I knew I could count on you, Dom," I said.

"Flattery will get you nowhere."

"I'm sorry to call you in the middle of the night like this but I need help."

"And when you need help Mommy said to find a nice policeman, right?"

"You bet." In the background I heard Rosie's voice. I could make out a questioning tone but not the words, though I heard his reply.

"It's Thea. Suggesting a nocturnal rendezvous." Rosie spoke again and then Dom came back to me. "Rosie says you wouldn't call unless it was important and I should stop giving you a hard time."

"She's right."

"Rosie is always right," he said. "What's up?"

I didn't know where to begin but gut instinct led me to say the right thing. "Someone tried to kill me."

"Again? I thought you'd vowed to reform. Take only safe work and leave the dangerous stuff to us."

"I tried, Dom. But the person who tried to kill me just called and wants to meet her. I've got to go, Dom."

"Why?"

"Because they've got a hostage. A student."

He sighed. "Where?"

"Sedgwick. The Bucksport School."

"Did you call the police?"

"Twice. The chief is taking the night off and this is sensitive. Send in a screaming horde of patrol cars and who knows what might happen."

"So sensitive you should risk your life?"

"I'm not risking my life. That's why I'm taking you. Look, can we talk about this on the way? This woman poisons people. She's got a kid in there . . . and she said she couldn't vouch for what would happen. . . ."

There was a long silence on his end. I could hear him breathing. I could picture his plain, serious face, his forehead creased with a frown. Dom didn't look like much unless he smiled, until you saw him close up. When I met him I thought he looked like an accountant but that was before I noticed his eyes. Dark blue, sharp, and knowing. All his experience was in those eyes. They were always moving and always seeing. He was a regular guy, flawed and stubborn and opinionated, not some superman, but he came as close as anyone I knew to being one of my heroes.

"Dom, please. . . ." There was a tremble in my voice I couldn't conceal.

"Okay," he said finally. "I'll come. I was about to make Rosie here the happiest woman in the world but she can wait. Patience is the eternal burden of the policeman's wife."

That time I heard Rosie's words quite clearly. A most unladylike "Fuck you, Florio."

And his reply. "That's what I was trying to do, Rosie." Then he sighed again for the lost pleasures of his night. "Where do I meet you?"

CHAPTER 25

THE NIGHT WAS thick with fog. It hovered around the lights and pooled in the hollows, making the whole world soft. Christmas lights, shimmering through the white haze, had the amorphous, melting quality of M&M's in soft-serve ice cream. They were pretty but I wasn't in the mood for pretty right now. There's nothing pleasant or Christmasy about going to meet a murderer. I'd done it before, I knew what could happen, and I was sick with fear. Scared enough so that I took the extra precaution of looking for the strange silver car. Maybe Ellie had an accomplice—Chas, for example. Or maybe the missing Chris Fuller was stalking me, seeking revenge for his lost job. The car was there, parked under a streetlight. I walked over and peered in. Empty. If I was being stalked, it was in a desultory fashion.

Even with heated seats and the heater on full blast, my hand, when I held it against my face, was like a block of ice. I should have been working on a clever plan for how I was going to get in and out of there safely while persuading Ellie to turn herself in but my mind was verging on mush. Fear will do that. I used to scoff when I read about people doing stupid things under stress. Now I nod wisely.

If anyone was going to make a plan, it would have to

be Dom. I could barely push enough thought through my head to do the basics necessary for driving. Luckily, I'd done the drive to the Bucksport School so often my car knew the way down 128 from the North Shore to the western suburbs. The car behind me must have felt less secure; it stuck to my tail like a remora. It was annoying but people do that in fog, just pick out a set of taillights and follow them. I've even been known to do it myself.

I snapped on the radio for company and was rewarded by being invited to rock around a Christmas tree. For once it sounded more inviting than what I was doing. It just showed how a change in perspective could affect one's appreciation of music. I would rather have been doing that, or twisting the night away or even willingly done the mashed potato or the electric slide if it meant I didn't have to go see Ellie Drucker.

I didn't feel that I had any choice. Rocky and Dorrie, the ones who should have been on this errand, were temporarily AWOL while I was, as Ellie had pointed out, about to ruin her life. Besides, there was poor Josh Meyer, whose bony knees, heaving shoulders, and ravaged face had roused my maternal instincts, in the clutches of a woman who had demonstrated her willingness to kill. Thea Kozak, always the slave of duty. I had just about reached my limit on this job, though. I shoulda stood in bed and let George do it.

But as I'd often observed, George never seemed to be available. No knights in shining armor were dashing to my rescue. My mother would say this was the consequence of too many years of insisting I could do everything myself. Maybe she was right but I still thought independence, even if it came at a high price, was worth it. Most of the time.

Besides, it wasn't entirely true. True, Andre wasn't going to be there but Dom was and he was as solid and trustworthy and competent as anyone. Even if he was married and old enough to be my father, I could imagine accomplishing my mission and swooning in his arms.

The trouble was I could also imagine him giving me a stern swat on the rear end and admonishing me to stop feeling sorry for myself and to go call Andre. That's just how it is. Cops stick together. At least I knew that Dom wasn't coming for Andre's sake, though he would have if Andre had asked, he was coming for mine. I wouldn't be doing this without Dom as my lifeline.

His big maroon car was idling quietly at the turnoff to the Bucksport School. I parked behind him and he got out and walked back to my car, getting in on the passenger side. He didn't say anything until he'd turned on the light and studied my face. Then he felt my hands. "Why are you doing this?" he asked. "This isn't part of your job. We can march into the Sedgwick police station and demand that they handle this."

"She's got a kid in there, a student, and I'm afraid of what she may have done to him. Or what she may do if someone else shows up at the door." I couldn't quite keep the tremble out of my voice. I was all too aware of other times when I'd unwittingly put myself in danger. This time I was going in forewarned.

"Cops are trained to handle situations like this."

"And what if they blow it? It's all my fault that he's in there—"

"And why is that, may I ask? Because you told him who dunnit and sent him off to get revenge?"

"Of course not."

He affected an accent. "Ah, Saint Theadora, who causes the sun to rise and sets the winds in motion. Who causes the would-be killers to confront the has-been killers and who—"

"Shut up, Dom. I'm scared out of my skin and I think I'm going to throw up. You want to call the cops again, call the cops."

"Is that what *you* want?"

"I want to be home in bed. I don't want to blow this. I want a happy ending—"

"All very well, but what were you planning to do in there?"

"I thought I might trade myself for Josh. He's just a kid."

He whistled softly. "You and Lemieux were made for each other, you know that? You've both got too much hero and no common sense."

"He's got plenty of common sense," I began.

"And you?"

"I just want to talk to her. To see if I can get her to let Josh go. We'll call the cops when we get there. I just want a few minutes to . . . I don't know . . . to try and fix this without a big shoot-'em-up scandal. Bucksport has had about all it can take. But Dom," I said, hesitating, "I don't have a plan. . . ."

"The plan is simple. You go in, you assess the situation, and if she doesn't want to give herself up, you leave."

"What if she won't let me leave?"

"Then you holler and I'll come in. Why don't I just come with you?"

"She might not let me in. As long as you're there, Dom."

He squeezed my arm. "For you, Princess, I am always there."

At that moment I could have hugged him and gone home. For a fleeting instant, the world was safe and perfect. But the clock was running and Ellie's vague hints about Josh loomed large in my mind. I knew what sort of things she did to people. I knew what they could do. So we would call the Sedgwick cops again. But I was going in. "Let's go," I said.

"You're sure?"

I thought about all the times I'd been accused of being too certain, too pigheaded, too determined to have my own way. "Would you accept almost sure? I just don't want to risk anything happening to him . . . to Josh. And she . . . she might not be alone." It wasn't so farfetched to think that Chas, having caused the problem in the first place, would rally to his wife's support.

"Okay. You go in and check things out, but that's all. No heroics, understand? I'll be right outside the window. Scream and I'll come in."

Why was he giving in so easily? Didn't he know how scared I was? I really wanted him to come with me; I was just afraid that if he did, she or they would see him and immediately do something awful to Josh. That's what hostages were for, to protect bad guys. I couldn't risk it. If Ellie Drucker was willing to do awful things to Laney and to Carol, what was there to protect Josh? "How are you going to get in?" I asked.

"If you can't open the door for me, I'll come through the window. Don't worry. I'll manage." He shut off the light and opened the door. "We'll take my car," he said.

"But I have a phone—" I started to argue with him, Thea the control freak to the end, but of course he had a full battery of police communications equipment in his car. Either of us was capable of dialing 911. He could probably do a lot more. Plus he had a trunkful of useful gear. I took a deep breath, stopped arguing, and followed him, reminding myself that you don't ask someone to help you because of his experience and expertise and then refuse to let him use it. That was a fundamental truth I was supposed to have learned in my years as a consultant—you don't have to be an expert in everything, you only have to know how to find and use experts. I was just a slow learner.

Ellie had given me directions to her house, which was on a side road off the main drive. Before we pulled into the driveway, Dom cut the lights and we crept forward slowly. The driveway was almost invisible in the fog but the house lights gleamed like a beacon. I patted my pockets to be sure I still had my Mace, and opened the door. "Wish me luck," I said. This time I made no effort to hide my fear. My hands were shaking, my knees were knocking, and I felt an anxious adrenaline rush go through my body. "If I die, be sure to check out the cup of tea on the shelf in my office. Cold poison peppermint tea. And tell Andre I'm sorry."

"You're not going to die," he said firmly. The door closed and I was alone in the cottony darkness. In the distance I could hear the crunch of tires on the main campus road. At the door I hesitated, took a deep breath, and knocked. She must have been watching through the peephole. The door swung quietly inward before I'd even lowered my hand. Ellie Drucker stood there, dressed in a vast pink quilted bathrobe, a peculiar expression on her face.

"How nice of you to come," she said as though this were a social visit. "We've been waiting for you. This way, please." Still the gracious hostess, she stepped aside and motioned me into the living room. A quick glance told me that it was a comfortable room, well furnished with antiques, books, and paintings. Things that weren't bought on a teacher's salary. Ellie's money. So tightly held there wasn't even a little bit extra to buy a poor girl an abortion. But my overall impression was of cavernous, high-ceilinged darkness. Only a few of the lights were on. My gaze didn't linger on the decor, though, but went straight to the figure lying on the couch, trussed like a turkey, a streak of blood running from the scalp down onto the cheerful flowered upholstery.

I stared down at him, back at Ellie, and back at the silent figure on the couch. "That's not Josh," I said.

"Of course not," she said, dropping to her knees beside her unconscious husband. She pulled a tissue from her pocket and tried to wipe away the blood but succeeded only in smearing it around.

"Of course not," echoed a voice from across the room. There were no lights on at the far end. I peered at the barely visible figure sitting in the darkness.

"Josh?"

"Well, it's not the Good Humor man."

"What's going on here?" It was like biting into a

chocolate and finding it was a radish. "What have you done to Mr. Drucker?"

"You can call him Chas," Josh said. "He likes that. I've done nothing compared to what he's done to me." He paused for effect. "Yet."

"So you know about Chas and Laney?" I took a step toward him, trying to get close enough to see his face.

"D-d-don't . . . come any . . . closer!" he commanded in a shaky voice. "I don't want to hurt you."

"Then why am I here?"

"You're the detective. You tell me."

I shook my head. "I'm not a detective, Josh. That's what everyone said, but I'm not. I'm a consultant. I come in, I ask a bunch of questions, I write a report. I don't solve crimes." My voice betrayed me. It was small, shaky, and scared.

"Then I guess I'll have to tell you," he said, sounding surprisingly agreeable. "You're here as a witness."

"As a witness to what?"

"Vengeance!" He shouted the word and I jumped, knocking into a set of fireplace tools that rocked and clanged behind me. "Retribution. Payback. That filthy, manipulative, self-satisfied pig there on the couch used Laney and then killed her because her pregnancy would have embarrassed him."

"You don't want to do this, Josh—" I began.

"Oh, yes, I do. And I want you to watch because you're the one who just had to know what was going on. Couldn't leave me alone but you had to be in my face, all the time, trying to make me tell you who Laney's lover was, rubbing it in that I didn't know, like salt in a wound."

Behind me, Ellie Drucker was making low moaning sounds. "Mrs. Drucker, will you please, for God's sake, shut up!" There was a crash as something he'd thrown smashed into the wall behind me.

Ellie jumped up with a wail and planted her hands on her ample hips. "You stop that right now!" she said. "That was a priceless antique, Josh. Brought back from China in the—" Another object smashed into the wall. "Eighteen thirties," she finished in a small voice. "Please. . . ." She sank back down on her knees, cradling broken pieces in her hand.

"He didn't kill her, Josh," I said. "He was with other people, he couldn't have."

"Don't bother," Ellie Drucker said in a strangled voice. "I've already said everything there is to be said. He doesn't care."

"She's right," Josh agreed. "I don't care. It doesn't matter whether it was Chas who actually pushed her, or whether it was Mrs. Drucker. It's like a chain reaction. Like dominoes. He's the one who set things in motion. He didn't care what happened after that. He didn't care that she was scared or that she was alone or that she was humiliated and afraid of being hurt. He didn't care if she was sick or how she felt about her father knowing, even though her father was the only other person besides me who really loved her. He didn't think about any of that. He just wanted to screw a kid. A kid the same age as his daughter and he didn't want to have to use a condom because he wanted his dick to get the full benefit. Just a squirt and a groan and good-bye, sister."

"Oh, stop. Please. Stop talking that way," Ellie Drucker pleaded. "You make him sound like a monster when he's just a man who made a little mistake. Haven't you ever made a mistake, Josh?"

"Yes. Not hitting you right after I hit him. You're the one with the money, aren't you, Mrs. Drucker? And you're the one Laney had to go to and beg for it, because the big stud there was too much of a coward to give it to her. What did you say to her, anyway? 'Meet me by the path and we'll take a little walk out into the woods, get far enough from the campus so no one can see us, and then I'll give you the money'? Only instead you pushed her out on the ice and let her die!" His voice wavered. "Have you tried to imagine what that was like for her? I have. I've imagined it every day since it happened and I've dreamed it every night. Every time I close my eyes I can feel her icy hands grasping at mine. Every night I try to save her but it's always too late."

"It's not too late for you, Josh," Ellie said. "Just let us go and you won't get into any trouble, I promise you. Don't do something that's going to screw up your whole life."

"I already did that. I fell in love with Laney. And you already did that. The two of you. You used her and then you killed her."

"But we didn't! What can I do to make you believe me?" She threw out her arms, knocking herself off balance, and fell with a rousing thud. The coffee table overturned with a crash, scattering candy and knickknacks and books across the floor.

"There's nothing you can do," Josh said dramatically. "It's too late."

Ellie made no effort to get up. From the floor, she said, "It's true that she came to me for the money. I didn't agree to meet her anywhere. I told her I wouldn't give it to her and I told her to go to hell. No one made her sleep with my husband." Then she gripped the edge of the couch and pushed herself to a sitting position. "Don't you see, Josh? You've got the wrong people. We're innocent."

"Innocent? Innocent? How do you people figure that?" The words reverberated with incredulous scorn. "You'd better step over by the fireplace, detective," Josh said. "I don't want to hurt you."

He raised his hand and I saw, now that my eyes had adjusted to the gloom, that he was holding a gun. Even if Ellie Drucker had committed the crime she so vehemently denied, this wasn't the way to end things. And wasn't it about time for Dom to come flying through that window? What was I supposed to do? Holler? Scream? But if I screamed, Josh would shoot me. Better to keep talking.

Something crackled and shifted with a thud. From the

corner of my eye, I saw the remains of a fire in the fireplace. I fantasized a dramatic escapade involving fireplace tools and burning logs, but it required eyes in the back of my head. "Josh, who told you it was Drucker? Was it Rick McTeague?"

"Yes. He took me to dinner at the Sedgwick House. That's when he told me that Laney went away Columbus Day weekend with Mr. Drucker, and then he told me about the small feet."

Keep him talking. "He hadn't told you this before?"

"Unh-uh. No. McTeague likes secrets. You must know that. He thrives on them."

"So why did he tell you now?"

"He said he was feeling sorry for me." Josh made a sound that was almost a chuckle. "But it was really to liven things up. It worked, too."

Straining to keep my voice neutral, I said, "So you came back from dinner, got your gun, and came here?" I wondered if McTeague, the world's biggest voyeur, was lurking out there in the dark with Dom, each of them peering through a different window, with McTeague hoping Josh would shoot one or more of us for the experience.

"I didn't. I was upset. You know my dad's coming tomorrow. Christmas vacation is going to be a nightmare of cocktail parties and theater and everyone commenting on how much I've grown, like I was still six, and Dad's women friends trying to get me into bed. It's so sick! I was supposed to go back and pack but I couldn't face it, so I went over to the theater to see if Russ—Professor Hamlin—was there. I always go to Russ when I'm upset. Now that Laney's gone, he's my only friend."

"Rick McTeague isn't a friend?"

"Give me a break. He was a free meal. A chance to get off campus."

Keep him talking. Beside me, Ellie was edging toward the fireplace. I didn't know what she had in mind, but a distraction would be nice. "Did you find Hamlin?"

"Oh, yeah. He was there. Friday nights he likes to work on things. Time when he can be alone. Hey! Mrs. Drucker. Get back over by your husband. Now!" He punctuated the order by smashing another of Ellie Drucker's priceless antiques. Ellie gave a sob and crept back to the couch. Chas Drucker moved restlessly and groaned. Josh gripped the gun nervously, shifting it from one hand to the other.

"Did you talk about what you'd just learned from McTeague?"

"Of course. He's my advisor. I tell him everything."

"What was his reaction?"

"Wild. I've never seen him so mad. He said that if he were me, he'd get some sort of a weapon and march over here, shoot the Druckers and claim temporary insanity. He said if we didn't do something, the campus would close around them and protect them and Laney's death would just be written off as a suicide."

"What about Carol Frank?"

He brushed me off. "We didn't talk about that."

I might be a dim bulb sometimes, but the rheostat was slowly being turned and the results were both illuminating and terrifying. I understood what was happening.

"He's using you, Josh. You were set up."

At that moment, the lights went out.

CHAPTER 26

IN NOVELS, THE lights go out when a person is knocked unconscious, but I was fully conscious. I was standing in a room lit only by the remnants of a fire, and the sounds around me were like Fourth of July fireworks. There was the sound of Josh's gun going off, a chilling scream from Ellie Drucker, the smashing of glass and wood as someone came through a window. I moved away from the fire and into deeper darkness, tripping over Ellie, who was now sprawled across the floor. She screamed again and this time she went on screaming. Feet thudded against the front door.

I took another step backward and came up against something very hard and sharp right at the base of my neck. "Don't make a sound," a voice hissed in my ear. A hand grabbed my elbow and pulled me firmly backward. We went through a door and another and a cold, damp smell mixed with old fuel oil rushed at me. "Down the stairs. Very carefully, now. I wouldn't want to hurt you."

We descended the stairs with one of his hands on my shoulder and the other holding the knife at my neck. Partway down, I missed a stair and came down hard on my ankle. The pain seemed to come right through the top of my head. "Careful!" The knife jabbed and a hand went over my mouth. "Shut up. Don't scream, or next time it will be for real."

What was that for? Fun? I didn't ask. "Come on," he whispered. "Move it." Gingerly I lowered my weight onto the injured ankle. It was no picnic. Four more steps and we were at the bottom. Prodded by the knife, I limped through the darkness. He seemed completely at home. "Watch it." Grabbed my arm and steered me left, then right, and then we were at another staircase. "I played a blind man once," he said. "Summer stock. I trained by walking around down here. All right. Up we go. And please don't get any grandiose ideas about escape. I was a marine. I've been trained to kill with this knife. I could do it."

The door at the top of the stairs swung silently open. The air smelled faintly of WD-40. He'd been preparing for this. Through the light coming in the window, I could see that we were in a kitchen. "Stop," he ordered. He went and looked out. "Busy, busy, busy. Although it didn't quite go as planned. Josh has too great a flair for the dramatic. If he hadn't insisted on having you as his audience, things would have gone swimmingly. The unfortunate deaths of a faculty couple at the hands of a distraught student, followed by his equally unfortunate suicide, the whole complicated by a nice, messy fire."

There was a scuffing sound and then he pressed me into a chair. "Please take your seat and put your hands behind you." He accentuated the point with the knife tip at the base of my throat. He wrapped my wrists with enough duct tape to secure the *Queen Mary,* circled my mouth a couple times, taped my feet to the chair, and excused himself. "A moment," he said. "I think we could still use a little fire." So what I had smelled in the basement was gasoline. The hands that wrapped tape around my head still smelled of it.

Behind the tape, I gagged. Recalled a recent case where a child had smothered after being wrapped in tape. Was grateful I could still breathe. But where were we and where were the cops? Surely Dom must have noticed I was missing? Logic said that this was more faculty housing attached to the Druckers', that we must now be in Hamlin's place. But why had he brought me here and what was he going to do with me?

It didn't take a rocket scientist to figure this out. Just a slow-walking, slow-working educational consultant. Russ Hamlin, having set his protégé in motion, hadn't been able to resist hanging around to see what happened and so he could be there to deliver the coup de grace in the form of a fire. And being conveniently on the scene, he'd witnessed the moment when my own little lightbulb had gone on, and I'd said, "He's using you, Josh," understanding perfectly well that I now knew who was the possessor of the small feet, who had been pining hopelessly after Laney Taggert, and who had been the wrong person to turn to when she ran out of people to ask for money.

Josh and the Druckers were supposed to be dead but even alive they couldn't harm Hamlin. What could Josh say? That Hamlin had commiserated with him and agreed that in Josh's place he'd be inclined to seek revenge? There wasn't much that anyone could sink their teeth into. I wiggled my hands and feet, wishing I could sink my teeth into something that would set me free. But the reason people use duct tape is because it's so good at what it does—holding things securely together. Of course, if they ever found my body, they might find Hamlin's fingerprints on the tape. The police had just solved a crime that way recently. When this was over, Dorrie and Suzanne and I were going to have to retitle our book *Cinderella and the Duct Tape Murders*. Except that only Suzanne and Dorrie would get to write it.

Maybe if I rubbed my wrists against the edge of the counter? I tried to bump my way across the room, but it made a frightful racket, bringing Hamlin through the door just as the chair fell over, slamming me onto the kitchen floor. I bit my lip and my mouth filled with the salty tang of blood that I couldn't spit out. Hamlin knelt down and leaned into my face so close I could feel his chin brush my cheek. "You think you're so smart, don't you? I've heard how you bragged to Rocky about solving a bunch of murders. Big, bright professional consultant coming in here and pushing us all around with your questions. Before Dorrie came, this was a nice place and now look at us. We're all at each other's throats."

He waved the knife in front of my face. The whites of his eyes seemed to glitter in the dim light, his shadowed face fierce and demented. "I'd like to kill you right now but I have my future to think of. I'm not home, you see. I've left for the holidays. The only change of plans is that for part of the trip, I'm bringing a guest. It's unfortunate that we're so pressed for time. This would be the moment for me to reveal all the details of my dastardly crimes, would it not? Ah, but I forget . . . you're being surprisingly silent at the moment."

It was probably just as well that my mouth was taped shut because I had a lot I might have said, much of it unprintable. As it was, all I could do was glare.

"I sense disapproval, do I not?" he said, mockingly. "You can't imagine how it was for me, pining away after that darling girl, maintaining my chastity only through Herculean effort, only to discover she'd given herself, without great love or passion, but only out of curiosity, to that loathsome old fart!"

He's not that much older than you are, I thought. Awful as my situation was, I pitied Dorrie for having to be the leader in such a moral wasteland. Her predecessor had left her with more than a fiscal and admissions crisis, he'd left her with a moral crisis as well.

He stepped back, as though I'd asked a question. "Carol Frank? Well, that was a tragedy, since Carol and I were casual friends. But after she talked with you she came to me, confronted me, and said she knew about my feelings for Laney, she knew Laney had decided to ask me for money, and was there anything I wanted to talk about? I never thought of her as a stupid woman, so I was surprised. I don't think she realized . . ." He let the thought drop. "But, with what she knew, I had no choice. I could hardly sit by and let that foolish woman ruin my life." I tried to say something but of course it was just a mumble.

"Morality?" he said, placing his hand on his chest. "What has that to do with me? The actor's life is all pretense. But enough of that. We've got to be going. Of this, perhaps more later, at our leisure. Now . . ." He sat back on his heels. "I'm going to cut your feet loose and we're going to walk out to my car. A bit of a hike, I'm afraid. Naturally, my car isn't here. I know what you're thinking . . . you're thinking just as soon as we get outside you're going to make a break for it and head straight toward those cops. Perhaps this will ensure your cooperation."

He jerked open my jacket, pushed up my sweater, and jabbed the knife into my side just below my rib cage. I screamed against the duct tape, writhing in agony, while he bent down and cut my legs free. I twisted sideways and curled up into a ball, trying to stop the fiery pain. He crossed the kitchen and shut the door against the smoke that was beginning to fill the room. Outside, I could hear Dom calling my name. "Isn't it nice to know you'll be missed?" he said, grabbing my elbow and hauling me to my feet. I stumbled once or twice crossing the room. My ankle was badly swollen. I could feel it pressing against the boot.

He pushed me roughly up against the wall. "Now, no funny stuff, understand?" The knife blade touched my spine briefly. He didn't have to worry. I didn't find any of this funny. I should have listened to Rocky and Andre and let the big guys handle this. Probably Rocky wouldn't have figured out about Hamlin but maybe Carol wouldn't have gotten killed and Josh wouldn't have tried to be a murderer and . . . and . . . and. Now there never would be those laughing boys and willful brown girls.

I was bleeding. Not big-deal serious shock-inducing exsanguinating bleeding, just medium-sized painful wet goddamn-this-hurts nasty bleeding. But there was more in store. Hamlin was flashy and handsome and obsessive and self-centered and couldn't bear to be upstaged. He wanted to be the one to bring down the curtain on this act. I flashed back to another time, another place, another person with a knife. That time I had sat, drugged and helpless, while someone slit my wrists and left me sitting in a pool of my own blood. I remembered the pain as the knife sliced through me and my certainty that I was going to die. The horrible warm stickiness of so much blood. I wasn't going to let that happen again. I staggered down the steps and out into the misty night, deliberately tripping and falling, determined to leave at least a bloodstain in the snow. Looking for a chance to fight back. Knife or no knife, I would not go gentle.

Cursing, he hauled me up and I charged straight at him, ramming him with my head. We were battling in a wet, white, cottony world. I saw his arm go up, knew the knife was coming, and threw myself sideways. It came down, catching the leather of my jacket, but missing me. I kept on rolling through slushy wet snow, giving the half of me not clad in leather an icy bath, scrambled to my feet, and staggered on toward noise and light and safety, off balance from my bound arms, limited by my bad foot, unable to haul in the air my starving lungs needed through my bound mouth.

"Oh, no, you don't!" The words came from his depths, like the growl of some primitive thing, deep, guttural, furious. It was no contest. I only managed a few steps before he had me again, head forced back, knife against my throat. "You are not getting away from me."

Oh, yes, I was. Like John Paul Jones, I had not yet begun to fight. I stamped down on the top of his foot with my heel and I twisted my head down and sideways. The knife scraped my cheek, but as long as my head was still attached, I wasn't quitting. I stepped sideways and kicked him again and then I ran, to hell with my ankle, I ran. I could feel him behind me, limping and cursing. Even without looking, I felt him coil for the leap that would bring him up to me, as though in the fierceness of our battle, we'd developed some primeval connection, some primitive ability to sense each other in the darkness.

I sensed other bodies in the darkness. I felt Hamlin fall behind me under the weight of a bigger body and when my ankle twisted again and I fell, it was safely into the right set of arms.

"You're all wet," he said.

As soon as the duct tape was off, an experience not dissimilar from leg waxing except that it took part of my swollen lip as well and involved some creative cursing on Andre's part, I said, "Excuse me," turned my head aside and screamed. Then I said, "Thanks, I think you're fine, too. Where'd you leave the white horse?"

"It was a silver Datsun. I left it down the road a piece."

"And Dom?"

"He's capturing the perp."

"I just love that word."

"Capturing?"

"Perp. Perpetrator is good, reducing a vicious human being to a neutral term, but perp is even better. It sounds like a cute little fuzzy animal. There's nothing fuzzy or cute about that guy, though. What took you so long?"

"Just the usual stuff. An injured female, gunshot wound to the chest. An injured male, blunt trauma injury to the head. A psychotic student with a handgun, threatening to shoot himself, who needed to be restrained. A house without lights. A fire. Fog as thick as pea soup."

Several men had come around the corner with flashlights, lighting up Hamlin being led away in handcuffs. He turned an enraged face toward me. "You'll pay for this," he said.

"Wrong. You'll pay for this. This isn't playacting, Professor. This is real life. And real death."

"You'll see," he promised. Then his escort led him away.

He was replaced by Rocky, who, courteous and considerate as ever, shone his flashlight directly into my eyes. "Ouch! Can't you shine that thing somewhere else?"

"Are you all right?" he demanded.

"What the blankety-blank, blistering, flickering hell do you think, Rocky? Sure. Andre and I are going out dancing just as soon as I wash off all this blood."

Rocky rolled his eyes. "I don't envy you, buddy," he told Andre.

Andre pulled me tighter. It hurt and I didn't give a damn. "Too bad for you," he said. "This woman once took her clothes off before every major network in the state of Maine just to save my life. Can you beat that?"

"I don't think I can. Well, young lady, as soon as we get you cleaned up, we've got some talking to do."

"*We* aren't cleaning up anybody, Chief. I can do it myself. And if you call me 'young lady' one more time, I'm going to pop you one."

Andre was grinning from ear to ear. "Isn't she just the cutest little thing?" He knows how I hate to be called cute.

Dom came up to join us. "Sorry I took so long. Goddamned trunk lock jammed. I was wrapping my jacket around my arm to break the window that way when Jungle Boy here came flying past me and dove right through."

"My hero," I whispered.

"Which one of us?" Dom asked, ever the smart-ass.

"Both of youse guys."

A very possessive pair of arms pulled me tighter. I looked up at him. Jungle Boy had a cut on his forehead and a very determined look on his face. "I am not letting you go again. . . ." It was just like the end of one of those awful romantic novels where the heroine on the cover is always bursting out of her dress. I looked down quickly to be sure my own chest was covered. It was.

"Can we go someplace warm and dry, please?" I

begged. Andre's arms were warm, but my wet rear end was freezing.

"That's my girl," Dom said. "Preferably someplace with food."

"She's not your girl," Andre said. "You go find your own."

"Woman," Dom said. "I've got one."

"We're going to Dorrie's," Rocky said. "Follow me." He strode away, taking the light with him.

"Great guy. Great manners," Dom said. "You sure can pick 'em, Princess."

"I didn't pick him. I wouldn't have picked him if he'd been the last apple on the tree. . . ." I trailed off. I wanted a big cup of ice cubes to press against my swollen lip and Advil for my aching head. I didn't much feel like talking. "You were following me," I said. "That car I kept seeing. Was you?" The pain was reducing my conversation to a you-Tarzan-me-Jane level perfectly suited for conversing with someone labeled Jungle Boy.

"What else could I do? You wouldn't let me stick around and protect you."

I kept my head pressed tightly against him, listening to the rumble in his chest. "As I recall," I said, my voice faint, "you said 'Cease and desist,' not 'Let me protect you.' "

"I suppose you've never said something hard to back away from and then discovered you were wrong?"

"Just the other day," I said. "I've been trying to say I'm sorry. I've left messages all over the state of Maine."

"And carefully stayed out of danger, too, I've noticed."

"I need to sit down," I said. "I'm dizzy. My ankle hurts. I'm bleeding. Stop talking and kiss me." He laid a row of kisses down the side of my face and neck that left me breathless. Maybe all there was between us was sex and violence, but man, did we do that well. "I was thinking about the laughing boys and the little brown girls. How I might never see them. . . ."

"Historically, we Lemieuxs are a pretty fertile bunch."

I laid a finger across his lips. "Later." With Andre's help, I limped to the car and we drove to Dorrie's.

She answered the door hollow-eyed and haggard and immediately started fussing over me. I waved her off. "Just give me a washcloth and something dry to put on. I'll be fine." I hadn't said anything about the wound. A quick glance showed it ugly and gaping and definitely needing stitches, but I couldn't face that right now. I found gauze pads and adhesive tape in the medicine cabinet and did a temporary repair job. Then I carefully washed my tender, bloody face and limped out. Hopped, actually. I could no longer put any weight on my foot. The woman in the mirror had wild green eyes and lips like the Pillsbury doughboy. A thing of beauty and a joy forever. I didn't need cosmetics, I needed a veil.

I'm not so brave. I screamed when Andre pulled my boot off. He almost screamed when he saw my foot, while Dorrie scampered for ice. I was not going to be rocking around any Christmas trees after all.

"Okay, Sherlock," Rocky said, pulling up a chair and sitting down beside me. Good old Joe Hennessey sat down right behind him, pencil poised. I closed my eyes. Detectives, it seemed, couldn't always choose the company they kept. Dorrie had a chair. Andre was sitting by my head, holding my hand. Dom stood at the foot of the couch, arms folded. He looked ready to spring if Rocky stepped out of bounds. "What's the story?"

CHAPTER 27

SO I TOLD it like a story. "Once upon a time there was peaceful kingdom called Bucksport. At least, its inhabitants thought it was peaceful. All the inhabitants watched each other closely and clung together in a model of community. But underneath its civilized veneer, relationships had begun to rankle and fester. Marriages were troubled, fertility an issue, midlife crises abounded. There were intrigues and jealousies. The children of the kingdom were being neglected by the grown-ups entrusted with their care. The Queen of Bucksport, busy with her chancellor of the exchequer and her chamber of commerce, didn't see what was happening. Her staff kept it from her, as did her subjects. . . ."

My mouth hurt. "Can I have some water with lots of ice?" Dom went to get it. "Into the midst of this troubled community came a princess from another country. Talented, aloof, manipulative, and vulnerable, and she became the catalyst that fused all the community's problems. The teacher who had grown tired of his wife basked in the princess's admiration and determined to seduce her, not knowing that she had also decided to seduce him, just for the practice. A high-strung student fell in love with her, a love that was reciprocated, but he couldn't understand her foreign ways. Another teacher allowed himself to fall hopelessly in love with the princess, a fact of which she was unfortunately aware, and as she had a cruel streak, she allowed herself to tease and tantalize him. Two members of the nobility, discovering that the princess was pregnant, determined to have her baby for themselves. And thus, because it wasn't an idyllic kingdom, was the stage set for murder. . . ."

Rocky sighed and would have spoken, but Dorrie put a firm hand on his arm and whispered "Hush!"

"The princess, finding that her relationships with her new countrymen were puzzling to her, went to see one of the wise women of the kingdom, and confided her confusion. The wise woman, to keep a careful record, wrote all these confessions down—"

"Which goddamned confessions then went missing," Rocky said.

"I have them."

Rocky lurched forward, and he might have grabbed me and shaken me, except that there were two big, snarling men in his path. He subsided into his chair. "What the hell," he said. "How did you get 'em?"

"I found them in my mail slot when I was leaving tonight. She must have mailed them before she died, before Hamlin got to her. I don't know why he killed her. It's not that obvious, from her notes. Not unless you know he was in love with Laney, and how much he disliked Drucker. I haven't found anyone who'll say this, but I think she went to Drucker for money. He turned her down. Then, because she was Laney and she was desperate and couldn't see why she shouldn't do it, she went to Ellie, and Ellie told her to go to hell. She wouldn't ask Josh, just as a matter of pride. The Donahues were hovering like a pair of vultures, desperate to get her baby, so there was no help there. Her best friend, Merri, was openly disapproving. So who did that leave?"

No one spoke, so I answered my own question. "It left Russ Hamlin. Laney knew he was infatuated with her. She was in trouble and she needed help. It never occurred to her that the fact that she was carrying another man's baby, another faculty member's baby, would be anathema to him, when he'd worked so hard to keep his hands off her, to keep his lust to himself. It made him feel like a complete fool. I expect he made her reveal the identity of the baby's father as a condition of handing over the money. He may even have intended to give it to her, but when he heard it was Drucker, a man he despised, a man he felt was so far inferior to himself, he snapped. And he killed her."

"So then he tried to poison you because you were getting too close?" Dorrie said.

"That was Ellie Drucker," Rocky said.

"How do you know?" Dorrie asked. She ran a shaking hand through her hair. "How many murderers and attempted murders do we have on this campus? We might as well close this place and sell it for tract mansions. We'll never live this down." She looked as exhausted and confused as I felt, with a kind of sad, resigned helplessness I'd never seen before. "Look, I know this doesn't absolve me, but Thea, my whole career has just been ruined . . . poor Josh has been pushed beyond his limits . . . Carol is dead. You could have been, just because I was sure Delaney Taggert's death was no accident and I was determined to get to the bottom of it. I never should have asked you to come back and keep working on it."

"Are you suggesting it would have been better to ignore things and let Russ Hamlin get away with his crime?" Andre asked.

Dorrie sighed. "I'm just not sure anymore. I'm not sure what I think. That is, I'm not sure what we've gained by my determination to find the truth. Look at all the people who have been hurt. It's like tossing a pebble into a pond. The circles keep getting bigger and bigger and affecting more and more of the pond. Laney's death, a small pebble. Carol's death, a bigger pebble. And now there's Josh and the Druckers and Hamlin."

"But who threw the pebble into the pond?" Andre said.

"I don't know. If we hadn't accepted Laney, would it have been someone else? Was it Chas? Or Ellie? Or Laney? Or Laney's mother? Or maybe I threw it in because I wasn't watchful enough. I knew Chas was vulnerable. I'd even heard vague rumors abut him paying too much attention to some of his students, but I figured he was a grown-up, it was his problem, and besides, I was too busy trying to fix the school's fiscal mess and shore up admissions. I could even claim it's society's fault for oversexualizing everything and failing to support everyone's ability to say no."

"Can we get back to the facts here?" Rocky complained.

But Dorrie still needed to talk. She took a deep breath. "But which of those answers prevents this mess? None of them. I can learn how to keep it from happening again but the cost of the learning curve is too high. Two dead. Three injured. Four faculty members gone. Plus Carol. Forgive me for sounding self-pitying, but no one is ever going to want me to run a school again."

"That might depend on how you handle things," I said.

"That's my girl," Andre said, patting me. "A consultant to the end."

"I hope the only end is the end of this discussion," I said. "I'm tired. But one question. How do you know it was Ellie who tried to poison me?"

"You're always tired," Rocky said. "She said so."

"She said I was always tired?"

"She said she tried to poison you. I guess she thought she was going to die and wanted to clear her conscience."

"Excuse me," Dom said, "but if you don't need me anymore, I've got some unfinished business at home. You know what Rosie's going to say when I tell her about this?"

"What?"

"She's gonna say she told me you wouldn't have called if you didn't need help. I don't know." He surveyed the crowded room. "Looks like you've got a hell of a lot of help."

"Dom. Believe me. I needed you."

He winked and bent down to kiss me. "Any time, Princess. Life with you is never dull." Then, as he straightened up, his face changed. "Why do you have blood all over your sweater?"

I pointed a shaky finger at Andre. "Because he broke my heart."

It was Rocky who lunged forward, pushed up my sweater, and showed the world my blood-soaked makeshift bandage, which he then peeled off to view the wound.

"Don't let them put me in the hospital," I said.

"Don't worry. I won't," Andre said. "I'll drive you to the ER for stitches and then we're going home."

"Wherever that is. My mother is still waiting to know if you're coming for Christmas dinner."

"Then we've got a problem, because my mother still wants to know if you're coming for Christmas dinner."

"So what do we do?"

"Draw straws. Flip a coin. Or we could just stay home in bed and watch *It's a Wonderful Life*."

"I like the stay-in-bed idea but everyone will be mad at us." I was ready for bed. Right now. I felt as though someone had played kick-the-cat with me. I closed my eyes, shut out the commotion, and let Andre's hand be my only connection to the room.

"We're tough. We can take it," he said.

"Deal," I said. "I got you a great Christmas present."

"Me, too."

Ellie Drucker survived, as did Chas, while Josh quietly withdrew from school and spent some time in a private institution. The morning after the debacle chez Drucker, Dorrie called an all-school assembly and publicly announced the firing of Drucker, Hamlin, and the Donahues. I wish I'd been there. Suzanne, who was, says it was the best presentation by a head of school she's ever seen. Sorrowful, humble, deeply caring, and certain that the welfare of the students required prompt and decisive action.

Dorrie and Rocky's relationship is rocky, owing, in part, to the incredible hours she works, but her job did survive. The trustees decided that her caring and courage and willingness to put the students' needs before her own were what they wanted in a headmistress, so she stayed on at Bucksport. Ellie pled guilty to avoid the circus of a trial. Russ Hamlin, theatrical to the end, escaped while being transported to a hearing, stole a car, and jumped off the Mystic River Bridge. I heard that Chas and his daughter Angie were moving out of state. Sure she was the one who gave him up, but maybe he knew he'd deserved it. I don't know what happened with Dom and Rosie after he went home but I have a pretty good idea.

As for me and Andre, we ended up spending Christmas day in bed watching old movies and indulging in the pleasures of the flesh, waiting for the rain to stop. His mother was understanding; my mother was not. When it cleared, we went down to the beach and tried out our four new gloves and two new baseballs. It looked as though we were a match made in heaven, unless it was in the sporting goods store. My aim was off, which Andre claimed was because I throw like a girl. I told him it was because I had a bruised ankle and stitches. For Christmas dinner we had a caviar omelet, champagne, and chocolate cake, and then went back to bed to talk about our future, with no promises and lots of hope.

Available by mail from

Available by mail from

THIN MOON AND COLD MIST • Kathleen O'Neal Gear

Robin Heatherton, a spy for the Confederacy, flees with her son to the Colorado Territory, hoping to escape from Union Army Major Corley, obsessed with her ever since her espionage work led to the death of his brother.

SOFIA • Ann Chamberlin

Sofia, the daughter of a Venetian nobleman, is kidnapped and sold into captivity of the great Ottoman Empire. Manipulative and ambitious, Sofia vows that her future will hold more than sexual slavery in the Sultan's harem. A novel rich in passion, history, humor, and human experience, *Sofia* transports the reader to sixteenth-century Turkish harem life.

MIRAGE • Soheir Khashoggi

"A riveting first novel.... Exotic settings, glamorous characters, and a fast-moving plot. Like a modern Scheherazade, Khashoggi spins an irresistible tale.... An intelligent page-turner." —*Kirkus Reviews*

DEATH COMES AS EPIPHANY • Sharan Newman

In medieval Paris, amid stolen gems, mad monks, and dead bodies, Catherine LeVendeur will strive to unlock a puzzle that threatens all she holds dear. "Breathtakingly exciting." —*Los Angeles Times*

SHARDS OF EMPIRE • Susan Shwartz

A rich tale of madness and magic—"*Shards of Empire* is a beautifully written historical.... An original and witty delight!" —*Locus*

SCANDAL • Joanna Elm

When former talk show diva Marina Dee Haley is found dead, TV tabloid reporter Kitty Fitzgerald is compelled to break open the "Murder of the Century," even if it means exposing her own dubious past.

BILLY THE KID • Elizabeth Fackler

Billy's story, epic in scope, echoes the vast grandeur of the magnificent country in which he lived. It traces the chain of events that inexorably shaped this legendary outlaw and pitted him against a treacherous society that threatened those he loved."